MW00446143

ENTRAPMENT

INFIDELITY - BOOK 4

ALEATHA ROMIG

NEW YORK TIMES AND USA TODAY BESTSELLING AUTHOR
OF THE CONSEQUENCES SERIES

ENTRAPMENT

Book 4 of the INFIDELITY series

Copyright @ 2016 Romig Works, LLC

Published by Romig Works, LLC

2016 Edition

ISBN 13: 978-0-9968394-1-9

ISBN 10: 099683910

Cover art: Kellie Dennis at Book Cover by Design

(http://www.bookcoverbydesign.co.uk)

Editing: Lisa Aurello

Formatting: Angela McLaurin at Fictional Formats

All rights reserved. No part of this book may be reproduced or transmitted in any form or by any means, electronic or mechanical, including photocopying, recording, or by any informational storage and retrieval system, without the written permission from the copyright owner.

This is a work of fiction. Names, characters, places, and incidents either are the product of the author's imagination or are used fictitiously, and any resemblance to any actual persons, living or dead, events, or locales is entirely coincidental.

DISCLAIMER

———•O•———

The Infidelity series contains adult content and is intended for mature audiences. While the use of overly descriptive language is infrequent, the subject matter is targeted at readers over the age of eighteen.

Infidelity is a five-book romantic suspense series. Each individual book will end in a way that will hopefully make you want more until we reach the end of the epic journey.

The Infidelity series does not advocate or glorify cheating. This series is about the inner struggle of compromising your beliefs for your heart. It is about cheating on yourself, not someone else.

I hope you enjoy the epic tale of INFIDELITY!

ENTRAPMENT

—●○●—

"The snare is set—leaving friendships, lives,
and futures dangling in the balance"

ENTRAPMENT continues the epic new romantic suspense series
INFIDELITY, featuring Lennox "Nox" Demetri, Alexandria "Charli"
Collins, the Montagues, and the Demetris.

The thrills, heat, and suspense continue to add up…

One chance meeting

plus…

One sexy, possessive alpha and **one** spunky, determined heroine

plus…

One week of uncontainable, unbridled passion

plus…

One impulsive decision

times…

Two declarations of love
divided by…
The sum of intertwining pasts, lies, and broken rules
equals…

ENTRAPMENT

"Infidelity - it isn't what you think"

Don't miss this latest novel in the Infidelity series from New York Times and USA Today bestselling author Aleatha Romig. The classic twists, turns, deceptions, and devotions will have readers on the edge of their seats, discovering answers that continue to pose questions. Be ready to swoon one minute and scream the next.

Have you been Aleatha'd?

ENTRAPMENT is the fourth of five full-length novels in the INFIDELITY series: Betrayal, Cunning, Deception, Entrapment, and Fidelity.

*This series does not advocate nor does it condone cheating.

PROLOGUE

●─○─●

End of Deception...

CHARLI

SIGNATURE CRIMSON FLOWED upward from the starched white collar of his shirt as Alton Fitzgerald stopped midstep and turned my direction. "It appears as though the prodigal daughter has returned."

I didn't stop walking until I was right before him. "I want to see her."

"You'll have to understand that I have no intentions of slaying a fatted calf on this occasion simply because you've decided to grace us with your presence."

"What happened?" I asked.

He looked over my shoulder toward the SUV as a limousine pulled past it and up to the edge of the walkway.

I turned back to see both Clayton and Deloris standing beside the SUV, looking as though they were both ready to run in my direction.

"Come home and we'll discuss this. *Alone,*" he emphasized the last word.

"Discuss it now. I don't want to go back to the manor. I want to see my mother."

Alton's tone lowered. "You see, Alexandria, that's the problem. For too long you've been coddled. Your days of getting what you want are over. It's time you acquiesced to your future, the same way Laide did."

I shook my head. "I don't know what you're talking about."

1

"Of course you don't. You've been too wrapped up in your own frivolities to worry about what's important. Perhaps if you hadn't been off in New York, you would have been able to help your mother. Now her fate is in my hands."

"What the hell does that mean?"

I cringed as he reached toward me and placed a hand on my shoulder. My stomach turned as he inclined his face closer to mine and his warm, putrid breath filled my nose.

"Turn around, Alexandria."

I did, not because I wanted to obey him, but because I needed to breathe fresh air. Brantley was standing near the open door to the limousine.

Alton spoke near my ear, his hand still holding my shoulder. "If you want to see your mother, or if she has a chance of ever being released from this facility, you will get in that car and do as you're told."

I looked back toward Deloris and Clayton.

"Alexandria, I won't ask again."

My eyes closed, blocking out the afternoon sun as I clenched my teeth and shook his hand away. With a deep breath, I took one step and then another. As I walked the plank to my own death, I said goodbye to Charli.

Alexandria nodded to Brantley and climbed into the backseat of the limousine.

Before the door was shut, encasing us in the cool, dim interior, my phone vibrated with an incoming call.

"Give me your purse," Alton said with his hand extended.

I lifted my sunglasses to the top of my head and stared. "What? No."

Tears prickled my eyes and I turned quickly as my face stung from the slap of his palm against my cheek.

What the hell?

I sent daggers flying from my eyes as I blinked away the moisture.

"Your mother is no longer a factor. Listen to me the first time and I won't need to be sure of your attention." Alton extended his hand again. "I don't repeat myself."

When I didn't move, he reached for my purse, his glare daring me to stop him.

Stupid! Why did I get into this car?

With the scenery moving beyond the tinted windows and the limousine in motion, I sat statuesque, trying to contemplate my next move.

Alton removed my phone and gave me back my purse.

I held my tongue, as I'd been taught to do, as he turned off its power and placed it in his pocket. Though my thoughts were filled with too many things to register, Chelsea's text message came to mind. I hadn't erased it. If Alton turned on the phone, he'd see it.

"Alton," I tried for my most respectful tone. "Please tell me about my mother."

He leaned back against the seat, seemingly composing his response. "Your time in New York is done. Your mother wanted a Christmas wedding. I think if Suzy gets started on the plans, it can still be accomplished. The only variable will be if Adelaide is well enough to attend." Alton sighed, cocked his head to the side. With a straight-lipped grin, he added, "I suppose that's up to you.

"Welcome home, Alexandria."

ENTRAPMENT

—•◦•—

Is it really cheating if you're doing it to yourself?

ALEATHA ROMIG

CHAPTER 1

ALEXANDRIA

I TRIED TO process Alton's words…

Christmas wedding.

Suzy.

His question…

Will Adelaide be well enough to attend?

And finally, his declaration…

Welcome home.

The words formed phrases in my native language. I understood each one individually, but not combined. Their meaning—in the order spoken—was beyond my comprehension. With the sting of his slap still tingling on my cheek, I pressed my lips together and waited for more, for him to explain what he'd said, what he'd decreed.

I'd played this game too many times—I knew the rules and the outcomes. My few winning moments had come in my mother's presence. She wasn't here. I was alone with Alton in the moving limousine. Not completely alone, because Brantley was behind the clouded glass, though no matter the reason, he'd never intervene.

I swallowed my thoughts and retorts. They'd only earn me another slap. Even in times of confusion, the old me—the one who understood her predicament—knew that if I were to survive, self-preservation and common sense needed to overrule impulse.

Now that I'd willingly entered Alton's trap, survival was my new goal.

The wheels of the limousine turned and time passed, but Alton didn't offer anything more. No explanation. No enlightenment.

With each ticking second, the silence loomed around us, settling like a cloud. The muted hum of tires against the pavement drowned out our breathing. There were no words or piped-in music; even Brantley remained silent, his silhouette beyond the clouded window barely moving. It was as if most of the world had stopped, leaving me a captive unable to affect the future.

Mile after mile, the car continued forward, undoubtedly taking us to Montague Manor, away from life and—almost literally—toward death. Charli couldn't live behind the iron gates and tall stone walls. She wouldn't survive.

Summoning Alexandria, I turned toward my mother's husband. His lips thinned as his attention moved from the side window to the screen of his phone. Though I stared, not once did his beady eyes turn my way or his words offer an explanation. By the smug satisfaction in his expression, he appeared confident that he had my acceptance or at the very least, my compliance. My neck straightened as I realized that in my stepfather's mind, I'd already acquiesced to my future *as my mother had done*.

What the hell did that even mean?

Taking a deep breath, I lifted my chin. "Will you explain yourself?"

His gaze turned my direction as his smile faded. "My mistake. I assumed a Stanford graduate would understand a simple statement. But by all means, Alexandria, I can dumb it down for you. After all, I've been doing that for your mother for the last twenty years."

Copper coated my tongue as I applied the pressure necessary to bite back my retort.

"As I stated," he offered in a most condescending tone, "we will discuss this at length once we're home."

Stifling my disgust, I called on my childhood training and did my best to equal his patronizing pitch. "Perhaps I need to make this simple for you also.

You see, I have a home, in New York. I have classes and a boyfriend. Despite what you assume, I can't *acquiesce* to anything that will interfere with any of that."

Instead of being offended, Alton smirked. "It's you who doesn't seem to understand. Alexandria, you don't have a choice."

This can't be real.

I continued to stare, waiting for the telltale crimson to rise from his collar. In some strange way, its absence frightened me more than its predictable presence. The anger, his normal barometer, was gone. In its place was an arrogant confidence that sent a chill down my spine.

"Do you have anything to say?" Alton Fitzgerald asked.

To an outsider, his question could be construed as an offer of enlightenment. That wasn't what my stepfather was doing. His inquiry served no other purpose than to bait me into saying something—anything—to warrant another of his slaps.

Taking a deep breath, I tried for another angle. "Please, tell me about my mother."

"In due time."

Suddenly, I startled. A shrill ring filled the interior of the limousine. As Alton reached for his phone, he nodded my direction, pressed his pale lips together, and wordlessly silenced me.

"Hello, Suzy."

Suzanna Spencer was Bryce's mother and my mother's best friend. Would Suzanna tell me what was happening? Surely she was worried about my mother. That had to be why she was calling Alton.

With a conscious effort to appear as though I wasn't listening, I turned toward the window. The muscles of my neck tightened as the scenery beyond the glass became increasingly familiar. No longer near Savannah's city proper, the roads were now more rural. Canopies of trees created dimmed tunnels as Brantley swiftly drove us in and out of sunlight.

Mulling over each of Alton's responses, I searched for a morsel of information. With each statement, I came up empty. Each sentence, each response, was calculated and well thought out.

As the strobe of light continued to illuminate, I contemplated what I'd been told thus far. Both my mother and Jane had mentioned that things in Savannah were changing; however, with each mile we moved nearer to Montague Manor, I knew that wasn't true.

Settlers created these paths hundreds of years ago. Horses and wagon wheels had carved the Georgia clay, their tracks making what would later become today's paved and pristine roads. Though the settlers wouldn't recognize the current hardened black surfaces, the trees lining the route were still the same.

It was another example of the Savannah way: change without actual change.

Alton continued his conversation with his back toward the car's back window, leaving me seated to his left. My seat faced the side, directly across from the door that had led to my current imprisonment. My gaze wandered from window to window.

My lips came together as I suppressed a gasp and my pulse quickened. I shouldn't have been surprised by what I saw in my peripheral vision, but I was. My childhood had a way of doing that—isolating me—but from where I sat I could see from the corner of my eye that I wasn't alone. A few car lengths behind the limousine was Clayton's black SUV.

What did Deloris think she could do, run the gate at Montague Manor?

That would never happen. Alton's employees were too well trained. They'd never let Deloris and Clayton pass.

I clutched my purse, wishing for my phone. If only I could send a text… let Deloris know not to try. Her efforts would be futile, possibly instigating other problems.

Why hadn't I shared more with her about the operations of Montague Manor?

Then again, there was a part of me that wanted her to try, wanting her and Clayton to storm the gate. I imagined the guards calling the police. When they arrived, I'd tell them the truth—that I'd been taken against my will and my mother was in danger. In the story forming in my head, the good people would win and the bad ones would lose.

That was how fantasies worked.

This wasn't a fantasy or a fairytale.

This was Montague—I knew too well that the bad would win. They always did.

Alton's conversation went on as I continued to try to glean any news of my mother. Other than a comment or two saying he'd tell Suzy about *that situation* later, nothing about my mother was mentioned. He mentioned Bryce's name but not Chelsea's.

Momentarily I closed my eyes and tried to decipher the puzzle being laid before me. Pieces were being moved, but I couldn't make out their destination.

For only a second before Alton powered off my phone, I'd seen the screen. It was Deloris's name. She'd been the one who'd called, undoubtedly wanting answers, wondering what I'd done by getting into this car and why I'd done it. I wanted to believe she was talking to Nox, messaging him, or somehow relating what had happened.

Why did I get in this car?

The question ate at my insides until a hole remained.

It was a familiar void, one I'd carried for most of my life, one that up until recently, allowed me to cope and survive. It took away my emotions. I worked to fill my lungs, to fill the emptiness with air. I would survive. I've done it before.

But this time was different. This time I had help. Though Alton may believe I was alone, I wasn't.

Nox was with me.

I reached for my necklace and ran the platinum cage up and down the chain. He may not be with me physically, but he was there. I was with him—a small dot on his phone, but *there* nonetheless.

Nox knew many of my secrets, my shadows, and he still loved me. I loved him. That was something that I'd never before had. It was something my mother never had. The knowledge that I did—I do—gave me strength.

The void inside of me shrank as Nox's love rushed through my veins and swirled with my own regret. I opened my eyes, wishing I could go back in time. Wishing I could undo my decision to get in this car.

Suddenly, I stiffened my neck, straightened my shoulders, and held my breath. It was the involuntary response to the simple movement of Alton's arm.

The corner of his lips rose. His gray gaze momentarily met mine as he dramatically lifted his wrist and pulled back the cuff of his suit coat. "We should be to the manor in less than ten minutes," he spoke into his phone. "Have everyone assembled in my office. I'm done with this farce."

I exhaled as he disconnected his call, mad at my own show of weakness. My flinch had shown vulnerability. I needed to be strong if I held a chance of saving my mother.

With a thin grin, wide enough to expose his stained teeth, Alton reached out and patted my knee. "Patience, as soon as we get back to the manor, Father will explain everything."

I fought back the rebuttal and concentrated on the reason I'd gotten into the car. I zeroed in on my mother. Alton could say whatever he wanted about my future. It wasn't his to decide. However, what he'd said about my mother's fate was accurate. As her husband, her future was in his hands. No doubt he had the legal documentation to back his power.

He already had power over her shares of Montague. How difficult would it be for him to obtain more, the power to make all of her decisions, especially if she'd been deemed legally ill?

There was so much I needed to know.

Who admitted her to Magnolia Woods?

From some of my reading, I knew that the legalities changed if someone admitted him- or herself to a facility as opposed to being committed by another.

"My mother?" I asked again.

"You see, she has a problem."

I waited.

"As time passed and your mother requested your return, she became more and more distraught." It was the same word my mother had used when I questioned her about Bryce's accusations that she was ill. "None of us realized the extent to which she'd fallen, the state of depression that she was in. Perhaps it was because your mother never complained. We didn't see it until it was too late."

"What do you mean *too late*?"

"Her behavior became…" He paused. "…odd. Very unlike the Laide we all knew. She drank more than usual, but not only that. It wasn't just the constant wine—that wasn't out of character. It was that she suffered more and more headaches and asked Dr. Beck for stronger and stronger painkillers."

My lips pressed together as he doled out small bits of information.

"She stopped taking the medicine the doctor prescribed, the one that kept her migraines away. We can only suspect it was because she wanted the stronger drugs."

I shook my head. "She's always drank, but she's always handled it well."

"There were a few incidents." He laid his head against the seat. "I almost hate to tell you."

My mouth dried. "What? What incidents?"

"Laide began hallucinating. She'd drive somewhere, refusing to be driven, and then not know where she was. She started to forget, well, everything and fabricated tales that made no sense at all. This hospitalization is for her own good."

"Did she agree to Magnolia Woods herself? Was this her idea?"

Alton scoffed. "It's obvious that the simplest of decisions are now beyond her ability. Dressing, showering, eating…"

My chest ached. It was clear that she hadn't admitted herself. "Please, I want to see her."

He shook his head. "She wouldn't know you."

"What do you mean *she wouldn't know me*? I'm her daughter."

"The doctors say that it'll take time. The combination of drugs and alcohol can't be stopped suddenly; the withdrawals could be life-threatening. She's lost weight and cutting off what her body craves would be dangerous for her heart."

"Her heart? She's never had heart problems."

His eyes narrowed. "Alexandria, how well do you really know what's going on with your mother? Maybe if you'd done as she requested, if you'd come home, gone to Savannah Law, or been here, you might have seen the signs. You might have seen them earlier than we did. But you didn't. You were selfish and now… now the narcotics have damaged her heart and mind."

Tears welled in my eyes as I tried to remember recent conversations. I sought anything that could refute what he said, but I couldn't think of one rebuttal. In the recent past, my mother had seemed scattered. She'd said things about duty and information, about changes... none of it made sense. That didn't mean I'd thought she was losing touch with reality. I'd thought she was desperate. Maybe she was. Maybe she needed me and I didn't hear the reality behind her pleas.

"Thank you."

His brows rose. "Yes?"

"For telling me." I knew how to play this damn game. "Please let me see her. I don't care if she doesn't know me. I want to be there for her now."

"New York?"

I wanted to say that it wouldn't go away.

I prayed that if I spoke to Dr. Renaud, my opportunities would remain at Columbia. I wanted to believe that Nox would support my decision to help my mother, but I didn't know if any of that were true. "I'll contact Columbia. They offer teleconferencing of lectures. I only have another month of this semester before finals." The accommodating words tasted vile on my tongue. "And then if I have to, I can look into transferring to Savannah."

"There's more," Alton said, "things that you'll soon understand, but for now, that's a start."

Just as I began to believe I'd done what I needed to do, said what I'd needed to say, if only to buy me some time until I could get to my mother, Alton's tone changed.

"I expect to be obeyed."

The dreadful taste left behind by my vile acceptance of my near future bubbled from my stomach to my throat. I shivered at the finality of Alton's decree.

"I may not be your father," he went on, "but you will, from this point on, show me the respect that comes with that title. No one sees Adelaide, except through me. There have been decisions made in the past that affect your future as well as your mother's and Montague's. It's not within your ability to argue these decisions. They're done."

The car slowed as the large iron gate moved to the side. I fought the urge to look through the back window to see if Clayton and Deloris were still behind the limousine. I feared that if I did, I'd alert Alton.

"They won't be allowed in," he said with more than a hint of disdain. "Ever."

My heart sank as I turned to the back window and watched the gate close. The limousine's tires bounced against the long driveway as we moved beneath the giant oak trees.

"When we enter the manor," he continued, "go directly to my office. Suzy and Bryce will be there. I have a few things to discuss with the front guards. Remember what I said. Your refusals and disrespectful tone are done. Don't make me refocus your attention again."

I fought the nausea twisting in my gut as the car came to a stop on the circular cobblestone driveway.

Before the door opened, Alton leaned closer, his hand once again on my knee. "In each directive, Alexandria, I want you to ask yourself two questions."

His words were heavy chains, securing my obedience as well as my captivity. I didn't dare speak for if I did, I'd surely say something I'd regret, something to cause him to *refocus* me.

"Ask yourself," he went on, "do I want to see my mother? And do I want her to get better?"

The door opposite me opened, flooding the interior with light. Though it came with a blast of warm Georgia autumn air, my flesh prickled with a familiar chill.

Before I could move or speak, Alton squeezed my knee. "I'm waiting."

Swallowing the bile, I replied, "I want to see her and I want her better."

"Very well. Remember that." He motioned for me to get out first.

Lowering my sunglasses over my eyes, I accepted Brantley's hand.

"Welcome home, Miss Alexandria."

Not acknowledging his words, I looked up and up toward the tall walls filled with windows. There was no need to correct the name Brantley had used to address me. Instead, I forced myself forward, step by step, as my flat shoes moved over the cobblestone toward the opening front door.

15

CHAPTER 2

——●○●——

NOX

DETONATIONS OF RED.

Flashes of white.

Explosions—visible to only me—momentarily hindered my vision. Blinking, I tried to make sense of Deloris's text message.

"ALEX GOT INTO A CAR WITH ALTON FITZGERALD. WE ARE FOLLOWING."

Though the plane ascended higher and higher, my heart fell to an abyss, the place where my stomach used to be.

I read it again.

The words refused to change.

Emotions boiled within me, creating a turbulent concoction capable of destruction. I looked toward the small window, expecting to see swirling clouds, but saw only the deceiving blueness of a complacent sky. Despite the misleading calm, disbelief, hurt, and rage swirled through my body, rushing through my blood, tightening my chest, and weakening my knees. Unconsciously, my fingers balled, creating fists that needed to connect with something—with anything—as I increased the pressure on the phone. Surely it would crack and shatter.

I read the words again and again.

They didn't make sense.

Charli wouldn't do that. She wouldn't willingly get into her stepfather's car.

Something terrible had happened.

I'd witnessed her apprehension and disgust when it came to Alton Fitzgerald. She'd shared her fears and some of her stories. He was the other devil, the one she spoke of. No matter what he'd done to her or not done to her in the past, being with him was dangerous. She knew that and so did I.

Charli wouldn't willingly go with him, not after she'd promised me she'd stay safe.

I clenched my teeth, hearing her words in my mind, her promises... her lies.

When she refused to wait for me for this trip to Savannah, Charli had promised she'd stay with Deloris.

According to this text message, she hadn't.

That's what the words on my screen were telling me. Deloris's message confirmed that Charli had done the one thing I forbade her from doing. She'd put the one person whom I'd entrusted to her care in danger.

She'd willingly sacrificed herself.

I needed to understand why.

I needed to speak to her, but I couldn't.

Since the plane had just left the ground, I couldn't make a call until we were high enough for the Wi-Fi to be activated; however, that didn't stop my rant. Pounding the tabletop before me with the butt of my fist, a tirade of words spewed forth. The outburst, infused with obscenities, echoed uselessly through the cabin.

Wisely, Isaac remained quiet, rightfully assuming I'd share more when I was ready. The flight attendant, though, was new. She didn't know me.

"Mr. Demetri, is everything all right?" she asked, her eyes bigger than dinner plates as she hurried around a wall and moved toward me. With each step she teetered one way and then the next, her body thrown off balance as the plane continued its ascent.

"No! Nothing is all right. Go sit down before you fall. There's nothing you can do."

"Sir," she said, looking down at the phone still in my hand. "If we're not yet out of the range of cell towers, we will be soon, but once we have Wi-Fi you'll be able to Face Time."

I reined in what little self-control still remained. This wasn't my first flight. "I'm aware."

"However, if you don't want to wait, the plane has a satellite phone. Would you like to use that?"

What? Why didn't I think of that?

Because I'm too stunned to process.

"Yes. Get it right away."

Her knees buckled as she maneuvered toward the cockpit, her hands supporting her one way and then the other.

"I'M CALLING ON THE SATELLITE PHONE. I WANT DETAILS!"

I sent the text to Deloris, not caring if it would send or if she would get it. Just pushing the letters gave me something to do.

As soon as the flight attendant placed the satellite phone in my hand, I began dialing the longer-than-normal string of numbers. With each second that I waited for the connection, my blood pressure rose another notch. The rush coursing through my veins filled my ears with an internal roar, muting the engine's drone.

Ring.

Ring.

Ring.

"You have reached—"

Though the plane continued its climb, at the sound of *her* voice, my stomach took another nosedive. Hitting the disconnect button, I called Mrs. Witt. She probably should have been my first call, but I needed to try to reach Charli. I wanted to know that I could.

Now, I knew that I couldn't.

As the satellite phone again waited to connect, I reached for my own phone and pushed the app on Charli's tracker.

Nothing.

My mind reasoned that it wasn't because she was unreachable. She may have gotten into a car, but she wouldn't take off the necklace. There was nothing on the app, because we didn't yet have Wi-Fi access and the cellular service was unavailable.

As soon as the satellite phone began to ring, Deloris answered, "Lennox we're following her…"

"What the hell happened? Where is she? Where is that bastard taking her? Why the fuck did she get in his car? Why didn't you stop her? Did he threaten her?"

"She's a few hundred yards ahead of us on the street. We're making our way out of the city. According to her tracker, her heart rate is elevated, but otherwise, we believe she's safe. According to the GPS it seems as though we're headed toward her home."

"Her home?" I asked incredulously. "No, Deloris, her home is in New York."

"Her *family* home," she corrected. "I told her not to go to him. I called after her. I've told you before that Alex has a mind of her own."

"Did he force her? Where the fuck was Clayton?"

"He was here. He still is—with me. We were merely a few feet away. She insisted on talking to Mr. Fitzgerald. I couldn't hear their conversation, but I imagine it was about her mother." Deloris spoke fast, barely taking a breath between each statement. "She's a patient at a facility called Magnolia Woods. They said she is stable, but I couldn't get any further information. I'm working on accessing their database. The staff refused to allow Alex access to her mother.

"Alex was right to assume it was Mr. Fitzgerald's doing. He was there. I spoke with him briefly. He refused to do more than that. He made it clear that Alex wouldn't be allowed in unless through him. I was about to explain that all to her when he came out of the facility. She didn't listen—"

"And you…?" I interrupted.

"We observed her conversation from a safe distance, but as soon as she stepped toward the open car door, we both went after her. Lennox, it happened quickly. By the time we reached the car, the doors were closed and it was moving. We hurried back to our car and followed. We *are* following."

"Have you called her?"

"Of course. I called immediately. She didn't answer. I've tried several more times and it goes straight to voicemail."

"I tried, too. I can't even see her tracker app."

"I can," Deloris reassured me. "Like I said, other than elevated heart rate, her vitals appear normal."

I leaned back and closed my eyes. Behind my lids I saw her—my Charli. A collage of images bombarded my thoughts. As if we were still together, I saw her, still sleeping this morning in our bed. The image helped me breathe. My chest rose and fell as I recalled her scent, flowers and perfume, the perfect mixture. I hadn't awakened her. Instead, I'd slipped from the warmth of the covers to let her sleep. She didn't need to wake as early and I had things to do.

Even after my workout, she was still asleep. She'd been working diligently this last week on something for class, something that took most of her time. I'd never questioned or demanded more of her. Law school was too important to her. That made it important to me.

The rock forming in the pit of my stomach hardened. What would happen? What would this mean for her classes? What did that asshole of a stepfather have planned?

"Deloris," I said when her end of the line went silent, "get her. I don't give a damn what you have to do. Run their fucking car off the road. I don't care. Just get her."

"Do you have any idea of the repercussions of something like that? The Fitzgeralds are powerful. I'm not saying more so than the Demetris. I'm saying it's different."

"I don't give a fuck!"

The flight attendant peered around a wall near the front of the plane and just as quickly disappeared.

"We're in Savannah. This is their world. Let us follow. We'll try to get in, but I've seen pictures of her home. It's very well protected."

"From the outside," I said.

"What does that mean?"

"It means, she doesn't want to be there. It means she's safer outside of that prison. That's what she calls it. Deloris, we can't leave her there."

"I'll do all I can."

"Do more. And have a car waiting for me. If you're not allowed in, I'll get in. I won't stop until she's in my arms."

And then, after I've held her tight and reassured her that everything will be okay, I'll redden her perfect ass for putting herself in danger and frightening everyone.

"Do it!" I yelled, interrupting something Deloris had been saying.

Disconnecting the signal from the satellite phone, I checked my cell phone. The Wi-Fi was now working. With only a sweep of my finger, I opened her tracker app and found her blue dot.

Fuck! It was moving. The GPS zeroed in, allowing a map to materialize around the dot. I sat helplessly as the blue dot moved along Georgia roads.

"I'm coming to get you, Charli. And then…"

The blue dot slowed, yet at the bottom of the screen I could see that her pulse was increasing.

I enlarged the map, zeroing in on her location.

The dot moved again. It was a private lane.

Deloris was right. That bastard took her back to Montague Manor.

I sent a message via Facetime.

"I CAN SEE SHE'S AT MONTAGUE MANOR. LET ME KNOW IF YOU GET IN."

CHAPTER 3

———●○●———

ALEXANDRIA

EACH STEP WAS a piece of every nightmare I'd ever had.

Though my exterior remained calm, the perfect Montague, my insides twisted and pushed upward... filling my throat with the acrid taste of dread. I swallowed continuously as I put one foot in front of the other. I inhaled as a sense of drowning overwhelmed me. Looking around, I knew that no one within the manor would throw me a life raft. I was alone in a sea of people.

Eyes peered my way briefly before looking respectfully down. The walls of the grand entryway were lined with Montague staff, obedient soldiers at their posts, reinforcing Alton's unquestioned command. People I recognized—both from my past as well as my last visit—and many more that I didn't stood at their positions, creating a path toward Alton's office.

"Hello, Miss Alexandria."

"Welcome home, Miss Alexandria."

My anxiety built with each greeting. Knots upon knots formed in my stomach as my heart raced. Pressing my lips together, I dutifully nodded toward the familiar and unfamiliar faces. Memories in this same hall—of my haircut as well as other injustices—flashed through my thoughts momentarily, mixing the past with the present. Each recollection was a cue, well played by my stepfather, to reinforce that this was his domain and in it everyone bowed to him.

My designated path through the foyer took me past the grand stairs and toward Alton's office. With each step I lost a shred of my newfound independence. The pieces were breadcrumbs that could lead me out... but breadcrumbs were transient and easily swept away. Soon they'd disappear, just like Charli.

I straightened my shoulders. Alexandria Charles Montague Collins was home.

Seeing the last member of the staff positioned near the door to Alton's office made my feet still. The lump that had formed in my throat burst as tears teetered on my lids. Her dark eyes said volumes, yet not a word was initially spoken.

This wasn't the place or the time.

I knew that.

Nevertheless, with everything inside of me, I longed to fall against Jane's chest and be wrapped in her embrace.

"Not yet, child. We will. We'll talk. I'll help. I always have."

Her rich supporting tone filled me, though her lips never moved. No one else heard her encouragement; it wasn't spoken with her lips but with her heart. Yet through our connection, I heard every word. Not only heard, but I took it in, willing it to give me the strength to continue.

Nodding ever so slightly, I lifted my chin.

Let the dog-and-pony show begin.

Jane nodded. Not enough that most would notice, but I saw.

Swallowing past the dryness in my mouth while wishing away the moisture in my eyes, I stood before the large door.

"Miss Alex, I'll get your room ready."

Her true voice washed through me, a river of warmth in this cold, dark place. I turned toward Jane. *Alex.* Unlike every other greeting, she'd called me Alex.

"Thank you, Jane. I'll be there as soon as I can."

Our gazes met in silent communication as the door to Alton's office opened, diverting my attention.

"Alexandria, come in," Suzanna's voice cut in, taking away the warmth and insulation of Jane's greeting. Something in Suzanna's tone was different. I couldn't pinpoint it, but if she were heartbroken over my mother, in that millisecond I didn't sense it.

While I debated my greeting, I stepped through the threshold and stopped.

Nothing could have prepared me for whom I saw.

Standing near the large windows was the one person I never expected to see in my house, not without my invitation. As she turned my direction, I scanned my best friend. Out of context, people and things become unfamiliar. How, after four years of living side by side with the woman before me, could she suddenly seem a stranger?

I didn't know nor could I fathom.

Silently, indignantly, her posture straightened. Her petite, toned body, modestly covered with a pink linen dress, stiffened. The simple but elegant dress hugged all the right places. It was lovely, but not a style she'd ever before worn. Her hair, now a shade of auburn, was smartly twisted behind her head, and her shoes were the perfect accessory. Around her neck was a simple string of pearls.

Chelsea Moore was beautiful.

She always had been in my eyes.

Yet today was different. Staring back at me wasn't my best friend, but a sad, haunting reflection. If we'd been dressed to match, I may have even entertained the idea that I wasn't seeing her, but my own image reflecting in the large window.

However, the day wasn't done. The sun outside was still shining and the windows weren't dark. The room went silent as we stared at one another. In her hazel stare were too many emotions to register.

I was here, in Savannah, in Montague Manor, because of her text message. Yet in that moment my overwhelming thought was relief that I'd finally found her. I had visual confirmation that she was well. The other people in the room, Bryce and Suzanna, faded into the surrounding mist as I hurried toward Chelsea.

"Oh my God, Chelsea." I reached for her shoulders and pulled her close.

Her head shook as she stiffly accepted my embrace.

I pushed her to arm's length. "What the hell is going on?"

"Alex... Alexandria," she corrected. "I'm sorry." Never had she called me by my birth name.

Bryce stepped closer. "It's nice of you to *finally* join us."

The small hairs on the back of my neck stood to attention at his greeting. He sounded more like Alton than himself. The knots in my stomach tangled tighter. This was a fucking nightmare, one I didn't see ending soon.

"Yes, Alexandria, welcome home." Suzanna's greeting returned the entire room to focus.

I moved my gaze from Chelsea to Bryce to Suzanna and finally to the room. Everything was the same as it had always been. The unchanged bookcases covered the walls while heavy draperies fell beside the windows. It was but another piece of the Montague fortune, regal and ostentatious.

To me the beauty was absent. It had never been present. In my mind, the ornate woodwork and bold regal colors were muted by shadows. Never had I held the appropriate esteem for the finery of Montague Manor. It wasn't a mansion. It wasn't beautiful. It was a prison and the reality was too overpowering to ignore: I was once again its prisoner.

My chest expanded, pushing my breasts toward my blouse, but I couldn't inhale. Something had changed. As I struggled to fill my lungs, I realized it was the air. It felt different.

Is that even possible? Does air *feel* like anything? Can it be felt?

It wasn't as if a breeze blew. On the contrary, the air in Alton's office was still, heavy, and stagnant.

As I looked around the room at the occupants and the surroundings, they all moved. I once again had the sensation of being the odd person out, the only one without stage cues. This time I wanted them. I wanted a script in my hand or a teleprompter in the corner—anything for direction.

Hell, I'd take a damn compass.

My phone had a compass, but Alton still had that.

Coming to my rescue, Suzanna motioned toward the long table. "Dear, let's all sit. Your father will be here soon."

I shook my head. "Suzanna, what can you tell me about my mother?"

"It's good that you're here. She needs you."

"What does that mean? Alton said she's… she's mixed up?"

Suzanna reached for my hand. "Alexandria, I hate to be the one to tell you this, but she's delusional. I suppose as her friend, I should have seen it. I didn't. I'm sorry."

Without giving it too much thought, I pulled back the heavy chair—my assigned seat—and sat. "For how long?"

Suzanna's lips came together and her eyes dimmed. "That's the thing, we aren't sure. Now we're questioning everything. Has she said anything to you that seemed out of the ordinary?"

As I contemplated our last few conversations, Bryce sat at the far end of the table and Chelsea sat a few chairs down from me. As Suzanna hovered near my mother's seat—the place a Montague had always sat—the arrangement felt wrong.

"Can you think of anything that she may have said that seemed odd?" Bryce asked, rephrasing his mother's question.

My head moved from side to side as I stared at him. "Why are you here? And you?" I asked Chelsea. "I mean, fine, Suzanna, you're Momma's best friend, but I don't—"

"Family, dear," Suzanna said, lowering herself to my mother's seat. "We're all fam—"

"That's my mother's—"

"And we were asked to be here," Bryce added before I could make my protest known.

"*Told* to be," Chelsea muttered under her breath.

By the way Bryce turned toward her and his expression flashed, he'd also heard her.

"Wait," I said. "I want answers." No longer content to stay seated, I pushed my chair backward and stood. "This isn't from my mother, but from… Facebook… news articles… what the hell is the deal with the two of you?"

Chelsea's chest rose as her chin fell. The stagnant silence resumed until Bryce met my gaze.

"We're glad you're home. I love you."

I placed my hands on the table. Wrinkling my nose, I narrowed my eyes and stared his direction, as if by squinting I could understand his words. "Obviously," I mocked.

"No, Alexandria, I do. I always have." He looked at Chelsea. "She knows. I never lied to her. But you wouldn't talk to me. You wouldn't respond to me. Over the last four years I traveled many times to California to see you."

He what?

"During those trips, Chelsea met with me. She would tell me that you didn't want to see me, explaining how busy you were."

He laid his arm on the table toward Chelsea. Though her gaze hadn't looked up from the table, she lifted her hand and placed it in the palm of his. As their fingers intertwined, he continued, "We grew close. It's been going on for a few years. We never intended for it to go this far, but well, I had to explain to the courts that I couldn't possibly be the person responsible for Melissa's disappearance. I was in California with Chelsea."

"What?"

He lifted her hand and brought her knuckles to his lips. The action revived the knots in my stomach, tightening and re-forming in gaggles of tangles.

"Didn't Melissa go missing around the same time that Chelsea was hurt? Do you know who hurt her?" I asked.

Still, my best friend's gaze stayed fixed upon the table.

"I know that I was glad I was there for her," Bryce said. "I only wish I wouldn't have left her alone that night."

"B-but you called me from Atlanta the next day. I remember your saying that. I was in the airport on the way to see her. You couldn't have been in California."

"I was. I lied. We still didn't want you to know."

My knees gave out as I slid back to the chair. "Chels? Tell me. You've never lied to me. Bryce has. I want to hear it from you."

A tear fell from her hazel eyes as she finally met my gaze. "I'm sorry. I have lied to you."

A weight landed on my chest, its heaviness crushing me as I scrabbled for breath.

"Do you two…? Do you love each other?"

"I told you," Bryce said. "I love you. I always will."

"What the fuck? You're a pig. You're holding *her* hand and professing your love for *me*? That doesn't make any sense. And you're some sick fuck if you think it does."

"Alexandria! Language," Suzanna reprimanded.

I momentarily turned toward my mother's friend. After only a second, I shook my head dismissively and turned back to Chelsea.

"I don't believe you."

"It's true," Chelsea confirmed.

I tried to recall, but the pieces weren't fitting together. "But in your hospital room, you said he was there and that you didn't recognize—"

"I knew you'd run into him in the lobby. I wanted to throw you off."

"No, no… this isn't right. It doesn't make sense."

"Why?" Bryce asked defensively. "You can be screwing someone on the side, but I can't?"

"Are you kidding me? Lennox isn't on the side." My volume rose with each phrase. "And besides, you've been screwing people *on the side* since we were in high school. I recently heard about your behavior at the academy. Chelsea, Millie, how many of my friends? Does it turn you on to know you're fucking my friends?"

"I don't know; does it turn you on to know you're with a criminal?"

"Children!"

Suzanna's reprimand went unnoticed as I countered, "He's not a…"

My words faded away as we all turned toward the opening of the office door. The air that was just heated plummeted to an uncomfortable chill at Alton's icy stare.

"Alexandria," he said, calling me out over Bryce, "that'll be enough! It's time you start behaving like the Montague you are and not some spoiled brat or brokenhearted schoolgirl. You have a position to maintain, which doesn't include tirades." He took a step into the room and shut the door behind him. "The staff can hear you all the way to the foyer and beyond. Your mother would be disappointed at again another example of your poor behavior." He placed his hand on my shoulder. "Don't make me correct you again in front of family and friends."

Daggers flew from my eyes as my skin was repulsed by his touch. It took me a minute to realize that Alton had the same effect on Suzanna and Chelsea that he had on me. Both of them were perched on the edge of their seat, waiting for the king's next decree.

Slowly he walked to the highboy and lifted a crystal decanter. Pouring the amber liquid into a tumbler, he sighed. Silence prevailed as he lifted the glass to his lips. His eyes closed and Adam's apple bobbed as he drank, never pausing until the contents were gone. Again he poured, but this time he turned back toward the table. With his tumbler over half full, he carried it to the head of the table and moved his gaze from Suzanna to Bryce to Chelsea and finally to me.

I wanted him to say something to Suzanna about where she was seated, but he didn't. Instead he took a deep breath and sat.

"This is better. I expect continued silence as I explain."

CHAPTER 4

——●○●——

ALEXANDRIA

ALTON'S VOICE RESONATED through the office. "What I'm about to say may come as a shock. It may seem archaic, but I guarantee it's true and legal. Ralph Porter volunteered to be here to show you the documentation, but I told him it wouldn't be necessary. No one in this room would refute my claim."

It was a dare, one I wasn't stupid enough to accept. I had no idea what Alton was about to say, but whatever it was, when I could, I would most certainly be requiring documentation.

"This all began after Russell Collins died," Alton went on, speaking to me. "Your grandfather was concerned about the future of Montague—everything Montague. You can understand how anxious he was about leaving it in Adelaide's hands. He wanted to know, needed to know, that a capable man was in control. He chose me."

"*He* chose you?" The words slipped out before I could censor them.

Alton's gray eyes captured mine. "Do not interrupt. Do you remember your two questions?"

Do I want to see my mother? And do I want her to get better?

"Yes," I said, raising my chin.

"Unless your answer to either of those is no, do not speak until I'm done. Is that clear, Alexandria?"

How the hell do I answer that?

I nodded.

"Very well. As I said, your grandfather chose me. I've always had Montague's best interests at heart. As CEO and the majority shareholder in Montague Corporation, I've spent the last twenty years seeing to its success."

I wanted to point out that his shares were really my mother's and mine, but now didn't seem like a good time.

"Charles was a smart man. He didn't believe in leaving anything to chance, not Adelaide's choice in a husband, nor the next generation."

The casual jumper I'd worn to class this morning had a long-sleeved top and on my legs were gray tights. The outfit was perfect for the cooler New York weather. In the SUV waiting for Deloris outside Magnolia Woods, it had been too warm. Now, in the depths of Montague Manor, I was once again chilled. As his statement settled over me, goose bumps materialized under the long sleeves and knit tights. "W-what does that mean?"

I jumped as Alton's palm slapped the shiny surface of the large table, the reverberations echoing as a reminder of my required silence. I pressed my lips together and focused on him. No longer did I care that Suzanna, Bryce, and Chelsea were present. In the depths of my bones I understood that whatever Alton was about to say would have life-changing repercussions.

"As I was saying…" He took another drink of his whiskey. "…even the next generation. As was the case with Charles and Olivia, Adelaide and I won't live forever. Montague is a family-owned corporation. It always has been. It remains so. The majority of stock must be held by Montagues. Charles's last will and testament provided that in the case of only female heirs, their husbands would have the voting power over their stock. I've had the proxy for your shares, Alexandria; however, that will end when you turn 25. Prior to that time, it's essential that you marry so that your husband can be proxy of your shares."

Marry? What the hell?

My mind immediately went to Nox. We weren't ready for that step. Besides, I doubted that was Alton's plan. As his decree sank deeper into my soul, I understood that this whole thing was archaic and felt confident that my grandfather couldn't dictate my future from his grave. No one had that right or privilege. This had to be illegal.

"We…" Alton gestured toward Suzanna. "…had left it up to your mother to inform you of your duties and responsibilities as a Montague. She failed… as she has in so many other things. Currently she's ill, gravely so. The doctors are working to rid her body of the toxins she's willingly ingested. They aren't certain that she'll ever fully recover, but one thing is certain: without your compliance, she won't."

A stunned silence fell over the room. Alton had everyone's undivided attention.

"Alton, tell her the best part."

I turned toward Bryce and his self-assured expression. He didn't look like a concerned friend who'd recently learned of my mother's infirmity. Instead, he looked like a child about to receive a gift. My skin crawled with trepidation of what, or more accurately, who that gift would be.

I turned back to my stepfather.

"Charles didn't leave your marriage or the future of Montague to chance any more than he did your mother's. Heaven knows, the sorts you've been hanging around with lately would be the end to a reputable company like Montague. That relationship is over. It's time you did what is expected—"

My fingers instinctively went to my necklace, rolling the diamond-dusted cage between the tips of my fingers and confirming the connection that Alton claimed was forever severed. Fury and heartache filled my soul. This wasn't right. The pressure within me built.

Warning be damned.

I needed to move or I'd blow, vomiting right there on the table. Hurriedly, I moved my chair back and stood, shaking my head. "No, this isn't real. It can't be happening. There is no way in hell I'm agreeing to any of this."

I looked around the table. All of them seemed calm, as if they weren't hearing this news for the first time. Then it hit me. They weren't. Everyone here knew this—even Chelsea.

"You're all crazy if you think I'll go along with this."

"Alexandria!" Alton stood, but just as quickly Bryce did too.

In one or two steps Bryce was beside me, spinning me toward him and away from Alton. "Your grandfather chose me. I've seen the will. Truly until recently, I had no idea. No one told either of us because they wanted it to be real. Alexandria, think back to *us*... to the us we were when we were younger. It was real. It can be again. We have an advantage that your parents never had. We have a past. We can have a future."

My knees weakened and the room tilted. Bryce's grip on my shoulders kept me upright. I peered beyond his shoulder. Still sitting at the table, virtually unmoving, was Chelsea, watching this scene play out before her. How did she fit into this? None of it made sense.

"Alexandria," Alton's stern tone came from behind me.

I began to pivot his direction.

"No," Bryce said, keeping tight his grip and not allowing me to spin, "she's confused. Give her some time."

I stared up at Bryce.

What was happening? Why was he standing up to Alton on my behalf? Had anyone ever stood up to Alton?

I couldn't recall it happening in my presence.

Bryce's grip slipped to my arms and though it lightened, it stayed steady. "Alexandria, we'll work this out." It was the tone of my friend, my childhood playmate, and the person who shared my past. And then, releasing his hold, in one swift move he placed himself between Alton and me. Reaching back, his hand went to mine as his chin raised and he met Alton eye to eye. "That's enough for today."

I was too stunned to fight or to remove my hand from his grip. In the short time since I'd entered Alton's car, my fight had found its hiding place. I wanted to believe it wasn't gone, rather that I knew when to let it out. Now wasn't the time.

Crimson seeped from Alton's collar. "There's more she needs to understand."

"Give her time."

"She doesn't have time."

"She doesn't have weeks or months, but she has hours and days. I'll take her to Magnolia Woods this afternoon and then tomorrow we can discuss it more."

Magnolia Woods. I held my breath.

"Adelaide can't have visitors," Alton said, "not for the first forty-eight hours."

Bryce didn't give up. "She can if you say she can."

My lips remained sealed as the two went back and forth. I was a voyeur, one who understood that in this world my voice held no power. If I spoke, no one would even hear.

"No," Alton decreed. "Alexandria can't leave the manor until we have everything around her secure."

Bryce turned back to me. "You know what he's talking about, don't you?"

I wasn't sure I knew anything. "I-I'm not sure."

"Your life has been in danger. It *is* in danger. We need to be sure you're protected."

"I am," I volunteered. "Clayton won't allow..." My words faded with the expression on both men's faces. "That's it. You're afraid if I leave the grounds that Lennox's people..."

"We need to be sure."

Bryce squeezed the hand he still held. "You see, it's not us stopping you from seeing your mother. We could go now. You could see her, but we can't risk your safety. It's because of *him*."

"My safety? Lennox's people won't hurt me."

"They've already tried."

My attention went back to Alton.

"What are you saying?"

"The shooting in Central Park was an attempt to get you out of his life. You're not wanted there and being with him or seen with him ever again is dangerous and forbidden."

"No, you can't do that. Besides," I protested, "that's not true. The shooting was a domestic thing. The woman's husband was taken in for questioning."

"It was a ruse," Bryce said. "Alton hired private detectives to dig deeper. The shooter was hired by Demetri."

My head moved from side to side. "You're lying. Nox was there. I saw how upset he was. He would never hire anyone to hurt me, and why would he risk his own life?"

I remembered his declaration of love that very morning. I recalled his concern, obsession, and need to know that I was safe. Then I recalled the lies that had been spread over the last few months: the apartment break-in, Bryce's letter, Chelsea's attack.

"You're trying to scare me, just like the letter. It won't..."

Bryce released my hand and reached for my cheeks. Though I wanted to pull away, he was all that stood between Alton and me.

When my gaze met his, he said, "Listen to us, Alexandria. We have proof. Lennox Demetri didn't hire the shooter; his father, Oren Demetri, did."

"N-no..."

"The entire family is dangerous."

"They're criminals," Alton said, his booming voice filling the room.

I pulled away from Bryce and turned back to Alton.

"Lennox is not a criminal."

"Being associated with the Demetris makes you linked to their connections," my stepfather said. "The shooting wasn't a risk. The criminals in bed with those people could take out one man in a crowded stadium. Having you hit while at the same time missing his son wasn't even a concern for the likes of your so-called boyfriend's father. The only glitch came with the misstep of some unfortunate woman pushing a stroller."

"No. I spoke with Oren."

"What?" Alton's voice bellowed.

Bryce again faced Alton, his chest growing with each second as his neck and shoulders stiffened. "We're done for today. Let Alexandria rest. She's not going anywhere. Once security is set, I'll take her to her mother."

"That won't be for a day or two."

"Is that your word?" I asked.

Alton's brow furrowed. "My word?"

"That in a day or two I'll be able to see her?"

He looked from me to Bryce to Suzanna and back to me. "Once everything is secure."

"I need my phone. If you want to assure that the Demetris don't storm this place, you need to let me talk to Lennox."

He scoffed. "No. No one, especially the likes of him, will storm my home. Montague security, like everything else Montague, is superior to that of those criminals." He lifted a brow. "No letters will be left for you in here."

The whirlwind of emotion I'd held back broke free. Tears came to my eyes at the crushing wait of the situation. "It was you. You placed that letter full of lies on my desk."

Alton shrugged. "It wasn't me. I wouldn't enter that den of iniquity."

"I have to talk to him."

"There's nothing to say. Go to your room."

"I'm not a twelve-year-old."

Suzanna stood. "Alexandria, get some rest. Tomorrow, photographers are coming. You need to look your best."

"What?"

"Yes, we need professional engagement pictures. After all, the announcement will be on Monday's society page."

Monday? This was Thursday.

I turned toward Alton. "I have class. I need to contact Columbia about the teleconferencing."

He looked at his watch. "It's after four in the afternoon. You can contact them tomorrow in my presence. Nothing will interfere with these plans."

"But... I need to speak to Nox."

Bryce let go of my hand and took a deep breath. "Don't mention his name again."

"What?"

He turned toward Alton. "Done for today?"

"Fine. Take her to her room and come back here."

"Wait? I can go..."

Bryce again reached for my hand. "Just learn when to keep your mouth shut," he said, pulling me toward the door.

I looked back in time to see Alton lean toward Suzanna before Bryce opened the door and continued his unwelcomed advice.

"It'll make this go a lot easier."

The cool air of the hallway reawakened my spirit, and I pulled my hand away. The members of the Montague staff were no longer lining the walls.

The grand entry was empty except for the sound of our shoes on the marble floor.

"I don't need your advice or your help. I've done this before." I stopped, affirming my stance. "Bryce, you can't possibly think I'll go along with this."

His cheeks rose as he reached again for my hand. Though I tried to pull it away, his grip was stronger. "Don't fight it, Alexandria. I more than think you'll go along with this. I know you will. You'll go along with everything, because if you don't, there will be repercussions that only you could have stopped." His lips thinned. "You'd never allow that to happen."

"Are you now threatening my mother too?"

"No. That's all Alton. Soon you'll understand. When you do, you'll be smiling like the blushing bride-to-be. Now, let me walk you to your room."

I managed to free my hand. "I'm capable of finding my own way. And you sure as hell aren't joining me in there."

Bryce shook his head. "I will accompany you. Alton doesn't want you finding anyone else or attempting to leave. You know that isn't possible, don't you?"

I didn't answer as the weight of his words held me captive. Silently we climbed the grand stairs. At the top we both turned the corner down the hallway leading to my room. Once we were there, Bryce reached for the handle.

"Don't leave your room. Alton will let you know when you can. It's for your own safety," he added.

I took a step over the threshold but immediately turned toward him. "Do not come in here."

Bryce smirked. "Always the proper lady, except when you're spreading your legs for trash like Demetri."

My palm stung as it contacted his cheek. Just as fast, Bryce seized my wrist. "Hmmm, maybe I should thank him. I didn't realize you liked it rough."

"Let go of me."

"Don't get too confident," he said. "I'll be in this room. Not just in here: I'll live here. I'll be your husband. Even before then, you'll reconsider that invitation, because, Alexandria, I'm all you have here. And as I said before, you don't want to be responsible for what will happen when you disappoint me."

"What the hell does that even mean?"

"You'll see." And with that, Bryce gestured for me to step back. When I did, he pulled the door shut, leaving me staring at the white wood as the tumblers in the lock turned.

CHAPTER 5

ADELAIDE

VOICES CAME AND went, but their words were lost. I wasn't sure when it happened or how, but the stress and formality of life had been washed away on a cleansing wave. Nothing mattered, not even my own consciousness.

My head no longer ached with the pounding that kept beat to my heart. Lights no longer blinded, and my body no longer convulsed.

In a place I didn't recognize, surrounded by voices I didn't know, I was content.

Such a strange word, content.

It didn't mean happy nor sad. It was the even keel of emotion, a plateau with no peaks or valleys. It was serenity and peace.

In the recesses of my mind, I recalled a plan to end my own life. Maybe I had. Maybe this was the afterworld. Was there really no heaven or hell, was it simply a sedentary satisfaction that took away the joys and pain of everyday life?

"Mrs. Fitzgerald, you have to drink. If you don't, we'll need to reinsert another IV. You don't want that, do you?"

In the purgatory of contentment, I was still chained to the name I wanted to forget. I'd hoped that God would allow me to go back to the name Montague, to leave Fitzgerald behind, but alas, this wasn't heaven. It must be hell. Another of my hopes dashed.

"Mrs. Fitzgerald…"

I didn't answer the voice. I didn't try to comply. I was neither thirsty nor hungry. The pricks in my arm were only momentary and then the rest could occur without my help. The voices didn't need my help. My daughter didn't need my help. My husband certainly didn't want my help. The reality was clear: I was useless to them and to myself.

I had no desire to reach out to them or even to decipher where I was. It was all beyond me. Inward was the way to go.

"ADELAIDE, OPEN YOUR eyes," the deep rumbling timbre woke me from my dreams.

The handsome face before me surpassed any dream my mind could possibly create. My cheeks rose as I lifted my lips toward Oren's and reached for his scruffy cheeks.

"I love waking with you."

"You could do it every day. Just say the word."

My chest ached with heaviness, not from his broad chest covering mine, but from the weight of life and responsibility.

His kisses came quicker, a rapid attack on my lips and cheeks. "Stop that."

"What?" I asked, looking into the depths of his light blue eyes.

"Don't think about it. Don't think about the future. I'm sorry I said what I did. I know your decision. I understand. Let me see the beautiful smile that just woke, not the sadness my offer brought."

Rubbing my palm over his cheek, his morning beard abraded my skin, reminding me of the sensation of his same scruff on other parts of my body. There was something about this man, something I'd never before experienced that left my insides twisted in a constant state of need.

"I love your offer."

"Your eyes say differently."

Reaching for the sheet, I wiggled away, pulling it against my bare breasts. "Please, Oren, please stop asking me… reminding me that there's a life out there, one I never imagined."

He threw back the covers and turned away. "How? How could you live this long and never know that you can be happy?"

It was a loaded question. Instead of answering, I went for humor—as if there could be humor in what we were saying. "Are you calling me old?"

His neck twisted as he craned his face back in my direction. His piercing blue eyes drank me in. I must be a fright, first thing in the morning, my hair in who knows what condition after a night filled with passion. Subconsciously, I reached for my hair to smooth the tangles.

In mere moments, Oren was back, our noses touching and my hand in his grasp. "Old, no. Beautiful, vibrant, and full of life. Forgive me, amore mio…" He kissed the knuckles of the hand he held captive. "…for wanting to see you smile. For wanting to be the one who makes you smile. For feeling so damn honored to be with you, beside you…" More kisses. "…inside you. When I'm with you, I don't feel like the peasant who's pretending to be a prince. Adelaide, with you I'm a prince, a king, and you're my queen."

"Take me, my king." The words were barely out when Oren did as I asked. Consuming me, shielding me from the world beyond, and filling me until there was no room for anyone but him. Tenderly yet possessively, we became one. Where one began and the other ended was beyond my comprehension. We fit together as if we'd only survive with the other. Alone we were but half of a whole.

Our short getaways, our small reprieves, left me tender and satisfied as I'd never known. My body ached for what Oren could give me, yet after a night or even an afternoon, I was marked in a way that I feared would be visible.

Never had lovemaking been like it was with him. In the past, it had been sex, and I did what I had to do. With Oren it was technically the same act and yet it couldn't have been more different. I longed to please him and to be pleased by him. Feelings and sensations that I'd only read about detonated inside of me. Sounds and words slipped from my lips as the world around me exploded until there was nothing left but charred remains.

The one thing I longed to say, I kept hidden. I couldn't call out his name in passion, though it was on the tip of my tongue. It was too great of a risk, too much of a danger. One slip, one misspoken word, and my world would implode.

Wrapped in a soft robe, my hair freshly washed, I gazed across the small round table as I held a steaming cup of coffee to my lips. Oren Demetri might have been nearly thirteen years my senior, but there was nothing about him that said old. In years he was a little older than my husband, and yet in his mid-fifties, Oren was more handsome than anyone I'd ever known. His firm body, trim waist, and broad shoulders rivaled those of a much younger man. His jet-black hair held the perfect amount of white, creating the distinguished look that only men could carry.

"When will I see you again?"

"I don't know," I answered honestly. "It's too hard for me to plan."

He reached across the table and covered my free hand with his. I stared at the contrast in our skin. Though I doubted he spent much time in the sun, mine paled in comparison.

"You know I'll do whatever I can. Just let me know."

I nodded as the familiar sense of dread bubbled up from my toes, filling me with trepidation at my return home. "I know. I also know this isn't fair of me to ask of you."

"It isn't fair of me to ask you to give up your life." His cheeks rose. "But I'll do it until you agree."

"Alexandria…"

"Would get along well with Lennox. I'm certain of it."

I scoffed. "Oh please. She already has one arranged marriage in her future."

"That's not what I meant. She sounds like a strong-willed little girl. It would do Lennox good to learn he isn't always the top dog."

"If only she had a brother."

"She could."

I stood, taking the cup of coffee with me. "I can wish, but that's all it will ever be. If you can't agree to that—"

Oren's strong arm encircled my waist from behind and pulled my back against his chest. Closing my eyes, I lingered in his embrace, allowing his aftershave to mark my senses and fill me with his scent.

"You won't get rid of me that easily. I just worry about you… with him."

Spinning, I lifted my chin to see into his blue eyes. "That's why I need to go home today. He won't be back until the day after tomorrow. There's a chance he won't even know that I left the manor."

"But if he does?"

"If he does, I have my story. The Metropolitan Museum of Art has a new El Greco exhibit. As a member of the Savannah Art League, I volunteered to preview it. There's talk of part of the exhibit traveling. We're in the process of submitting a grant to have some of it showcased at the Telfair."

"When do you have to leave?"

"Later tonight. I was going to go to the Met first."

"May I accompany you?"

It was New York City. The museum would be filled with thousands of people. Would anyone know me?

Oren's expression darkened. "I understand if you don't—"

Lifting myself up onto my toes, I kissed his lips, quieting his words. "Mr. Demetri, I hesitated for no other reason than I never took you for the art type."

"And why is that? I've lived in and around New York my entire life. I've learned to appreciate the finer things." He pulled me closer. "And with each taste, I want more."

"If you're sure you don't have work and won't be bored."

"I have work, but it can wait. And bored, with you? I don't think that's even possible."

"I'M GOING TO lift you. You need to change positions."

Who's lifting me? Where?

"Let me go back," I said. The request came out before I could censor my response. Maybe this isn't purgatory, not if I can go back to Oren. Maybe this is heaven.

"Ma'am, you can go home when the doctor thinks you're ready."

I blinked as light and unfamiliar scenery filled my field of vision. "W-where am I?"

"Magnolia Woods. You've been here for almost a day."

"A day?" That didn't make sense. I looked from the round face of an unfamiliar young man to the pinch in my right arm and assessed a multitude of clear tubes and various long needles unsuccessfully hidden behind lines of tape. "What is that? I don't want it." I reached for the tubes. "Take them out."

The man in blue scrubs reached for my hand. "Don't touch those."

"But I don't want it."

"You don't know what it is."

"Whatever it is, it's made a whole day go away. I don't want that. Where's my husband? Where's my doctor?"

"Dr. Miller will be in later today."

"Dr. Miller?" My mind was fuzzy, but I wouldn't forget my doctor. He'd been my doctor for most of my life. "Not Miller. My doctor is Dr. Beck."

The man painfully squeezed my hand that he still held. "If I let go of your hand, will you leave your IV alone or do I need to restrain you?"

"Restrain me? Do you know who I am?"

"I think the real question is if you know who you are."

"Of course I know who I am. I'm Adelaide Montague Fitzgerald."

"Well, Adelaide Montague Fitzgerald, your doctor's name isn't Beck, it's Miller, and if you so much as pick at the tape covering those needles, I won't think twice about restraining your hands to the sides of your bed. Is that clear?"

"Who do you—?"

"My name is Mack. I'm one of your nurses here at Magnolia Woods and you'll learn to listen to me. I don't make idle threats."

I turned away from Mack and back toward the IV. "What's in there?"

"Whatever Dr. Miller says."

"I need to get up."

"Yes, ma'am, that's why I sat you up. You can't get out of bed yet, but they want you sitting."

"What do you mean I can't? I can get out." I reached for the railing.

Mack pushed my shoulder back. "No. You can't. You're restricted to your bed until they get your tests back."

"What tests?" With each statement, my mind seemed to clear.

"Mrs. Adelaide Montague Fitzgerald," he repeated my name with an unnecessarily patronizing tone, "our job is to get you clean. We don't care how many names you have. You're the one who filled your body with all kinds of chemicals. It'll take some time, but we'll get you clean."

"I-I haven't…" Or had I? Did I finally take those pills, the ones Jane took away from me? There were so many blank spots in my recent memory. "No, this isn't right."

"Tell me what pills you've been taking."

"I haven't taken any pills except my migraine prevention."

"Don't lie to me. We'll have the results soon."

"I-I'm not lying."

"And wine. How much wine have you been drinking?"

"What?" I reached again for the railing. "I want out of here. I want Dr. Beck. Where's my family?"

Shaking his head, Mack walked to the boxes that created a wall of monitor-looking things near the IV. "Just relax. You're getting upset. I'll up your dosage and you'll be all happy again."

"I don't want..." I reached for my arm. "S-stop..."

Warmth filled my veins, weighing down my limbs and stopping my rebuttal.

"That's it. You sleep."

As the room began to fade, my left arm was lifted and a cold bracelet closed over my wrist.

CHAPTER 6

—•○•—

NOX

ONLY BRIEFLY DID the slam of the shutting door echo in the waiting SUV as Isaac secured his seatbelt. Seconds later he spoke, "Sir, I have GPS that'll take us directly to Miss Collins."

There wasn't any need to fill him in. He'd been with me since we took off for Savannah. He'd witnessed my tirade and the subsequent return to my senses.

Shedding my suit jacket, I settled against the backseat. The damn Georgia heat only added to my angst, each degree pushing my temper higher and nerves tighter.

"Just a minute. I'm getting Deloris on speakerphone. Let's find out if there're any new developments." It was wishful thinking, but that's what had happened since I learned of Charli's decision to enter her stepfather's car—I'd wished. I'd wished she'd waited for me. I'd wished she wouldn't have done it. I'd wished I'd find her waiting in our hotel suite, a silky nightgown covering her petite body, with a glass of whiskey awaiting my arrival.

However, according to the blue dot on my app, none of those wishes would come true. I'd told Charli once that life wasn't a fairytale and I wasn't Prince Charming, but in my wishes, I imagined storming the castle and freeing the princess. That's what she was to me: my princess.

"Yes, sir," Isaac answered, keeping the SUV idling in place.

As we waited, the hum of the air conditioning created a cooling breeze, slowly changing the interior from stuffy and unbearable to merely uncomfortable. Deloris's phone began to ring over the artificial cool, its chime coming not from the speakers but from my phone.

Her voice came through loud and clear. "Lennox, you've landed."

"We have. Now I want to get Charli. I see on the app that she's still there."

"She is," Deloris admitted. "I still can't reach her by phone. It appears to be turned off. As I told you, the house has a gated entrance. I was told in very specific terms that we wouldn't be admitted onto the grounds. The guard even knew our names. He mentioned you and said he had orders not to allow your entrance either."

My chest tightened as she continued to speak.

"Is there another way onto the property? Surely everyone doesn't use the front gate."

"Yes. I've been studying the maps and satellite images. I'd assume that every entrance is at the least monitored and at the most, guarded or gated."

"Damn it. If nothing else, I need to get word to her, let her know we're working on this, that we haven't abandoned her."

"Lennox, I've tried to reach Chelsea. Her phone is off too."

I hadn't thought of her. "Do you think she's there? Why would she be there?"

"I don't know if she is. She's the one who sent Alex the text message about her mother. I figured if I reached her, we could confirm Alex's safety. Right now, all I can tell you with one-hundred-percent certainty is that according to the necklace, she's inside the manor, her pulse is still elevated, and her respirations are quick."

Fuck! Fuck!

"Send Isaac your location," I said, "We'll meet you after we go to the manor. Just that word, manor, sounds like a fucking horror movie. I don't like it."

"Lennox—"

"Don't tell me not to go." I nodded to Isaac as he put the car in gear. "I have to make an attempt. I have to try. If I don't get in, then at least I can tell her I tried. I can't look her in the eyes if I don't."

Her golden eyes.

Deloris sighed. "I understand. I just sent Isaac the location of the hotel. You have a suite. I hope you bring her back with you."

I hoped that too, maybe even wished it. How long had it been since I'd put my faith in things like hope and wishes? Those words had faded from my vocabulary after Jo. Now that they were back, they were anything but encouraging. They were a carrot dangling at the end of a stick, perpetually out of reach yet just visible enough to make me try. They were words of uncertainty and words I despised. Yet for Charli, I did hope. I did wish. But I knew that wouldn't be enough.

If the positions were reversed—if I were the one who had Charli—I wouldn't let her stepfather within fifty feet of her. I hadn't. For the last few months I'd done everything possible to keep her safe and away from that asshole who was capable of casting unwanted shadows in her beautiful golden eyes.

I had to think about a plan, about the future. "In the meantime, what are you doing?" I asked, not allowing myself to think of Charli stuck in a place she loathed as much as she hated her childhood home.

"I went back to Magnolia Woods," Deloris explained. "The staff was unusually uncooperative, but that wasn't why I was there. I was there to infiltrate their internal database."

"Tell me that you were successful."

"I was. I had to manually extract information; firewalls prevented it from being accessed online. Now that I've breached those, I can see everything, including all of Mrs. Fitzgerald's records."

"And?"

"I'm sifting through it all as we speak. I'll tell you more in person."

"So this wasn't a ruse just to get Charli here? Her mother really is sick?"

"She is. They have her on some strong medications. I'm trying to learn more about them and some of their other notations as we speak. I'm much better with hacking than I am with these medical terms."

I nodded as the scenes outside the windows changed. As the large trees and Spanish moss grew thicker along the side of the road, I imagined having Charli beside me, the two of us, together, on the way to visit her mother. That's how it should have been. If only she'd have waited.

Imagining.

Wishing.

Hoping.

This wasn't me. I was a man of action.

Clenching my fists, I vowed not to stop until those words were replaced with the reality of Charli Collins being where she belonged.

"SIR, WE'RE GETTING close. Mrs. Witt sent a few alternative entrances. Do you want to try those or go to the front gate?"

"Front gate." I almost said that I don't do things through backdoors, that I'm too open and upfront for that. I almost asked if Isaac had me confused with my father, but before I could say any of that, I realized that for Charli, I'd fucking climb a fence or maneuver under a gate.

Could that be the difference between Oren and me? Could it be that I'd never had the motivation to sneak around and do backdoor shit? I'd been too hung up on appearing better than him, when in reality I wasn't. As the SUV moved forward, I knew without a doubt, there was nothing I wouldn't do to get Charli back in my arms.

Nothing.

If that made me like Oren Demetri, then fuck it.

The SUV slowed as we turned onto a lane lined with oak trees draped in Spanish moss. The house—or fucking manor—wasn't visible, only trees and a tall wrought-iron fence with a guard building beside the gate.

Of course, it wasn't just a speaker. Alton fucking Fitzgerald had an actual guard at his gate. What the hell? Did he think he was like the King of Savannah?

Suddenly, I recalled introducing Charli to Oren. I remembered him saying that Charli was royalty, genuine American blue-blooded royalty. I'd had no idea. Even after I'd learned that about her lineage, I never imagined this type of money or home.

The reality set my blood to boil. How the fuck did someone from this heritage end up at Infidelity?

Because of Alton Fitzgerald, that was how.

As the SUV approached, an unfamiliar churning began in the pit of my stomach. Royalty. Fuck. Charli wasn't someone who should have been at Infidelity. She was someone who deserved the best. My bloodstream filled with a sense of inferiority I hadn't felt in years. It was the memories of Jo's parents and their low opinion of me.

If I was no better than Oren's son, hailing from a family of dockworkers, then who the hell did I think I was demanding Charli's release?

Before I could consider my answer, the SUV rolled to a stop as it pulled up to the gate.

"Mr. Demetri?"

Isaac's simple use of my name was exactly what I needed. I wasn't the simple son of a dockworker. I was Mr. Demetri, Lennox Demetri. I'd worked hard to get where I was. Fuck, even my father had worked hard. We may not have come from generations of money, but we earned ours. I'd paid for it with hard work and sacrifice, and I sure as hell wasn't sacrificing Charli.

I nodded in the rearview mirror toward Isaac as my window lowered and a man stepped from the small guardhouse with a tablet in his hand.

"Do you have an appointment?" he asked.

"No. I'm here to see Char-Alexandria Collins."

"Your name, sir?"

"Lennox Demetri."

"I'm sorry, Mr. Demetri, Miss Collins is not accepting guests at this time."

"At this time?" I asked. "When do you anticipate she'll be accepting guests?"

He looked down at his tablet. "Your name again?"

Motherfucker knew my name. Nevertheless, I kept my raging emotions in check. "Demetri, Lennox Demetri."

His eyes opened wide in recognition. "Sir, she left a letter for you should you come by."

I took a deep breath. "I haven't just *come by*. I'm here for her, to get her."

The man stepped back into the guardhouse and came out with an envelope. On the outside penned in female handwriting was one word: *Lennox*.

My brow lengthened. "You say that this is from Miss Collins?"

"Yes, sir. She gave it to me herself. She also asked me to tell you not to return. She said the letter would explain everything."

Lennox.

There's no fucking way that Charli would write a note or letter to Lennox. Hell, even Mr. Demetri would have been more plausible. "When Miss Collins handed this to you herself," I asked, "what was she wearing?"

"Excuse me?"

"What was Miss Collins wearing?" I'd left before she was up and dressed for class. However, I knew her closet, her clothes. I knew how her dresses hung in all the right places, how fucking sexy she was in soft pants and a sweatshirt. I'd know if he were lying.

The man's head shook as he looked back at the tablet. "Um, it's not my job to notice her attire. It's actually inappropriate."

"Her hair? How was she wearing it?"

"Sir, your questions are inappropriate."

"Are you an employee of the Fitzgeralds?" I asked.

"Yes, sir. Obviously."

"And your job is in security?"

"Yes."

"Yet you're unobservant?"

"No," he replied. "That's not what I mean. I mean that looking at Miss Collins like that, paying attention to her clothes and her hair could…"

"Could what? Get you fired?"

"Sir, Miss Collins would like you to leave and not attempt to return. Mr. Fitzgerald has also stated the same wishes."

I bet he had.

I nodded toward the guardhouse. "Do you have the ability to call the house?"

"Yes."

"Do it. Call the house. I'm not leaving until I speak to Miss Collins."

Perspiration dotted the security guard's forehead and upper lip. "Sir, you can be escorted off the property. This is privately owned…"

I gripped the edge of the envelope tighter. "Call. If *she* tells me to leave, I'll leave." Isaac's eyes caught mine in the rearview mirror.

As the guard stepped back inside the small building, I eased open the flap of the envelope. The one page unfolded as I freed it from the envelope.

Lennox,

I know this seems sudden, but it isn't. My mother needs me. Don't try to reach me. My phone is off. I need time with my family.

I need more than time and space. I need—no I want—to do what I have known I would do my entire life. I can't do that and continue seeing you. We are done. Forget about Del Mar. Forget the rules.

Go back to New York. Send my school things. Everything else you can keep or burn. I don't care. Move on with your life.

I am moving on with mine.

Goodbye,

Alex

Rules.

My eyes locked on that word as my teeth clenched. It wasn't her, but who would know about the rules?

"Sir," the man outside my window pulled my attention away from the letter, the writing, and words. I didn't want to look away. No longer was I a CFO of Demetri Enterprises or even a concerned boyfriend. I was a detective, deciphering each clue.

Did the writing look like it could be hers? It could. It was similar, feminine. However, the wording made me skeptical. Fuck skeptical. I don't know how in the fuck they knew about the rules, but in my heart, I knew this letter wasn't written or even dictated by my Charli.

"Yes?" I finally replied, pulling my gaze away from the letter and narrowing it toward the guard.

"Miss Collins said to tell you that the letter is self-explanatory and to please leave."

The ends of my lips rose. "Are we being recorded?"

The man's Adam's apple bobbed. "Why?"

"It's a simple question. I want to know if Mr. Fitzgerald will see this."

"I'm not sure who will…"

I peered up to the roofline of the small building. Just under the eave was a protruding dark dome. I cocked my head to the side. "Please tell Alex that I got her letter and hear her loud and clear. This isn't over."

"Sir?"

I tapped Isaac's shoulder. "We can go." I turned back to the guard, his complexion paling by the second. "Tell Mr. Fitzgerald to rest assured, we will be back."

CHAPTER 7

---o---

ALEXANDRIA

IT TOOK ME a few seconds to process... the turning of the tumblers... the rapid beating of my heart...

I was locked inside my childhood bedroom.

My heart continued to pound, the beat no longer contained in my chest, but hammering in my ears.

Slowly, I turned, not stopping until I made a complete circle.

My room—the familiar wallpaper.

My bed—the floral cover and eyelet skirt and canopy.

My windows—their draperies pulled, bound by ropes of satin to reveal the cobblestone driveway below.

Everything was as it had been, months ago, years ago... forever.

Unchanged.

The thought of thriller movies and books itched at my consciousness. Had I ever left? Had I ever been free? Or in some sick twist of fate, was I where I'd always been and everything else—Nox, Stanford, and Columbia—was but a dream, an illusion?

As shadows of the past lurked in the dim corners, I reached for my necklace. The diamond-dusted cage did more than roll between the pads of my fingers. It was my reassurance and confirmation that I had been free. I had lived a life away from Montague Manor.

I took a deep breath.

Though a million thoughts of friends, foes, and family ran through my mind, with the necklace in my grasp, I momentarily closed my eyes. Behind my lids I saw Nox's light blue eyes swirling with emotion. The swirls weren't an indication of the passion I craved or even the anger I anticipated. The concoctions of blue were filled with pride and appreciation.

Never once had Nox demeaned my dreams. His constant encouragement, whether I was reading a ridiculously boring case study or working into the early morning on a paper, was omnipresent. "You can do this, princess. I know you can. Not only are you beautiful, you're the most intelligent woman I know. I'm coming for you, but in the meantime, you've got this. You're smarter than them. I'm coming and I love you. Don't let the shadows win."

It was like when I'd seen Jane. She hadn't spoken her encouragement, yet I'd heard it. My rapid pulse slowed as I opened my eyes and turned another circle. His deep voice was so real it reverberated through me, to my core, yet I was hearing with my heart and not my ears.

Swallowing the continually rising bile, I assessed my situation. The current problem at hand wasn't my mother, Chelsea, or even the accusations that Nox's father was responsible for the shooting. I couldn't do anything about or for any of them if I were locked in my bedroom. I had to concentrate on my current predicament.

As my slow spin came to a stop, I was once again facing the door.

That prick had locked it from the outside.

My teeth clenched and shadows faded as my indignation grew.

I wasn't a child capable of being sent to my room, yet that was what had happened.

And for a moment, I'd allowed it. Now, I recognized the error of my thinking. My childhood room wasn't exactly the same. As a child—and up to and including my last visit—I'd been the one to lock my bedroom door from the inside. It had been my security, knowing that the door would stay shut and unwanted visitors would stay out.

This time was different. The door had been locked from the outside.

I crouched low, leveling my eye with the lock. The keyhole provided a small glimpse—a peephole—to the corridor. A sigh escaped my lips as I shook my head. Either Bryce was an idiot and didn't understand the function of skeleton keys and locks or he'd taken the key on purpose to allow me to escape.

One more time, I turned and scanned the room. It was time to learn if it really were unchanged.

Making my way to my dresser, I opened the bottom right drawer. Inside were clothes I hadn't worn in years, neatly folded in small stacks. Running my hand to the back of the drawer, I brushed the tips of my fingers along the drawer's seam. My lungs forgot to inhale as I moved them from left to right, and then, the tip of my fingers brushed it.

One of the extra keys.

Skeleton keys…

Within Montague Manor, they were all the same. It had been a fact that had led to many sleepless nights, but this time, now, it brought a smile to my face. I wasn't locked in nor could I be, as long as I possessed a key.

I hurried to my jewelry box, still sitting atop a bookcase near my old television. It looked just like it had years ago, not even a speck of dust. Opening the delicate top doors, I revealed the uppermost compartment. It was designed with lines of indentions. Each one was made to hold a ring. Small silver rings as well as those with birthstones filled some of the indentions. With only a pinch of the green velvet, I lifted the false bottom to reveal the hidden compartment. A smile formed as I peered down at another key.

Over the years, I'd acquired quite the collection. I was certain there were at least three or four others hidden throughout the room.

With the first key secured in my pocket, I replaced the velvet lining and left the second key hidden. Of course, none of them would work if Bryce had left the key askew in the other side of the lock. That was unless I had the long needle-nosed instrument to turn the key from within. The tool was shaped like an ice pick, with a curly tip. I believe it was originally used as something that aided in buttoning shoes—a long time ago. Unlike my supply of keys, I no longer had the funny-shaped device. I had one at one time, but during my last visit I'd noticed it was missing. At that time it didn't seem important. After all,

I hadn't planned to return.

Now, here I am.

Regardless of whether or not I had the long-nosed, twisted instrument, as long as there wasn't another key in the lock on the other side of the door, I was free. More importantly, or at least equally important, with a key, I could keep the lock secured from my side.

When I turned again, the telephone on the bedside stand caught my attention. Rushing forward, I lifted the receiver. When I was younger, the phone had mostly been used for intra-house communication. My mother would call or Jane. I could call the staff to bring me whatever I needed. Calls could be made outside of the manor, but mostly I'd used my cell phone for that.

Lifting the receiver to my ear, I listened. It's amusing how one holds his or her breath in anticipation, as if the breathing could obscure the distinct pitch of a dial tone. There was nothing to conceal.

No dial tone.

Only silence.

Repeatedly, I pushed the long skinny button on the cradle. Nothing. As I reached for the cord, I noticed what should have been obvious. It was missing. The telephone wasn't plugged into the wall. It was merely a decoration or perhaps, a taunt to highlight my isolation.

"You can do this, princess." The deep timbre reverberated in my soul.

Patting the key in my pocket, I hung up the useless phone. I needed to bide my time until later and sneak downstairs to a telephone that worked. When I did, I'd call Nox. I'd hear the tenor that I loved, not in my mind, but through the receiver.

Once again, I fingered the small platinum cage hanging from my necklace and closed my eyes. If I could hear him, perhaps he could hear me. I spoke with my mind and my heart.

Nox, I'm here. I'll come back to you, I promise. I have to see my mother. I have to be sure she's safe and getting better. Please don't give up on me. I need your strength and encouragement.

If only I hadn't insisted that the necklace not have an audio connection to Deloris or Demetri security. When I'd made that request, I'd been concerned about people listening to our private moments, but now... Now, I wished with all my might that I could speak to him, to let him know I was safe and would return.

Marry Bryce!

The absurdity of Alton's proclamation washed over me. Pacing the length of my room, I shook my head.

Ludicrous!

What made Alton and Bryce think that I'd go along with this archaic edict? As if my grandfather could dictate my future from his grave. It was ridiculous.

Do I want to see my mother? And do I want her to get better?

I sank to the edge of my bed as Alton's questions returned to my mind. With a sigh, I lay back and stared up at the underside of the canopy. What was happening with her? What drugs had she taken? Why would she do that? How did her condition get this out of hand without anyone seeing or noticing?

My eyes opened wide as I quickly sat and moved my gaze to the door.

Shit! The key was still in my pocket.

The tumblers turned. Their clicks filled the silence, interrupted only by the once-again increased beat of my heart. My gaze darted from side to side as I contemplated my next move. I could run to the door and try to insert the key.

I'd waited too long. That wouldn't work.

I could run to the bathroom and lock that door.

Again, too late.

As the door began to move inward, I knew my only option was the same as downstairs. Face Alton head on.

Standing, I swallowed and lifted my chin.

The dark skin of her hand was the first thing I saw. Her beautiful big brown eyes were next.

"Miss Alex..."

I rushed forward. With each step my fight and strength evaporated. By the time her arms embraced my shoulders, tears coated my cheeks and my body liquefied against her bosom.

"Hush, child. We need to talk."

Nodding, I took a step back as Jane turned and closed the door. Once she did, she inserted a key and turned it until the tumblers locked. Another small twist and the key was secure, only able to be removed from the other side with the long gadget.

When she turned back toward me, Jane opened her hand. In her palm was another key. "For you."

I willingly took it, not explaining that I already had one in my pocket and others hidden around the room. Instead, I reached for the silver key and tightly squeezed it in my own fist. "Thank you, Jane."

"You're a smart lady. You don't need a lock to keep you here."

I nodded. "I don't want to be here, but I-I can't leave until I see Momma."

Jane reached for my hand and walked me back toward my bed. At the foot there was a long bench covered in light-yellow crushed velvet. As we both sat, she said, "That's what I mean. You need to show him that you ain't leaving. The door can be left wide open and you're not going back to New York."

New York. Just the words hurt my heart.

"I don't know what to do."

"Yes, you do. Your momma needs you." Jane squeezed my hand. "Child, she needs you more than she's ever needed anyone. You're the one, the only one, who can help her."

I wiped a tear from my cheek. "Tell me about her."

Jane's lips came together.

"Jane, don't hold back. I need to know."

"Child, she's a strong woman. I know you may thinks she's not, but she is. Heaven knows he don't think so. But she's more than strong." Her brown eyes beamed. "She's smart. She tried to do what's right. She did. Don't you ever doubt that. And she loves you, more than life, more than herself. You."

"What happened?"

Jane shook her head. "I don't know. She had pills from Dr. Beck. They help when she has her migraines. She had..."

"What? She had what?"

"A lot of them, but here's the thing. I took them. She gave them to me for safekeeping. She'd been taking this other medicine, the one that keeps the headaches away, and they were happening less and less. I had her pain pills. I still do."

Jane stood and paced to the window and back. "I took all her prescriptions except the preventive ones. She was trying. I see her with water not wine." Jane shrugged. "I don't know. Then she start acting funny... strange-like. Saying things and getting confused. I called Dr. Beck and he came out here, more than once. But it got worse, not better. It don't make sense."

I couldn't follow. "What doesn't make sense?"

Jane stood, letting out a deep breath. "Mr. Fitzgerald, he got mad at Dr. Beck. He say that Dr. Beck wasn't helping but making it worse. I couldn't say anything. It's not my place."

"What would you have said?"

"I would have said that it wasn't him—Dr. Beck wasn't making it worse. The doctor would talk to me. He knows I love your momma. I'd do anything to help her."

My heart fluttered at her words. Jane was the glue that kept my momma and me together. She wasn't an employee. I'd never seen her that way. When she said she loved, it was real and deep. It was the kind that made you feel warm and safe. Knowing that she'd been that for Momma made me smile.

"Dr. Beck, he was worried," Jane went on. "Your momma told him she wasn't taking pills and honest to goodness, she wasn't drinking like she used to... but... then she would."

"I'm not following."

Jane sank to the bench. "I can't say what I think. I ain't got no proof."

"What do you think?"

"I think your momma be a smart lady. I think she started to know things, things Mr. Fitzgerald didn't want her to know. And I think she... she's ill and she needs help. She needs you."

The anger I'd suppressed to be the obedient Alexandria that Alton required flooded my bloodstream, reminding me of who I really was. I stood and stared down at Jane. My question came out harsher than I'd intended. "Tell me. Do you think *he* did something?"

Jane's eyes opened wide.

"I mean something *new*," I clarified. "He wouldn't poison her? Would he?"

She lowered her chin as she shook her head. "I never thought so. I didn't. I did everything to take care of her. Now with Dr. Beck's questions and how fast it all happened... I don't know."

I was now the one pacing. "Is Dr. Beck still seeing her?"

"I don't think so. I hear Mr. Fitzgerald and Miss Suzanna talking. I think Mr. Fitzgerald, he fired Dr. Beck and Mrs. Fitzgerald has a new doctor at that Magnolia place. But before that, Dr. Beck run tests. He said it wasn't making sense and he wanted to know what was in her blood. He said the results take time." She peered up, moisture filling her dark eyes. "I don't think he has the answers yet."

"Jane, I need to talk to Dr. Beck."

She nodded. "Child, I got his number. But I think my phone's being watched." Her eyes widened. "I mean listened to." She shook her head. "Can they do that? Or am I going crazy too? Maybe we all crazy?"

I scoffed, thinking of Deloris. "Oh, no, Jane, you're not crazy. I know they can do that. I'm not sure Alton knows how, but I'd guess he could pay someone. He took my phone. I don't have any way to call, and Dr. Beck isn't the only one I need to call."

"That young man?"

I nodded as a sad smile filled my cheeks. "I need to let him know what's happening. He's, well..." I contemplated the best way to describe Nox. "...protective. I can't imagine what he's thinking or going through. Somehow I need to let him know that I'm okay. And then, there's school. Alton said he'd let me call Columbia tomorrow, but I need my own way of communicating without him listening to every word."

"I don't think my phone is your answer. You know how your momma used to call you on it?"

"Yes."

"She stopped doing it. Said if she did, he'd know. I don't know if he did or if it was part of the crazy. She never said more about it, but it scared me. So when you called this morning, I wasn't sure what to say."

I sighed. That made sense as to why she sounded so strange.

"What about now?" I looked up at the ceiling. "You don't think they can hear us now, do you?"

Her eyes followed mine. "I-I ain't never thought about that."

"I don't even know what to look for."

Jane closed her eyes and shook her head again. "If they can, we'll know soon enough."

We both turned toward the door. Silence prevailed as we stared. When it didn't move or even rattle, we both took a deep breath.

Her hand went to her chest. "Honest, Miss Alex, I don't know what to think or feel. I don't know if it real or not."

"What do you think Momma knew that Alton didn't want her to know? Was it about him and other women?"

Jane blew out a long breath. "No! Well, yes, she knew that for a long time. She'd say if some whore would help him out, more power to her. It'd be one time she don't have to."

My eyes widened. "My momma said that?"

Her cheeks rose. "Yes, sorry. I guess I thought you were old enough to hear that."

"I-I guess I am, but oh my. If that's not it, what did she know? Do you have any idea?"

"I don't know exactly. But it has to do with your marriage to Mr. Spencer."

I put my hands on my hips. "I'm not marrying Mr. Spencer. I'm not marrying anyone right now, but if I did, it wouldn't be him."

Jane tilted her head to the side. "It'd be that young man?"

I shrugged. "We haven't talked about anything like that. We've only been dating since... well, we met last summer."

"But you like him? You're living with him?"

I couldn't hide my smile. "I do and yes. I have an apartment, but as I said, he's protective. I'm safer at his apartment. Besides, I want to be there."

"Not here."

"No, Jane. I want to be with Lennox, but I'm here for Momma, and I'm not leaving until I know she's going to be all right."

Jane stood and walked toward me. Reaching for my hands, she smiled.

"Child, I ain't never been happier to hear your voice than I was when you called. How did you know? I was praying. Was it God? Did He tell you to call?"

My stomach twisted. "Something like that."

"Praise the Lord. Miss Alex, I know you can help."

"I hope so, Jane. I hope so."

CHAPTER 8

—•○•—

ALEXANDRIA

THE HANDS OF the clock moved painstakingly slowly as the sky beyond my bedroom morphed from Georgia sapphire blue to a deep, velvety black and eventually filled with stars. Sitting in the sill of the giant window, I watched the driveway. The cobblestones were no longer illuminated with lights. They'd all been turned off near midnight. Now, nearing two in the morning, only the silvery shadows cast by the moon lit the property in front of Montague Manor.

There wasn't much to see. If my bedroom faced toward the back of the original plantation, I could watch the lake and the fields beyond. However, my view was limited to the front. I'd imagined Clayton's SUV barreling toward the manor.

It hadn't happened. Not one car had come up the drive, not since I took up my post. One had left. I'd watched from behind the curtain. I was a spy trying my best to understand this strange yet familiar terrain.

The car had left after Jane's visit, after dinner had been brought, and after the sun had set. I'd stood perfectly still as the black sedan drove to the door. I didn't know the driver, yet he wore the customary uniform. It was when the passengers made their way down the broad steps that I knew he worked for the Spencers. The first to come into view was Miss Suzanna, flanked by Alton.

My stomach churned as he guided her toward the car, his hand securely placed in the small of her back.

Friendly gesture?

I wondered, until he leaned closer to kiss her goodbye. It was on her cheek, but something felt wrong, as if it were more than friendship. I had a sinking suspicion that their camaraderie wasn't based upon common concern over my mother.

However, before I could let my thoughts linger, my attention quickly diverted to the next couple: Bryce and Chelsea. Judging by the time, nearly nine o'clock, the four of them must have enjoyed a nice dinner here at Montague Manor.

My heart ached and mind questioned my new reality. I was sequestered to my bedroom while Chelsea dined in the Montague Manor dining room. The question turned to indignation as Bryce helped her into the backseat and she turned toward him and smiled.

The simple expression was the twisting of a knife, one I hadn't even realized had been inserted into my heart. How does one suffer a stab wound without knowing? I couldn't answer. Nevertheless, in that moment, seeing her smile up at Edward Bryce Carmichael Spencer, the flesh of my chest tore as the blade plunged deeper.

I'd hoped for more information from Jane, but she hadn't been the one to bring my meal or retrieve the tray. I didn't know the young lady, though she fit Alton's profile: young, attractive, and silent.

Each passing minute and hour, my mind swirled with the reality around me as well as what was happening away from Montague Manor. Though I had the ability to leave my bedroom, I worried about the possible repercussions. Would Alton suspect that Jane had given me the means? What would that mean for her? Why hadn't she been back?

I waited and bided my time until the nighttime silence settled over the manor.

During my wait, I'd realized that other than seeing Nox's telephone number once on a Post-it note in Karen Flores's office, I'd never known the digits. Instead, I'd relied upon my phone to hold that vital information. Though I racked my brain, the numbers were nowhere to be found.

I contemplated locating my phone. Would Alton take it with him to the master suite? Could it be in his office? For hours I paced and contemplated until I found myself settled on the giant windowsill overlooking the main entry and exit of Montague Manor.

At some point, I searched my purse and wallet. What had I done with that Post-it note? Had I saved it? If I had, I couldn't find it. However, tucked away behind a credit card in my wallet was a business card, one I'd been given in case of an emergency, one that when I'd received it, I'd considered less of a lifeline and more of an anchor, one that I'd feared had been capable of drowning me in my poor decisions.

Now, after two in the morning, with Deloris's card and number secured in the pocket of my robe, it was time to search for a telephone. During my childhood, each and every room had been wired for the house phones. Within the manor were multiple lines and direct buttons to access the staff. The phone system was much like what a large hotel would still have today.

The tumblers clicked as I turned the key. Their echo seemed louder than it would ever have been during the day. Twisting and pulling the crystal doorknob toward me, I peered out into the hallway. Part of me feared there might be a guard sitting outside my room, but there was none. As quietly as I could, I closed my door and relocked it. If anyone came by and tried the handle, they would hopefully assume I was inside.

The corridor was dark and silent, except for the occasional small nightlight between every few doors, illuminating the way. I inserted the key and opened an empty bedroom. With a click of the light, I saw that the bedside stand was devoid of a telephone. Quietly, I repeated the task, room by room. Not one contained a telephone. Apparently, even Montague Manor moved with the times. Everyone had gone cellular.

When I reached the end of the hall, I second-guessed my plan. I could stay on the second floor and make my way to the library. The downside was that it was closer to Mother and Alton's suite. The upside was that it held less of a chance of meeting staff. Then again, at this hour would anyone be awake?

As I lingered, my heart beat rapidly, creating a cadence like a drumline or a firing squad. I refused to decide which one.

Staying close to the wall, I made my way down the grand stairs one step at a time, allowing my eyes to adjust to the darkened foyer. I'd left my slippers in my room, deciding instead that I could be quieter in bare feet. Step by step, I moved closer to the ground floor.

I forced myself to inhale and exhale, certain that if I didn't, I'd pass out before finding a way to reach Deloris. Like the second level, the first floor was quiet. Only the hum of the air conditioning dominated the air as I moved along the corridor I'd walked earlier in the day. Alton's office was risky, but I knew without a doubt it contained a telephone.

I took a deep breath as I reached for the door handle. Would it be locked?

I pushed the door inward and it opened. Peering inside, I once again held my breath, a part of me fearful that he'd be present. Shadows lurked in the darkness, their presence were felt more than seen. I stepped within and waited for my eyes to adjust. At least in the hallways there'd been indirect lighting. Alton's office was black. Even the draperies appeared to be pulled, blocking the moon's rays. I pushed the door closed behind me as the latch clicked closed.

I debated on turning on the lights, knowing that there was a lamp on a nearby end table between two high-backed leather chairs. My thoughts went to the setup of the room. Twenty-four years of experience combined with an embedded memory of this room allowed me to walk without colliding into anything. Perhaps the unwillingness of Montague Manor to change had its advantages.

I fumbled for the switch.

Light was faster than sound, yet before my fingers twisted the knob, I heard the footsteps.

"Oh!" I stifled a gasp. My heart that had slowed to normal speed jumpstarted, the jolt sending shock waves throughout my body.

An arm went around my waist as a hand covered my lips. In a fraction of a second, I was held tightly against a hard body.

"He said you'd try this." Bryce's low growl came near my ear. "I told him you were smarter than that. I guess I was wrong."

I'd seen him leave with Chelsea. How was he here?

His warm whiskey breath teased my neck, sending chills from my spine to my bare toes. I fought against his hold.

"Please, Bryce…" My words came out muffled by his hand.

Without thinking, I quickly bent forward and snapped backward with all my force. The back of my head collided with his face. What did it hit? His nose? His chin? At the same time my elbow met with his stomach.

Ooaf.

It wasn't a word but a sound as his grip loosened. Without pause, I broke free and raced for the door.

The sliver of light shining beneath the large door was my goal, my finish line or perhaps my start line. Once beyond, I imagined screaming for help as I ran back upstairs. Lunging forward, my bare feet tripped on the plush carpet as they were captured. Helplessly, I fell forward, ending my race before it began.

My arms flew out, barely catching myself and saving my face from hitting the carpet as Bryce pulled me backward, causing my robe to move upward moments before he landed on top of me. I fought to breathe as his weight covered my back. Slowly he moved, a deep laugh filling the darkened office as he readjusted, the entire time keeping me pinned as he straddled my body.

"Damn, you nearly broke my fucking nose." His breath and words were close as he leaned down, pulling my head backward with his fist in my hair.

"Let me up," I demanded.

Kicking my feet I met air as Bryce released my hair and grabbed my shoulders. I was helpless as he turned me over, holding me down, straddling my waist, and securing my arms at my side.

"Asshole," I spewed. "Let me go."

For a split second, in the lightening darkness, his face and outline of his broad shoulders came into view. From the shadows around his eyes, I feared he'd slap me as Alton had done. Instead, he painfully seized my chin. "Shut the fuck up, Alexandria."

When I didn't respond, he leaned closer. "Even though I was wrong, I can't tell you how fucking happy I am to finally have the right one."

"What?"

The word was barely out when his hand went from my chin to my lips, crushing them painfully against my teeth until my chin was down as far as it could go. The telltale taste of copper alerted me to blood.

"I told you earlier," he said, his warning slowing in a menacing tone, "you need to learn to keep your mouth shut. Now is an excellent time to give that a try." He bent forward until our noses were nearly touching. "Can you do that? Can you listen for just a minute?"

My head barely moved as I attempted to nod.

Again, his laugh filled the office. "I like your spunk almost as much as your willingness to submit. We'll have more fun than I'd imagined."

It wasn't only his words that twisted my stomach, but the realization that his erection was probing my stomach as he leaned down.

Slowly he lessened the pressure against my mouth. I sucked my bruised lips between my teeth as he sat taller.

"You have two choices," Bryce said. "I let you up and we talk about whatever it was you were going to do, or I keep you here and call your father. I have my cell phone in my pocket. Think about it: do you really want him to know he was right?"

It wasn't only that I didn't want him to call Alton. More importantly, I wanted him off of me. "Let me up." When he didn't move, I added, "Please."

His knuckles caressed my cheek. "That's the Alexandria I know, polite and genteel."

Though internally I shivered, I did my best to remain still. "Bryce, please don't do anything that will ruin us. Please help me."

His chest heaved with indecision. "Us? Really, Alexandria? Are you now saying there's an us?" He moved his attention from my face to the lapels of my robe. Brushing them aside, he revealed my nightgown.

My stomach twisted. "Bryce, you don't want it to be like this."

His eyes opened wider. "How do you want it to be?"

I wanted it to be never, but that wouldn't get him off of me. "You know I don't want it." His knees applied pressure to my wrists secured at my sides as he sat taller. "But," I added, "if it's in our future, I want it to be special."

Bryce leaned down. "Was your first time with him special?"

Pinned beneath Bryce, I was at a definite disadvantage; nevertheless, I couldn't answer him forthrightly and tell him that despite being treated like a slut, my first time with Nox had been magical.

I couldn't think about Nox and our first time. I couldn't think about Del

Mar or Highway 101. I couldn't think about the gas station or later in his suite. I had to concentrate on Bryce and getting him off of me. "I could ask you the same question, but the *her* would be rather ambiguous."

Bryce's chest expanded as he took a deep breath, lifted his weight to his knees, and then swung to my side. Scrambling as fast as I could, I crawled backward and stood. But before I could run for the door, Bryce backed me into one of the leather chairs near the light.

His tone was low and slow. "We're getting married. I'll have you, and I'm not spending the rest of my life apologizing for fucking willing participants." He reached again for my chin. "Alexandria, I believe you were reaching for that light. Do it. Turn it on and see what you did to me."

"Bryce..."

"Do it!"

I fumbled again for the switch, my moist fingers having difficulty grasping as I turned the small knob. Fearful of seeing what I'd felt against my stomach, I closed my eyes before the light registered.

He again squeezed my chin. "Open your damn eyes. Look at me."

Taking a deep breath, I did as he said. With his grasp of my chin, he had my face directed toward his. It wasn't what I expected, but I soon realized what he wanted me to see.

"Y-your cheek?" I said, lifting my hand to the raised knot, now a shade of deep pink.

He closed his eyes as I ran my fingers over the contusion.

When his eyes opened, he turned and sank into the other chair, on the opposite side of the lamp. "We may have to postpone our engagement pictures."

"Good idea," I said.

"Postpone. Not cancel," he clarified as he leaned back against the high back and sighed.

I nearly laughed at the sight of his mussed blond hair. Normally he was one of those preppy-looking men without a hair out of place. I took a deep breath and focused on my mission. "Bryce, this isn't going to happen."

His gray eyes opened wide as a smile broke across his face. "I'd tell you not to fight it, but damn, I think I like it when you fight." He rubbed his own cheek. "But I'll need to do something to ensure you don't leave marks, at least not ones that show."

My eyes fluttered closed in a silent attempt to stop the bile. "I need to make a call. Please, let me call a friend. I just need to tell her that I'm all right."

"Her?"

CHAPTER 9

---•○●---

NOX

THE DAMN PINGING of my iPad brought me back to reality. I ran my hand through my hair as I tried to make sense of the sound. It was dark, the middle of the night, yet the sound wouldn't stop.

Ping.

Ping.

I'd finally fallen asleep after a few too many fingers of whiskey. It didn't seem to matter how much alcohol I consumed—it wasn't enough to wash away my guilt at not being able to help Charli. I should be with her. She should be with me.

Her crumpled letter, the one that both Deloris and I knew wasn't from her, lay on the bedside stand beside my bed. Though she hadn't been the one to write it, its presence gave me a sense of connection. Next to the letter was my phone. I'd sent her multiple text messages and even left a couple of voicemails. My mind told me it was useless, but I couldn't seem to stop.

I continued to reason that when she finally turned on her phone, she'd see that I'd tried, that despite the roadblocks, I'd done my best to reach her and wouldn't stop.

Pulling myself from my stupor, I opened my tablet. My personal messages were multiplying by the second. Each one was from Deloris.

What the hell?

Was she sleeping on a button?

I opened the first, second, and then the third. They were all the same.

"ALEX IS ON THE PHONE. COME TO MY ROOM."

The sheets around my legs were suddenly restraints hindering my movement. Kicking them away, wearing only gym shorts and a t-shirt, I rushed from the lonely bedroom and through the front room of my suite. Without stopping for shoes, I grabbed the room key and hurried out into the hallway. A few doors down, I came to Deloris's room. I would have known the number, but with the door slightly ajar I could hear Deloris's voice.

The next voice I heard momentarily stopped me in my tracks. I would have recognized it anywhere. Taking a breath, I barreled inside. The door bounced against the inside wall.

"What—?"

Quickly, Deloris turned my direction, pursed her lips and put her finger to her mouth.

"Of course…" she said. I couldn't remember what Charli had asked; I'd been too astonished to hear her voice.

"I want to speak to her," I whispered.

Deloris shook her head as she asked, "Alex, can you repeat that? I think we have a bad connection."

Charli's voice filled Deloris's room. "Can you hear me now?"

"Yes, can you tell me again what you said? Are you sure you're all right?"

"I'm fine. I wanted you to know."

"Ch—"

This time it was Deloris's hand that stopped me as she thrust a note my direction.

Don't talk. She's on speaker and she's not alone.

Who the fuck is with her? Is it her stepfather? Who and why? It's two-fucking-thirty in the morning. Why isn't she alone?

Those were my unspoken questions as I pressed my lips together and listened.

"How's your mother?"

I marveled at the calm in Deloris's voice. It wasn't mirrored by her body language. Standing in a robe, she was uncharacteristically rigid.

"I-I don't know yet," Charli answered. "I want to go see her, but I need your help."

"My help? Of course. What do you want me to do?"

"Go back to New York."

Fuck that!

I spun like a caged lion as I silently pleaded to Deloris, hoping that telepathically she'd hear my rebuttal.

"Alex, how will that help?"

"Alt—my family—is concerned that if I leave the manor something could happen to me."

"You know that we'd never allow anything to happen."

"That's the thing," Charli said, "they're afraid you'll be the cause. I can't see my mother until they're assured that I won't be taken, by you or Lennox."

Lennox. She did it again. Could the letter have been from her? Was this her way of letting us know that she was speaking under duress? The letter may not have been her, but the person on the phone definitely was. I didn't only know her voice, but her sounds, moans, and pleas.

I shook my head—so much for telepathic—as Deloris's eyes widened, looking my direction.

"Is my word enough that we've left or do they need more?" Deloris asked.

"Um, I trust your word, but…" She paused. "…they would like proof. A flight manifest showing that you, Lennox, and Clayton have left Savannah."

"Fuck," I mumbled under my breath as I turned away.

"How can I reach you?"

"You can't."

"Excuse me?" Deloris asked.

"I can't use my phone right now, and I don't have access to my email. You can send the flight manifest to altonfitzgerald at montaguecorp dot com."

"What about this number? Can I call you back on this number?"

"No, this is my stepfather's home office. He wouldn't be pleased."

"I don't fucking care…"

"Deloris," Charli said, "please tell me you're alone or I'll need to hang up."

"It's the TV, Alex. I thought I'd muted it." Deloris's glare stopped anything else from escaping my lips.

"Do you still want Lennox to follow your instructions in the letter you left for him at the gate?"

"Letter?" She paused again. "Oh, yes. Please."

"All of your clothes or only the summer ones?"

What? The letter had said only supplies for class.

"Um," she answered, "all, I suppose."

"Alex, you know all you have to do is—"

"Deloris," she interrupted. "I need to go, but first, I wanted to say thank you, to you and everyone. Please do as I ask. I need to see my mother and until you're gone, I can't. And tell…" Her voice bubbled with emotion, tearing at my heart. "…*him* that I'm sorry. This is the way it was always supposed to be, what I was supposed to do. I just didn't know it. I didn't understand. Now I do. We were never supposed to happen."

It took every ounce of my strength to stay quiet. I wanted to scream at the phone, at Charli, at whoever the fuck was with her. She wasn't telling the truth. I knew more than her voice, moans, and pleas. I knew her heart. We *were* supposed to happen.

Why the hell would I end up in Del Mar? Why the hell would I go to the large pool? It was fate and whatever shit she was being fed couldn't stop that. It wouldn't stop us.

"Alex—" Deloris began.

"Goodbye."

The hotel room filled with silence as we both stared at Deloris's phone. The call was done.

"What the fuck?" I asked.

"She was obviously being coached. I just don't know who was with her."

"Why did she call *you*?"

"She didn't say," Deloris answered. "But at the least we confirmed that she didn't write the letter."

"We never thought she did. What I want to know is how did the person who wrote it know about rules?"

Deloris shrugged. "Would Alex have told someone?"

I ran my hand through my hair, still moving, spinning in place. "I don't know. She hasn't had much contact with anyone but her mother and a woman named Jane."

"What about Chelsea?"

"What about her?"

"Would she know that? She was with Alex in Del Mar."

I couldn't think or reason. "Maybe. What did she say before I got here?"

"Not much. She said that she arrived to the manor safely, and that she'd dropped her phone. It wasn't working right now."

"That's fucking bullshit. She didn't drop it. I mean it's not on, but I don't believe she dropped it."

Deloris shrugged. "Lennox, she obviously sounded... coerced."

"No shit. She also referred to me as *Lennox* in that conversation," I said. "I think that means something."

"It's your name."

"It's not what she calls me. She's giving us clues, clues that whoever is with her wouldn't understand." My chest tightened as I pulled at my own hair. The pain in my scalp was to help me think. "Fuck, Deloris, they're making her say things she doesn't want to say."

Deloris stood, meeting me head-on. "She called. I'd venture to guess it took some work on her part to do that. I'd also guess that there was more in that conversation than either of us heard. I recorded it. I'll go back over it, a million times if I have to. I won't stop until I've deciphered every one of her meanings."

"I'm not leaving Savannah without her."

"Just because we leave doesn't mean we have to stay gone."

My eyes closed as I sank down onto the sofa. "If we don't leave, they won't let her see her mother."

"Wait..." Deloris said as she pushed buttons on her phone. The recording of the call began to replay in snippets:

"My help… by you or Lennox… they'd like proof. A flight manifest showing that you, Lennox, and Clayton have left Savannah." Deloris hit rewind and replayed the last sentence. "A flight manifest showing that you, Lennox, and Clayton have left Savannah."

Deloris's eyes widened. "Did you hear that?"

"Yes," I said dejectedly, "twice, or I guess, three times."

"No. Think about what she said. Who needs to leave?"

"All of us."

"Lennox, that wasn't what she said. She named me, you, and Clayton."

The puzzle Deloris was showing me began to make sense in my tired, heart-wrenched mind. "She didn't say Isaac. Maybe she doesn't know he's here."

"Or maybe she knows, but no one else does. After all, Clayton and I were seen at Magnolia Woods. You were seen at the gate."

"Isaac was with me."

"He was a driver, behind a window. He could have been from a rented service."

"Isaac can stay while we leave?"

Deloris nodded.

MY BACK TENSED as Clayton drove Deloris and me through the gate into the private airport.

"This pisses me off," I said for the hundredth time.

"You've mentioned."

I turned toward the window, seeing the Georgia red clay as the sun made its way above the horizon. "We're giving in to him. I fucking hate it."

"We aren't. We're helping Alex by doing as she asked."

"She didn't mean it. I know she didn't."

"Give me time, Lennox. Give her time. There's a game going on here and we unfortunately aren't familiar with the rules. The thing I keep reminding myself is that she is."

"Rules?" I repeated. "When was the last time you spoke to Chelsea?"

"It's been over a week."

I turned toward her. "If she wrote the note, maybe she was giving us a clue too? Maybe she is familiar enough with the Montagues that she knows the rules, enough that could help?"

"I'll keep trying. I haven't been able to reach her since Alex... since yesterday. One thing's for sure: Alex is familiar with the rules and with Mr. Fitzgerald," Deloris confirmed. "I'm sure she told you in confidence, but the more I know about her childhood, the mansion, about everything Montague, the more I can help her."

I recalled Charli's honesty, how she'd said she wanted to tell me about her shadows. She said her honesty wasn't so I could right the wrongs done to her, but so that she could show me she trusted me with things she'd hidden from others.

"I don't know what will help you."

The car stopped on the tarmac, near the Demetri Enterprises plane. As Clayton opened the rear door, Deloris said, "I'll go get the manifest from the airport and have them send it to Mr. Fitzgerald. I'll meet you on the plane."

Each step toward the stairs was harder than the last. Each step up seemed like quicksand, its muck sucking me back to the Georgia clay. I stopped halfway up the stairs and looked out at the landscape. Beyond the airport the land was flat, the expanse mostly filled with the lightening sky.

What was Charli doing? What was she enduring?

I recalled the night in our apartment when she first shared.

"Did he abuse you?" I asked.

She didn't hesitate with her answer: "Psychologically. Verbally. I was never good enough at anything. Always an embarrassment. Never the Montague I should be."

Fuck!

That was what she was saying on the phone. This was what she was supposed to do and be. I didn't know what that meant, but that was it. I knew it—in my heart, in my soul—and it frightened me, not for me, but for her.

Whatever was happening wasn't what she wanted, but what she was supposed to do.

If only I'd pushed more.

But I hadn't, and now I was at a loss.

As I gazed out the window looking for Deloris, it hit me. She was wrong. I wasn't the one who could answer her questions, but there was someone who could.

Pulling out my phone, I searched my contacts. The name had to be there. I'd called him at least once before. My watch read 7:26. Maybe if I hurried, I could catch Patrick before he left for work.

CHAPTER 10

———— ●○● ————

ALEXANDRIA

"ALEXANDRIA? ALEXANDRIA?" MY name echoed through my tired mind, punctuated by raps upon my bedroom door.

I pulled myself from my bed, wrapped my robe around me, and made my way to the door. "Hello." My voice sounded sleepy even to my own ears.

"I'm coming in."

"Suzanna?" I asked, though I knew it was her voice on the other side of the locked door.

Last night, after my call to Deloris, Bryce insisted on returning me to my room, only after I relinquished my key. I tried to explain that I wouldn't leave; I'd only wanted to make a call. He wouldn't take no for an answer. Thankfully, he had taken no for everything else.

Each time we were together, it was as if there was a power struggle going on within him: his desire to please Alton versus being the Bryce of my childhood. Since it was feasible that Alton would eventually learn I'd made the call to Deloris from his phone, Bryce could counter, saying he'd orchestrated my dialogue as well as confiscated my means for further escape. Giving him the key was a no brainer. When I'd explained that it was one I'd had hidden in my room for years, he didn't seem to question. I didn't mention there were numerous others waiting to take its place.

I turned back to the clock. It was nearly ten in the morning.

A new panic washed through me. Had Alton left for Montague Corporation? Had I lost my chance to contact Columbia?

I took a step back as the tumblers clicked and Suzanna unlocked the door. As the door opened, she instructed the same staff girl from last night to enter, pushing what I assumed to be my breakfast, or at least, a cart with an assortment of covered plates, a carafe, cups, and glasses.

Pulling my robe closed, I watched as Suzanna directed the girl where to place everything and then instructed her to leave. Once we were alone, Bryce's mother turned toward me, her expression filled with artificial compassion.

"Alexandria, how are you?" Each word dripped with her saccharine-coated Southern drawl.

That was her lead in?

I forced my bitchiest smile. "I'm peachy. Thank you so much for asking. After all, you just unlocked my door to enter. Doesn't that sound like fun to you?"

"Really…" She sat opposite the tray at a small table in my room and lifted the silver dome. "…dear, you should eat. I heard you had an eventful night."

I lifted my brows. "It's nice that Bryce discusses things with his mother. I'd like to do the same."

"Look, the cook made you pancakes. You've always loved pancakes."

I wrinkled my nose. "Not since I was seven." I sat and reached for the carafe of coffee. Though there were two cups; I only poured mine. By the time I stirred in the cream, Suzanna huffed and poured her own cup.

Bitch, I'm not your maid. I didn't say that. Instead, I offered the small pitcher. "Cream?"

Reaching for the pitcher, Suzanna said, "Darling, you really do have the ability to make this better. It's up to you."

"If it's up to me, I want to see my mother and go back to New York." It wasn't what Jane had told me to say, but it was the truth.

"That's not what I mean. I mean, you and me, we should be friends. Your father has requested that I plan your wedding for the Saturday before Christmas." Her eyes lit up. "That's Christmas Eve. Can you imagine how beautiful it will be? Now, think about it. We don't have much time. Who do you want to stand up with you? Every girl imagines her dream wedding. Tell me about yours."

After taking a sip of her coffee, she nodded knowingly. "Just because this is rushed, doesn't mean we have to skimp. Your father wouldn't hear of that. He wants the biggest, grandest wedding Savannah has seen in years... decades even. This is monumental—the Carmichaels, Fitzgeralds, and Montagues, all becoming one."

I grimaced over the rim of my cup as she enthusiastically spoke. I had visions of the newscasters who were able to describe the destruction of a mass disaster with a smile on their faces.

Five thousand dead as a tsunami devastates... on a lighter note, the Miss America pageant will go on as planned.

"...really can be an epic event. I've started the guest list—"

"Excuse me," I interrupted, reining in my sarcasm. "There's no Fitzgerald in that equation." I stood ready to say that I'd rather marry a Fitzgerald than a Carmichael, when an idea hit me. "Patrick."

Suzanna stared. "What?"

"I want Patrick Richardson to stand with me."

"Well, of course, he could be a groomsman."

"I didn't say that," I corrected. "I want him to stand *with me*." I shrugged. "I would probably have chosen Chelsea, but you can see where that may be a bit uncomfortable. I'm no longer close to any of my classmates from the academy and those at Stanford didn't know about... well, this." I motioned around the room. "I want Patrick."

"Dear, we'd need to discuss that with your father. I know he isn't pleased with the life choices Patrick has made."

Infidelity or being gay? I'd go with Infidelity, since homosexuality wasn't actually a choice. Then again, Infidelity was a secret, so apparently it was Patrick's sexuality that Alton didn't approve of.

I tilted my head. "I don't want to know how you know what Alton thinks, but if you call him *my father* one more time, I'll spill my coffee all over your lovely cream dress."

"Alexandria! I'm trying to help you."

I slammed my nearly empty cup onto the table. "Let's get something straight. I don't want to marry your son. I have never wanted to marry your son. I won't marry your son, but I will play this damn game to get to my mother. Now how about you stop pretending to be my best friend and you start being Momma's?"

She stood. "I-I'm simply aghast."

As she fluttered around my room, with her hand near her throat, I sat back in my chair and laughed. It started as a simple giggle, but as the seconds passed the rumble grew to a resounding full-body laugh.

Finally, she cleared her throat. "You don't seem to understand. This wedding is happening. Don't you want a choice in choosing your wedding dress?"

"You're right, I don't understand. How about instead of giving me a choice in dresses, I get a choice in grooms?"

She squared her shoulders. "Alexandria, I came here this morning to help you."

Standing to meet her, I asked, "Why don't you tell me about my mother? Better yet, since you have the key to my freedom, why don't you take me to my mother? Let me see her condition for myself."

Her tongue darted to her lips and she nodded. "I-I think we should concentrate on where we can do the most good, where we can make the most progress. As it is, we have less than two months before you and Bryce say your vows. There are showers that need to be planned, registries that need to be completed, and a honeymoon planned. You'll be pleased to know I've secured the Presbyterian Church…"

I narrowed my gaze. "Are you serious?" The Presbyterian Church was one of the oldest, most historic churches in Savannah. It didn't seem possible that she could reserve that on such short notice, especially on Christmas Eve. The donation must have been enough to cover my law school for the full three years, including my housing. Well, at least now I knew where my trust fund went.

Setting her coffee cup on the table, Suzanna brushed the imaginary lint from the skirt of her dress. "Alexandria, your *father*…" She emphasized the words, daring me to reach for my coffee. "…expects you in his office at noon. The photographer was due here at two for your engagement pictures, but it seems as though that needs to be postponed." She took a step closer and lifted a brow. "Perhaps you and Bryce could manage to keep marks limited to places covered by clothing, at least for the near future."

"I was fucking fighting him—"

Her palm neared my cheek, but just as quickly I leaned away, saving myself from another slap and seized her wrist. Clenching my teeth, I squeezed. "Don't think that you ever can strike me."

She pulled her wrist away, rubbing the area I'd just held. "You may have been off gallivanting around the world and your mother may have coddled you, but, Miss Collins, you're back in Savannah and proper ladies don't say *fuck*. From this time forward, that word will be stricken from your vocabulary either willingly or by force. The choice is yours."

"Do you even give a fuck about my mother?" I opened my eyes in question as well as disobedience.

"Laide is my best friend. Of course I care. Don't you understand, Alexandria? I'm here with you, putting up with your insolent behavior for *her*. Do you think Alton would do this? The answer is no. He would not and will not put up with your disrespectful conduct. I'm here to help you and help Laide. I guess the question is… Do you give a *fuck* what happens to her?"

It was Alton's question, restated.

Suzanna turned on her heels and walked toward the door. With her hand on the crystal handle, she added, "I'll leave your door unlocked. Shower, dress, and be in your father's office before noon. If your answer to my last question is yes, then don't be a second late."

I wanted her gone. I also didn't want to obey anything she, Bryce, or Alton said, but I was trapped. "Suzanna?"

"Yes?"

"He said I could call Columbia. Is he here? I could go down and call my faculty advisor now. I've already missed a class yesterday afternoon and another this morning."

She eyed me up and down. "A proper lady doesn't walk around Montague Manor in a bathrobe."

After twisting the knob, she opened the door and just as quickly disappeared as the door closed.

I TURNED THE key from my side of my door and returned it to my jewelry box. I couldn't make myself go into the bathroom and shower knowing the door could be opened. I had visions of emerging from the bathroom to someone—anyone—in my room. I doubted it would be Alton, but then again, anything was possible. In my opinion, Bryce and Suzanna were equally unacceptable visitors.

Before my shower, I'd moved the cart with my breakfast back into the hallway. The key was a risk, a way to alert others that I had another. I'd hoped that placing the cart in the hallway would stop the young girl from trying to enter my room.

As I looked for clothes, I realized that it didn't matter that the things I'd packed in New York were with Deloris and Nox. My closet was full. There were both clothes that I'd left in Savannah as well as new ones. Even the bathroom cabinets were filled with my choice of cosmetics. I remembered that Jane had unpacked for me during my last visit, but with each new discovery, I feared there was another explanation, someone else who helped to plan for my return.

No one else would have known my preferences so exactly except the person who'd shared my life and my apartment for the last four years. Everything was correct, all the way down to the brand names and colors of eye shadow. I didn't want to think that Chelsea purposely sent me the text message to lure me back to Savannah. I rationalized that even if she had, given my mother's condition, I was glad I was back.

Besides, if Chelsea hadn't contacted me, would anyone have even told me about my momma?

As I prepared for my command performance in Alton's office, it occurred to me that although my closet and cosmetics were satisfactory, I didn't have everything that I needed. I needed my backpack, school supplies, and birth control medication.

The absence of my medicine gave me another idea. Perhaps it was as farfetched as having Patrick in my wedding—that would never happen—but it was worth a try. I needed my birth control medicine. If Alton wouldn't let me have my things from New York, there was only one alternative: I would need to see Dr. Beck—alone.

Taking one last look in the mirror, I shrugged. The simple dress and flat shoes were a compromise. I'd have preferred jeans and a light sweater, but I was playing his game. If I were sequestered to the manor, my attire wouldn't matter. My goal was to get to Magnolia Woods. For that, I needed to look my part.

With a deep breath, I made my way toward Alton's office. It was the same path I'd taken during the middle of the night, minus the check of neighboring rooms. Though the passages were brighter during the day, the Montague Manor shadows never fully evaporated. They lurked within the dim and less-traveled passageways.

I fought to breathe as blood drained from my cheeks. It was 11:50 as I lifted my hand to knock on the office door. I had always despised this room, and here I was, entering it for the third time in the last twenty-four hours.

I may have thought it before, but the dog-and-pony show was now in full swing.

CHAPTER 11

NOX

I PACED NEAR the windows of my office. The world beyond the glass continued to move. Small cars created ribbons of traffic, and tiny dots of all different colors walked along the sidewalks. The colors of the dots were created with jackets and coats, hats and gloves, possibly even scarves. While the early afternoon sun cast shadows on the ribbons and dots, it did little to warm the air. But this was New York. The residents were tough and would persevere. Despite the late October breeze blowing fiercely between the buildings, all of the dots moved forward, onward as if my world weren't on the brink of imploding.

I was from here, born in Brooklyn, raised in Rye. I was resilient, yet I didn't feel that way. Instead, I felt defeated. Why was I back in New York?

How could I face Charli one day, admitting that I'd left her... in that house of horrors?

Nothing about my brief talk with Patrick this morning alleviated my level of stress. We hadn't had much time and he had a prior obligation. That was why the two of us had a dinner meeting scheduled for tomorrow. Nevertheless, during our quick chat, he'd confirmed my unspoken fears. With each response, I had the sickening realization that I hadn't grasped the depth of Charli's despair when she first arrived in New York. I could make excuses.

I could blame my own rage, but that didn't change the fact that she'd been in pain and I hadn't recognized it.

That wouldn't happen again.

According to Patrick, the loss of Charli's trust fund was sudden and recent. She'd told me about it, but not in detail. She'd said that her mother and Alton Fitzgerald had taken it. What she hadn't told me was that they offered her another option. Her alternative to being penniless was to transfer to Savannah Law, marry Edward Spencer, and live at Montague Manor.

My Charli hadn't caved to their will. She'd fought them... and found Infidelity. Though the company was supposed to be a secret, it seemed as though it was truly the worst-kept kind. Patrick was the one who'd told Charli about it. He still assumed I was her client. In his mind, that made the topic open for discussion.

As I watched the ribbons and dots, I palmed my temples. My head ached from both too much whiskey and not enough sleep. Sleeping hadn't been an option after Charli's call.

There was something else that bothered me. Patrick had said more than once that he was happy Charli had found me and that we'd been paired together. He didn't know what an ass I'd been, how I'd treated her, chastising her for a choice and decision that should have been praised. Not that I do or did condone Infidelity, but she should have been applauded for standing up to the injustices she'd endured. That wasn't what I'd done. Instead, I'd belittled and punished her.

What made it all worse—ten times, a thousand times, a million fucking times worse—was that now, despite it all, she was back under their roof again. The independence she'd exerted was taken away from her in an instant. Patrick had no doubt that somehow they'd sucked her back in. He did question the possibility of ever truly freeing her, especially as long as her mother was ill. A black hole, he called it.

I didn't argue, though I vehemently disagreed. I'd free her if it were the last damn thing I did. But first, my goal was to understand my opponents. I wanted to know every detail, from the layout of Montague Manor—the grounds and the house—to the way Alton Fitzgerald took his coffee. I wanted to know everything.

I'd learn as much from Patrick as possible and once I did, I'd free her. And then I'd spend the rest of my life atoning for my unacceptable behavior. Never again would she feel trapped. Never again would she be sucked into the Montague darkness. I'd do anything and everything to fulfill one promise I'd made her. I'd said it when I was upset, but I meant every damn word.

Alexandria Charli Montague Collins is mine. She belongs to me. I'm not a good man, but I'm the only fucking bad I want near her.

That had been my promise and my threat. I wouldn't rest until I made it her reality.

For the millionth time, I opened the tracker app on my phone. Her blue dot was still at the manor. As soon as it moved, I'd alert Isaac. He had access to the same app. I knew he was also watching, but it made me feel better to see her, even if she was a blue dot.

I even spoke to the blue dot: "Charli, I may have left Savannah, but know it was only because you asked. It's only because it'll help you see your mother. Don't think of me as being gone. I'm still with you and you're with me. Stay strong, princess. I'll get you back… this bad man needs you. You're my good, my light."

The beep of the intercom beckoned my focus toward the speaker on my desk phone and away from the tracker app. "Mr. Demetri, your father is on line two."

If I stood perfectly still, could I ignore Dianne's message and pretend I didn't hear her?

I took a deep breath, said a silent prayer that I was up-to-date on whatever the fuck he was going to ask, and pushed the button. "Thank you, Dianne. I'll take his call."

Easing myself into my desk chair, I lifted the receiver and pushed the connection for line two. "Oren."

"Lennox. Tell me what's happening."

That was such a broad request. My mind scrambled with what he could possibly be referring to. "There's a lot happening. Care to narrow that down?"

"I could ask about the distribution centers you promised Carroll or the way you outsmarted Davis with the House bill, but I'm more interested in why two separate private Demetri-contracted planes went to Savannah. I'm interested in why five people went to Savannah and only three returned to New York." His tenor uncharacteristically slowed. "I'm interested in why Miss Collins didn't return. I was under the impression she was a studious person, intent on her law degree."

"How the fuck do you know this?"

Oren's volume rose. "I'm the damn CEO of Demetri Enterprises. You may think I'm sitting in London not paying any fucking attention, but I see everything. Every manifest is copied and sent to me. Every proposal goes past me before it goes further. I started this company from nothing—"

I pushed back against the chair, my temper and temperature rising exponentially. "I know!" I interrupted. "I've heard this fucking speech. Get to your point."

"Why is Miss Collins in Savannah without you?"

I ran my hand through my hair. I must be not only sleep-deprived, but also fucking delusional, because for a moment I imagined hearing genuine concern in my father's voice, concern over my life, my girlfriend, perhaps even more than how it related to Demetri Enterprises. "Why the hell do you care?"

"So it was just a fling? A conquest? You threw her away, or did she leave you?"

My head moved from side to side. "You really don't want to have this conversation with me right now."

"Mr. Demetri," Dianne's voice came through the speaker.

"Hold on, Dad," I said leaning forward and hitting the button. "Not now, Dianne. I'm still on the phone."

"Sir, Mr. Demetri—"

I lifted my eyes to the opening of my office door, momentarily stunned as my father entered with Dianne half a step behind.

"Sir, he's here."

Slamming the receiver down, I replied, "I can see that." My stare sent daggers toward my father. Fuck him. He didn't have any idea what I was going through.

As our eyes locked, I expected the daggers in return. I expected some arbitrary lecture about how my name was associated with his company and in reality it was his name on the letterhead. I expected anything other than what I saw. In the split second since he'd entered, the arrogant prick I expected was gone. In my father's pale eyes was something I hadn't seen in years.

Emotion. Concern. Perhaps even helplessness.

"Dianne, close the door. Give us a minute."

Oren placed his phone in his pocket.

"You didn't think you should've started that conversation with *I'm here?*"

"Tell me what's happening. Don't bullshit. I want to know."

"Why?"

He walked to the chair near the sofa. The one he always used, the one facing the door.

"Son, that's a long story."

CHAPTER 12

—•○•—

ALEXANDRIA

As THE DOOR opened, Bryce met me face to face. For only a moment I forgot to walk; instead, I stood mesmerized by Bryce's face, more accurately, by the large egg-like elevation on his left cheek. I fought to pull my gaze from the purple contusion to his eyes. Once I did, my lower lip disappeared between my teeth.

"Sorry." As soon as the apology left my lips, I regretted uttering the word. I wasn't sorry that I'd head-butted him. I was sorry that he'd caught me, wrestled me to the ground, and gotten aroused. I was sorry I'd allowed him to choreograph my conversation with Deloris. I could go on and on with my regrets. Head-butting him wasn't one of them. Shrugging, I added with a grin, "Not really. Maybe you should think twice before you tackle me again."

His eyes narrowed and voice lowered to a whisper. Cocking his head toward Alton and Suzanna, he said, "This is another instance when you should keep your mouth shut."

Bile swirled in the pit of my stomach as I took a breath and stepped through the threshold.

"Mother," Bryce said.

Suzanna nodded. "I'm glad you could make it on time. I see your ability to tell time has improved, Alexandria."

Bitch.

I summoned my most accommodating tone and even allowed a bit of Southern drawl to sweeten my response. "Thank you for noticing. It was difficult without my phone, but at least the clock in my room works."

"Hmm," Suzanna said, pursing her lips. "Well, Bryce has asked that we give you and your father some privacy." She looked toward her son. "He hopes that with fewer distractions, you'll understand."

I was in a strange quandary. I didn't want Suzanna and Bryce present, yet I didn't want to be alone with Alton. Yesterday, Bryce had stood up to Alton on my behalf. I'd never seen anyone do that, not even my mother. That didn't mean I wanted to admit I wanted him here.

Instead, I focused on my indignation at their insinuation. "I'm capable of understanding, distractions or not. It's the absurdity of the information that has me thrown."

"I don't have all day," Alton announced as he sat behind his desk.

So this wasn't going to happen at the table—another gray area for me. Each unfamiliar move seemed to throw me off-kilter.

Bryce stepped closer and reached for my hand. "Would you rather have us stay? Me stay?"

I didn't want him to ask, nor was I willing to admit to anything. Retrieving my hand, I shrugged. "It seems to me that I'm the only one who doesn't know all the information. Just tell me so I can go see my mother."

"That hasn't been—" Alton began.

"They're gone," Bryce interrupted. "You showed me the manifest."

My heart sank with the knowledge he so casually offered. I was truly here without them. Nox and Deloris had done what I'd asked, leaving me alone. I held out hope they'd caught my message about Isaac. However, as I faced this room, it didn't matter. I was alone. I reminded myself to concentrate on my mother.

Alton's eyes narrowed toward Bryce in some unspoken exchange. Finally, he said, "That doesn't mean it's safe."

"We'll take security. I won't leave her alone."

"Alexandria," Alton said, "sit down. First things first."

"I agree," I consented as I eased into a chair across from his desk. "First things first: you promised me a call to Columbia."

"It's done."

"What? What do you mean it's done? You said I could call."

"The day is half over. I assumed an institution as prestigious as Columbia Law would do business at a more reasonable hour and I was right."

"What did you say?"

Alton leaned back and lifted his brow. "It was an interesting conversation. I spoke with a Dr. Renaud."

"Yes, she's my faculty counselor."

"She was surprised to hear from me, again—your father—in connection to your records."

My stomach twisted as I recalled telling her that Alton had no say over anything regarding me. "You have to understand, I'm an adult. I should have been the one who called."

"While that's debatable—"

"It's not," I interjected. "Talking to parents is against university policy. She has to talk to me."

He waved his hand. "The subject is irrelevant. After a brief discussion and reminders, the situation is resolved. You're now on a family-emergency leave."

"What does that even mean? How will that affect this semester?" Panic filled my bloodstream. "I can't go on leave. I'll finish from here. I can watch lectures online and communicate with my professors via email and teleconferencing. I only have a little over a month left until the end of the semester. I don't under—"

Alton lifted his hand. "Enough. I took care of it."

"Really, dear," Suzanna said, her words once again filled with sugar. "You'll be too busy. What, with the wedding arrangements and of course, your mother, you don't have time for school."

I turned toward Suzanna, my jaw clenched in helpless frustration. "I can make time."

Alton opened a manila folder on his desk and gestured toward the chair beside me. "Suzy, sit. Bryce, pull over another chair. Brantley is waiting to take us back to Montague Corporation. The world doesn't stop because Alexandria has decided to grace us."

I didn't decide to grace them. I was kidnapped, tricked, and captured.

Momentarily, the loss of Columbia drowned out the commotion of everyone sitting around me. I turned toward Bryce. "You're going back to work? What about going to see my mother?"

Before Bryce could respond, Alton began. "I explained the groundwork yesterday. Basically, your grandfather legally secured the future of Montague by tying up loose ends before his death." He handed me a piece of paper.

Leaning forward I took what he offered, curious yet dreading what I was about to read.

"This is a section of Charles Montague II's last will and testament," Alton explained. "It's a copy. You can imagine the magnitude of the actual document. This is the part that concerns you."

I stared down at the words. The room quieted, taking a collective breath, as I read.

Article XII - Provisions for Montague holdings

If at the time of my passing these provisions have not been satisfied, it is the responsibility of my heirs, Adelaide Montague Fitzgerald and Alexandria Charles Montague Collins, to willingly and legally satisfy the following criteria at the appropriate dates. Failure to do so will result in the loss of all inheritance, including but not limited to assets, property, shares, personal properties, and the residual remainder of my Estate.

As is now the case, it is essential that Adelaide Montague remain married to Alton Fitzgerald for the remainder of their earthly lives. As Adelaide's husband, Alton Fitzgerald will have all rights set forth as the primary stockholder in Montague Corporation. If either party files for divorce or attempts to end the marriage, all Montague holdings revert to Alexandria Collins.

Upon the death of either A. Fitzgerald or A.M. Fitzgerald prior to the coming-of-age of A. Collins, all Montague holdings will be held in trust for her until the age of twenty-five or until she has completed a college degree, whichever comes first.

Once the age or degree completion has occurred, in order for A. Collins to inherit the Montague holdings and assets and to fulfill the requirements set forth in this legal document she must adhere to the following:

Being of the legal age of twenty-five (or having completed her college degree), Alexandria Collins must agree to a legal union with a husband who too will represent her and their biological children's shares in Montague Corporation as well as in the running of private Montague assets.

It is my desire, and thus forth the determination of this last will and testament, that A. Collins will marry Edward Bryce Carmichael Spencer, the son of Suzanna Carmichael Spencer, as outlined below.

E. Spencer must first complete undergraduate and graduate school and prove himself worthy of Montague Corporation. Upon completion of his postgraduate degree, no more than eighteen months may transpire before their union.

Upon their marriage, controlling interest in all things Montague will revert to A. Collins and E. Spencer, with provisions for the continued support and oversight by A. Fitzgerald and A.M. Fitzgerald until the time it is determined that either or both is no longer competent.

If this union does not occur, all Montague holdings and assets will be liquidated. The assets will henceforth be bequeathed to Fitzgerald Investments, leaving both heirs and their descendants without Montague assets.

If the marriage of A. Collins and E. Spencer fails to survive, resulting in divorce or premature death, all Montague holdings and assets will be liquidated and henceforth bequeathed to Fitzgerald Investments, with one exception: in the instance that a male heir exists over the age of twenty-five, the designated heir will retain all holdings and controlling interest.

If it is found that anyone mentioned in this article willfully and purposely hinders my wishes, that beneficiary will be stricken from receiving his or her share of the inheritance.

Once I'd finished, I didn't look up. Instead, I read it again from the beginning, looking for something I'd missed the first time. With each paragraph dictating my life and essentially the lives of my children, my head moved from side to side. If this were a test question, I'd answer that it was illegal.

Finally, I looked up and said what I was thinking. "This can't be legal."

"I assure you, it is—beneficiary stipulations."

"This is why my momma never left you?"

Alton's brow furrowed. "Why, Alexandria, would you presume that your mother wanted to leave me?"

"Wait!" I said. "She can't die. She has to get better. It says in here that if she dies—"

"Your mother won't die," Alton said. "I told you to ask yourself if you wanted to see her and if you wanted her better. Dying isn't nor was it an option."

I stared in disbelief, remembering Jane's concerns. Instead of asking Alton if he'd hurt my mother, I changed the subject. "Where is Jane?"

Alton's head twitched. "What?"

"Where is Jane? I saw her briefly after I arrived." I could have said 'was kidnapped and locked in my room,' but I didn't. "Where is she? I haven't seen her since."

"I don't know the location of each member of the household staff. That's your mother's duty and obviously she isn't currently capable."

"Then who's overseeing the staff?"

"It'll be your job as lady of Montague Manor, once you and Bryce marry, which is another reason for a leave from your studies. This is a big estate."

Because hiring cooks and gardeners was more important than my degree? Staying focused, I asked, "Who's doing it now?"

"I am," Suzanna volunteered. "I'm doing all I can to help your mother."

I turned her way. "Where is Jane?"

"She's no longer with Montague."

There wasn't enough gravity in the atmosphere to keep me seated. "What? Why?"

Alton lifted his hand. "The two of you may discuss household staff and budgets after I leave. The information in that document is as simple as I can make it. Tell me, Alexandria, do you plan to fulfill your responsibility as a Montague?"

How many times had my mother asked me a similar question? Yet never had she explained exactly what would be expected of me as a Montague.

"When was this archaic document written?"

"After your mother and I married, nearly twenty years ago."

Standing behind my chair, I held tightly to the formed back, squeezing the leather until the tips of my fingers blanched. "I was four and my future was dictated?"

Bryce shrugged. "Mine was too, but I'm not fighting it."

"Why?" I asked louder than I should. "Why aren't you fighting it? Why would you want to go along with this plan? Do you want to be married to someone who doesn't love you?"

"This is business, not love," Alton said.

Bryce stood and faced me. His gray eyes swirled with sadness. "No. I want to marry my best friend. I want to marry the pretty girl who used to swim with me in the lake. I want to marry the beautiful girl who accompanied me to the dances at the academy, who visited me at Duke. I want to raise children with her and have them attend the same academy. I want to hold her hand as our son swims and our daughter runs. That's what I want."

I couldn't form words, not in coherent sentences.

He reached for my hand. "I know this seems out of left field, but really it isn't. You know I've always wanted to marry you, long before I knew about this stupid will. I've loved you since we were children."

"Bryce?" Suzanna asked.

The world moved in slow motion as Bryce's Adam's apple bobbed and he fell to one knee. I took a step back when he released my hand and reached into the pocket of his suit coat.

"No, please don't do this," I whispered.

Undeterred, he removed a small box from his pocket and opened it to a diamond engagement ring. The stone was huge. I wouldn't say it was pretty or stunning. It was big. Other than my mother's, I couldn't recall seeing a bigger center stone. The diamond sat in prongs on a platinum rather than yellow-gold band. That alone told me that it wasn't my mother's ring.

"Remember," his voice cracked with emotion, "when I told you I had a ring at Duke?"

I nodded.

"This isn't it."

"It isn't?"

"No. This diamond belonged to your grandmother, Olivia. With your mother's help, I had it reset in a more modern setting. See, Alexandria, this is what she wants, too." He swallowed again. "I'd be honored if you'd wear it, if you'd wear it forever and be my wife."

My head moved from side to side. "Bryce..." Tears filled my eyes. "...I don't love you." I hesitated, but continued. "I love someone else."

The muscles and tendons in Bryce's neck tightened. "You heard Alton. This isn't about love."

I looked back at Alton. Suzanna was beside him with tears in her eyes.

Is she nuts?

I concentrated on Alton. "If I say no? If I refuse?"

"Magnolia Woods expects payment. You're free to walk away from Montague, but what will happen to your mother?"

"But she can't die. You said that."

"Oh, I thought you'd learned by now that there are fates worse than death."

CHAPTER 13

OREN

WHERE TO START?

Maybe at the end?

My gaze held tightly to Lennox's as years' worth of memories swirled, creating a cyclone that threatened to blow our fragile relationship to pieces. I'd never intended to share this part of my life. That's not true. I would have done anything to truly share it—with Adelaide, Lennox, and Alexandria. That was before.

After it ended, the way it ended... it was never anything my son needed to know... until it was.

Until now.

When Adelaide left me the final time, she'd made it perfectly clear that we were done, forever and always. The only solace I found in her goodbye was the pain I saw in her beautiful blue eyes and sadness I heard in her voice.

If that makes me more of a bastard, then I guess I am. I would have moved heaven and earth for that woman, but she never allowed it. I couldn't have given her the life she had. Instead, I could have given her more. Not in money. I would have given her the love and respect she deserved. I did for years... until I couldn't.

Honestly, I couldn't blame her for leaving me, not after what I told her. It was one thing to be in love with a man with a dubious past and equally questionable present. That could be easily overlooked as long as the particulars were arbitrary. It was another—too much—to learn that the objectionable past intersected with hers.

Who the hell was I kidding?

It hadn't intersected: it had collided.

I walked away that day with my head held high, knowing that I'd done what I had to do. I'd done not only what was expected of me, but what was required. I couldn't face a future with Adelaide without telling her the truth—the whole, painful truth. It turned out to be more than she could handle.

Outwardly I was stoic. It was inside that I ached... more than ached. When she told me to leave, when I walked away, Adelaide Montague took what was left of my heart and humanity.

Angelina was gone. Lennox was running Demetri Enterprises, and my Adelaide had told me to go, never to return. When I thought life couldn't get worse, it did.

The markets crashed. My justification began to disintegrate before my eyes. Every move, every decision, everything I'd done, everything I'd agreed to, was for Lennox's future and for Demetri Enterprises. In my mind, the two went hand in hand. I'd built one, neglecting everything else for the other. And then, in two months, the value of it all dropped over fifty percent.

Only on paper, the newscasters said. That wasn't the truth. I understood how businessmen in the 1920's found solace in jumping from their office windows. More than once, the thought crossed my mind. I'd endured too much: Angelina's death, Adelaide's rejection, and the drop in Demetri holdings. Lennox was married and had what was left of Demetri Enterprises. I was no longer needed.

I'd said I was moving to London for the company. After all, it was a global financial crisis and if we were to survive, Demetri needed to be at the epicenter.

That wasn't the entire truth. I wanted to be away. I couldn't face the day-to-day emptiness any longer. Lennox had Jocelyn. Silvia was content with them and her own life. For the first time in my life, no one needed or cared what I did or where I went. It was the coward's alternative to jumping to my death. I'd seen too many men take their last breaths. I couldn't do that, but I could fade away.

For years I did. I tried to forget the two women in my life—the two who had left me—and distance myself from the son who didn't know me. It wasn't his fault. I'd never tried. That wasn't who I was.

In the beginning, I worked diligently to distance myself, geographically as well as emotionally. I deleted the applications that allowed me visual access to Montague Manor. The cameras were outdated and the software was archaic by today's standards. Who's to say the cameras weren't eventually found?

Old man Montague, as Vincent had called him, never had cameras installed in the master suites. He was looking at the main living areas as well as office space in the home and at Montague Corporation. It pained me to view even the ones of the main floor, seeing Adelaide wandering aimlessly from room to room, always with a glass in her hand.

Never did I see the woman in my memories. The smile she wore while in her home was faux, a cheap imitation. I'd seen the real one, the designer original, the one that lit up her blue eyes. I'd heard her laughter and knew that what she showed to those who should be closest to her wasn't genuine. It was too painful, like the twisting of a knife. I couldn't watch any more of it.

Now, with the recent turn of events, I wish I could. Then again, I doubted the system could even be supported by today's networks, not without a remodulation of the entire system. It wasn't like I could send a crew to Montague Manor and announce that their home-security cameras needed to be upgraded.

Though many memories of Adelaide replayed in my head, one that never left me was of her concern over her daughter's future. She was continually concerned over her father's wishes for Alexandria's future, her predetermined marriage to be exact. From all of Adelaide's accounts of Alexandria, I never doubted the girl's ability to fight. It seemed as though she'd been doing that most of her life, ever since I took away her defender.

That thought ate at me, over and over, through the years.

And then Lennox suffered a tragic loss. Of course he didn't turn to me. I'd never turned to him.

It was a long shot, a pipe dream, a way to unite us once again. Leading two people to the same resort was easier than being sure they'd connect. Neither of them suspected a thing.

I'd taken Adelaide's daughter's defender from her when she was too young to understand. Lennox had lost the women he held most dear. Bringing the two of them together was perhaps a shot at redemption, one last attempt to right a wrong that in reality could never be righted.

If I understood what Adelaide had said, if Alexandria married someone other than the young man her grandfather wanted, the Montague fortune would be given to Adelaide's husband.

I'm a selfish bastard, but that scenario didn't sound unappealing. My hope was that if that happened, that bastard would leave Adelaide. She would no longer be of any use to him. If that happened then I could offer her a new life—if she would have me.

It had been years since she'd learned my secret. Perhaps time truly did heal all wounds.

It had all worked even better than I'd planned... until now.

Something had happened and I was at a momentary loss. It was time to come clean with Lennox and offer my assistance. It was time that father and son stopped working opposite sides and became a team. If one Demetri could accomplish the things each of us had, then together we could be unstoppable.

"Dad, what is it?"

"Do you have anything stronger than water in this office?"

Lennox's eyes narrowed. "Are you ill?"

"No." I stood and walked to the windows. The early evening traffic was starting to build. It was late in London, yet here I was in New York. "I need to tell you something, something I should have told you before."

"Is it about the company?" he asked, standing.

I ran my hand through my hair. "In a way, but not like you think."

"Fuck, Dad, I'm not thinking anything. Say something. I have a shitload of things going on right now. If you can't tell me, then go back to London and we'll talk another time."

"I wanted you to meet Alexandria."

Lennox took a step back. "What the fuck are you talking about?"

"She needed you. You needed her. I don't know why you let her go back to Savannah, but you need to go get her."

His eyes widened. "I don't know what the fuck you know about Alex or Savannah, or any of the cryptic shit you said at the house a few months ago, but I tried. I went to her house. It isn't a house—"

"It's a castle," I said, completing his sentence. "Is she there because she wants to leave you?"

"No!"

"Then why?"

Lennox turned a small circle. "Why the fuck do you care?"

"I've cared for a long time." I took a deep breath. "Alcohol?"

Lennox nodded and walked toward a sideboard. Pushing a button, a panel in the wall moved, revealing a well-stocked selection.

I lifted my brow. "Nice. I approve."

"Hmm."

His back was toward me.

"I guess I don't say that enough."

Lennox turned toward me with two tumblers of amber liquid in his hands. "Never, actually. I went for straight up."

"Lennox, I was never a good father."

"Or a husband… do you want me to go on?"

I took one of the tumblers. Swirling the liquid, I contemplated my reason for flying to New York. Two swallows or was it one? The smooth oak-flavored whiskey only burnt for a second before it was gone. I handed him back the glass. "I'll take another."

Lennox didn't answer as he turned and refilled my drink.

"There have been two women I've loved."

His shoulders moved. "Too bad Mom wasn't one of them."

When he turned back my way, I said, "If you were anyone else, you'd be lying on the floor right now."

He extended the drink. "Go for it, Dad. I've had a shitty few days."

"Your mother was my first love. You don't understand what happens to people when life interferes, but it never took away our love. I loved your mother until the day she died. When she died she took a part of my heart with her, a part that will always be hers."

Lennox took a deep breath, swirled his drink, and tipped the crystal to his lips. Equally as quickly, his tumbler was empty. "I do know."

My chest ached at his tone. "I'm sorry. You do. And you're too young to live with that. That's why Alexandria was—no, *is*—good for you."

Lennox refilled his glass and asked, "The second? During, before, or after Mom."

I shrugged. "During but after."

Gulping the fiery liquid, he slammed his empty tumbler on the counter and walked back toward the chairs where we had been sitting. "I don't want to hear it. I don't give a fuck who you cheated on Mom with."

"During, because I never stopped loving Angelina. I met the second one after your mother and I divorced." My cheeks rose in a sad smile. "Angelina even knew. She asked me. She said she could tell I was happy in a way I hadn't been for a while. You may not understand this, but she approved. We loved one another enough to want the other to be happy."

"So you didn't cheat?"

"Not with anyone who mattered. That's all I'll say on that."

Lennox shook his head. "What did you mean that you wanted me to meet Alex? We just randomly met. It wasn't arranged. I didn't even know who she was. She didn't know who I was. Did she?"

My head moved from side to side. "I don't think so."

"Then what?"

"I knew she needed someone. You needed someone. It seemed like a good idea."

"How could you possibly know what she needed or needs?"

"She needs you. Tell me what's happening and let's help her together. I don't know her stepfather, but what I do know is that I don't trust him. From what I've seen and heard, Alexandria is a smart young woman. Because of that, she's a threat to him. She'll need more than smarts to get out of the trap that was set for her when she was young.

"I know you have no reason to trust me or turn to me, Lennox, but I can help. I want to help."

"I'm going to ask this one more time. Why?"

"Adelaide Montague."

CHAPTER 14

ALEXANDRIA

TAKING A DEEP breath I turned from Alton to Bryce and back. "No."

For the first time since my return to Montague Manor, I'd stood up for myself. If that wasn't satisfying enough, watching the signature crimson rise from Alton's collar made it the entire package. Perhaps if I continued to push, Mr. Alton Fitzgerald would have his own cardiac event? If he did, an alternate provision to my grandfather's will would go into effect. The thought was my mini-Christmas and for only a moment I reveled in it.

A loud thump filled the room as Alton's palms came down hard on the desk.

"Alexandria?" Bryce was now standing.

"Two questions," Alton growled.

"Yes and yes," I replied.

"It doesn't appear as though."

"Appearances?" I lifted my brow. "Is that your goal?"

"No," Alton answered. "What's yours?"

"Seeing Momma and her getting better."

"Then put on the damn ring."

When I looked at Bryce, he had the ring out of the box, the band pinched between his thumb and finger as he stared down at the stone. Many would consider it beautiful. I should, but I didn't. I should relish the idea that it was my grandmother's. However, something about my recently acquired knowledge regarding her husband and how he'd damned not only me and my future children, but also my mother in a questionably binding document soured my appreciation.

I extended my hand toward Bryce, palm up. It wasn't the romantic proposal one dreams about. It wasn't the man I loved, down on one knee, slipping the band over my finger.

Slowly, he released the ring to my grasp. I lifted my hand up and down. The damn ring was actually heavy.

If I wear it, will I need to start lifting weights with my right arm to keep my definition even?

It was a silly thought, but strange things passed through my mind while the real world continued on a crash course toward disaster.

Anticipation filled the air as all eyes were on me.

"Put it on," Alton repeated as Bryce and Suzanna waited.

"Let's negotiate," I offered, setting the ring on Alton's desk and sitting back down.

"Alexandria, I don't have time for your childish—"

This time I lifted my hand. "Hardly childish. I'm negotiating for my future as well as my mother's." Before he could speak, I sat erect and continued, "I will be able to go see her—*now*. I have clearance to visit her regularly." His mouth opened, but I didn't stop. "My door is no longer locked from the outside. I agree to stay here in Savannah, but I won't be a prisoner."

I turned toward Suzanna. "I'll take over the household staff and that includes reinstating Jane. And I will personally contact Dr. Renaud. I will complete this semester online. If that isn't possible, then I'll do what needs to be done, including traveling back to New York."

"No New York," Alton countered.

"I need to speak to her."

He nodded.

"And I'll have access to a car. Let me clarify: a car, not a driver. If I'm playing this damn game, you'll need to trust me."

"I don't. I never have."

It was my turn to shake my head. "I've found only untrustworthy people have a problem trusting."

"You'll go back to him."

My chest rose and fell. "I want to. I won't deny that. I need to explain things to him so he doesn't think I just left arbitrarily. But no, I won't go back. I'll make sure Momma is all right first."

"First? What about the wedding?" Suzanna asked.

"We can plan it."

"Alexandria?" Bryce asked again. "What does that mean?"

"Right now my answer is no. I'll wear the ring. I'll play the part, but I can't agree to marry you."

"Then your mother will lose everything." Alton spoke without a hint of concern. "I hear there's some top-notch indigent care being offered at a local homeless shelter."

The temperature of the room elevated. "Do you agree?" My question wasn't for Bryce. I wasn't even bringing him in on the conversation.

"Don't you think you should be talking to your fiancé?" Suzanna asked.

My head tilted to the side as I stared at Alton. "Did you negotiate your marriage with my mother or with my grandfather?"

He nodded. "Very well. Put on the damn ring."

It seemed heavier than the first time as I lifted it from the shiny surface of the desk. Prisms of color danced across the reflection as the stone caught the artificial light. Closing my eyes, I spoke to Nox. No one else could hear, but I prayed that he could.

This isn't real. Let me explain. Please know that I'm doing what I have to. I love you—only you.

I slipped the band over my knuckle, hoping that maybe it wouldn't fit, that it would need to be sized, but no. It was perfect.

I turned toward Bryce. "Take me to my mother or I'm going alone."

His gaze moved from me to Alton and back. "I'll take you."

THE EARLY AFTERNOON sun warmed my skin as Bryce and I stood

awkwardly silent just beyond the front doors. Though I'd been outside yesterday, as I filled my lungs with the fresh air, I had a sense of relief. With each breath I longed for more freedom, more than just from my room or the manor, but for the freedom that came with California and New York.

The diamond ring on my hand was my reminder that freedom was currently beyond my reach. No longer would I know the exhilaration of independence, not until I figured a way out of this obligation—this life sentence.

First I had to see my momma.

The dark bark of the oak trees caught my attention. In New York, the leaves were changing colors or even gone this late in October. Here, the black bark and wide-reaching limbs held tightly to the deep green leaves. As a child I rarely gave it thought, but now the fact that not until the new leaves came in the spring would the old ones fall seemed ironic.

In New York, each season was different—a fresh start. Here, the old ways held tight until the new pushed them to their death. I was the new. The season of old leaves was about to end.

"Do you really want to manage the staff?"

I turned my sunglass-covered eyes toward Bryce. "What?"

He shrugged. "It's a good thing, I think."

"What are you talking about?"

"You told Alton you want to be in charge of the household staff. Is it just for Jane, or do you want to do it?"

It was hard to hide my thoughts—my nose itched to scrunch and my lips to purse—but if I was going to do this, I needed to try. Keeping my expression as sincere as possible, I replied, "It's both. Don't you remember how wonderful Jane always was?"

Bryce nodded. "Yeah, I liked her."

"I more than like her. I love her. She's devoted her life to this house. There's no reason to dismiss her now."

We both turned to the sound of tires as they turned upon the cobblestone. From the garages, a black sedan approached. Bryce's hand moved to the small of my back. He leaned toward my ear and added, "Since she was your nanny, I suppose she'd be good with our babies."

It was impossible to hide the disgust from my expression. Thankfully, I was facing the car. I took a step away from his touch. "Bryce, I'm not ready—"

Reaching for my shoulder, he turned me toward him. In an instant, my childhood friend was gone. "I'd be worried about no sex, since you were always so determined. I got it. You had issues. I respected that. But now, Alexandria, things have changed."

"Nothing's changed. I don't—"

The tendons in his neck stretched, coming to life under the skin. "Everything has changed. You've spread your legs for him: you will for me."

"And how would you know that?"

"Lennox Demetri…" Bryce said the name I was forbidden to utter. "…doesn't seem like the type to have a live-in roommate without benefits."

I lifted my chin toward the front of Montague Manor. "The difference with this situation is that I'm not living with you. I'm in my own home." I shrugged. "Don't worry. There are plenty of bedrooms. Maybe you can bring Chelsea. I'm sure she'll keep you busy."

His grip on my arm tightened with each phrase. I should have stopped talking. This could be one of the times he'd spoken about. Yet like the bile rising from my stomach, once the words began, I couldn't stop. "Or how about you fill the manor with your whores? For example, Millie. She'll be devastated that her wedding will be overshadowed by ours, but maybe you can make it up to her."

"Are you done?" Bryce's words came through clenched teeth as a driver I didn't recognize stood patiently with the back door to the car open.

"For now."

"Get in the car before I change my mind about taking you to Magnolia Woods."

I shrugged away from his grasp and turned toward the car. I'd wanted Bryce to drive, but since we were getting in the backseat, it appeared that we would have company.

As soon as the door shut, Bryce angled himself toward me, his face millimeters from mine. "You'll be ready, trust me. I'm not marrying a virgin or an ice princess. I'll give you time." I fought the need to flinch as his breath filled my lungs and his knuckles caressed my cheek. "You'll soon figure out, I'm either your only friend or your worst enemy. Think about it, *fiancée.*" His hand dropped from my cheek to my thigh. "I think you'll decide that spreading these legs willingly for me will be in everyone's best interest."

I covered his hand with mine and pushed. "Don't make me head-butt you again."

My neck straightened as his lips covered mine. Soft and warm. Mushy. I didn't move, not an inch. Bryce pulled back and shook his head. "You'll learn."

I quickly turned toward the window, refusing to look his way. The car slowed as we neared the gate. When it did, my heart leapt as I noticed the SUV waiting on the other side. Had Nox and Deloris found a way? My fingertips ached to touch my necklace.

And just as quickly, disappointment washed away my hopes.

Now seat-belted next to me, Bryce placed his hand again on my thigh, this time near my knee. He tipped his head toward the large black vehicle. "That's more Montague security. Alton's not taking a chance on anything happening to you."

"How very kind of him."

"Yes, Alexandria, if anything happened, we couldn't wed and then where would that leave Adelaide?"

Thankful I was still wearing the sunglasses, I made myself turn his direction. "I still don't get it. What do you get out of this?"

"What do I get?"

The sedan was open, yet the driver wasn't even a thought in my mind. Maybe it was the way I was raised? Montague employees heard without hearing. Perhaps it was Nox's openness in front of Isaac and Clayton? No matter the reason, I spoke without concern for the man's thoughts or ability to hear.

Glancing backward as we drove along the main road, I got a quick look at the driver and passenger of the SUV. They were two men I didn't recognize.

Sighing, I turned toward Bryce. "Yes, what do you get? A loveless marriage. Why? Obviously, other women are interested."

"One day you'll realize that I don't want the other women. They've just...

I don't know… kept me occupied. I've wanted you since I can remember. And with this gift from your grandfather, I get you." He gestured forward to the driver. "I get all of this—the manor, the corporation, and Alton's approval. I get it all."

"Why would his approval matter to you?"

Bryce shrugged. "I guess because I'll never have my real father's. Doesn't it mean something to you? You know what it's like not to know your own father."

I hated that Bryce knew me so well.

"I do, but no," I answered honestly, thankful that he'd taken his hand off of me. "I've never had Alton's approval and I don't give a damn about it." I remembered Oren mentioning my father. "I'd rather have my real father's. And though I never can, I'd like to think he'd approve of the decisions I've made."

As soon as I spoke, I knew that I'd said it right.

Made.

Past tense.

Because the decisions I was making and might continue to make weren't ones that I believed my father or anyone else would find acceptable. Not if what Oren and my mother had said were accurate. Not if I was truly like Russell Collins.

With each mile toward Magnolia Woods, I allowed my mind to drift. Russell Collins. He didn't often cross my mind. Had his marriage to my mother been brokered like her and Alton's? What decisions had my momma ever been allowed to make in her own life?

CHAPTER 15

―●○●―

ADELAIDE

"Momma?"

The murmur of voices filled my ears. I couldn't make out their words or even if they were talking to me. I didn't want to care. I wanted to go back to my memories, thoughts of him, thoughts I hadn't allowed myself to entertain for years. Oren was calling to me, but so was she.

My baby.

My daughter.

My Alexandria.

Was she a dream? A memory?

They were all mixing together. It was difficult to keep them straight.

"Adelaide."

"She doesn't know… We've tried… She was fighting…"

The murmurs continued as I tried to reason. The bed where I lay was different. I wasn't in my room—our room. And then I remembered.

The unfamiliar room.

The man.

The bracelet.

My eyelids fought to blink, to move.

Was I still wearing the bracelet? I thought I was, but everything was detached. Even my Alexandria's voice.

"Momma, can you hear me?"

I can hear you? Where are you? The responses formed in my mind, but I couldn't make my lips or tongue articulate the sounds. Dead weight. Falling. I was sinking and I couldn't make it stop.

Was this what quicksand was like? An unstoppable force dragging me down, each moment deeper than the last until an all-encompassing presence surrounded me. Comforting, yet suffocating.

Alexandria called out again.

This time there were more than words. A touch. A warm touch that momentarily stilled the ice-cold free fall.

Though I couldn't speak, the touch of her hand on my cold skin was an answer to my unspoken question. She was here. My Alexandria was here.

I'm not alone.

If only I could talk to her, touch her, and let her know I was okay.

I would be now. She was here.

When did that happen? When did the mother become the child?

Though it was rarely I who'd comforted Alexandria in the night or saved her from bad dreams, now she was the one to rescue me. Not from bad dreams—my dreams were my solace. Alexandria would rescue us both from our reality.

"Momma…"

I love you.

I couldn't speak. My body no longer responded.

The effort was too much, too monumental.

I surrendered to the dreams. It wasn't really surrendering, not to the quicksand, not to the sensation that dulled my senses. I was relinquishing the fight and giving myself time to re-emerge, time to work my way out of the muck and find my way back to a life I wanted to live.

I'd fought too hard to fully surrender. It was what was expected of me, but I was ready to be done with what was expected. I wanted more.

Allowing my body and mind to give way to memories, I passed the baton to Alexandria. She would fight for our future while I concentrated on having one.

"Adelaide."

Alexandria was beyond my reach, but Oren wasn't.

I lifted my tired eyes to the most stunning blue—soft yet intensely light—and at the same time, filled with their own darkness. I could gaze into their depths for days, but alas, we didn't have days. My cheeks rose in a grin seconds before I lifted my lips to his.

"Where were you?"

The fresh air swirling around us was clear, yet I hadn't been here. I'd been lost in an unfamiliar place. How could I make him understand? "What do you mean?"

"I was talking to you, but you seemed far away."

My head moved dismissively from side to side. I could never get used to the way Oren Demetri saw me, saw into me. It was strange and foreign, exposing me like no other person had ever done. Neither Russell nor Alton had ever tried to see me, to know me. I doubted that even my mother had truly seen me. Only Oren Demetri.

Though Oren and I'd been seeing one another for years, our time spent collectively hardly amounted to a month.

An hour of stolen time. A day or maybe two. It was the most we could arrange. Though we both wanted more, we willingly settled for what we could get.

"I could tell you a lie, but I don't think you'd believe me."

Oren reached for my hand and pulled me closer. The world around us was oblivious to our plight. What did they see? Two middle-aged lovers? An old married couple? Or perhaps the truth: two people in love, trapped in bodies and lives that laughed at our plight. We weren't young and the world wasn't ours for the taking. We'd both been wronged, hurt, and disappointed. We'd seen the possibilities and we'd settled for so much less. Yet in spirit while together, we were young lovers. The experience was foreign while continually new and exhilarating.

"Why would you lie to me?" Oren asked.

I pondered my response. "Because it's what I do."

We began to walk, hand in hand, along the water's edge. The state park was virtually empty of visitors this early in the year. Too cool... except for the wildlife. We both smiled, momentarily distracted by the serene sight of deer grazing in the distance. Oren tugged my hand, pulling us to a downed tree, close to the intracoastal waterway. Judging by its smooth texture, I imagined the tree had been horizontal for nearly as long as it was vertical.

"I don't believe you."

The breath caught in my chest. It was a reflex reaction to being questioned, something I avoided at all costs with my husband. But one look at the hand holding mine and I remembered this wasn't my husband, though I wished he could be. Exhaling, I shrugged. "It is. It's what I was raised to do. A proper Southern lady never complains or speaks of her problems, not in public, not to anyone outside her immediate circle."

Small lines formed near the corners of Oren's eyes as his cheeks pushed higher and higher. "Well, tell me. How much closer do we need to be, than what we were an hour ago in the cabin, for me to be considered inside your immediate circle? Because it seemed that we were very close." He shrugged. "If you know of a way to be closer, I'm open to learning."

Warmth filled my cheeks, not from the spring breeze, but from his words and tone. The way his deep timbre settled over me calmed the quaking his earlier statement had induced. "No, I'm most certain I don't know of any way to be closer." Feeling uncharacteristically playful, I added, "And I'm most certain it is you who has taught me."

He lifted my knuckles to his lips. "No, Adelaide, I'm constantly the student when it comes to you."

"Then we've learned together."

"Then what was the faraway look?" Oren asked again, not letting the subject drop.

"Too many things." I took a deep breath. "I almost don't want to ask, but how is Angelina?"

The light in Oren's eyes faded. "Not well. She's holding on for Lennox's wedding, but I'm afraid…"

I waited, silently offering him the strength to continue. In most instances it was reversed: Oren usually gave me the encouragement to go on, but this was different. This was his first love. I wasn't jealous of Angelina Demetri. Perhaps I was, but only because I envied her name, not her. Oren loved her, and I knew he loved me.

Despite that they were no longer together, he never once said anything unkind about his ex-wife, even during our first meeting after his divorce. Theirs was a relationship I longed to have. I marveled at their love and maturity. They'd grown together and apart. They'd created a life they both adored. They created a baby boy who was now a man. I'd listened to Oren's stories, ones he told with a sad smile. Through those I'd felt his joys and pains.

When they were younger, Angelina had been his dream, but with her came more than he ever imagined. I'm certain that through the years and stories, Oren has spared me the details. Nevertheless, I now understood why Alton called the Demetris criminals.

At the same time, never in Oren's presence did I feel that he was anything less than a knight in shining armor. I'd pondered the injustice that someone who did what was expected of him and what he had to do could be considered a criminal, when someone else did what he did, not for love, honor, nor family, but rather for money and power, and that man was considered a business tycoon.

"*Afraid?*" *I encouraged when Oren stopped speaking.*

"*That she won't make it to the wedding. I've tried to talk to Lennox, but it's like talking to a wall. He won't speak to me about his mother.*" *Oren shrugged. "I understand. In his eyes I'm the villain. I'll take the title, but I don't want her to miss the wedding.*"

My heart broke a little at the emotion in his deep voice. "Why are you the villain? You aren't a villain."

"*Oh, Adelaide, have you not listened through the years? I am. I'm the worst.*"

I palmed his cheek, enjoying the soft beard growth. He'd forgotten to pack a razor, and though it embarrassed me to admit it, I loved the feel and not only on my hand. "No, you couldn't be the worst. You're a good man, Oren Demetri. Angelina knows that. I know that. One day Lennox will too."

Tenderly he moved my hand to his lips. Soft kisses rained over my skin. "It's the way of this generation. We're to blame; Angelina and I knew that. We didn't want him to be indebted as we had been. Somewhere in the process, he lost the respect for his family and elders.

"*But he's alive. He's strong. He's getting married and will have children one day. His life is free from the chains that still bind me but will soon be broken for Angelina. We don't regret a thing.*"

I marveled at his selflessness. "When is the wedding?"

"*Summer.*"

"*They can't move it up?*"

He shook his head. "Adelaide, I don't know. He won't talk to me about it— something about Jocelyn's parents. I know Angelina and Sylvia are helping. Everything I know is through Angelina. The last time we spoke she was too weak to talk for long."

I kissed his cheek. "She knows you care."

"*If every cent I'd ever earned would save her...*"

"*You can't save everyone.*"

"*I can save you... if you'll let me.*"

The weight of my life fell heavily upon my chest, knocking the air from my lungs. I inhaled, trying to fill them. As I did, the view of the waterway caught my attention. "I've lived in Savannah my entire life and never been to this park."

"You're changing the subject."

"How very astute of you, Mr. Demetri."

"It's beautiful. I'll buy a cabin here if I can see you more often."

I giggled. "It's a state park. I don't think they sell cabins."

"A big enough donation and one could be mine."

My smile fell. "No."

Oren pulled my chin toward him. "Why do you give him that power?"

"What power?"

"He wouldn't know if I donated to a park."

"You don't know. He's connected—his thumb is in every pie. You can't understand."

Oren smiled. "I understand. I understand more than you know. Money talks."

I pulled away. "And most of it is mine. Yet I can't do a thing."

"You can," he reminded me. "You can let me save you."

CHAPTER 16

NOX

"YOU KNOW? HOW do you know?" Patrick asked, staring at me over the tall glasses of beer.

My head throbbed—literally. My forehead. I suspected the vein on my brow was visibly pulsing, the telltale sign of my frustration. The damn thing throbbed in time with my aching temples and clenched jaw. "I didn't know it had happened. I knew it was supposed to."

"You knew she was supposed to marry that ass and you let her leave?"

I lowered my tone as I leaned across the small table. "I didn't *let* her leave. She left to visit her mother who supposedly is ill. I told you before: she makes her own decisions. I was on my way. And I didn't know about the arrangement until after she left. If she only would have waited."

Patrick studied me for a minute before speaking. "Patience was never one of her virtues. She can be impulsive."

"That's not always bad."

"I'll take your word on that. The other day after you called me, I called my mother. She didn't know anything about Alex and Spence. She didn't even know Alex was in town. Then she called me this morning with news of the engagement. How could you have known before her?"

"I didn't know anything had happened. I didn't fucking know they were

119

calling family members. I only found out the other night about the last will and testament."

"What will?" Patrick asked.

Fuck!

I closed my eyes and forced myself to take a deep breath. "It's an arranged thing. I don't know if Charli even knew about it. If you don't, she probably didn't."

"I don't know anything about a will. Whose will are we talking about, Aunt Adelaide's? She's not that ill, is she?"

"Everyone should have a will. But no, not her mother's. Has Charli said anything to you about marrying Edward Spencer?" I hated voicing the question, using the words *marrying* and *Edward Spencer* in the same sentence.

"Yes, but not in a positive way. It was part of their conditions I told you about for her trust fund. She said it flippantly…" His tone mimicked Charli's. "…hurry up, marry Bryce Spencer, and carry on the bloodline. *Chop-chop…* make some babies."

My heart wrenched at the thought. That wasn't happening. I didn't give a damn who'd received engraved announcements, it wasn't happening.

"Besides," Patrick continued, "she can't do this, not while she's under the agreement."

I shook my head. "I don't think she wants to. I believe she's being railroaded somehow. Do you think she'd do this to save the manor or Montague Corporation?"

It was what Oren remembered, what Charli's mom had told him, something about duties for Montague. As Oren spoke, I recalled Charli using similar wording after a conversation with her mother—duties and obligation. When she had, she was as confused as Patrick appeared to be now.

The whole thing was so fucked up!

I refused to think too much about my father with Charli's mother. I couldn't come up with a better description than… fucked up.

But there was something else, something I never imagined. It was the tone of Oren's voice…

I hadn't heard that level of passion or compassion in my father's voice—ever.

"I don't think she gives a shit about either one," Patrick said. "I know she doesn't care about the manor. She hates that place."

"Why? Be honest with me."

"So you'll do what? Storm the gate?"

"If I fucking have to. I went there—"

"And let me guess. They wouldn't let you in?"

"I was informed that 'Miss Collins wasn't receiving visitors.'"

Patrick shook his head. "I'm going."

"You are?"

"I'd been thinking about it since you called, but then my mother gave me the perfect excuse. There's going to be a party, a week from tonight, to announce their engagement to the social elite of Savannah and beyond."

"I've got a week to stop this."

Patrick's lips curled upward. "I seem to remember something about a week... in Del Mar, right?"

"That was different."

My thoughts went back to my father. After what he'd shared, even Del Mar felt tainted. I couldn't think about his claim of bringing Charli and I together. It didn't matter anyway. Having us at the same resort didn't guarantee what had happened. The connection between us was organic attraction, pure and simple, a primitive draw. We'd both felt it, an irresistible pull. Oren may have orchestrated our presence—sending me there on business and having some woman tell Charli where to stay—but approaching her chair was all me.

As I imagined Charli lying there in the Southern California sun, her e-reader and big hat, the skimpy bathing suit... I missed some of what Patrick was saying.

"...the corporation. Why would she give a shit? They've never cared about her dreams."

"Tell me what I'm up against. How can I get in the manor?"

"You can't. It's simple. The place is fortified like Fort Knox. My uncle is... damn..." He grinned. "...there are so many ways to end that sentence, but I'll go with meticulous."

"About...?" I prompted.

"Everything. Almost compulsively. He's been married to Alex's mom as long as I can remember. Even that. He acts like he's a Montague, like everything Montague is his. He holds on to everything with an iron grip. He's a grade-A control freak."

I exhaled. "Then he's met his match."

Patrick shook his head. "I'd venture to guess he thinks he's already won. After all, he has her back. According to my mother, she's wearing Spencer's ring, some family heirloom. The engagement party is being planned. For something of this magnitude, the manor will be filled to the gills with not only the cream of Savannah society, but I'd imagine the guest list will also include people from all over—anyone who wants an invitation to the wedding will be present. There will also be security, a shit ton of it."

"It's bullshit."

"It is and all I can think about is how much Alex hates this shit. Dog-and-pony show. That's what she used to call it. We used to make fun of the pretense. Now they've got her in a starring role."

"And you're going to attend this farce?"

"Cy and I both."

"Good. She needs you. Do you think you can get her alone?"

"I'm going to do my best. Tell me something first. Why are you so worried? Is it the agreement? If she tells Uncle Alton, he could expose Infidelity."

"I'm worried because I love her. It has nothing to do with the fucking agreement."

"You're not going to go back on it, are you?"

What a fucking dumb question. "I'm not asking for my money back, if that's what you mean. She won't say anything to him about it." *Besides she's no longer involved and more than likely, he already knows about the company.* I didn't say that last part, but according to Deloris, Alton Fitzgerald's secretary is an employee. And then there's Chelsea. Theoretically, Alton shouldn't know about that, but obviously Spencer does. Infidelity: the worst-kept secret.

"What will were you talking about?"

"If you don't know, I'd suppose you aren't meant to."

Patrick's eyes opened wide. "Are we trying to get her out together or not?"

"Don't tell anyone."

"Lips are sealed."

"Her grandfather's will has a provision dictating her marriage to Spencer and following a specific timetable. We don't know the particulars, but my assistant is working on it. The problem is that back when the old man died, nothing was electronic. It's much harder to get actual paper documents."

"Damn, that lady's good."

"She is," I agreed, though she hadn't been the one to give me that information I was sharing. I reached into the breast pocket of my jacket and pulled out a small cell phone. "Try to get this to her. I'm sure they've taken hers."

Patrick reached for the phone and charger and nodded. "She got lucky getting assigned to you."

"No, I'm not a good person either, but I'm the only bad I want around her. Charli belongs to me and I'm going to get her back. A woman like your cousin doesn't change her mind during the course of three days. Three days ago she was in our apartment, in our bed. That doesn't even scratch the surface. Think of what this is doing to her education. She's worked too hard for this."

I leaned forward again. "If Spencer so much as touches her, I'll kill him. I'm not talking murder-for-hire. I'll take him out with my bare hands."

"And then you'll be in jail and Alex will be alone or worse yet, abandoned at the house of horrors."

"You're right." I cocked my head to the side. "I'll miss the satisfaction, but I know people."

Patrick shrugged. "I believe you. Truth is, other than his mommy, I doubt he'd be missed and you'd be doing the world a service."

"No love lost?" I asked. "If you all grew up together, shouldn't you know Spencer?"

"I do, and no. No love lost is right. He's a snake and if I thought you needed it, I'd contribute to the murder-for-hire fund. I know a few women who might chip in too."

"If you keep saying things like that, I'm back to storming the manor."

"Some of the accusations against him are more conjecture than substance, but not all... Take that current thing with that girl from Northwestern. I can't believe he's going to beat that rap. No matter what that ass does, he always walks away smelling like a rose." Patrick looked down at the small cell phone still in his hand. "I've tried several times to call her. All I get is voicemail."

"She called my assistant and mentioned that she dropped her phone, but I don't believe her." I took a drink of my beer as Patrick tucked the small phone and charger in his pocket. "Tell me about the manor."

"House of horrors."

"I hate that name."

"Well, you should. She does. What do you want to know?" he asked. "It's bigger than a fucking palace. The grounds go on forever. It used to be a tobacco plantation. I guess it still kind of is. I mean they still grow tobacco but it has more: gardens, pool, tennis courts, lake, woods..."

"They're not letting me in the front gate. Tell me how I can get on the grounds. If there will be a crowd there next Saturday, one more person shouldn't trigger a red flag."

"I don't know if you can. Uncle Alton will probably have a 'WANTED' picture of you posted in every room." He narrowed his eyes. "Give me a minute. I'm trying to think. It's been years since I wandered around that place, way back when we were kids."

I pulled out my phone and opened an email from Deloris. "This is the aerial view of the property. Does it bring anything back?"

Patrick reached for my phone and swiped the screen, moving the image around; he enlarged and reduced the size systematically. As he studied the image, I took another drink of my beer and imagined Charli engaged to Edward Spencer. Swallowing became difficult as the pressure in my throat built.

She hadn't given into them when they left her penniless. I needed to know what had caused the change. I needed to know why she'd agreed to this dog-and-pony show, as Patrick called it.

"See this?" Patrick asked, pointing to the image.

Though it was grainy, I could make out a dirt access road. Deloris and I had noticed it before, but we weren't sure if it was monitored or even accessible.

"Yes, do you know if it's monitored?"

He shook his head. "It didn't used to be. It's about a fifteen-minute walk from the house to this wooded area." He pointed again. "This road runs through it and connects to a little-used country road. I think the name is Shaw or something like that. A long time ago the road was used by the workers who tended the fields and picked the tobacco. Now that's mostly done with machines. Of course, they still need workers, but when Uncle Alton took over, he didn't want just anyone to be able to come and go on the property. He added another entrance, closer to the curing barns. That one has another guardhouse and workers sign in and out. This old road hasn't been used for as long as I can remember, except to sneak Alex on and off the grounds a time or two."

For the first time since Charli entered that car, a smile tried to break my bleak expression. "You snuck her away from the manor when you were younger?"

"Only a few times. She's younger than me, but sometimes during boring family events, we'd escape for a few hours. We'd drive to town, get ice cream or catch a movie. I'd drive separately and after the mandatory family shit, I'd claim some excuse to *leave*." He used air quotes on the last word. "She'd tell everyone she was going to bed and then we'd meet back on that road. At the time, we went there because we knew it wasn't monitored. I don't think Aunt Adelaide or Uncle Alton ever found out.

"Jane probably knew," he added.

"What's the deal with her?"

"Who, Jane?"

I nodded.

"Nothing. She was Alex's nanny when she was younger, probably her best friend."

"Do you know her last name? Why isn't she helping to get her out of this?"

"I don't know her last name. She's just Jane. If anyone could help, it would probably be her. She was always good at keeping Alex's secrets."

I got a small bit of comfort just knowing that Charli had someone she could trust.

"Tell me the truth, because if you say yes, I'll fucking storm the damn gates."

Patrick's eyes opened wide.

"Do you think they've hurt her... or will?"

His chest rose and fell as he considered his response. "It depends on your definition of hurt. Montague Manor is a messed-up house. Alex knows the rules, the ones about not talking. She never said specifically what went on. You've got to understand how this works where we're from. We don't talk about things. They happen. Everyone knows, but nothing is formally said. But I do know that she's always hated my uncle. Hated. Like the two of them can barely stand to be in the same room. So for her to get into his car willingly... for her to agree to his terms... it's big.

"I always got the feeling that whatever happened between them when she was younger was more psychological, but still, she lived with it for most of her life. That shit has lasting power whether she wants to believe it or not. My uncle's not a great guy. I remember hearing my parents talk about his and Aunt Adelaide's marriage. They thought Alex's mom would leave him, but she never did. It's part of that control-freak thing."

"Does your aunt really have a drinking problem? Is that legit?"

"I can't once remember her without a glass. But in all honesty, if I were married to that man, I'd be drinking too."

"Get Charli the phone," I said. "And let her know I'll be on that old road. She just needs to get to me and I'll get her out of there."

Patrick nodded. "I'll try, but I'd guess she has her reasons for being there. She didn't cave to them over the whole trust fund thing. I'm guessing it has something to do with Aunt Adelaide. My mom didn't have much information on her, only that she's ill. Remember, we don't talk about things like that." Pat took another drink and lifted his brow. "Informally, hell yes. I'm sure my poor aunt is the talk of the social circles. My point is that Alex may not want to leave."

His words churned the beer in my gut.

"I need to know," I said. "At least I need to talk to her. I'll do it on that phone, but I'd rather do it in person. I'd rather look into her eyes when she tells me why she got in that fucking car. You've got to go to that party and get to her. How about the house? You could call there."

Patrick nodded. "I could, but I think it's better if I don't. You don't know my uncle. My chances of getting near her are better if he has no idea that we're already close. If I show my hand too soon, I could be added to the do-not-invite list."

"Then we could crash the festivities together."

"Cy's pretty excited to see the manor. He's also worried about Alex."

"Then don't get uninvited."

CHAPTER 17

—●○●—

ALEXANDRIA

I SAT QUIETLY perched on the chair opposite Dr. Miller's desk at Magnolia Woods. Though Alton was in the chair beside me, I occupied my time with taking in the surroundings. The office was large for an institution; however, I'd venture to guess that at one time it had been a home, a grand Georgia mansion. The dark oak paneling gave a warm yet regal feel and the large windows, unblocked by drapes, looked out upon the lush, scenic grounds.

It was supposedly the best private facility in the state. According to the brochure I'd taken from the reception area, many clients came from out of state and even internationally to experience the skilled and caring staff as well as the luxurious surroundings. Even now out on the lawn were many clients, walking the paths through the gardens and enjoying the mild autumn air and sunshine.

If only Momma could be one of them.

She wasn't.

Before going to our meeting, Alton and I visited Momma's room. She was the same as she'd been yesterday and the day before. Only briefly did her eyes open as if recognizing my voice, but then just as quickly, she was asleep.

I wanted to believe she'd get better. I wanted to talk to her and let her know I was here. Instead, I smoothed back her hair, noticed the sprinkling of gray that had never before been visible and made a mental note to find out about the facility's salon or learn if I could bring a beautician to her. It wasn't much, but I knew how important appearances were to my momma, and no makeup and gray roots were not what she would want.

I held her hand and talked. With Alton present, I told her about my moving to Savannah and about making plans for a Christmas Eve wedding. I never said I was engaged and avoided using Bryce's name. It wasn't necessary. Alton was there to fill in the blanks.

"I did it, Laide," he'd said. "I told you I would. It's all going to work out. Alexandria understands her responsibility and is ready to take her place where she belongs."

I knew better than to contradict him.

That didn't mean that I agreed, only that I'd avoided further confrontation.

My goal was to meet and talk with Dr. Miller. If I had to play nice to do that, I would.

"Where is that man? Doesn't he know I have a schedule to maintain?"

Alton's impatience pulled me from thoughts of my mother. "The receptionist said he had an emergency, but that he'd be here as soon as possible."

Alton stood and paced about the office. "Two more minutes and we're leaving. I have better uses of my time..."

His words trailed away as the door opened.

"Mr. Fitzgerald," a tall, handsome man said, nodding toward Alton.

Alton extended his hand. "Dr. Miller, I was just telling my daughter—"

"Yes, your daughter," Dr. Miller said as he turned my direction and extended his hand. "Alexandria? Isn't that correct?"

His shining brown eyes scanned me before settling on mine as we shook hands.

"Dr. Miller, we heard you have information regarding my mother?"

"Yes." He made his way to the other side of the desk as Alton retook the chair to my left.

No longer shining, his expression dulled as his words slowed. "I understand that you, Mr. Fitzgerald, are a busy man. I'll get right to the heart of the subject."

I sat taller, scooting to the edge of the chair, my back and neck straight with my knees and ankles together and my hands neatly folded on my lap. It was the perfect posture, yet inside I was a bundle of nerves, each one stretching and snapping as the tension built.

Dr. Miller opened an old-fashioned folder upon his desk. "The blood tests indicate high levels of the opioid hydrocodone. We're running further tests that will indicate the length of exposure and at what levels."

"Why is that significant?" Alton asked. "You know what she took. Isn't that all that matters?"

"Knowing is part of the plan," Dr. Miller said. "It's a good thing you brought her here. An overdose of this nature can be fatal."

I sucked in a breath, though my lungs remained empty. This was real. It wasn't a ploy. I blinked away the moisture and concentrated on Dr. Miller's words.

"Fatal?" I asked.

"Yes, Miss Fitzgerald."

"Collins."

"Collins, I'm sorry. Well, thankfully, your father realized the severity and sought treatment. From her previous records from…" He thumbed through the papers in the file. "…Dr. Beck, Adelaide's normal body weight is anywhere from 122 to 119. Currently she weighs 109 pounds. Loss of appetite and nausea are early signs of hydrocodone overdose. Other symptoms include confusion and weakness." He turned toward Alton. "Didn't you say that she had been acting confused?"

"Yes, saying things that made no sense. She even drove to local places and would become lost. I'd receive calls that she was out and about. I'd send someone to get her and later she'd have no memory of the incident."

Dr. Miller shook his head. "Mrs. Fitzgerald also had a blood alcohol concentration of 0.22%."

"Is that high?" I asked.

"The legal limit for driving in Georgia is 0.08%. Your mother's level was almost triple that content. Most people are unconscious at 0.30%. A significant factor is that we didn't take her blood for over an hour after she was admitted. The body metabolizes alcohol at a rate of 0.016% per hour." Again he turned to Alton. "You brought her in during the late morning. Was it usual for your wife to drink early in the morning?"

Alton shook his head. "Doctor, I'm usually at work when my wife wakes. I don't know how early she begins drinking. It did seem as though she had been consuming more as of late."

"It's the combination," Dr. Miller explained. "Mixing opioids and alcohol creates a depressed state. The two chemicals interact in a way that creates negative effects. The opioids slow the central nervous system, decreasing respiration and pain signals. Vicodin also contains acetaminophen, which blocks the pain signals. That's why it helped with Adelaide's headaches. Alcohol is also a depressant, slowing respiration and other body functions. It's different than Vicodin, but both put strain on the body and organs, especially the liver. We have more tests scheduled to assess her liver enzymes as well as the function of her other organs, including her heart."

"Her heart? Does she have heart problems?" I remembered Alton saying that she did, but I wanted to hear it from the doctor.

"The combination of opioids and alcohol creates hypotension. The slowing of the heart muscle leads to abnormally low blood pressure. Just as high blood pressure is dangerous for the heart so is low blood pressure. We haven't fully assessed the damage that Mrs. Fitzgerald has done to herself."

"Why is she sedated?" I asked.

"The process of detoxification is tricky. Your mother's body has become accustomed to the toxins. Removing them has its own array of side effects: irritability, anxiety, headaches, nightmares, and insomnia. The primary nurse assigned to Mrs. Fitzgerald has noted episodes of anxiety and paranoia while attempting to minimize the current medication. It's for your mother's own good and comfort to sleep through the difficult process."

"Is she in pain?"

"No, Miss Collins, your mother is blissfully unaware. The midazolam in her IV is keeping her from experiencing the brutal reality of her choices."

"How long will she be medicated?"

"I can't answer that," Dr. Miller said. "We're doing continual tests. The liver enzymes will be essential. If it's too damaged, if the enzymes are too high, we will need to rethink our treatment. We don't want to cause additional damage."

"Doctor," Alton said, "do whatever you need to do. Money isn't an object."

"She's a lucky woman. This treatment is not always covered by insurance and can be quite costly. Once the toxins are removed from her body, intense counseling will be necessary."

Alton turned toward me. "Alexandria, don't you agree that your mother should have the best care that money can buy?"

My respirations came quick and shallow. I'd hoped for a miracle. I'd prayed that when I arrived at this place, I'd find my mother the vital woman I remembered. Instead, she was exactly as Alton had said.

"Alexandria?" he asked again. "Dr. Miller and I are waiting for your answer. Do you agree that your mother should continue treatment here at Magnolia Woods?"

Do you agree to sacrifice your life and happiness to save your mother? That was the real question he was asking.

Swallowing, I nodded at Dr. Miller. "Will you please keep me informed?"

Dr. Miller's gaze moved quickly from mine to Alton's and back. "Your father is the only one your mother listed on her HIPAA form, but this is a private facility so as long as he gives his approval, we can speak directly with you.

"Mr. Fitzgerald?"

"Alexandria?" Alton asked again, his tone strained by the repeated attempts to get me to answer.

"Yes and yes," I said, still not looking his direction.

"Test results come to me first," Alton said. "Daily communication can be shared with our daughter. I'm sure she'll have more time to spend with her mother than I."

"Very well, Miss Collins, I'll be sure that information is added to your mother's chart."

CHAPTER 18

ALEXANDRIA

COMPROMISES.

That was the word I liked to use as I assessed my plight.

I hadn't given in to every mandate nor had I blazed my own way. Five days of compromises. Five days of avoidance. And most of all, five days without any contact from Nox.

With each passing day, I'd begun to wonder if he'd given up on me. Did he think about me as I thought about him? Had he heard what I'd done, the compromises I'd made?

I worked to block out the thoughts of him—the sound of his voice, touch of his hands, warmth of his lips, and even the aroma of his skin. It was difficult during the day, but at least then I had distractions. At night it was impossible.

Though I'd spent each night after the first alone behind my self-locked bedroom door, in my mind Nox was with me. My hands would roam, recalling his mastery. Moans fought to tumble from my lips as my fingers became a sad substitute in mimicking his skills. There were even times when my body would quake as I imagined his blue gaze upon my exposed core, watching and approving as his deep voice directed, pushing me higher over the brink.

But alas, the fantasy always faded.

Reality left me cold, lonely, and faced with the stark reality of his absence. A warm washcloth did little when compared to the heat of his tongue, lapping the essence from my moist thighs.

I pushed the thoughts away and inhaled the warm afternoon breeze. I'd found one of the smaller courtyards at Magnolia Woods to be a nice, quiet place to catch up on my studies. Isolated and remote, it was reserved for family and not frequented by clients. As with most afternoons, I was alone as small wisps of auburn fluttered about my face and I concentrated on my new tablet.

It was part of the compromise Alton and I'd made. After our meeting with Dr. Miller, I was granted access to Columbia and all the accounts associated with my schooling: email, class groups, and lecture videos. I'd spoken with Dr. Renaud and received clearance to complete this semester's studies via Internet. I wasn't sure if her concession was based on protocol or if she was tired of dealing with my new drama. Either way, I was happy to finish my semester.

While Alton mentioned that he'd paid for the semester, I reminded him that the second semester was paid as well. When he responded that there was still time to drop those classes, instead of arguing, I changed the subject. It was my new plan: denial. I didn't need to answer negatively or affirmatively as long as I avoided precarious topics.

Completing my classes was acceptable to everyone involved as long as I also attended to my new responsibilities. The one I'd asked for—the household staff—had taken care of itself.

One phone call and I had Jane reinstated at Montague Manor. Though Suzanna had terminated her employment, Jane hadn't actually left, claiming she needed time to find housing. After all, she'd lived at the manor for over twenty years. It wasn't easy losing a job and a house. Despite Suzanna's wishes, Jane didn't lose either.

As it turned out, Jane had helped my mother with the staff. She knew everyone and knew each one's responsibilities. Other than the need for my approval, the job was hers. I promoted her to house manager, giving her not only the title, but also a nice increase in salary. After all she had endured over the years, there wasn't enough money in the Montague accounts to repay her. Nevertheless, I intended to give it a try.

Another of my responsibilities was currently sitting on the terrace table beside my tablet's keyboard. I couldn't type with the ostentatious rock on my finger. The damn thing would swivel and type its own notes if I wasn't careful. I dutifully wore it when in the right company. That primarily meant Alton, Bryce, or Suzanna. Other than in their presence, it often found its way into my pocket.

Though I negotiated for a car, it hadn't happened. I reasoned that it had been only four days since our discussions. Without a car of my own, my getting to and from Magnolia Woods was dependent upon drivers and came with an extra car of security.

Each visit to Magnolia Woods seemed harder than the last. I held tight to the hope that once Momma was through the worst of her detox, she would be able to be weaned off the sedative. With my new tablet, I'd thoroughly researched the medications that Dr. Miller mentioned. I'd hoped to find something to indicate that it was all a farce, but nothing gave me that hope.

The hours spent at the facility made me both sad and happy. Sad at her condition: her mumblings didn't make sense. Dr. Miller had said that nightmares could accompany the detox, and yet I had the feeling she was content, perhaps even happy, in whatever world she was living. The positive side to that was she didn't need to be restrained. The first day Bryce had brought me here, her wrists were secured to the bedrails.

If the medication kept that from happening, I couldn't argue.

The courtyard was a break in the mundane, a time for me to breathe fresh air while Momma continued to rest. I found solace in being away from Montague Manor. It wasn't as if I had many options, at least not ones approved by Alton, but Magnolia Woods was one.

Though I wore the ring, I continued to shut Bryce down. It had been less than a week. I'd spent four years avoiding sex with him, and yet he was more determined than ever.

His cheek was mostly healed—which was good, considering our engagement pictures were scheduled for Thursday afternoon, Suzanna and I had an appointment with an exclusive wedding planner on Friday, and the grand announcement party was on Saturday. It was the stair-steps of shame: smaller at first and increasingly difficult.

I could smile for a camera and perhaps feign excitement for the plans, but an entire evening of entertaining seemed too much.

"Miss Collins?"

I turned toward a familiar voice and all at once, my sadness washed away in a flood of relief. "Isaac!"

"Shhh," he prompted, looking from side to side.

"How?" I followed his darting eyes and lowered my voice to a whisper. "How are you here?"

He offered me his hand. "James Vitoni, ma'am."

I took his hand. Had I ever known his last name? Where did Isaac come from? "Mr. Vitoni?"

"My father is a patient here. I happened to notice you sitting alone and wondered if you could use company."

"Your father?"

"Yes. Unfortunately, I've been out of the country off and on for the last three years and just recently learned of his dementia. It's sad. He doesn't recognize me."

"Because…?" I asked in a whisper.

Isaac lifted one brow with a slight grin. "He's never seen me before in his life. It was the best we could do."

My chest filled with the warm breeze as my cheeks rose. "My security is outside. They don't come in with me."

"I've been watching."

We kept our voices low as we spoke.

I swallowed. "Does this mean he hasn't given up?"

Isaac's grin became a full smile. "Ma'am, have you ever met my boss?"

"Yes, I'm glad to say I have."

"Giving up is not in his repertoire."

"I've always been a fan of persistence."

"Then let me be the first to say, you've found the right man."

Isaac's gaze left me and went to the tablet and then beside the tablet.

I reached for the ring and standing slightly shoved it into the depths of a pocket. "I-I need to explain."

Isaac shook his head. "He knows."

The newfound relief evaporated. "He knows? How? It hasn't been announced."

"He knows about the will. He knows about your mother. He wants to hear it all from you."

Tears teetered on my lower lids as I imagined his thoughts. "Tell him I didn't want…"

Isaac touched my hand. "Miss Collins, please don't. We can't bring attention to our conversation. I've been watching your security. They don't always stay outside. Periodically they enter the facility."

"They do?"

"Yes, ma'am, you're being watched, and I should get back to my father."

"Are you really visiting someone?"

"Yes, but like I said, he doesn't remember me."

I shook my head. "Isaac, I can't talk to him. Alton will know, but tell him I love him. Tell him I'm working on a plan. Getting my mother well is the first step."

"James," Isaac corrected. "I'll tell him." His voice rose, "But like I said, he isn't remembering. It's very sad."

Before I could question, we both turned to see one of Alton's men entering the courtyard.

"Miss Collins, is there anything I can get you?"

I lifted my chin. This was one of the drivers. I wasn't even trying to learn their names. It wouldn't matter. They rotated multiple times a day. I'd decided it was a ploy to keep me from getting close to anyone. "Time," I replied. "I'm not ready to go back."

"Miss, Mr. Fitzgerald phoned. You're expected back to the manor in an hour."

"Then I still have twenty minutes." I turned back to Isaac and extended my hand. "Mr. Vitoni, nice to meet you. I do hope your father gets better because memories can be a great solace."

"Yes. It was nice to meet you, too. Perhaps we'll see one another again."

"I hope so," I said, gathering my tablet and book and placing them in a backpack. Turning to Alton's man, I said, "I'll be in my mother's room for the next twenty minutes. There's no need to follow me or come back inside. I'll be out to the car in time."

"Yes, ma'am," the driver said.

Just as I was about to enter my mother's room, I turned back toward footsteps.

"Miss Collins, I believe you left this on the table."

Isaac extended a small light-pink pouch toward me. Before I could protest, he added, "I believe it fell out of your backpack. I'd hate for you to lose it or have it fall into the wrong hands." He tilted his head toward the right. Above his head was a translucent black nub, obviously a camera.

"Thank you, Mr. Vitoni."

I slipped the pouch into my backpack and joined my mother. A few minutes before I was required to be outside, I slipped into the public bathroom near the front of the facility. I'd already noticed the cameras in my mother's room. I supposed that they could be justified. These were patients that required monitoring. I'd even noticed one in her private bath.

Closing the door on a stall and assuring my privacy, I opened my backpack and removed the pink pouch. It was small, about the size of an eyeglass case. Slowly I unsnapped the front. Inside was a small cell phone and charger.

The small stall melted around me as tears blurred my vision. During the months Nox and I had dated, he'd showered me with many gifts, but nothing filled me with the joy and relief of the small disposable phone. I couldn't call now. It wasn't safe. But I would—I could. I finally could.

With shaking hands, I stuffed the phone and charger deep into an inside pocket of the backpack and then filled the pouch with lipstick and lip gloss. Tossing it back into the backpack, I worked to suppress the first real smile on my face in nearly a week and made my way out to the waiting car.

CHAPTER 19

ALEXANDRIA

FOR THE ENTIRE drive back to Montague Manor my mind was filled with Nox. These weren't the same images I conjured in my bed. These were real.

Lennox Demetri was more than sex, though I adored everything that man did and would do. Together we'd continued to search for my hard limit, but as of yet, no matter what he suggested or what we tried, we'd failed to find it. Though I always knew that no was an option, thus far, I'd not found the reason to say it.

In the last few months, Nox had become so much more than the man at Del Mar. He'd become my best friend. It may be too soon to say soul mate, but he was close.

He'd not only filled my days and nights with passion, but also with love and security.

I looked to the front seat. The men Alton employed didn't create the sense of safety I felt when with Nox, or even what I'd felt during the few minutes I was with Isaac. To the man driving the car, I was a job, an assignment. With Nox I was half of a whole. From the way he'd ask me about my day, to the way our fingers intertwined as we walked, we completed one another. I'd read about connections like ours, and they sounded like a fantasy—ours was a reality. The phone buried in my backpack proved it. Even separated, we were one.

I rolled the platinum diamond-covered cage between the pads of my fingers and sighed, knowing that Nox hadn't given up on me. He knew what was happening and was still trying to help me.

Of course he knew: he had Deloris. I didn't know how she did what she did, I was just glad she did. Not only that, they'd figured out my clue, letting them know that Isaac had avoided Alton's radar.

As I watched the passing scenery and contemplated calling, I found my cheeks raising, bringing a smile to my lips. I needed to get myself under control, but the anticipation had me almost giddy. For the first time since I'd entered the limousine last week, I had real hope, knowledge that soon I'd hear Nox's deep voice. I thought about my explanation. I wasn't naive enough to think he'd like it, but he would accept it, as I had accepted his explanations.

My smile grew shy as I considered how things might be different if we were talking in person. I fidgeted against the leather seat as I imagined his hand reddening my behind. The phantom sting shouldn't turn me on, but it did. I'd taken real punishment in my life, and what Nox delivered was not the same. I'd willingly take his hand or belt, because when they delivered the burn, it was but a precursor for the high that would follow.

I squeezed my thighs tighter as my mind filled with sensual thoughts.

The scenery alerted me that Montague Manor was near, lessening my fantasy and smile. I would explain everything to him, from the will to the engagement ring. I'd tell him the truth and share my plan. In the days that I'd been in Georgia, I'd spoken to those around me. I'd answered questions and made small talk. I'd agreed to a life I didn't want and I'd even indulged Suzanna in her quest for planning.

When our paths crossed, as they occasionally did, I'd said a few words to the person I'd considered my best friend. And whenever possible I'd talked in small snippets to Jane. However, since our heartfelt reunion that preceded her dismissal, we'd kept our discussions generic and focused on the household activities.

Through all of that, I hadn't shared. I hadn't opened up.

At first I was worried that my room was monitored. After all, my new tablet was. When Alton gave it to me, he'd said it was only for use with classes and made it clear that he'd know if I used it to contact anyone else. I hadn't, but I had done a search for microphones and monitoring devices.

I had a plan that if questioned, my research was for a class case study. The truth was I'd wanted to see what the devices looked like, how small they could be. I was overwhelmed. The average person on the street could purchase small almost-undetectable cameras. 'Nanny Cams' is what many of them were called—outlet covers, clocks, picture frames, and even light bulbs. Some were fitted in electric razors, belt buckles, and makeup mirrors. If the possibilities were that limitless for the average person, I couldn't fathom what a professional could obtain.

It took me an entire evening, but I searched every square inch of my room. I unplugged my clock and unscrewed every light bulb. I even unscrewed outlet covers. My mind told me I was paranoid, but my heart wouldn't let me stop looking.

I didn't find a thing, nothing unusual.

That didn't mean that I planned to talk to Nox in my room. Fighting back the smile, I decided that a nice long walk in the gardens was definitely in my future. First I had to learn why I'd been summoned back to the manor.

We passed through the gate, leaving our trailing SUV behind and approached the manor. As we came closer, Bryce stepped onto the front porch. A quick check of my watch told me it was only a little after three in the afternoon. He should be at work, not here. Quickly, I fumbled for my new ring and shoved it on my finger. With the excitement of the cell phone, I'd completely forgotten.

As the tires rolled slowly over the cobblestones, I searched for answers. Why was he here? What had happened? Since I'd just left my mother, I knew she wasn't the issue. As the car got closer, I made out Bryce's expression—his rigid features, ruddy complexion, and clenched jaw—and knew that something had.

The car had barely come to a stop when my door opened. It wasn't the driver who'd opened it; he was still in the front seat. The man at the door's handle was my fiancé, barking orders as he opened the door wider. "Alexandria, get out of the car now."

What the hell?

"Bryce? What the—"

"Now!" He repeated, shoving his hand my direction.

Rebelliously, I avoided his touch, reached for my backpack, and eased myself out of the car. Before I could ask again, he gripped my upper arm.

"Tell me you're not that dumb."

"Tell you what?" I asked, turning toward him while trying to free my arm. "Bryce, let go of me."

"Get used to my hands on you, darling, and take my advice." He leaned down, his menacing whisper spewing warm, moist breath close to my ear. "Don't say another word. I sure as fuck hope you're not as stupid as he thinks."

My heart raced with my possible crime. I'd played their damn game. I was wearing the ring. Had the driver told them about Isaac? No, James. James Vitoni, that was his name.

Pulling me forward, Bryce dragged me into the manor and through the entryway. Digging my heels in did little to slow his process. The marble floor created a skating rink for my flat-soled shoes. "Stop it!"

Bryce's steps stalled and he looked down at me. His hold of my arm didn't loosen though his glare took the pain away. Blood drained from my cheeks as I stared at this man, the one I thought I knew. My circulatory system forgot to work as the world wavered and I fought to remain conscious. This stare, this expression, wasn't Bryce. This was my stepfather reincarnate. Rage and wrath surrounded him, oozing from his every pore. It wasn't only visible in the depths of his gray eyes. It was palpable. The sting returned as more of my arm's circulation was cut off.

"What, Alexandria? What is your excuse this time? I've stood up for you. I've fought for you to see your mother and take your damn classes, and this is what you do?"

The air around us was filled with a sickening scent. It was like the heavy, calm dampness before an intense electrical storm. The tiny hairs upon my arms and back of my neck stood to attention, small soldiers prepared for a battle. It was coming... I just wasn't sure why.

"What? What do you think I've done? I've done everything you and Alton said. I don't know what you're talking about."

His jaw clenched as he stared down at me. "I fucking hope you're telling the truth. Not only for your own sake."

Goose bumps materialized like needles pricking my skin as my tiny soldiers prepared for battle.

Bryce didn't wait for a response as he pulled me toward the office.

Alton's expression matched Bryce's as we crossed the threshold.

"Alexandria, sit."

Bryce shoved me toward a chair at the long table.

Rubbing the feeling back into my arm, I stumbled toward my newly assigned seat. "What the hell is—?"

I hadn't noticed Suzanna; however, as our eyes met and the sting of her slap resonated from my cheek, she had my full attention. I stood taller. "If you ever strike me again, I will see you on the floor." My threat rumbled through the regal room.

"You are a Montague," she began, undaunted. "It's time you started acting like it. Crude language will not be tolerated."

"And who the fuck do you think you are?"

This time I caught her hand before it connected, squeezing her wrist.

"Alexandria..."

She didn't finish her plea as Bryce seized my shoulders from behind. "Sit," he said, pulling out the chair he'd shoved me toward earlier. "Mother, step back."

I turned in time to witness Alton with my backpack, unbuckling the main compartment. I hadn't even realized I'd dropped it.

"Would someone tell me what you're doing?"

"I recognized him," Bryce said.

"Who? You recognized who?" As I voiced my question, I recalled Isaac with me at the hospital when Nox and I'd gone to see Chelsea. Isaac had stayed with me while Bryce wanted to talk.

"Don't play dumb. It doesn't suit you," Bryce said, his arms crossed over his chest as Alton turned the backpack over and emptied the contents onto the table. The pink pouch Isaac had handed me was like a beacon under the glowing ceiling lights as my tablet and book slid to freedom.

"What are you doing?" I asked Alton. Turning toward Bryce I said, "I don't know whom you're talking about." I scrunched my forehead. "Do you mean the man at Magnolia Woods? Are you all this pissed because I had a conversation with a brokenhearted son of another patient?"

I waited, but the cell phone didn't appear. The inner pocket where I'd placed it had a zipper. I prayed I'd closed it.

Alton handed Bryce the pouch. "Make this easier," Bryce said, holding the pouch. "Alexandria, tell us what he gave you. You can still help your mother."

I sat taller. "I *will* help my mother. That man, James… somebody… Vitoni, I think he said, is the son of a patient at the facility. He said his father doesn't even remember him. I don't know what you're insinuating."

"He works for *him*," Bryce said. "I remember him from when I visited Chelsea."

Though the way he worded that made my skin crawl, I remained focused. "I guess he does look a little like Lennox's driver." I'd been forbidden from saying his name, but damn it, I could throw words with the best of them. "Call the facility. Ask. His last name was Vitoni. I'd assume that's his father's last name too. That's usually the way it works." I said the last part while eying Alton.

The pouch was still in Bryce's hand.

"Open it," I prompted. "It's my lipstick holder. It must have fallen out of my backpack while I was sitting in the courtyard. That man saw it and brought it to me."

"And he just happened to know where you were headed?" Bryce asked.

"Do you people have nothing better to do than watch surveillance footage day and night? You should get a better pastime. I promise I'm not that exciting."

Bryce handed me the pouch. "Last chance. Tell us the truth and you don't have to open it."

This time I stood. "I don't *have* to do anything." I unsnapped the pouch and dumped two tubes of lipstick and one of lip gloss onto the table. "I'll do it to prove you're all assholes." I quickly turned toward Suzanna. "Don't even think about it."

She pursed her lips and shook her head.

"Sorry, dear," I replied, my tone mimicking hers as I sat again. "I didn't sign up to be your daughter-in-law, but since it looks like that's the plan, maybe you should fucking get used to me."

"Alexandria!"

Bryce once again seized my shoulders from behind. "Apologize."

What the hell?

Though his grip tightened, I remained mute.

Finally, I said, "I don't think I'm the one who needs to apologize. Let go of me and tell me you were wrong. That guy wasn't whom you thought. The pouch is simply a lipstick holder, and this whole interrogation was unnecessary."

Alton spoke over everyone. "I just sent an email to Magnolia Woods. If there isn't a patient there with the name of Vitoni, this isn't over."

I started to stand, but was quickly pushed back down. "Stop touching me!" I yelled at Bryce.

Leaning close, he whispered loud enough for everyone to hear, "Now's the time to stop talking, but don't worry, darling..." His threat dripped in syrupy sweetness. "...when I do touch you, you'll enjoy it."

My stomach rolled.

"Well, shit."

We all turned toward Alton.

His chest widened with a deep breath. "Dennis Vitoni has been a patient at Magnolia Woods for the past seventeen months. His son, James, was recently located and has been with his father for the last two days."

I shrugged away Bryce's hands. "If we're finished, I have more schoolwork to do."

"No," Suzanna said. "We have a driver waiting to take us to a quaint little boutique in Brooklet. They have the best wedding dresses in the South."

I shook my head in disbelief. "You can't be serious? I'm not going with you to look for wedding dresses."

"Would you prefer if Chelsea joined us?"

"No."

"You do realize that the wedding is in less than two months and nothing has been decided. We're going to meet with the planner tomorrow. He needs colors. You need a dress. Who is standing with you? Bryce, who is standing with you? The church is set, and given the time constraint, your father and I have decided it would be best to have the reception here."

I was trapped in an alternate universe. Only minutes ago I'd been screaming at this woman and now she was chatting on and on about wedding plans.

"The party is Saturday night?" I tried to deflect her quest.

"Yes," Suzanna answered.

"Shouldn't that be your concern right now? The other stuff can wait."

"We're leaving," Alton announced, picking up the backpack off the floor where he'd dropped it and throwing it onto the table. When he did, the phone's charger sailed across the hard surface.

As Bryce started to reach for it, I stood and reached for his hand. "Can we talk before you leave?"

His eyes narrowed as he stared down at me.

My heart beat erratically as I searched for anything to divert his attention. "Please." I tilted my head to the side. "I don't want you to leave upset. I understand that the man resembled the driver at the hospital, but as you heard, he's just the son of an ill patient. He's distraught over his father. You can understand that, right?"

I reached for the tablet and one by one put everything back into my backpack, including the phone's charger.

"Now, Bryce," Alton said, "or take another car. I'm leaving."

I put my hand on his arm. "Alone?"

"And then you'll go with my mom?"

I nodded, hating myself for what I was doing, yet thankful I'd saved the phone.

"I'll be to Montague Corp. soon."

"Hurry, dear," Suzanna prompted. "The driver is waiting. You can freshen up in the car."

I didn't respond to Suzanna, keeping my eyes on Bryce. The room lost its life-giving air as Alton and Suzanna stepped from the office. It was the first time either had done as I'd asked, and in doing so, they were leaving me alone with Bryce.

CHAPTER 20

NOX

"THEY'RE WATCHING HER every move," Isaac reported.

I gripped the cell phone tighter as I leaned forward and placed my elbows on the desk—so much for concentrating on Demetri Enterprises. That was all right. Oren was in the office down the hall, doing what I should be attending to. For the first time I could recall, his help didn't seem suffocating or intrusive. As much as I'd always hated to admit it, my father did know the ins and outs of Demetri Enterprises. I didn't always agree with his tactics, but they were what had gotten this company up and running.

"Were you able to talk to her? Give her the cell phone?" My heart seized waiting the millisecond for his response. It was like the day she'd become mine through Infidelity, only a million times worse. I was supposed to be working then too, but the thought of her in that hotel room or in the car, knowing that Isaac had spoken to her... I couldn't *not* see her.

This was worse. I couldn't see her. I couldn't talk to her. Not if she didn't have a phone. I didn't care that I'd given another phone to Patrick. He wouldn't see Charli for four more days. I wasn't sure I'd make it one day more without hearing her voice. Four more days would be impossible.

"Yes to both questions," Isaac said. "The cover is working well."

Getting Isaac established as the son of one of Magnolia Wood's patients was ingenious and Deloris's idea. From all she could deduce, the patient and his son were estranged. The son lived in Oregon and traveled frequently to China on business. Currently he was overseas. Though the son, James, had been contacted numerous times by the Magnolia Woods' staff, there was no record that he'd ever visited or signed in. The only visitor the patient had ever had during his stay was an attorney.

Deloris sent Isaac all the information she could uncover. Isaac knew his pretend father's life history, financial information, and even his passwords. He knew the names of cousins and uncles. The lonely man's plight worked to our benefit.

On her one call, Charli had told us to leave Isaac behind. We'd done what we could to use that to our advantage.

"More. Tell me every word she said."

The man had a photographic memory, apparently that included audio too. I couldn't fathom that Charli would even consider that I'd give up on her. It was because of them. In five days they'd begun to wear her down.

"She said to tell you she loves you, and she's working on a plan."

It wasn't her voice, yet I could hear it. I could hear the sweet melody as she told me she loved me, as her smile blossomed and beautiful golden eyes shone. The memory was so intense it was as if she were with me, not a phone, not Isaac's voice.

"The only plan that matters is getting her home," I said. "At least in the meantime, the cover story can keep you near her, since that seems to be the only place they allow her to go unaccompanied."

"Sir, she doesn't go *anywhere* unaccompanied. That's what I was saying. Not only is there a driver, there are always at least two other people nearby."

I didn't want to think about that, about how she argued when I'd insisted on my security. That seemed like years ago, not months. At that time, I'd had no idea that her response was based on personal experience, that she was all too aware of the intrusion. Fuck! There was so much about my Charli that I'd wrongly assumed.

I took a deep breath. "Do you have any information on the access road I told you about?"

"I've checked it out. At one time, the location may have been a vital artery for the estate or plantation but not any longer. It's literally a mile from anything other than woods and fields. Since this year's tobacco crop has already been harvested, the labor workforce on the plantation is down to bare bones. Those that do still work there seem to be working in the curing barns."

"Do people still do that?" I asked. "I'd have thought it was done with machines."

"From what I've seen there are fifteen men that sign in on weekdays and three that sign in on the weekend. I haven't been in the curing barns so I'm not sure how it's done. They all enter on another road, closer to those barns."

"Are you saying you've been on the estate?"

"I've parked in the wooded area. The trees make a great cover, even if there is any aerial observation. From there, I've walked some. I've thoroughly searched the old road and found nothing that indicates it's monitored. It has an old gate that partially covers the road, but the chains holding it closed are rusted and broken. The road itself, the shaded part under the trees, is covered with an overgrowth of moss. It's as if it's been forgotten by the twenty-first century."

That sounded perfect to me.

"Can you get close to the manor?"

"I haven't tried to go beyond the woods. With the crop harvested, the vast fields are rather wide open. I can go during the night if you want me to."

I did, but I didn't want him to get caught. He was my only current connection. As detached as he was, Isaac was all I had until Saturday.

"No. As long as I can get to the road from the outside and Charli can get there from the estate, I'm going to have to wait until Saturday."

My answer killed me a little on the inside. I wanted to be her knight in shining armor. I wanted with everything in me to storm the gate, but it would have to wait. Gallantry wasn't worth losing the war over. Alton had her. He'd won a battle. I'd had her safe. That was my win, though at the time it wasn't her own family I thought I was protecting her from. Isaac said she looked safe. If she could hold out a little longer, we would prevail.

I turned at the sound of the door to my office opening.

"Dianne told me you were on a call with Isaac," Deloris said in a stage whisper. "I told her not to bother you."

I nodded. "Do you want to talk to him?"

"Put him on speaker."

"Isaac, Mrs. Witt is here." I hit speaker and laid the phone on my desk.

"Mrs. Witt," he replied.

"Isaac, have you seen Chelsea Moore?"

"Not since the Sunday after Alex arrived. I've been monitoring the front gate and she was in a car with Edward, his mother, and a driver. I haven't looked for her. I've been concentrating on Alex."

"Why?" I asked.

Deloris took the seat opposite my desk and leaned toward the phone so we could both be heard. "She just called me."

There was something ominous in her voice. "What about?"

Deloris's expression was solemn. "She wants out. She's scared." Neither Isaac nor I spoke. "She said it's been worse since Alex arrived, a lot worse."

"What's worse? You never said there was a problem."

"Apparently under the letter of the Infidelity bylaw, she has legitimate grounds for canceling her agreement."

I knew the Infidelity agreement. I knew the one reason to terminate it. There was only one.

Abuse.

"That motherfucker! Get her out. Isaac, find her and get her out."

"Wait," Deloris said.

"Wait?" I asked. "No. She's Charli's friend. We got her in this mess. We have to get her out."

"I said she wants out, not that she's ready to leave."

I narrowed my gaze. "What the hell does that mean?"

"She's afraid that if she leaves..." Deloris sat taller and took a deep breath. "...she's afraid if she leaves that instead of her, Mr. Spencer will hurt Alex."

I sprung to my feet as I paced to the other side of the room and back. "What the fuck has he done?"

"I can get her," Isaac volunteered. "She doesn't have the security detail they have on Miss Collins."

I turned toward Deloris, praying for some kind of encouragement, something. Her expression was grave.

"Both of them," I said. "I want them both out."

"Then what about her mother?" Deloris asked.

We both turned as my office door opened again. Fuck! It was a damn party.

"I thought we were doing this together?" Oren asked, closing the door again.

I waved him in as Deloris sat taller.

"What did you just say about Alexandria's mother?" Oren asked.

I swallowed. I hadn't told my father about Chelsea or about the connection with Infidelity. "There's something we didn't discuss."

He made his way to the other chair near my desk, moved it so the back was toward the far wall and sat. With his arms crossed over his chest, Oren said, "Tell me."

I looked at Deloris, but she was looking at me. I took a deep breath and sat again at my desk. "I'll explain more later. For now, Alex's roommate during college was a woman named Chelsea Moore. We had an idea regarding the House bill and a few other things happening with the legalization of marijuana..."

"You offered her something undercover?"

I was shocked at how his mind had jumped to the right conclusion. "Yes."

"Does Alexandria know you put her friend in this position?"

"No, but that's only the tip of the iceberg. For the placement to work, she needed to go through a company, a companionship company—"

"Infidelity or full-fledged prostitution?"

"Infidelity," Deloris answered. "She was supposed to go to Severus Davis. It was all worked out and then the shooting happened and well, sir, it was me. I let the ball drop."

"That isn't the point," I interjected. "The point is that Chelsea was then assigned to Edward Spencer."

Oren dropped his crossed arms and sat taller. "The man engaged to Alexandria? Doesn't that render the Infidelity agreement null and void?"

"No," Deloris answered. "Severus is married. The profile Chelsea agreed to uphold included pairing with married men. She's still under a one-year obligation, even if this wedding would occur."

I shook my head. I hadn't thought of that. "But there are grounds to nullify her agreement."

"He's hurt her?" Oren asked.

"How do you know so much about Infidelity agreements?"

"Son, you invested a shit ton of money in that company. Of course I know what it's about." He nodded toward the phone. "Is that your man?"

"Yes. Isaac, my father, Oren Demetri, has joined this discussion."

"Yes, sir. Hello, Mr. Demetri."

"Can you get this girl out of there?"

"Yes."

"I'm afraid it isn't that easy," Deloris went on. "Miss Moore doesn't want to leave without Miss Collins. She fears for her safety if she isn't there."

"Then get them both. Do it now."

"Dad, there's more. If Isaac gets the two ladies, it leaves Adelaide alone."

"Bullshit, take her too."

"Sir, she's very ill," Isaac said. "I've seen her. She's not coherent."

Oren took a deep breath. "We'll get the best doctors. She won't be alone."

"There are complicating factors," Deloris said.

"What the hell—?"

My phone chimed with an incoming call. On the screen was the name MISS COLLINS #2 PHONE.

"Isaac, Charli is calling. I'll call you back."

I didn't wait for his response as I swiped the screen. "Charli?"

"N-Nox, I-I'm so sorry…"

CHAPTER 21

ADELAIDE

SHAKING... UNCONTROLLABLE...

It rattled my bones and my teeth...

Pounding... like drums...

Sounding in my temples until I ached. Not only my head—everything—every part of me.

The world didn't make sense. Thoughts and truth jumbled until fiction became factual and reality became make-believe.

There were voices, Alton's, Oren's, and even Alexandria's. They came and went in a fog of uncertainty.

Yet Oren and Alexandria weren't really here; they both had to be part of a dream, my mind playing tricks, hallucinations. They came and went in my consciousness or was it my unconsciousness? The voices seemed real, taking on new tones and cadences.

The past mixed with the present until they blended into one. Had they really come? Oren and Alexandria? Or could it be that those were the two I longed for, wished for, needed, if only to say goodbye. Surely I couldn't go on much longer, not like this.

Somehow the world around me became cold and sterile, a place I loathed—even more than my home and my husband. Those were familiar.

This was not. Why would they leave me here? If hell were truly levels, I'd descended lower than ever before. I needed to go home, even wanted to go back, but I was sinking faster than I could crawl to the surface.

Please don't leave me here. I'm not done.

My father and mother told me from the time I was young that I had responsibilities. I clawed at the darkness, needing to get back. There was more I needed to do. I felt it... but I couldn't recall any particulars. The memories wouldn't come. They stayed just out of reach...

Time passed in undefined segments. Yes, science may say it was all related to the sun and rotation of the earth, but that wasn't true. There were times that I recalled that I'd wanted to last forever, yet greedily time moved forward at uncharted speed. Weeks became days and days hours. And then there were those instances that dragged on and on, as if the earth had slowed both its rotation and spin. Hours lasted for days and days for weeks. Weeks became months... months became years.

Wherever I was, in this sterile place seconds moved like hours, each one dragging on and on until years were passed, beyond my reach... or was it only days? The boredom ate away deliberation until nothing existed—no topics or thoughts—nothing except a void, a black hole of consciousness.

I searched for memories... faces... names. I tried to count, to recall events. I wouldn't go quietly. I refused. Drowning in the pits was not my end. I would fight to return, claw my way up from the depths. No one else could save me, not this time, not that anyone ever had. As always, it was up to me, and I wanted it—for my daughter, for my love, but also—for the first time—for me.

And then...

I was present.

Tears filled my closed eyes with the relief. The bed beneath me was familiar. I was in my suite at Montague Manor. And yet, the familiar setting didn't fully relieve my anxiety. It should have, yet the uneasiness was there, bubbling through me, twisting my world. Something wasn't right. My sealed eyelids opened, if only a bit, as I stole a glimpse around the room. My stomach heaved as the lines of woodwork, doorframes, and molding weaved and bowed.

My suite that had forever been inanimate slowly came to life.

My rational mind told me it wasn't true, yet I saw it. I felt it. The energy was real and stifling. The beige walls were once again covered with wallpaper from the past. The ivy print on the once stagnant wallpaper grew before my eyes. No longer contained to its parchment, it twisted and twirled, growing and filling the suite, creating a jungle of obstacles.

"Jane." My plea was soft at first, but with each request my volume rose.

The one-word name sparked wicks of explosions strategically placed within my brain. Pain—like small detonations—obstructed my vision. I couldn't see the vines for the blinding white light, but I knew they were there. I felt them touching me, my ankles my wrists, binding me.

I thrashed at their touch.

"Jane!" I called louder still, battering the vines away.

"Jane…"

Covering me, strangling me.

A low laugh rumbled through our suite. I wasn't alone. Alton was here.

"Please," I begged. "Please make it stop."

"Laide, my Laide."

I couldn't see him, yet his touch was real. Knuckles caressing my cheeks, uncharacteristically gentle. I hated asking for his help, but I couldn't refrain. "Please, help. Get Jane."

"Jane isn't here. Neither are you… neither am I. You're delusional."

No!

I shook my head, but this time it barely moved. The ivy had matured, its vines thick and coarse as rope covering the bed, wrapping me in their grip. "Get them off! Please get them off."

"What? What are you talking about?"

Warm tears leaked from my closed eyes. I couldn't pry them open, the light was too bright, the pounding too severe. That didn't mean I wasn't aware. I was. Like insects scattering across my skin, the vines continued to weave and wrap; alive and possessed, they tied me to the bed, covering my legs, body, breasts, and arms. I couldn't move.

Oh God!

The foliage was infested. True insects scattered with tiny legs and feet, crawling, eating, and nesting… on me… in me. I feared speaking, afraid they'd enter my mouth. My nose was vulnerable as I blew from my nostrils. Like a bull, I tried to keep them away. My ears and hair crawled with hundreds of thousands of bugs.

I spit my request, "Help! Please, make it stop. Not my face, don't let them on my face."

No one answered. The only sound above his fading laugh was the buzzing and hissing as the infestation continued.

My heart thundered in my ears as I struggled against the vines and insects. With my energy depleting I waited, scared to live and terrified to die.

Did I lose consciousness? I wasn't sure. The buzzing was gone, yet my skin was on fire. Every inch itched with the venom the tiny beasts had left behind.

I was still bound, unable to ease the growing need to scratch. My screams and pleas echoed in the distance until the explosions in my head became literal flames, burning my skin and hopefully the vines.

"Help me. Make it stop. Put it out!"

If only I could move, unwrap the vines, but I was bound in a fire… a sacrifice to a god I didn't know.

"Please, not my face."

"Mrs. Fitzgerald, no one is covering your face."

I blinked once and then twice: the suite was gone and so was the fire. Yet the stench remained, deep within my lungs, the odor of burning flesh. Was it mine or the insects? Had the fire scared them away?

No longer hot, cold water lingered upon my skin. Chilled to the bone, the trembling resumed. My dressing gown clung to my breasts and legs. Yet the moisture did little to relieve the itch and burn that I'd endured as a result of the abusive vines and insects.

Still bound, I turned from side to side, seeking relief. "It itches," I tried to explain. "Please free my hands."

"Do you promise to leave the IVs alone? You've been pretty out of it for the last few days."

"Days?"

My eyes slowly opened, expecting the excruciating pain. Instead, my vision was met with a dull ache. The explosions had ended. My open eyes found only destruction and devastation, the remnants of a battle lost.

"Jane?" I asked, though I knew I wasn't in my suite. I prayed she wouldn't leave me.

"No Jane here," the man's voice replied.

I wanted to cover myself. It wasn't proper to be in this place, wherever it was, with a man I didn't know, wearing a dampened gown. I couldn't. My arms were trapped and body heavy.

"Please, I won't touch the IVs."

Each second that I waited irritated my skin. It crawled with the memory of the infestation. Surely I was covered in marks, bites, and scratches. Like the flames, I longed to soothe it; my entire body prickled. If only I could scratch. If only I could soak. That was what I needed, to soak in a bath.

I needed Jane.

My left arm was the first to be freed, yet it weighed too much to be of any use, falling to the bed and refusing to move. My mind sent instructions, telling it to move, to scratch, to abrade my irritated skin. If only I could, I knew it would bring relief. But, alas, my own limb laughed at my inability.

Pushing with my feet I was able turn my entire body, a little bit at first and then more. The movement helped my back. No doubt the ivy had wrapped totally around me. There wasn't a place that didn't need relief.

"Mrs. Fitzgerald, you need to hold still."

"Itches. My whole body."

"You're soaked in sweat. DTs do that."

DTs?

I couldn't comprehend what he meant.

D and T, what was that?

And then it began... the rumble of an impending earthquake. Starting at my toes, a tremor like I'd never felt before. It grew until my entire body quaked. Loud and primitive, a roar filled the room, its vibrations threatening to shatter the windows and still my erratic heart.

Was the jungle back? Were there animals?

Alarms and buzzers... voices... so far away.

Oh God.

My teeth were going to break: they chattered so hard. I couldn't stop them from gnashing until my jaw became rigid.

All control was lost.

I was here. I felt it. I knew it was me—even the roar—and yet my body was an entity of its own. Tension faded, expelling my bodily fluids...

Oh dear Lord, please help me.

My heavy arm was lifted and then...

Blackness... and calm.

CHAPTER 22

—•O•—

ALEXANDRIA

THE CLAY PATH beneath my shoes was lined by stripped tobacco stalks for nearly as far as the eye could see. I'd ventured beyond the lawns, gardens, tennis courts, and past the pool, until the harvested fields were all around me. The manor was but a dot in the landscape, and I prayed that I'd found the place beyond Alton's security.

In my solitude, for the first time in nearly a week, I wasn't alone. Fingering the tracker necklace, Nox's voice reached beyond my ears to my heart. The tidal wave of relief brought on by his presence, even though only through the phone, staggered my steps.

"I'm so sorry... I didn't want to..." My feet stilled as I gripped the small phone tighter. My blurry gaze darted about the landscape as I tried to catch my breath, determined not to cry any more than I already was. I couldn't waste our precious minutes as a broken-down mess.

"Princess, it'll be all right."

His tone rumbled through me, weakening my knees until I collapsed upon the hard Georgia clay.

"You don't understand," I said, barely able to get the words out before my voice broke. "I-I kissed him."

"What?" His one-word question held no judgment. Instead, there was restraint, as if Nox were doing his best, not only to stay calm himself, but also to keep me that way too. That was what he did: despite what would be his justified anger or hurt, he still put me first.

"When Isaac gave me the phone, Bryce recognized him—"

"Shit!"

"But," I continued, "the Vitoni thing worked. Alton checked and it all was verified. I don't know how you did it, but thank God you did. I convinced Bryce that even though he might have looked like your driver, he wasn't. They searched my backpack." I hiccupped a suppressed sob. "They're watching my every move. I hate it. It's so much worse than…" I didn't want to say worse than him, because that wasn't what I meant. I understood Nox's need to keep me safe. Alton's need wasn't based on protection but on control. It was different.

"Clayton?" Nox offered.

"I want Clayton back."

"Is that the only person you want back?"

"Oh God, no. I miss you so much. There are so many things I need to tell you."

"Tell me *why*. That's what I need to know."

Exhaling, I laid my head back upon a grassy patch near the path and looked up at the blue sky. Small white clouds moved slowly across the expanse, forming shapes and images that continued to change and morph. The small vision exemplified my life. No matter how much I hated that things stayed the same in Savannah, things that I wanted to remain the same changed and morphed like wisps of clouds.

I wanted Nox, New York, Columbia, and even Clayton. I missed Deloris, Lana, and my classmates. I missed our routine. I missed the life we'd made.

Another cry bubbled from my chest. I'd tried to be strong around Alton and Bryce, even Jane, but this was Nox and I couldn't do it anymore. I couldn't pretend, not with him.

"My mom, oh, Nox, she's so sick."

"Princess, you're not alone. You know that, don't you?"

I nodded as tears coated my cheeks.

"I'm watching you," he continued. "You're a blue dot, the most beautiful blue dot I've ever seen. Clayton and Deloris are watching you too, and so is Isaac."

His words, their timbre, washed through me, taking away the shame that had been left from giving into Alton's demands and refilled my depleted strength.

"I was afraid you'd give up on me."

"Never. That's not even an option."

"When I saw him... James," I said, recalling his fake name. "You'll never know how much it meant to me. Despite all I've done, seeing him made me feel like you still believed in me."

"Of course I do. I always will."

A reassuring silence settled over us. Just hearing his breathing calmed me.

"It's good to hear your voice," Nox said, "but I'm a greedy son-of-a-bitch. I want more than your voice. I want every part of you. We're getting you out. We have a plan."

I closed my eyes. Everything inside of me wanted to let him come and get me, but I couldn't. "Nox, you can't."

"You're wrong. I can. We have it all worked out. During the party on Saturday, Patrick is going to help—"

"Stop." I couldn't listen to his strategy and go through with mine.

"No, Charli, you need to listen. It'll work. According to Patrick there'll be a lot of people."

"Nox, I can't leave. If I do, the provisions of the will go into effect. I can't do that to my mom."

"Have you seen the will?"

"I've seen the part that's important. I want to see the whole thing, but I'm biding my time. You don't understand how tyrannical Alton can be. I can't rush it."

I hadn't even been able to arrange an appointment with Dr. Beck. Nothing was within my control.

"Fuck, Charli, you haven't rushed anything. It's been five days. That's not rushing." His voice softened. "Talk to me. Are you safe? Has anyone hurt you?"

Instinctively I reached for my arm, the place where Bryce had gripped it.

The skin was tender, making me wonder if it would bruise. And then I lifted the tips of my fingers to my left cheek. It seemed to be everyone's target. Maybe that was because Alton and Suzanna were both right-handed. I couldn't overthink it.

"Charli?" My name came as a question and a warning. Nox wanted an honest answer, and he wanted it now.

"No," I choked out my response.

"No, you're not safe or no, no one has hurt you?"

"I'm fine, Nox. Really. I just miss you. I miss my life. I-I don't want this to be my life, but it has to be for awhile."

"You're killing me. What about Columbia? What about your dreams?"

I loved that he cared. "I spoke with Dr. Renaud. I'm watching classes via teleconferencing and submitting my work online." Nox sighed. "Thank you for my school things, they arrived yesterday."

"Did you find everything?"

I lifted my head. "Tell me there wasn't anything in there for me. By the time it made it to me it had all been inspected—*for my safety.*" My tone alone on the last part said more than my words.

"No, princess. I wanted to. I wanted to write you a ten-page letter. I wanted to tell you how much I love you and how we'll get you out, but I was advised against it. That sounds like it was good advice."

"It was. They're watching everything. They saw Isaac—I mean, James—give me the case. I don't know what made me hide the phone and put lipstick in the case, but if I hadn't, I wouldn't be talking to you now."

"It's because you're smarter than them, than the whole lot of them." It was like his encouragement that I'd imagined, only better. "Charli Collins, you can do this, you can save your mother and yourself. Deloris is working on getting your grandfather's will. The problem is that it's only on paper. If it were electronic, she'd already have it."

"Nox, I love you. Please remember that. I wish we were together. I wish I were in your arms."

His tone lowered. "Princess, if we were together, by now you'd be over my knee."

My cheeks rose. "As long as I ended up in your arms."

"You'd start there and finish there, but in the middle, I'd redden your beautiful ass for putting us both through this hell. Tell me why you got in that car."

"I told you. My momma is sick, so much more than I ever imagined. If I didn't go with Alton, he wouldn't let me see her. If I don't do as he says, he'll let her suffer. He'll take away all her money."

"Isn't it hers? That's what Deloris has said."

"It is," I confirmed. "According to the part of the will I saw, if I don't marry Bryce and stay married to him..." The words hurt, not just saying them, but also knowing what they must be doing to Nox. "...all of Montague will be liquidated and the assets diverted to Fitzgerald Investments. That includes the corporation, the manor, the investments—all of the assets. Everything. My momma and I'll be left penniless."

"You know I wouldn't let that happen."

"I can't... I can't accept that from you. My mother isn't your responsibility. Neither am I. And you know that if this just concerned me, I'd walk. I did when they took my trust fund. If she were well, I'd seriously consider it. But she isn't."

"You *are* my responsibility." His tone was final and decisive. "And with you comes whomever you want. Your mother will never be indigent."

"That's the word he used."

"He's a bastard and he's playing on your emotions. Charli, let Patrick help you get to the old road, the one where he used to pick you up after family gatherings."

My chest swelled, not only with the memories, but also the idea of Nox and Patrick talking, planning, and working together to support me. I considered his offer. It would be easy to be saved, to be rescued. But Nox had told me he wasn't Prince Charming, and I refused to be the damsel in distress. This was my fight. I needed to see it through, not just for me, but also for my momma.

"I-I can't. It won't work. It's a long walk from the manor to the road. By the time I get back, they'll notice. I can't possibly be gone that long during the party."

"Fuck, you aren't going back. While I'm getting you, Isaac will get your mom. It'll happen before anyone knows what hit them. Then you'll both be safe. We'll get her all the medical care she needs in New York."

I took a deep breath. "I want that. With all my heart, I want that, but if we leave, he wins. I don't give a damn about Montague, but it's what my momma has worked for her whole life. He can't win."

"He won't. You do what you need to do to get to me on Saturday. Just don't fucking kiss him again."

My skin prickled with shame. "I had to think of something. He was about to find the phone. I tried to distract him. I'm so sorry."

"Don't be sorry. I hate it. I hate the idea of him in the same fucking room as you. Touching you. Kissing you." Each phrase was deeper, like a growl. "I hate *it*, Charli, but it's him. I don't hate you. I don't blame you. I want you safe. And while I know firsthand how distracting you can be, come up with another distraction.

"You should probably know that once you're safe, he's going down and so is your stepfather. They aren't winning, unless body bags are prizes."

Why didn't that upset me? It should, but it didn't.

"Nox, this isn't your battle; it's mine. I have to fight it."

"Princess, you can, with me by your side."

"I'll call you whenever I can. I can't make any promises. Just know that I'm safe."

"One more thing," Nox said. "Take care of Chelsea."

My neck stiffened. "Why would you say that? You have no idea. I can't even process. She helped them, luring me back here. She barely looks at me, and she's with—"

"I know more than I can say, especially now. We need time to talk, but she's trying to help you."

"No, Nox, she isn't. She's living my life. She used me for four years and I never saw it. I thought she was my friend. She's no better than them."

"Princess, you have every reason to lash out, but she's not the right target."

I sat up as my volume rose. "Fuck that. You haven't seen her. Ask me to stay safe. Fuck, ask me to stab Alton in his sleep, but don't put Chelsea on my watch list. I'm sure as hell not on hers."

"You've said it yourself: things aren't always what they seem. Would I lie to you?"

"I don't know, Nox, would you? Because this seems out of left field."

"No, I wouldn't and I haven't."

"Then tell me why I should take care of her? As far as I'm concerned, she and Millie can start their own harem. Let them be Bryce's distraction. I don't care."

"Do you trust me?"

Nox's question set my mind spinning to every time he'd asked me that, to satin bindings, hot wax, and crops. My skin tingled and core clenched. "Yes, I trust you."

"Then do it—help her. Saturday night we'll start with you in my arms."

"I-I can't promise..."

"I can. I love you, Charli. Hold on until Saturday."

"Nox, I love you, too. I probably should go. Please don't give up on me."

"Never."

Begrudgingly, I disconnected the call, wiped my tear-stained face, and attempted to pull myself together. The severed connection ripped a hole in my chest, creating a void that longed to be filled. For only a few minutes it had. I could have talked to him forever, but my mind was a ticking clock, and for today, my time was about to run out. I needed to get back to the manor.

Sadness and fear bubbled through me, paralyzing me to my near future. The road Nox mentioned was closer than the manor. Could I go there and call him, have Isaac come today?

My body tingled with excitement... I could.

No. I couldn't.

Like a clear sky after a storm, the excitement disappeared. All energy was gone. For only a moment my weary body collapsed back onto the grass. Overhead, the white clouds were filling with colors: multiple shades of pinks and purples.

Dusk was looming on the horizon.

Saturday.

Hold on until Saturday.

I could do that. I could make it for four more days. I'd survived five, but at what cost?

The impending twilight propelled me up and forward. I couldn't be late for dinner. Heaven forbid. It was always at seven.

As I began walking back toward the manor, my thoughts returned to the scene in Alton's office. I detested what I'd done, but saving the phone and speaking to Nox made it worth it.

The end justified the means.

It wasn't a legal defense, but sometimes it was true.

Seeing the phone's charger sail across the shiny table had made my heart skip a beat. In that second I knew one thing: I hadn't zipped the inside compartment and the phone could easily be next.

When I'd moved my lipstick, I should have secured the phone. But then again, I'd never expected the search and interrogation. I'd never imagined that I was being so closely watched.

The crimson shades of the Savannah sunset intensified as I continued walking, not seeing the world around me, but reliving this afternoon's scene.

I searched Bryce's gray eyes, looking for a sign of the person I used to know, a clue that the boy I'd considered a friend still existed somewhere beneath this Alton clone.

The shutting of the door echoed through the silence, alerting us that we were alone.

Bryce looked from me to my backpack and to me again. "Why?"

"Why what?"

"Why don't you want me mad?"

My mouth went dry as I looked up to him. "Because you were right." His eyes opened wider. "About what you said the first day you took me to see my mom. You said that you were either my only friend or my worst enemy. I seem to have enough of the latter; I could use a friend."

"A friend?" he asked, lifting my left hand and looking down at the diamond.

My eyes closed, lingering in the darkness, encouraging me to continue. "I never asked for more."

"Sometimes life gives us surprises, gifts we never knew we wanted or in my case, never knew were possible. You see, Alexandria, you're my gift. I've wanted you and you've shut me down, time after time. Yes, I dated the great Alexandria Montague Collins. I had a

reputation, but never did I get from you what I wanted most."

I tried to move away, but my body was captive between him and the table. *"Can't we go slowly?"*

He caressed my cheek. *"How fucking slow do you want to go? Any slower and we'd be in reverse. You're not a scared kid and I'm not a fumbling teenager. I know what I like. It'll happen. And you'll like it too. Let's get past that and move on."*

"I don't want our first time to be something we're getting past."

His thin lips twisted into a smirk. *"Darling, things have changed. It's time you learned to accept it. You aren't in charge of this. The only reason I'm not fucking you on this table right now is out of respect for what we once had. Each time you screw with us, each time you think you've worked a way out of this, another bit of that respect is chucked out the proverbial window."* He took a step toward me, but there was nowhere for me to retreat. The table's edge bit into the back of my upper thighs as his hips pressed closer. *"It's up to you, because I'm ready to take you and make you mine. I'm ready to wash all memories of Demetri from your mind. Because once my dick is buried inside of you..."* His smirk grew at my uncontrolled grimace. *"What's the matter, darling, you can dish out the language to my mother, but you can't take it?"*

I swallowed the bile. *"Go on, Bryce, if it makes you feel like a real man to threaten to rape me, go on."*

"I'm not threatening and I'm not going to rape you. I'm going to make my fiancée mine. I'm going to fuck you so good, you won't remember ever being with anyone else."

I was certain that wasn't possible.

"This wasn't the discussion I had in mind," I said, *"when I said I didn't want you to leave angry."*

"Then what do you propose, Miss Collins?"

I willed the repulsion to diminish. It was just a kiss, a means to save the phone, a means to get to Nox. I could do it.

"A kiss, a real kiss."

Bryce stood taller. *"I want to make love and you're offering me a kiss? That's kind of like offering a starving man a cracker. It may sustain me, but it won't ease the hunger."*

"With Chelsea around, I doubt you're starving."

He shrugged. *"McDonald's is hardly satisfying when I have caviar in the palm of my hand."*

I took a deep breath, hoping to get away from the food analogies. I didn't want to think about him and Chelsea. Not that I gave a shit who he screwed as long as it wasn't me. Then again, maybe I did care, enough to also wish it wasn't her.

"I get it. I'm not in charge. I understand that the decision is now yours." With each phrase his expression softened. "But I also believe that we're more than fiancés. We were friends. It's something Alton and Momma didn't have. I'm asking you to please not ruin that, not to take that advantage away. I meant what I said: I want you as my friend, even after we're married."

The words came easier than I expected.

"You scared me when I got home." I went on. "I don't like seeing you that way. I want my friend."

His hand slipped behind my head, down to my neck. As it did, all hopes of a chaste, friendly kiss evaporated.

"Show me, Alex."

I exhaled. Alex. For the first time since I'd returned, he called me the name I wanted to be called. Lifting my chin, my lips met his. With everything in me, I wanted to back away, but I was trapped. Instead, I closed my eyes and imagined full, possessive lips, ones below light blue eyes.

Bryce's tongue pushed against the seam of my lips.

With a warm tear descending my cheek, I granted him access. It was a small concession, I reminded myself. I'd kissed him before when we were young. I'd given in this much. This was no different. This was for Nox. This was for the phone.

With increased fervor, Bryce's fingers entwined in my hair and he pulled me closer, bruising my mouth and flattening my breasts against his chest. I struggled to breathe as his tongue probed. My body fought the urge to fight, to take in air and rid myself of his invasion.

When Bryce finally loosened his grasp, his gray eyes searched me, looking for my true emotion. I was slowly blinking mine open, only showing small openings to my thoughts. I couldn't let him see my feelings and I was too upset to hide them; instead, I lowered my chin, rested my forehead against his chest, and concentrated on breathing, each inhale deeper than the last. While I worked to keep my revulsion at bay, Bryce stroked my hair with a newfound gentleness, one he hadn't shown during the kiss.

I'd calmed him, if only for a moment.

"I want this too," he said.

An answer wouldn't come, not without crying. I simply nodded.

Bryce lifted my chin, forcing our eyes to meet. "I'm not mad anymore."

"Friend?" I managed to ask.

"Fiancé."

"Thank you." I didn't know why I was thanking him, but it seemed right for the mood we'd created. "For being patient."

"My mother is waiting for you."

I nodded again, lifted my backpack, and walked toward the door.

"I'll run this up to my room, and then I'll be out." *After I brush my teeth and gargle for ten minutes.* I didn't add the last part.

Bryce reached for the bag. "I'll take it. Mom said you have an appointment."

I forced a smile. "Yes, for wedding dresses. I appreciate your offer, fiancé." I lifted myself to my toes and brushed my lips over his. "Alton is waiting for you. Of the two, I think your mom will be the easiest to pacify."

With his eyes wide and a growing grin, Bryce shrugged. "You're probably right. I'll see you tonight. We'll be back."

Damn, couldn't he eat at his own house? "We'll?"

"All of us. I'm hoping this new—or renewed—friendship is still present."

Did all of us include Chelsea? I didn't ask. Instead, I took a step toward the stairs. "I'll see you tonight." Before he could answer, I hurried upward with my backpack in hand and visions of cool mint toothpaste.

CHAPTER 23

———•○•———

ALEXANDRIA

AS I MADE my way toward the manor, images of the afternoon scene with Bryce were easily overshadowed by thoughts of Nox and our call. I'd stowed the phone and charger in an old storage shed beyond the tennis courts. It was seldom used since no one played tennis. The small building held rackets and balls as well as maintenance equipment. It was also supplied with electricity, so I could keep the phone charged.

I didn't want to leave it, but I feared taking it back into the house. Closing and latching the old shed, I turned toward the manor. From a distance, the windows' golden glow likened it to a Thomas Kincaid picture, an inviting image with the warm illumination contrasting the cooling Georgia evening.

It was an illusion.

As I entered through a back patio door, there was no welcoming warmth filling the cool air. Only the clatter of dishes and staff from the kitchen and dining area gave the mansion life. I avoided the office and sitting rooms as I slipped inside and glanced at my watch.

I'd made it in time with minutes to spare. Circumventing the main hallways, I scurried up the back stairs near the kitchen toward my room. As I rounded the last bend, I nearly ran into Jane. Her large hands cupped my shoulders while a relieved smile overtook her face.

"Child, thank the good Lord. You had me worried. Mr. Fitzgerald's been asking for you."

The memories of Nox faded like my expression as my nerves jumped to life. "I went for a walk. After the afternoon with Suzanna, I needed air."

She tugged me up the last few stairs. "Hurry. I'll tell him you're getting ready. Dinner's soon."

"I will." I lowered my volume. "Do you know what he wants?"

"Something about your momma. That place called here for you too, when you're out with Miss Carmichael."

"But I came back and no one said anything."

"Child, you was here and then gone. I went to your room and you were out of here."

I took a deep breath and released it slowly. "This is why I need a phone. You need to be able to reach me."

Jane turned down a hallway toward my room, leaving me half of a step behind. "Keep doing like you doing. It'll come." She stopped at the door and inserted the key. Pushing the door wide, she continued. "I don't know what they want. But you're helping her. I know you are."

"Thanks, Jane."

"Now hurry."

I smiled. "I thought I was now your boss."

"You always have been." Her shoulders straightened and eyes brightened. "But now I'm the house manager."

"Yes, you are."

"Love you, child... Miss Alex."

"I love you, too."

She lowered her voice again. "That fresh air did you good. The smile on your face was mighty pretty as you were coming up those stairs."

It wasn't the air that had given me the smile, but Nox. I shrugged, not willing to share him, even with Jane. "The land has always been one of the things I liked around here. It's beautiful. I could walk around all day."

"Okay, that sounds good." She winked. "Cause if I was to guess, you was thinking about someplace besides here." She gently pushed me through my doorway. "Now hurry. You need to be downstairs in seven minutes."

"Yes, Miss House Manager."

With that, I shut the door, pulling my own key from my pocket and locking it again from the inside.

Hurriedly, I splashed my face, added fresh mascara and lip gloss, and ran a brush through my hair. A few clips and it was styled. Slipping out of my jeans and light sweater, I pulled a blue dress over my head, and stepped into a pair of pumps.

As I took one quick look in the mirror, the pearl necklace bobbed over the neckline. The illusion I'd created wasn't too bad for a four-minute makeover. Just as I was about to head back downstairs, I remembered the lack of warmth at Montague Manor. Autumn was trying to break the lingering summer heat. Generally it was a futile effort as long as the sun shone, but with nightfall, autumn found victory. I turned back to my closet for a sweater when my doorknob began to turn.

It could rattle all day and all night, but unless the person had that funny little gadget, it wouldn't open. Taking a deep breath, I called, "I'm on my way."

"Alex?"

The sweater slipped from my grip and fluttered to the floor.

I stepped closer to the door. "Are you alone?"

"Yes," Chelsea replied.

The calm Nox had given me slipped completely out of my reach as hurt, anger, and even jealousy bubbled to life inside of me. Turning the key and opening the door, I stood resolute in the frame. "If you're coming to assure I make it to dinner, as you can see I'm on my way."

Chelsea nodded as a tear escaped her sad hazel eyes. "I-I see. That's not why I'm here. I hoped I could slip away…"

"And what? Spy on me? Tell Alton and Bryce more about me?" I gestured toward the suite. "You obviously filled them in on my favorite products. No one else would've known."

I blocked her forward motion, keeping her in the hallway.

"Alex, I know what it looks like. I know what I've said, but I love you. You're my friend. This wasn't supposed to happen."

I shook my head. "You have a funny way of showing it. What is it with all my supposed friends who think the best way to get to me is to screw Bryce?"

"I-I should go…" she said, turning away.

The pain swirling in Chelsea's eyes reminded me of what Nox had said, how he'd told me to take care of her. "Wait. What wasn't supposed to happen? Why are you still here anyway? I mean, how does it look now that Bryce is engaged?"

Swallowing her tears, she lifted her chin. "It looks like I'm a whore." Her eyes closed as more tears escaped. "And I am."

I don't know if it was the raw emotion in her voice, the honesty, or what Nox had said, but something in the way Chelsea held herself broke a piece of my heart, starting a crack that had the potential to shatter the anger and hurt I'd been harboring.

I reached for her shoulders. "What happened to you? Where's my Chelsea?"

She shook her head, still not looking at me. "I can't tell you. I can't tell anyone. We don't have time… I just couldn't spend another meal with you… hating me."

As I wrapped her in my arms, four years of togetherness began to chip away at a few months of separation punctuated by a few days of disgust.

Slowly she pulled back, mascara streaking down her cheeks.

I reached for her hand. "Come in here. Clean up or they'll know."

Chelsea nodded and followed me inside. As she did her eyes opened wider, taking in the suite.

"Have you been in here before?"

"No, I didn't even know for sure where I was going. I saw you come in from the back of the house. I excused myself and followed you up the stairs. Then I waited until Jane left."

Chelsea followed me to the bathroom and reached for a tissue.

"I almost chickened out," she added.

"Chelsea Moore doesn't chicken out of anything."

Her cheeks fell. "She does now."

When she threw the tissue to the counter, I closed the bathroom door and reached for her hand. "Did they make you text me?"

"Your stepfather did. Bryce knew, but Mr. Fitzgerald told me what to say."

"And you did it?" My chest ached.

Chelsea turned away, only meeting my eyes in the mirror. "You've seen her. She needs you. Without you, she would've gotten worse. I know you've hated your mom, but I think there's so much more."

I pursed my lips and widened my eyes.

In barely a whisper, I said, "Unless this is part of their plan, stop. I've looked everywhere, but I can't shake the feeling this room is bugged. We might be safe here in the bathroom."

Swallowing she stood taller. "Oh God..."

Fear, confusion, even terror... the emotions leaped from her hazel eyes. "I-I..."

My heart told me that everything I saw was honest. My Chelsea wasn't a good actor: she never had been. She'd always been the one to say what she thought, the fresh air that had inflated my life raft when I'd moved west. I looked down at my watch and back to her reflection. "We need to go. Let me try to handle this. Can you go along with me?"

Maintaining our whisper, she met me face to face. "Honestly, I don't know. I'll try."

"Please, Chels. We can do much more together than apart. We've already proven that."

"Fucking jail break?" she asked with a hint of her old self.

"I've been told you're kick-ass."

She shrugged. "Maybe I can remember how, as long as I have my best friend by my side."

CHELSEA SLIPPED DOWN the back stairs while I waited and descended the front. We were both late, not by normal standards, but this wasn't normal. This was Montague Manor.

"Where the hell have you..." Bryce's growl rumbled from the dining room as I approached through another entrance. The damn room had doors in all directions. It was designed for large parties. Guests could even enter from the terrace, if the French doors were open. Tonight they weren't, yet the drapes were open, giving a view of the lawns and lake.

The idea to see if the tennis courts were visible from the sitting room was a fleeting thought. Bryce's tenor zeroed my attention past Alton and Suzanna, who were already seated, to him. His question wasn't meant for me, though I recognized the tone. It was the same one I'd heard earlier in the day, but that wasn't what held my attention. It was the way he gripped Chelsea's arm that sent the small hairs on my arms to attention.

What the fuck was his problem?

Before she could answer, I entered. "It seems that tardiness is rampant tonight," I volunteered, taking some of the heat off Chelsea.

Ignoring her, I bravely walked to Bryce, meeting his agitated gaze with one of calm. "I'm sorry, I couldn't decide on which dress looked best." I turned a small circle. As our stare connected for the second time, I noticed his mellowing a bit.

He released Chelsea's arm as I took another step closer. "You were right," I cooed.

"I was?"

I lifted one brow and slowed my cadence. "You're back."

While Chelsea hurried to her seat, Bryce leaned forward to offer me a kiss. Our lips barely touched, when Alton's bellow saved the day.

"You're late. Dinner is being served."

My smile wasn't fake: it was ironic. Never could I remember welcoming my stepfather's intrusion as I did at that moment. Thankfully, Bryce appeared to misconstrue its meaning as he met my expression with a smile equally as large.

"Nice dress," he whispered as we turned to our assigned seats.

Silence and glances prevailed throughout the first two courses as Alton and Suzanna spoke about our wedding dress excursion. Why Alton was interested was beyond me. It wasn't as if he'd have carried on a long conversation with my mother had she been the one to shop.

After the main course was placed before us, I turned to Alton. "I was told you were looking for me?"

"Where were you?"

"Surely you know. Don't you see all?"

As his beady eyes narrowed, I continued, hoping to minimize my sarcasm. "On a walk. Other than Magnolia Woods and shopping, I haven't been outside. You're the one who told me to get used to being here. The part of here that I adore is the land.

"The fields look bare and sad. When was the harvest?"

"Really, Alexandria, do you think I worry myself with the planting and harvesting schedule?"

I shrugged. "Honestly, yes."

"Don't be late for dinner again."

"I wouldn't have been, if I hadn't been ambushed."

"Really, dear, you're so dramatic," Suzanna said. "Who ambushed you? Not Bryce. He was with us."

"No, not Bryce. Chelsea."

Chelsea's hand stopped mid-lift, the fork dangling in the air precariously above the fine china as all eyes turned toward her.

"That's where you were?" Bryce asked, obviously questioning Chelsea.

"Yes," I volunteered. "It seems she wants…" I lifted my glass of wine and took a sip, allowing the anticipation to build.

"What? What does she want?" Bryce asked.

"For us not to hate one another. For me to forgive her for her lies and conniving ways, for four years of deception, cunning, and betrayal."

"Alex?" Emotion choked Chelsea's one word.

"What?" I asked dramatically. "Isn't this what we're all about now… openness?"

"Yes," Alton answered.

"Excuse me?" I turned his way.

"Chelsea isn't going anywhere. It would be best for the two of you to… get along."

I furrowed my brow. "That doesn't work for me."

I avoided looking at my friend, knowing my words were inflicting pain, yet confident I was on the right path.

"I'm proud of you, Chelsea," Suzanna said. "I know what a difficult position you're in. Alexandria, this really would be the best. It would be perfect if you could show a united front on Saturday."

"Hmm?" I asked. "Maybe me on one side of Bryce and Chelsea on the other?"

"That would—"

"Not exactly," Alton said, interrupting Bryce.

"Then what... exactly?"

"Chelsea resumes her role as your friend and roommate."

"And stops sleeping with my fiancé?"

There were comments from both Bryce and Chelsea, but I wasn't listening to them. I was back to negotiating. For that to be successful, it had to be with Alton.

He lifted his napkin and dabbed his thin lips. "In public."

This time I turned the direction of Bryce and Chelsea. "You had sex in public?"

"No, Alexandria!" Suzanna interjected. "That's not what your father meant. He meant that what happens in private is... private. In public, Chelsea resigns herself to being your friend and Bryce's ex. She's part of your crowd now. The others will take their cues from you. If you don't show any animosity, the other girls will follow suit."

What was this, a fucking sorority? The Chi Omega of Savannah's upper echelon.

"What do you expect us to do?" I asked. "Have a sleepover and make up?"

It was Suzanna who answered. "I think that's a perfect idea. Maybe you could think about the maid-of-honor role too?" Her nose scrunched dramatically. "It's a much better solution than the one you proposed."

"Have you spoken to Alton..."

"No," she answered. "I was hoping..."

"That's enough," Alton proclaimed. "I don't care about the details. Chelsea is moving in here tonight."

"Wait a minute..." Bryce's words stalled as we all turned his direction.

Asshole. If I wasn't able to screw Nox, he didn't need to be screwing anyone either. Still, that consequence was merely the icing on the cake. My first goal had been to talk to Chelsea. If I gained her a reprieve from Bryce, all the better.

"Fine." Bryce threw his hands in the air. "Fine. If this is what you want, Alexandria... fine."

I couldn't give in too quickly. "I never said it was."

"I did," Alton proclaimed. "Now eat. When we're done, Chelsea can go get a few things from Carmichael Hall while I fill you in on your mother."

"My mother? I was there..."

"Her DTs are getting worse," Suzanna said shaking her head.

"What? She was sleeping comfortably when I left?"

Alton lifted his hand. "You were the one absent when I tried to speak to you. This will wait. I'm not letting the subject upset our dinner."

"The subject? My mother?"

"Alexandria."

"I need a phone."

Alton didn't answer, no one did. As if a switch had been flipped... heavy silence fell over the room, interrupted only by the occasional sound of forks upon china and food being consumed.

CHAPTER 24

OREN

THE VICTORIAN DISTRICT. That's what they called this area of Savannah. I'd been here before, to this exact house. In many ways, it reminded me of the brownstones in Brooklyn, but made of wood and with more color. In the darkness the colors were muted, but during the day, they were like a rainbow, blues and greens, even shades of pink. The houses were semi-detached, giving each a side yard, yet their floor plans were similar to what I had known. The structure was narrow, deep, and tall. Without the woodwork and architectural bric-a-brac, they would resemble the old shotgun style seen more frequently in New Orleans.

Through the years and with the renovations, the value of homes in this area of Savannah had increased significantly. And while being a secretary at the esteemed law firm of Hamilton and Porter in this historic city was a noble job, it wasn't what one considered lucrative. Not lucrative enough to be able to afford one of these townhomes. That took extra income, the kind not found on a tax return.

I peered up and down the quiet street. Nighttime had fallen hours ago, taking the residents inside and allowing quaint, old-fashioned streetlights to be the only source of illumination. The black iron fence separating the small front yard from the street wasn't locked. I'd already checked that. It seemed like she'd learn. It hadn't been locked the last time I was here either.

That little stretch of green helped the residents of this area believe they were better than the brownstones and many of the shotgun houses. These fine dwellers had a front yard.

I couldn't help but shake my head. Through the years it had become obvious that the things people considered important became trivial as the life they lived slipped away. The item on the grocery list with the star was no longer significant. The appointment at the beauty parlor was no longer paramount. The new car or green patch of earth no longer mattered.

Death had a way of refocusing both men and women.

The sad observation was that the clarity given to these misguided souls came too late for action. Perhaps there was solace in the knowledge or could it be remorse? If only the realization had come when there was time to rectify goals. That was seldom the case.

The gate creaked as I lifted the lever and pushed it inward. The slam as it shut behind me echoed on the empty street, awakening a dog a few doors down. Thankfully, after a few halfhearted barks to do his job, the canine forgot its interruption and quieted.

Historically accurate, the porch was as it had been a hundred years earlier. Revisions included new boards and paint, but not surveillance. There were no visual doorbells or cameras. My image would not be captured or saved.

With a handkerchief covering my finger, I pushed the round button. A chime played within, its tune barely audible at my distance. The unlit porch light should probably have been an indication that Miss Natalie Banks wasn't expecting visitors, but this was the South. Hospitality, even at a late hour, was inbred.

Keeping my face away from the side window, I waited as the interior entry filled with light. Seconds later, the door opened.

"May I…" Miss Banks's welcome stopped as our eyes met.

Recognition and terror were easily misconstrued. Perhaps it was that I'd witnessed them both, often in conjunction, one right after the other. Her gaze darted around me.

"M-Mr. Demetri?"

"No one has seen me, which is neither an advantage nor a disadvantage.

It's rude to entertain on your porch, Miss Banks."

She hesitated for only a moment before taking a step back. "Please, come in."

Nodding, I stepped over the threshold. Neat and clean, the foyer was narrow with the staircase to my left and a formal sitting room to my right. The solid oak floors glistened with the artificial light as Natalie Banks took another step backward on a narrow hallway that led past the stairs toward the kitchen.

"I'd forgotten what a very nice home you have."

Bobbing her head quickly she tugged at the hem of her shirt. "Thank you. Would you like something to drink? The kitchen is—"

My cheeks rose. "No, I'd like something else."

I hadn't been the only contributor to her unreported income, but I had made a significant donation after she helped to point Alexandria toward the resort in Del Mar, a far larger donation than the task was worth. That made us family.

Family watched over one another. They helped one another out. They repaid debts. Hers had just come due.

CHAPTER 25

———•◦•———

ALEXANDRIA

SEIZURES.

Alton had delivered the news as if he were giving me Montague's stock report, assuring me that I could visit again in the morning. Thankfully, I'd convinced Bryce to stay with me as I heard the news. I honestly had no idea what Alton had been about to tell me, only that I was trying to give Chelsea space to get her own things without his help.

She got Suzanna and I took Bryce.

Now, an hour or more later after more of a battle than I'd waged in five days, I was racing through the hallways of Magnolia Woods. When we arrived, I didn't stop to sign a registry or even speak to the woman at the front desk. This was after visiting hours and the woman was too busy painting her nails or reading some smut to notice as we passed by.

The only one we'd spoken to was the outside guard, who'd begrudgingly allowed us to enter.

"Alexandria, slow down."

I didn't listen to Bryce as my shoes slid over the tiles and I made the final turn.

"Ma'am?" A large man in scrubs said, scrambling to his feet from a chair near the window as I burst through the door.

"I'm Miss Collins, and you are?"

"Mack, Mack Warren, Mrs. Fitzgerald's night nurse."

The room was dim, illuminated by only the display of multiple monitors. Hurriedly, I stepped toward her bed and turned on the nearby lamp.

I gasped.

The lamp did little to help my vision. If anything, the scene before me blurred, as if a mist had settled over us, softening the reality. I reached for my heart as it painfully clenched and my stomach dropped to my feet. The woman on the bed was a shell of the mother I knew, even less than the one I'd left this afternoon. The vital lady in my memory was always dressed impeccably and the perfect belle. That lady was nowhere to be found.

The patient lying before me wearing a hospital gown that clung to her perspiration-drenched skin revealing her too-thin frame was a stranger. This person's brown hair was dull, matted, and damp against her scalp and her complexion a pale shade of gray.

I choked out my words as I reached for her hand. "Momma, I'm here. It's Alexandria." The coolness of her touch sent a chill through me as if I were holding an ice cube instead of her extremity. "It's going to be all right. You're going to get better."

Bryce came up behind me, his radiating warmth a contrast to my mother; though he wasn't touching me, his breath skirted my neck. "I-I'm sorry…"

I turned on him, lashing out on the only one I could. "Sorry? You're sorry? Look at her. I should have been here, not having some stupid family dinner. You knew about her seizures and didn't say a word. I don't want to hear that you're sorry."

He lifted his hands in surrender, but his eyes held both fight and a warning. His yielding was a show for Mack, but I'd take advantage of my temporary upper hand.

"Alex, I'm not the enemy here. When did I have the opportunity to tell you? You left the manor. I couldn't reach you. I tried."

Standing tall, I held back the tears as I turned again to my mother. Her skin beneath mine was clammy and moist. The longer I stood, the more my nose prickled and the rank air settled around us. I turned to Mack. "You're her nurse. Why haven't you cleaned her?"

"I-I didn't know if she would have another seizure."

My head swiveled from side to side. "What difference does that make? She needs a bath. If she has another seizure, then do it again."

Though his shoulders straightened, he didn't speak.

"You heard her," Bryce said.

I grimaced at his support, hating it almost as much as his opposition. "Forget it," I said. "Get me a basin with warm, soapy water and another with fresh warm water. I'll also need washcloths and towels." I turned to Bryce. "You'll need to step out."

"I can't leave you alone."

"Of course you can. I've been here for five days, most of it alone. Besides, Mack will be here. Go, give my mother some privacy." Dismissing him, I continued my orders to Mack. "I'll wash her. You change her bed and get me one of her nightgowns. Mrs. Montague Fitzgerald shouldn't be wearing a hospital gown. I can guarantee we're paying for better care than she's received."

His jaw clenched. "Miss, our clients may have money, but they're all the same: addicts. Her name isn't—"

Bryce began to speak, but I lifted my hand. "Mr. Warren, stop now or get a new job tomorrow." It may have been years since I'd been a pretentious snob, but old inbred habits were hard to forget.

"Did you misunderstand the lady?" Bryce asked when the nurse remained still.

Mack's gaze narrowed, but just as quickly, he began gathering supplies, moving to and from the private bath with the basins.

"Bryce, go into the hallway. I'll call you back as soon as we're done."

"Alexandria, you don't have to do this. That's what these people are here for."

"You're wrong. I do and I am." I turned back to Mack. "I want to wash her hair too. How do we do that in the bed?"

I pulled down her sheets.

"Oh my God! What the hell happened to her arms? They're a mass of scratches, and why are there bruises around her wrists?"

"It was her," he explained. "She'd been doing good and the restraints were off, and then all at once she started screaming. She was hallucinating, yelling about vines and insects, saying it itched. I cleaned some of the blood away after I got her restrained again."

I gently caressed blue and red marks on her dainty wrist. "She's what, one hundred and ten pounds? What the hell are you restraining her with?"

"That isn't it. She fought it, pulling and thrashing, before the seizures started. Once they did, her whole body fought. That's why they're bruised."

Each explanation tore at my heart. I lifted each wrist. It wasn't anything like the faint lines from Nox's bindings. My mother's wrists were irritated and inflamed. "Help me move her."

My mother was but a feather in Mack's arms as he rolled and lifted her, aiding me in cleaning her as well as changing the bed's clothes.

By the time we were done, she was clean, fully clothed in a pink nightgown with her clean yet damp hair combed over her shoulders. If it weren't for the catheter, I would have insisted on undergarments as well.

Compromises.

I found myself making them at each turn.

The bags of fluid hanging near the head of her bed had multiplied since I'd left earlier in the day. "What medicines have been added?"

"Anticonvulsants. They had to up the dose from what they first put her on, but the seizures finally stopped."

"I want to speak to Dr. Miller."

"It's, like, midnight. He's off call."

"How much do we pay for my mother's care?" I didn't let him answer. "I'm confident it includes a constant connection to her team."

"I-I don't know…"

"Call him. Get him in here or at least on the phone." I stared up at this man. "Now."

"I'm not supposed to leave her."

"Then use your cell phone, or leave her in my care, which is obviously better than what she's had, and go call him." I walked to the closed door. "Bryce?"

He nodded from where he'd been, leaning against the far wall, and walked toward me.

"Mack was just about to get ahold of Dr. Miller for me. Can you assure him we won't leave Momma's side?"

Bryce looked down at his watch. "Alexandria, it's nearly midnight. What can the doctor possibly do now that he can't do in the morning? Besides, we have pictures—"

Maybe it was my expression, I don't know. All I know is after our eyes met, Bryce turned toward Mack.

"Do it now."

"Yes, sir," Mack said, heading for the door.

"I fucking hate this patriarchal society," I mumbled as Mack left. "Savannah needs a lesson in equality."

Bryce shrugged. "I don't know. You seemed to be holding your own." He walked closer to Momma. "Look at her. She looks better already."

I pulled a chair closer to the bed and lifted her hand. Pushing back the soft silk sleeves of her nightgown, I showed Bryce one of her wrists. "Look at this."

His brow furrowed. "What the hell?"

"This isn't right. Please help me help her. Please. How would you feel if it were your mother in this bed?"

"I'd hate it. I'd do anything I could to help her."

"Then please don't make this harder for me, for her."

His chest expanded and contracted with deep breaths. "What? What do you think I can do?"

"You said it earlier. I'm not in charge; you are."

"I don't think you're talking sex?"

"No, I'm not. I'm saying Alton listens to you. I need a phone. I need this place to be able to reach me. I need you, him, and your mom to reach me. Jane…"

As I said her name, Mack reentered the room. "Dr. Miller said you can call him." He handed me a slip of paper with his number. "You just said something."

Taking the paper, I asked, "What?"

"Jane. That was a name your mother was calling out."

"She was talking?"

"Yeah, like I said. She was saying stupid stuff about vines and bugs, but she also kept calling for Jane. Is that your sister?"

"No, but if my mother wants Jane, she'll have Jane."

Mack shrugged. "I can't leave this room until my replacement comes in the morning. You can stay, but she's pretty drugged. I don't think she'll be fighting any more vines or bugs."

I lifted my hand toward Bryce, palm up. When his eyes opened in question, I replied, "Give me your phone. I'm calling Dr. Miller."

He began to hesitate, but it was short-lived. "Here," he said, handing me the phone from his pocket. "I'm listening to the conversation."

"Suit yourself. I'll put him on speaker and we can all listen."

The conversation was less new information and more confirmation.

Earlier in the day they'd lessened her medication, trying to lure her out of her drug-induced sleep. Dr. Miller said it isn't good to keep her that way. They'd hoped that she'd been unconscious long enough to have missed the severe delirium tremens—the DTs. But as she began to come out of the medicine, she became delirious, hallucinating and shaking. Before they could restrain her again, she attacked herself, scratching at her own skin. It took multiple orderlies, but they stopped her before she tore her face, once again restraining her hands.

That was when the seizures began. According to the tests, she had two severe ones. They used to be categorized as grand mal but now they're called tonic-clonic. It's the type of seizure that's characterized by loss of consciousness and violent muscle contractions. Dr. Miller explained that usually those types of seizures are caused by abnormal electrical activity throughout the brain, but in Momma's case they're believed to be a byproduct of the alcohol and opioid withdrawal.

By the time we left the hospital, I was too exhausted and upset to object to Bryce's hand on the small of my back or the way he helped me into the car. Though he'd driven, we had our customary security team of two individuals following close behind.

Once we were moving, Bryce reached over and touched my knee. It registered as wrong, yet I couldn't protest. Not because I was unable, but because my mind was with my mother, not on another violation of my space.

My problem seemed rather trivial in comparison.

"Don't yell at me," Bryce said, "but I am sorry about your mom. I've always liked her. She's been like my second mother my entire life."

I nodded as I watched the darkened scenes pass by the windows. "Thank you. Thank you for letting me call Dr. Miller."

"Friends and fiancés," Bryce said, his smile visible by the dashboard light. "I'll talk to Alton. I'm sure if he concedes, your phone will be closely monitored. So don't screw it up, but I'll do my best to get you a phone."

I reached down to where his hand still rested on the hem of my dress and put mine on top of his. The huge diamond glittered from the artificial lights. Red and green numbers made the dashboard look like some kind of control pit. His car was equipped with everything, yet I saw nothing. I was even too tired to consider the obvious overcompensation. "Thank you."

CHAPTER 26

ALEXANDRIA

A TUNNEL OF blue light shone from the headlights, illuminating the long driveway. The large oak trees bowed and the Spanish moss twisted. By the howl of the wind, it was more than a breeze. An autumn storm was brewing. With November nearly here, cold and warm fronts were battling for domination.

As Bryce stopped the car before the front steps of Montague Manor, he squeezed my hand. "I could come in with you."

"I-I don't know... if Alton would approve."

Apparently it was the right answer, at least one Bryce willingly accepted.

"Then let me walk you to the door."

"It isn't necessary. It's late. I'll see you tomorrow." I didn't linger long enough for a goodnight kiss; instead, I pushed the door open. When I did, the wind grabbed ahold, pulling the door from my grip and whipping my hair about my face. "Oh! It feels like a storm."

Stepping from the car, I steadied myself as I pushed the door closed. If Bryce had said anything else, I hadn't heard, not over the howling winds. Even in the darkness, lost leaves and pine needles swirled on the driveway, small cyclones preparing for a bigger event.

That was what I was doing, dancing to the music Alton and Bryce selected, biding my time for the big event. What would that event be, Saturday night or maybe my wedding?

The building storm no longer registered as I slipped inside and closed the large doors to the manor. I knew all too well that this place was a fortress, impenetrable to outside forces. Through the dimmed foyer and up the stairs, I made my way to my room. I longed for the phone from the shed and even considered going out to find it, but my body ached from the exhaustion and my heart hurt from the sight of my mother. Sleep was what I needed.

Turning the key, I pushed open my bedroom door as flashes of lightning shone from the unblocked windows. I rushed to close the drapes to keep the storm outside. I had enough turmoil within: Mother Nature could keep her mayhem outside.

Looking below, I sighed at the now-empty driveway. Thankfully, Bryce had left.

It was after midnight. Only three more days until Saturday.

My mantra...

I could keep him at bay for three more days, I was confident. However, if things didn't go as Nox planned, that timetable went from three days to seven weeks. Seven weeks until our wedding. Could I keep Bryce from sex for seven weeks?

With the second window covered, I turned and faced my dark room.

Sometimes clues went unnoticed. Signs were present, but things like storms and drapes demanded attention. Was it a sound or a feeling? I didn't know.

What I knew with increased certainty was that the small hairs on my arms weren't standing at attention because of the electrical storm outside my window. As a sense of dread loomed stronger than before, I realized that I hadn't locked my door. Somehow I'd been more concerned with the storm.

What was I sensing?

In my heart I knew that it wasn't only my nerves on high alert. Somehow I knew that I wasn't alone. Someone was in my room.

Why hadn't I turned on the light?

Blood rushed through my ears, muting the autumn storm. Breathing... had that been what I'd heard?

Survival. The continual flashes from around the draperies gave me snapshots of sight. The growing thunder rolled as I searched for a weapon. The key. The skeleton key was still in my hand. My mind swirled with the possible uses. Stab him in the eye, the neck… where were the most vulnerable points?

"Alex?" The voice came from the direction of my bed.

"Oh fuck. Chelsea." I reached for a lamp and twisted the switch. Sitting on my bed with her knees pulled up to her chest was my best friend. "What the hell are you doing?"

"They gave me a room down the hallway, but I-I guess… I wanted to talk to you."

Indignation grew disproportionately to her presence. My fist found my hip. "Or were you checking to see if I came home alone? What? Are we doing a three-way now?"

Her soft hazel eyes grew wide, swirling with shock, hurt, and disbelief. The emotions were all present, each one fighting for its chance to shine.

"I-I thought tonight at dinner was…" Her forehead fell to her knees, muting her words. "God, Alex. We can't get past this, can we?"

Lifting her tear-stained face, she pulled her knees closer. The action brought my attention away from her as a whole to her as my friend. The pajamas she wore were really a pair of shorts and the top was sleeveless. It wasn't different from what she'd worn for four years, but she was different. I flipped on another light.

"Oh my God," I said, my hand moving to my mouth, unable to keep the disgust from my voice.

Her eyes opened wide, meeting mine, as I went toward her.

Only a few feet away, I remembered my fear that the room was bugged. "Come with me."

Briefly, she hesitated before crawling from near my headboard to standing by the bed and following me into the bathroom. As soon as I shut the door with us both inside, I flipped the switch and the room filled with light, much more light than in the bedroom.

Her complexion was gaunt with her makeup gone. Without asking, I reached for her chin and pulled it toward me. "Oh Chels." I lifted the tips of my fingers to her left cheek, barely touching the remnants of green. It wasn't an obvious flinch, but she did. I let go and took a step back. Surrounding her upper arm was a dark purple handprint, complete with individual finger marks. It was what I'd seen in the bedroom, what had prompted me to bring her in here.

Tears filled my eyes as she slowly lifted her top. We'd been roommates for years. It wasn't as if we paraded around our apartment naked, but the occasional changing of clothes occurred in one another's presence, enough that we shouldn't be shocked by the other's nudity.

Yet as the hem of the tank top rose, my stomach dropped and my body forgot how to move. I couldn't speak or reach out. I couldn't do anything but stare at the multiple bruises, strategically placed where they'd be covered by her clothes.

Though my mouth dried, I managed to speak. "Why? What the hell?"

Pulling her shirt back down, Chelsea collapsed onto the edge of the garden tub. Down, down, and further down she went until her head was bowed, held only by her arms resting upon her knees.

"I-I can't... any... more." Her voice was uncharacteristically soft, muted by her position. She looked up, tears coating her cheeks. "I tried... for you, but... I've never been more afraid."

My legs gave out as I fell down and held onto her knees. "Then why? Why would you do this? Was it really for the money?"

Bristling at my touch upon her knee, she abruptly stood. "It's easy for you, isn't it? You've always had it. Even in school, even when they took it. You walked right from one bank account to another. That's fine. Make assumptions, Alex. Thanks for understanding."

"What the hell? I don't know what you're talking about. You're the one who stepped into my life. I never asked you to do it."

"Not you, but you said it would be all right. You said to trust her."

I shook my head. "I don't know what the fuck you're talking about. Look at you." Standing, I grabbed her slim shoulders and turned her toward the large mirror. Standing beside her, I said, "Look at your hair. Think about the way you dress. This isn't you. It's me—the Alexandria me. Did you lie to me for four years?"

She faced me, her eyes blazing. "Is that what you really think? What's the matter, are you jealous? It isn't enough that you have Nox, you don't want me to have Bryce? Well, fuck you. I'm done. I was trying to stay... to help... to take the heat... but fuck you, Alexandria Charles Montague Collins. With each passing day I see how totally screwed up this whole life is. I don't want it. It's not worth it. If that's what you think of me, then you're not worth it." She lifted her shirt again. "And good luck with this life. You're going to need it."

Allowing the top to drop, she reached for the doorknob. Just as quick I stood in her way.

"Chelsea, I don't get it. I don't understand."

"Of course you don't. Have you even tried?"

"Have I tried? No. I've been a little preoccupied with my mother."

"How bad is she?" Chelsea asked, concern infiltrating her anger.

"Bad. The DTs from withdrawal are wreaking havoc on her body. It's worse than I could've ever imagined."

She nodded. "You needed to be here. No one else would be watching after her, not like you." She shrugged. "Besides, I think he really does like you. I mean, if he's capable of it, it's you."

"How long have the two of you...? This started when? Our freshman year? Sophomore?"

Chelsea paced the small space, shaking her head. "Is that what you think?"

"It's what you said. It's what he said."

"I didn't have a choice, and him... he lies more than he tells the truth. I'm his cover for the Melissa Summers scandal. Did that story work so well that even you didn't see the truth?"

"I-I don't know."

"Alex, Bryce is a pig. I hate him."

There was a hint of something in her voice. I took a step back and looked at her. My Chelsea wasn't gone. Hidden under the auburn hair dye and expensive clothes, she was still there. When she was downstairs, she might not have been the same woman I'd lived with, but now hearing a bit of that spark, I knew in my heart that my friend hadn't been completely broken. Little by little she was trying to come back. "Why would you agree to this, to be his cover… to allow all of this?" I asked, motioning up and down her body.

"Agree? Allow? Is that what you think?" Indignation returned to her tone. "Are you going to *allow* it? Because I have news for you: it will happen."

"I'm not marrying him."

"Really? That's not what I've been hearing. Tonight at dinner Suzanna was going on and on about the perfect gown the two of you found."

"This place is an illusion. I've told you that before—forever. Nothing here is real."

"It feels pretty fucking real to me."

As Chelsea sank back to the edge of the tub, I recalled Nox's request, the reason I'd tried to get her here to Montague and away from Bryce, even if I wasn't sure I wanted that. "Chelsea, why would Nox ask me to help you?"

Her eyes lit up. "He did? When?"

"Um, the last time I spoke to him. He said something about things not being the way they seem."

She shook her head. "I don't know. It doesn't matter anyway. I can't do this. Just like Stanford. I can't even be a whore right. Just another item to add to my list of failures."

Again I melted by her feet. "Chels, you're not a whore or a failure. You're sleeping with a jerk, but that doesn't make you a whore. You're smart. They hired you at Montague for HR. I've always thought you were one of the smartest—especially when it came to street smarts—women I know."

She swallowed. "I-I wish I could explain. I really want to help you, but I have one out and I want to take it. Since you've been back, I-I can't do anything or say anything… he scares me." She reached for my hands. "Really scares me. He's said a few things. I might be wrong, but I think it was him in our apartment. If not him, he was involved. I don't know why and I can't prove it."

One out—what did she mean?

Before I could process, she was back to the subject of the attack in Palo Alto. "He would do it."

"I-I don't know if he's capable—"

With tears again filling Chelsea's eyes, she nodded. "Yes, Alex, he is. Tell me what happened the first day you arrived, during the night?"

It had only been days, but it seemed like much longer. I thought back. "I wanted to make a call."

"Nox?"

I shrugged. "Of course, but I didn't have his number. I had Deloris's." Chelsea didn't speak so I went on, recalling the night. "Alton had taken my phone. I was supposed to be locked in my room, but I had a key. I tried in this wing, room after room, but couldn't find a working house phone. It was the middle of the night, so I snuck down to Alton's office."

"And?"

"Bryce was there, waiting. He caught me. He pushed me to the floor..." Saying it aloud made it even worse than when I'd experienced it. "Somehow I convinced him to let me up and let me call. He listened to the call and afterward took the key and locked me back in this room."

"Were you relieved he didn't... take it further?"

I nodded. "Yes, he was... aroused. I was afraid..." I couldn't go on. Not with the way Chelsea was looking at me. "Why? Tell me. Did he go back to Carmichael Hall?"

"Yes."

"That's where you were staying?"

"Yes." Each response was quieter than the one before.

"Chelsea, what happened?"

She shook her head. "No. I'm not talking about it. No one needs to hear that and I don't want to relive it."

It was as if someone reached into my chest and squeezed my heart while someone else punched me in the gut. Oh God. What was she suffering for me? This couldn't go on.

I stood and paced, back and forth, as my plan and Nox's went through my head. "I can't tell you more, but I can help you. I can get you out of here."

"And then I'm leaving you. I don't want to—"

"No, you're not leaving me. You're giving me one less concern."

She shook her head. "Can I stay with you tonight in your room? I'd like for one night to sleep and feel... well... safe."

I'd never considered Montague Manor as safe, but if it could be that for Chelsea, who was I to stop her?

"Yes, but in the morning… we fell asleep talking. They can't know that we've made up. They can't suspect or they might figure out that you're leaving."

"I don't want to leave without you."

"I don't want you to stay."

As we climbed into bed, I asked, "How is your job at Montague Corporation?"

"Fake," she said as her head fell against the pillow.

"It's not real?"

She yawned. "You said it, Alex. Nothing here is real."

CHAPTER 27

———•○•———

NOX

IT HAD BEEN over a week since I'd seen my Charli asleep in our bed. Now I was a voyeur, watching from afar, through an electronic feed from Isaac's phone.

With everything in me I wanted to be there, to be sure she'd arrive and that the plan had a chance of working. Charli didn't know what was in store: it was too risky. For this to work, she needed to appear and be completely unaware.

From the limited view I could see the tea room. From Isaac's description, the restaurant seemed to be the epitome of girly. It would never survive in Brooklyn and maybe not even in Rye. From the lace tablecloths and tiny teacups to the crystal chandeliers and dainty cakes, I could list a thousand reasons why it was not my kind of place.

There was one reason that it was, and according to Isaac she'd just entered.

He whispered his commentary as I waited across town.

"She's with two others. I don't see her security. It seems as though you were right. As long as she's with Mrs. Spencer, she doesn't have her direct shadows."

"Good," I replied. "Isaac, my man, I kind of hate you right now."

197

"Because I get to drink tea out of a dollhouse-sized cup?"

"That, and you're seeing her."

"Boss, if all goes well, so will you. Soon."

"Tell me what you see."

"They're sitting. She's… she's…"

"What?"

"Smiling and talking. I don't know her that well, but it doesn't seem genuine. Not like I've seen her with you." He paused. "Not even like I've seen her alone. She seems tense, like she's nervous. Are you sure she doesn't know?"

"How the hell could I have told her?"

"Good point. They're ordering something and Mrs. Spencer is doing most of the talking."

"Is it just the two of them?"

"No. Chelsea Moore is with them."

I wanted to know more—what is she wearing, was her hair up or down—but the things running through my thoughts seemed trivial. I'd never voice them to Oren, but nothing was trivial when it came to my Charli.

"Sir, more coffee?" the waitress's voice transcended the phone.

I waited for Isaac to answer and said, "I thought you were drinking tea?"

"I had to man up somewhere. This setting you have me in is seriously threatening my man card."

"Get her to me and your man card will stay valid."

"Waiting."

As silence filled our conversation, I thought about why Charli was there—about her mother.

Since Deloris had infiltrated Magnolia Wood's system, she'd been following Charli's mother's medical records and notations. Mrs. Fitzgerald had recently regained consciousness, though she was still heavily medicated. The doctor believed the worst of the withdrawal symptoms were over. However, she wasn't able to keep down any food or drink. Instead they had her on intravenous fluids and nutrients.

The doctor Deloris had consulted asked for Mrs. Fitzgerald's previous records. Why they hadn't been sent in their entirety to Magnolia Woods didn't make sense. It also didn't matter. Mrs. Fitzgerald's regular doctor was online. It was only a matter of minutes before Deloris had everything. Currently, our consulting physician was mulling through years of information.

Oren was determined that we would have everything in place that she needed by tomorrow. He even had a room in Rye converted to a makeshift hospital room, a full-time nurse hired, and a doctor on standby. He believed an actual hospital was too risky, and I had to agree.

It seemed that Fitzgerald had Charli on constant surveillance, but not her mother, not Adelaide. Other than the regular security at Magnolia Woods, there was nothing extra. No personal guards. No additional cameras. No doubt, Alton Fitzgerald didn't feel that his wife's future was a concern, perhaps other than to keep her as bait for Charli.

Demetri Enterprises had a reputable and well-established security company under our umbrella. It had been in operation for over fifteen years. With their help and Deloris's hacking skills, the cameras at Magnolia Woods could be easily manipulated. Put on a loop, a determined amount of time could pass without anyone knowing that Mrs. Fitzgerald had been taken.

Our biggest concern was transport. However, now that she was conscious, the plan was falling into place.

Charli's voice penetrated the din of muted chaos in Isaac's background. I didn't think Isaac was that close to her, yet I heard a simple sound and immediately knew it was her. My heart stopped. Not literally, but I wanted more. More than just her tone. I wanted words and moans. I wanted it all.

Just as I thought I might not make it another minute, Isaac spoke, "Sir, it's happening. A hostess just brought Patrick and an older woman to the table."

"His mother," I confirmed.

"Miss Collins seems very happy to see her cousin."

"Good." The word came out on a sigh. That was what we wanted, needed, for her to be genuinely surprised by Patrick's early arrival.

I imagined Charli jumping up and hugging him.

I didn't only hate Isaac, but suddenly, Patrick was on my list.

"Sir, I'm going to pay and leave. Patrick saw me and nodded. All plans seem to be progressing on schedule."

"I hope you're right. You're sure you don't see her security?"

"Not inside the restaurant."

"Thank you, Isaac. Since you drank coffee and not tea, I believe your man card is safe."

"Thank you, sir."

The line went dead.

Now all I could do was wait here in this Savannah hotel suite.

We hadn't flown to Savannah, as would have made sense. Instead we flew to Macon and drove two and a half hours to Savannah. Our hotel was reserved under a fictitious name and we were only using cash. While I doubted Charli's stepfather's ability to know everything that was happening in his town, I wasn't willing to jeopardize the future of our plan.

Even having Isaac at the restaurant was a risk, but we needed visual confirmation, both that Charli and Patrick had arrived and for Patrick, that Isaac was ready with the next step.

CHAPTER 28

---•◦•---

ALEXANDRIA

I RELEASED PATRICK'S neck as tears prickled my eyes. "I've missed you."

"Well, not anymore, little cousin, I'm here." He reached for my hand and eyed the garish diamond. Wiggling his eyebrows, he said, "Let the celebration begin!"

He was too jovial, even for Patrick. My eyes narrowed.

He reassuringly squeezed the hand in his grasp. "What's the matter? Forget how to have fun?"

"Probably."

"Never fear, I'll help you remember."

"Alexandria," Aunt Gwen said with a quick hug of my shoulders.

"Aunt Gwen, what a surprise."

"Well, yes, Patrick likes a little fanfare."

My cheeks rose. "Yes, he does."

The wait staff pulled up chairs, creating places for Aunt Gwen and Patrick to sit. Once I was seated again, I asked, "Pat, I thought you weren't coming until tonight?"

"Cy couldn't come here until then, but I decided if you could have a family reunion, so could I."

"And we're so glad he did," Aunt Gwen said, patting Pat's knee. "Dear, how is Adelaide? It's so difficult to get any information from my brother."

"She's better. They think she's through the worst part."

Patrick's composure changed. "Is she… was she… is it really…?"

I nodded, not wanting to say too much. It wasn't right.

Chelsea reached for my hand, but before she could give me a show of support, I pulled it away, tucking it daintily on my lap. By the way Suzanna's lips pursed, our minor display hadn't gone unnoticed. In the past few days since Chelsea had moved to Montague Manor, we'd managed to keep our renewed friendship covert, as well as to keep her and Bryce's together moments to public only, at least to our eyes. We'd also managed to monopolize my time with pictures, dresses, caterers, and the like. He was becoming increasingly impatient, with both of us, it seemed.

As silence fell over the table, Aunt Gwen asked, "So tell me about the wedding plans? This is rather fast, isn't it?"

I lifted my cup to my lips, hoping if I sipped my tea long enough, Suzanna would take over. It didn't take long and she was on a roll. "It's because Bryce and Alexandria are too excited to wait." She widened her eyes. "No other reason. I hope people don't assume…"

My stomach twisted, curdling the creamer in the tea I'd swallowed. That was just what I wanted—people thinking I was having a shotgun wedding because I was having Bryce's baby.

Before I could respond, Suzanna went on, reciting the plans both set and those yet to be determined—dresses, colors, decisions, and indecisions.

"Don't you think red would be beautiful for a Christmas Eve wedding?" Suzanna asked.

"Yes."

"Well, Alexandria seems to be partial to black, but I think it's morbid for a wedding."

Gwen looked my direction as I shrugged. "Black is formal…" she replied in my defense.

I tuned them out, wishing I could talk to Pat, wishing I could find out what he and Nox had discussed, and basically wishing I were anyplace but here.

Abruptly, Pat stood and reached across the table. "Alex, let's go. I don't think your mind is on this conversation."

My heart raced. What was he doing?

"Besides, I want to see Aunt Adelaide. Let's go see your mom."

I looked from side to side, my eyes meeting briefly with Suzanna's. Fuck her. I didn't need her permission. "Um, yes, I'd like that, but I don't have a car."

"We do," Aunt Gwen volunteered. "Go ahead, you two. I can take a cab home."

"Nonsense," Suzanna chimed in. "Alexandria has too much to do—"

"To visit her own mother for an hour or two?" Aunt Gwen asked indignantly.

"No... well, her father..."

"Should be there too, but I suspect he's at work." Gwen turned to us. "Give her my love."

Patrick took my hand as he spoke to the table. "Do not fear, I'll personally deliver the princess back to the house of... the manor as soon as we're done. No harm, no foul. We just need to stop by my hotel and then on to the hospital." He kissed my cheek. "Thanks, cousin, it wouldn't be a family reunion if I didn't get to see my aunt." He turned to his mother. "Are you sure you don't mind?"

"Of course not. I do mind that you're staying in a hotel. You have a home."

Pat's cheeks rose and his nose scrunched. "Thanks, Mom. Baby steps for Dad."

Still holding my hand, Patrick tugged me toward the front of the restaurant.

"Wait," I said, stalling our exit. "What about my security?"

"Little cousin, you've got me. I'm as badass as they get."

Part of me wanted to wait for Suzanna's permission, but who the hell was that part of me? Not someone I wanted to be. I smiled up at Pat. "Damn right. I sure wouldn't mess with you." I reached playfully for his bicep. "Check out those guns." I turned back to the table. "I'll be back to the manor as soon as we're done."

"Alexandria," Suzanna said, "I'm not sure your father or Bryce—"

"Have fun," Gwen interrupted. "Be sure to tell Adelaide I said hello and let her know we're praying for her." Aunt Gwen waved us off as she turned back to Suzanna. "Have you decided on a caterer? You know I just adore…"

A long black limousine pulled up to the curb the moment we stepped onto the sidewalk. Hurriedly, Patrick opened the door and rushed us inside.

Taking in the spacious interior, I leaned my head back against the seat and sighed. It was the most free I'd felt in over a week. "Thanks, Pat. Are you trying to lose my detail? This kind of feels like it did when we were kids."

"Not quite. We aren't going for ice cream or a movie."

"No, but for a few hours I'm not being watched."

With the car now moving, he looked out the back window. "I think we may have ditched them."

I shook my head. "Not for long. They're bloodhounds."

"Do you have a new phone?"

"Yes, I just got it yesterday. I don't think you're on my approved list of calls."

He shook his head. "Girl, why are you letting them do this? Is Aunt Adelaide that bad?"

Tears moistened my vision. "She is. She was."

"She wouldn't want you selling your soul."

"I'm not. I have a plan."

After a few turns right and left, the car came to a stop.

Pat winked. "I have a plan, too. Let's go up to my suite and then we'll visit Aunt Adelaide."

"You're right," I conceded. "It's not the same as ice cream, but I'll take it."

"Before we do, can I see your new phone?"

Furrowing my brow, I opened my purse. "You're reminding me of Alton."

"Oh! Girl, never say that again." He took the phone from my hand and laid it on the seat. "GPS. This is how they're able to find you."

"And you don't want them knowing I'm going to your room, because…"

He handed me a key card. "Suite 2003. I figure twenty minutes to Magnolia Woods and twenty back. I'll visit for an hour." He leaned forward and kissed my cheek. "Consider this an early wedding present."

I could hardly comprehend his words. "What are you saying?"

Was he saying what I thought he was saying?

"Go. He's waiting. And take that chandelier off your finger."

"I-I can't. They'll know... somehow, they'll know."

Pat shook his head. "You're wasting time. And darling, you don't want to make that gorgeous man wait."

As I dropped the diamond ring into my purse, I looked at the phone. "If they call... they will, Pat. I know it. Either Bryce or Alton will call."

He waved me out of the car and away. "I haven't met a man I couldn't handle."

Just before opening the door, I leaned over and hugged him. "I love you."

"Yeah, yeah. I hear that from all the beautiful women. Sorry, sweetie, I'm happily taken." He winked. "And so are you... go."

As I stepped from the car, I looked up and down the street. We weren't at the front door of the Riverfront Hotel. The limousine had stopped at a side door. Touching the card to the sensor, the door opened. My heart rate increased as I went down a few stairs. Anticipation and fear mingled through my bloodstream as I stood before a bank of elevators.

The whole experience was very covert. No front lobby or bellmen, by the time the elevator doors shut, I hadn't even passed another guest.

With each floor the elevator ascended, my destination became more real. Like a schoolgirl, my palms moistened and heartbeat quickened. I glanced toward the shiny doors wondering if I looked all right. When I'd dressed this morning, I never imagined it would be for a reunion. By the time the elevator stopped, my knees wobbled like jelly, stumbling my steps.

The signs indicating room numbers were there—these rooms to the right and those to the left.

I had the sensation of floating, not walking. It happened so suddenly I hadn't had time to process. Nothing about the historic hotel registered, only room numbers as I searched for 2003. As I turned the final corner to the executive suite, the sound of voices—men's voices—murmuring behind me came into range.

One sound and my elation turned to dread.

Oh God. The sign for 2003 was right before me, but if I stopped and they saw me, I could be leading them directly to Nox. I couldn't do that.

Taking a deep breath and accepting my fate, I passed my destination and continued to walk, slowing my steps, each one dragging until the men were directly behind me.

"Miss?"

"Yes?" I asked, turning their direction. They were both wearing matching navy jackets with golden emblems on the lapel.

"Can we help you?"

"No." The word came out breathy as I expelled the air I'd been holding. "Thank you. I'm on my way to my room."

"If you need anything, just call." And with that, they were gone, beyond me, moving quickly down the long hallway.

As soon as they passed the bend, I turned around and hurried back to 2003.

As the card neared the sensor, the green light appeared.

Having the knowledge that I would again be face to face with Nox hadn't prepared me for the reality. Seconds, hours, days, a week... it seemed like ages since we'd been together. One conversation was all we'd been able to manage, and now...

My breathing hitched as the door opened.

CHAPTER 29

———●○●———

CHARLI

ELECTRICITY SURGED THROUGH me as Nox's hand met mine, pulling me closer until nothing separated us but two layers of clothes I desperately wanted gone. I was engulfed in his embrace. His strong arms surrounded me as his spicy scent enveloped us like a cloud.

"Princess…"

The only word uttered rumbled to my core as our lips found their way back to where they belonged. Strong and possessive, his lips dominated, took, and gave. It was the way a kiss should be.

I didn't wait for his tongue to probe, as mine sought out his warmth.

Moans and whimpers filled the suite as large hands tugged my hair, pulling my head backward and exposing my sensitive flesh. My body willingly surrendered and became putty in his hands and pliable to his touch. His midday scruff teased while his lips taunted.

Buttons were but an obstacle as I pulled at his shirt, freeing each one until my fingers could roam his chest. Mine splayed as they sought the heat and definition that encased his thundering heart. The rhythm beat its mating call as his breathing labored. Soon, it wasn't only his shirt that was gone: my dress was up and over my head, leaving my bra and panties as my only defense.

His kisses and caresses stopped for only a moment as Nox held me at arm's length, devouring me with his gaze. Unashamedly, his blue stare started at my high heels and slowly moved upward. Each moment was fire, burning my skin, leaving goose bumps in its wake until even my scalp prickled.

"You're so fucking beautiful." He turned me completely around. Once my circle was complete, he demanded, "Tell me he hasn't hurt you."

I shook my head... "I'm here. I'm fine." ... all the time praying he wouldn't notice my arm. It hadn't really discolored, but with Nox, anything was possible. The man had a sixth sense.

Not wanting him to notice, I took a step closer and reached for his belt. "Please, make me forget everyone but you."

Nox stilled, suddenly becoming an ice statue. Coolness rolled off of him in waves. Too late, I realized how my plea had sounded. "No, Nox. Only the kiss. That was all. But take that away, please. Fill me with you. Give me the strength to go back."

"I don't fucking want you going back."

I reached for his hand and pulled him toward what I hoped was a bedroom.

The curtains within were closed, blocking out the Georgia afternoon sun. If I pretended, we could be anywhere: in any hotel, in any part of the world. We could be back in Del Mar, New York, or perhaps on the moon. I didn't care, as long as I was with the man worshipping me, loving me, professing his love and admiration. Covering his lips with mine, I swallowed his words. They were meant for me. I'd keep them deep inside me, allowing them to fortify me when life couldn't.

I refused to think beyond us... beyond our bubble.

The soft bed bowed to our weight as we fell together onto the comforter. There were things we needed to say and plans we needed to make, but none of that mattered as my body screamed for what only Nox could give.

My bra disappeared as he captured and caressed my breasts. I writhed at his skillful touch. My nipples beaded as he sucked one and then the other. His lips moved lower, forever kissing, nipping, and biting until he was over my stomach.

"Princess, I need to get you home to Lana's cooking. Are they not feeding you?"

I didn't answer as his touch dominated my thoughts. Food wasn't even on my radar. My focus was overtaken with the sensation of panties moving from my hips, to my knees, and then beyond.

When had I taken off my shoes? I couldn't remember.

My legs willingly opened as he kissed my inner thighs.

"I missed everything about you, princess. Your scent, your taste."

My nails gripped the comforter as Nox buried his head at my core. It had been so long. I wanted everything about this man, but what I desired most was what I'd yelled for in a California gas station. "Please, Nox. Please, fill me."

He moved upward. The woodsy scent of his cologne mixed with my essence on his lips created an intoxicating cloud as his blue eyes sparked and he hovered above me. "Say it."

Blood rushed to my cheeks as I obeyed. "I want your cock."

Without hesitation, he granted my wish. My back arched as my core conformed to his invasion. Whimpers echoed, bouncing against the walls and blending with moans as I welcomed the delicious stretch. In and out, Nox plunged. Over and over, we moved in sync, one pushing until the roles reversed. Together we soared upward until we were the only two at the top of the peak.

In the distance there was a storm building, and yet neither of us was willing to seek shelter. Nox Demetri was the only refuge I desired. Surrendering to his expertise, I enjoyed the view as he thrust deeper and deeper, taking me beyond the mountain, higher up into the rumbling clouds. His broad shoulders strained as the tendons in his neck came to life. Muscle and definition encased this powerful man and I couldn't get enough.

I held on tight—to the bed, to him. He was both the wind beneath my wings and the anchor for my life's journey. I couldn't let go. Surely if I did, I'd fly away.

"O-oh, Nox!"

Beginning at my toes, my body stiffened, tighter and tighter until words no longer formed. Lightning and thunder from a late-night Georgia squall would never exude power like that of the eruption building within me.

I lost my grip, surrendering to the strength. Sounds of satiation spilled from my lips as I gave in to the detonations clenching my core—once, twice, too numerous to count. They continued overtaking my body as they created a wave capable of complete destruction, a tsunami of orgasmic proportion.

My mind was adrift with only us.

As the seas began to calm, I floated above the water and below the clouds.

I could go up or down, fly or swim. It wasn't my decision. Faster and faster Nox thrust, bringing me higher, back to the stratosphere. My body and mind were no longer singular but willingly joined with his. One more surge, and then, all at once, the suite filled with a guttural growl, a roar that resonated from the depths of his soul. His broad shoulders relaxed and we both drifted back to earth.

My entire body fell slack as Nox collapsed upon my chest, his thundering heart against mine. Pants and hums of satisfaction combined with our labored breathing until our hearts found their normal rhythm.

With him over me, in me, and around me, I was safe and secure, encased in a Nox cocoon. It was exactly where I wanted to be. My lids fluttered as I imagined falling asleep in his arms.

Easing out of me, Nox hovered above, shifting his weight to his elbows, and stared down into my eyes. I couldn't look away; I didn't want to.

"Stay with me."

Just like that, the spell was broken.

I pushed against his chest. "Nox, don't."

He rolled to his side, his gorgeous body fully on display as he ran his hands through his hair. "Don't? Do you fucking know what I went through to get you here?"

I reached for the comforter and pulled. Covering myself, I retorted, "Do you have any idea of the risk I took coming here?"

He sat up. "Charli, listen to me. Stay. We have everything set up for your mom and Isaac can get Chelsea. Don't go back. Don't put yourself at risk."

"You don't know what you're asking. I did what you said. I talked to Chelsea." My chin dropped to my chest. "God, Nox, he's hurt her."

Nox stood, his body rigid as his hands clenched to fists and the muscles and tendons in his arms bulged with the interior pressure. "Fuck this. You're not going within one hundred feet of that bastard. He's hurt Melissa and now Chelsea. There's no way in hell I'm letting you go back. You're not going to be next."

I stood, pulling the comforter with me. "I am. I don't care what you say."

"What?"

"You heard me. I'm sick of having everyone else decide what's best for me. I love you, Lennox Demetri. If you love me, you'll trust me."

"Trust me."

"I have. I do, but I know there's more to this situation than meets the eye. I feel it. I've talked to Jane. My mom, she was on to something before she got sick. I don't trust that bastard. Alton hurt her—I know it. And I don't just mean the abuse she's endured. I mean this illness. It's wrong. I'm not walking away and letting him win."

Nox reached for my shoulders. "Then fight him—from New York. We should have a copy of the will soon. If not tonight, tomorrow."

My neck stiffened. "How?"

"Does it matter?"

"Yes. It's not electronic. How can you—"

"Oren."

"Oren? You told Oren?"

"Charli, there are a lot of things I need to tell you—some things I've just learned and other things I've known."

I looked down at my watch. "Now isn't the time. I need to get back." My neck straightened. "I *am* going back."

"Tomorrow night I'll be on that road. Find a way there."

"I will. After what Chelsea told me, I can't leave her. Somehow we'll both get there."

Nox took a deep breath. "Fuck. She told you?"

"She was emotional—"

"Charli, you have to know that having her end up with Edward Spencer wasn't the plan. It was supposed to be Severus Davis. It all happened so fast."

My stomach dropped as I clung to the comforter. "What did you just say? What do you mean it was *supposed to be*... Davis... that's a name related to that Senate bill... right? The man at my party. Why? How?"

"Your party? I don't know, but yes, he's a lobbyist. It was supposed to be controlled."

"Shit, Nox." My words slowed. "Supposed to be? Have her end up with? Please tell me you're not talking about Infidelity."

His eyes widened as his Adam's apple bobbed.

"Lennox Demetri, what do you mean *the plan*? Did you lure my friend into Infidelity when you hate the damn company? Did you know what was happening to her all those months I was worried sick?"

He turned away, rubbing his palms over his cheeks.

"Answer me!"

He spun back, his jaw set with navy blazing in his eyes. "Yes. It was a stupid decision on all of our parts. Yes, she's in Infidelity. Yes, she has an agreement with Spencer. Yes, Deloris is the one who told her about it. It wasn't supposed to happen this way."

The muscles of my throat squeezed, choking off my first response as my knees gave out. I sank to the edge of the bed. "Th-that's what she meant when she said I'd told her to trust her. The *her* was Deloris. Oh God... I was part of it. You made me part of it."

"No. It was Chelsea's decision. We've offered her an out. She wanted to stay for you..." He squared his shoulders. "...and for the money."

My head moved back and forth as I scanned the floor for my clothes. Heat filled my bloodstream and my temperature rose. I'd accused my best friend of wanting money. I'd meant the Carmichael money, not Infidelity's.

Shit!

"I need to get dressed. I need to be ready when Patrick comes to get me. I can't stay with you, not if she's there... not if my mom is still there... I can't leave if those bastards haven't all paid for what they've done."

Nox reached again for my shoulders. "Charli—"

"Don't! This isn't just about the last week. This is about more. You saw me suffering. Hell, you came back to New York to comfort me when I was devastated over Chelsea's message and you knew! You didn't just know... you were responsible."

"I didn't know then. I found out... but not that night."

I waved him off as I found my bra and panties and put them on. "I-I can't deal with this, not until both she and my mom are safe."

"We'll get her. I'll send Isaac right now and then your mom."

I shook my head. "No, Chelsea is staying at Montague Manor. Isaac can't get close."

Stepping into my dress, I pulled the arms up over my shoulders, smoothed the skirt, and walked to the mirror. My hair was a mess—a sexy mess but a mess nevertheless. Ignoring Nox's pleas, I combed my curls, using my fingers, and straightened it the best I could. Finding lipstick in my purse, I applied a coat.

The diamond mocked me from the bottom of the handbag. Snapping the purse shut, I turned. "Goodbye."

Nox was now wearing his trousers, but his belt was unbuckled and his chest was beautifully displayed. I imagined how nice it would be to fall back into his embrace, absorb his woodsy scent and hibernate in his arms, to just allow life to go on outside my safe enclosure. Instead I stood resolute. "I need to leave."

"Not like this," he said. "I don't want you going like this."

My watch said otherwise. Patrick was probably waiting. Just as I was about to protest, Nox's phone chimed. Struggling to remove his eyes from me, he walked to his phone and lifted it.

After reading the text, he said, "It's Patrick." Defeat showed in his eyes and rang in his tone.

I may not be a princess and Nox may not be Prince Charming, but the clock had struck midnight. My time had run out. Straightening my shoulders, I repeated, "I need to go."

In two strides he was back, his hands encircling my waist as he bent forward. His nose neared mine. "Princess, I could make you stay."

"Tie me to the bed? Sorry, Nox, I'm no longer in the mood."

His chest grew as he inhaled. "This doesn't change a thing. This is over tomorrow. Tell me you'll be on that road. Tell me that tomorrow night I'll fall asleep with you in my arms."

"I'll do what's best, Nox. That's all I can promise."

CHAPTER 30

———•○•———

OREN

"MR. DEMETRI?" DELORIS WITT said, her inflection sounding more like a question, as if she were somewhat surprised I'd be knocking on the door to her hotel suite.

It wasn't like we had offices here in Savannah. We were dealing with the hand we'd been dealt. When she didn't ask me in, I went ahead with my current concern. "Where is he?"

If anyone knew Lennox's location, it would be her. Over the years, I'd had my doubts as to how efficient this woman was with the tasks Lennox entrusted to her care. After all, I'd witnessed more than a few of her blunders. Then again, I'd witnessed her successes. No matter which, I didn't doubt her loyalty to Lennox. That alone made her an invaluable employee.

However, as she stood resolute in the doorway, it seemed that her devotion to my son did not extend to me. As a matter of fact, it was obvious she didn't trust me, evident by the unnecessary amount of time she spent double-checking any information I shared.

While that would make some men suspicious, it moved Deloris Witt up a notch in my book. She was correct: I wasn't the most trustworthy person. I'd been known to do whatever needed to be done, damn the cost.

That said, I had my limits—hard limits. Doing anything to screw over my

214

son or my own company were on top of that list. By the way her eyes narrowed, Deloris Witt didn't know that. The way I saw it, by not trusting me she was showing good instincts. That was a person to have in Lennox's corner.

"Mr. Demetri, Lennox is indisposed at this time."

"What the hell does indisposed mean? I need to see him."

I opened my hand to reveal a pen drive—thirty-two gigs of information that no doubt took a certain secretary from Hamilton and Porter more than a few hours to scan. Many of the documents were pictures while others were hastily scanned with a hand scanner. I didn't give a damn how I got the information, as long as I got it.

The bar was tucked away from the historic, touristy area of Savannah. I saw Natalie Banks as soon as I entered, seated at the bar, wearing a plain blue dress and looking a little bit haggard. Easing up onto the empty stool beside her, I put my hands on the bar and looked straight ahead. Behind the rows of bottles was a mirror. There were golden scrolled letters upon the framed glass, but I couldn't make out their message as many were faded beyond recognition. I wasn't looking at the letters; I was looking at Natalie. Through the old mirror I made out her expression.

I wouldn't say she was happy to see me.

"Did you get it?" I asked quietly, still looking toward the mirror.

She didn't turn my way. "Do you have any idea what Mr. Porter or Mr. Hamilton would do...?"

"My answer's the same as it was last night. I don't care. The consequences are inconsequential to me, other than what will happen if you don't produce the documents I want."

"I have some money. My parents left me a small life insurance policy..."

She stopped talking, looking down into her drink as the bartender approached.

"Drink?" he asked.

For the first time, I turned toward Natalie and sized up what was in her glass. Based on the small size, it was strong and on the rocks. "Do you have Corsair?"

"Triple Smoke."

"I'll take it neat and another drink for the lady. Give her a double of whatever she's drinking."

Natalie's shoulders slumped before she looked up from the glass and nodded. As soon as the bartender walked away, she continued, "The policy isn't a lot, especially to you, I'm sure, but I can pay more... like on credit?"

I reached for a handful of peanuts from the little wooden bowl. Popping one in my mouth, I laughed. "No, I'm doing you a favor. Being indebted to me isn't what you want."

"I could lose my job. Worse... if Mr. Fitz—"

"Shhh," I growled under my breath. "I don't want to hear his name or have anything to do with that man. This isn't about him."

In the reflection I watched her eyes close.

"It was wrong," she confessed. "I knew when I was doing it, but I had to. He said I did."

She'd given me a synopsis last night at her home. While it may have been under a bit of duress, I'd found that, in general, information was often more accurate that way. Surprise interrogations didn't give people time to manufacture a story. Believable lying took time and effort. Telling the truth was much easier. And when people were put in a heated situation, it was usually the ugly truth that boiled to the top.

"You worked to gaslight Mrs. Fitzgerald..." I almost choked on the name. "...made the woman believe she was crazy, falsified legal documents, transferred her rights to her husband, and you're concerned that talking to me will risk your job?"

She lifted the glass, brought it to her lips, and drank. She didn't stop until the last bits of ice clanked in the otherwise empty tumbler. The way she grimaced and her neck tightened told me that whatever she was drinking wasn't her usual drug of choice.

Briefly she turned my direction. I didn't look into her eyes—the emotion or lack of it wasn't my concern. I was the monster and she was the prey. Nothing else mattered.

"No, Mr. Demetri," she said. "I'm not concerned about my job; it's my soul I'm worried about."

My cheeks rose as she turned back to the mirror. Meeting her gaze, I replied, "Then consider this your good deed, your repentance for sins otherwise unatoned for. Tell me, who else knows what you and your boss did... well, other than the husband."

"No one. Well..."

The bartender stepped up, placing the drinks in front of us. I reached into my pocket and laid a hundred-dollar bill on the bar. He nodded and walked away.

"Well?" I prompted.

"There was this intern who worked with Mrs. Fitzgerald. He doesn't know what we

216

did, but he knows about the codicil."

"Is he still employed by your firm?"

She shook her head as she lifted the glass and spun her wrist. "No. Another reason to worry about my soul."

"Then it seems that redemption is due."

"Please, don't tell anyone where you got it."

"Where I got what?"

Part of me expected copies, maybe boxes of papers. Instead, she reached into her purse and removed a pen drive. Though technology was wonderful, I would have liked to be able to see proof of what she was delivering. "How do I know this contains what I want it to contain?"

"Because, Mr. Demetri, you know where I live, where I work, and as you mentioned last night, where my niece attends school. She's a baby."

"Yes, beautiful girl. Not really a baby. Eleven, correct?" Before she could answer, I added, "That's a woman in many cultures."

Natalie sat taller though her shoulders resumed their slump. "It's all there. I haven't slept since your visit. It took me most of the night and some stolen time today, but I promise it's all there, even the power of attorney."

I lifted my hand, drawing the bartender's attention, tipped my glass and drained the contents—rich smoke with a hint of cherry and beech. Not bad for an American single malt.

"Another, sir?"

"No, I believe I'm done." I tapped the C-note.

"Change?"

I shook my head. "Nice doing business with you."

"Yes, sir."

I stood, pushing in the barstool. "Until we meet again, Ms. Banks."

"I hope not," Natalie said, low enough for only me to hear.

Winking in the mirror, I added, "Take care of that pretty niece."

Still standing at the door, Mrs. Witt looked at her watch. "I expect him soon."

"May I come in?" It seemed like a foregone conclusion, but obviously only to me.

Deloris stepped back and opened the door wider. The front room of her suite was transformed into a work center with multiple laptops, a hot spot, and a video feed of Magnolia Woods playing on the television. I was drawn to the feed, longing for more than a glimpse of Adelaide.

"Nice," I surmised.

"Thank you."

I took a seat in the far corner, in a spot where I could watch both the door and the room. "Tell me the truth, Mrs. Witt: you don't like me much, do you?"

She didn't miss a beat. "No, sir, I don't."

Her honesty made me laugh. "Well then, you won't be too upset to learn the feeling was mutual."

"Was?" she asked.

I shrugged. "You don't trust me. I'm not trustworthy. You have good instincts. I've always been good at technology, but it's moving faster than I can keep up." I nodded toward her setup. "Your skills are impressive. I've been watching what you do. I even put in a few questionable employees in my security department."

I smiled at her microexpression and added, "No need to worry. They never had any real access, but I knew you were watching."

Deloris sat opposite me. "You were testing me?"

"If I were, you passed. Not only did you fire and replace them, you did it without fanfare. No calls, no proclamations. I was impressed."

"I-I should have known."

"No, that wouldn't have been much of a test."

I leaned forward. "Tell me your thoughts on the shooting."

"A test?"

"No! Rest assured of one thing: I'd never take a chance with my son's life."

She nodded. "I do believe that. I've spoken with Silvia for some more insight. The jury is out on her, but obviously she's been with the Demetris for a long time."

I nodded. "Family. There's no need to question."

"All family is above reproach?"

"Family is family."

Deloris nodded. "My gut says the shooting wasn't family—Costello or Bonetti. There was nothing to gain, no statement to make. My money is on Severus Davis." Her head began to shake back and forth. "But I can't prove it. Ballistics, trajectory—nothing is helpful. The police are equally as baffled."

"Yet they had enough to suspect the woman's husband?"

"Suspect, not accuse. That's because we planted it all, circumstantial evidence. None of it would hold up in court. It was enough to take the heat off Lennox and Alex."

"Have you completely ruled out family?" I clarified, "I'm not talking Demetri. There was another person."

Deloris took a deep breath. "I haven't. I can't prove that either. Though I haven't seen the same honor regarding taking a risk with someone's life." She tilted her head toward the TV, making the muscles in my neck stiffen.

"The break-in?" I asked, refusing to lose focus.

"Which one?"

"Palo Alto."

"I believe it was Edward Spencer. He was there. He went to the complex claiming to be Alex's fiancé and they let him in. His fingerprints became a non-issue. It was handled very poorly."

"Lennox's apartment?"

"Alton Fitzgerald, I'm sure of it. He paid Jerrod to place the letter. Though his person told Jerrod it was because Mrs. Fitzgerald couldn't reach her daughter; I believe Jerrod thought he was being helpful."

"A mistake I can assume won't be repeated?"

"No, sir, it won't. I also believe that Alton Fitzgerald was trying to scare Alex into coming here to Savannah. When that didn't work, he resorted to using his wife."

The hairs on my arms prickled. There were few people I loathed who still walked this earth. I was ready to make that one less. "Melissa Summers?" I asked.

"Is currently safe."

I nodded, happy she'd confirmed my suspicions. "Currently?"

"Currently."

"Does Lennox know?"

"He hasn't asked. He mentioned that he wanted the problem to go away, so she did."

My cheeks rose as I nodded in admiration. "And Mr. Spencer taking the heat?"

She shrugged. "An unintended bonus."

We both turned as the door opened and Lennox and Isaac entered.

"What the hell?" Lennox asked. "Did something happen?"

His hair was windblown or was it just disheveled? And his shirt was wrinkled. Not terrible. It didn't look like he'd slept in it, but for Lennox it was unusual. "What the hell happened to you? You look like something the cat dragged in."

He flopped into a chair and looked up at the television. "Nothing. Anything new?"

"No," Deloris answered. "I was able to splice some video from two days ago into this feed. It appears as though she was there with Patrick."

Lennox nodded.

"The security?"

"Patrick lost them. When they headed toward the hospital, I called and he left. He picked her up on the back street. By the time Fitzgerald's men picked up the trail, Patrick and Alex were on their way back to the manor."

Lennox took a deep breath and turned my way. "Dad, what do you want?"

I wanted to know what in the hell they were saying. I wanted to know that they weren't dumb enough to risk everything so Lennox could dip his dick. I wanted to believe that Adelaide was in more capable hands than that.

However, with age comes wisdom and patience. This wasn't the time for a confrontation. Swallowing my questions, I pulled the pen drive from my pocket. "I thought we might go through this together and find out what exactly we're up against. There's an interesting codicil."

"A codicil?" Deloris asked.

"You got it? The will?" Lennox asked.

"Yes, I did. There's a codicil and some questionable signatures on recent power-of-attorney documents. I'm sure there's a hell of a lot more, but I haven't had much of a chance to go through it."

Lennox nodded. "I shouldn't have doubted you. How did you get old man Montague's will?"

I shrugged. "Perseverance."

Deloris stood and put out her hand. "May I have the honor?"

My lips quirked to a grin. "Can I trust you?"

"Not with your life."

With a scoff, I handed her the pen drive.

"You have your own copy, don't you?" she asked.

"Of course. Won't you have one also in a matter of minutes?"

"I doubt it'll take me that long."

CHAPTER 31

ALEXANDRIA

I SLIPPED INTO the limousine, let out an exaggerated breath, and collapsed against the seat.

"I'm not going to lie," Patrick said as the car began to move, "I expected a bigger smile. Someone isn't doing his job. Maybe I should have gotten you a vibrator instead?"

I shook my head. "Thank you, Pat. I-I..." Though I did my best to stop them, tears bubbled to the surface.

Breathe in and out... breathe in and out...

The words repeated in my head.

Patrick moved seats, wrapping his arm around my shoulder and pulling me close. "Christ, Alex, what's happening?"

Pat's cologne filled my senses as I worked to inhale my outburst. Instead of swallowing my emotions, my too-fast breathing stirred them up, making them fester and boil until they came out in big hiccupping sobs.

It had all been too much too quickly...

Nox.

My momma.

Chelsea.

Nox.

Infidelity.

Nox.

Bryce.

The wedding.

Nox.

Suzanna.

"I'm... so... tired," I managed to say between gasps of air.

Patrick didn't speak. Instead, he hugged me tighter.

"I-I can't... keep this up." It was the cleansing confession I'd wanted to make to Nox, the embrace and support I'd wanted from him, but I hadn't talked to him, not really. Our time was monopolized by our reunion—our reunification. It wasn't that I was complaining. I wasn't... my body wasn't. Making love had been another release I'd wanted, but now I needed more. "I'm tired of fighting."

Pat loosened his embrace and pushed a button to open the window between us and the driver. When it opened, the eyes of another stranger peered back through the rearview mirror.

Was it bad to long for some familiarity? This stranger wasn't Pat's fault; the car and driver belonged to Aunt Gwen and Uncle Preston. More tears squeezed from my closing eyes as I longed for Isaac or Clayton.

"Sir?" the unnamed driver asked.

"Is there an ice cream shop around here? I can't remember."

"Yes, sir, on Broughton."

I stared at Pat and shook my head. "No, we need to get back. You don't know how they get."

"Leopold's!" Patrick exclaimed. "I haven't been there... well, in years." Enthusiasm twinkled in his light brown eyes. "Come on, cuz. That's better than the DQ we used to get when we escaped the manor."

"I-I can't."

Ignoring my protest, Patrick informed the driver to circle back to Leopold's, closed the screen, and pulled the phone I'd been granted just the day before from his pocket. Swiping the screen, he put the phone to his ear. "No, this is Patrick again."

I couldn't make out what Bryce was saying, yet without words his displeasure emanated from the phone to the car. The prospect of ice cream or any other food became even less appealing.

"Of course she's here," Pat said, "but before I hand her the phone, we both wanted you to know we'll be a little bit late… We're stopping for ice cream." Patrick rolled his eyes at whatever Bryce said. "Nope. Not a problem." His responses came separated by short breaks. "Sure, but she's upset about Aunt Adelaide, make it worse and I'll…" Pat smiled "No, a promise."

His self-assured merriment was contagious, making my cheeks rise as I took the phone.

"Alexandria?" With one word, my glimmer of cheerfulness was gone.

"Bryce."

"Ice cream? Mother says there's a list of things to get ready for the party."

I sighed. "That's what the staff is for. She simply needs to tell Jane and it will be taken care of. Pat is determined to cheer me up."

"Cheer you up? What happened? How's your mom? Is she talking more today?"

Shit! I hadn't even asked Pat.

"Is she talking?"

Pat shook his head, his smile fading.

"Yes," Bryce confirmed. "You were there, weren't you?"

"Of course I was there. No, she's not talking, but she's calm." I said the last part hoping I was right. Pat nodded to confirm.

"This is all very stressful."

"You think?" I asked impudently.

"You don't need to be out all day. Come—"

I sat taller, my eyes on Pat. "You're welcome to your opinion, Bryce, but I'm not asking and neither was Patrick." The words gave my self-esteem a much-needed boost while at the same time planting a seed of dread. The shifts in his demeanor were difficult to predict. Nevertheless, I persevered. "We'll be back after ice cream. Instead of being upset, be happy that I'm keeping you informed."

"Really? Do you think I don't know where you are and where you've been?"

My stomach dropped.

"I'm sure you're getting up-to-the-minute reports."

"Since you don't need my permission, let me give you my advice: get back to the manor before your father."

My jaw clenched. "I'll take that into consideration. Goodbye." Before he could respond, I hit the red button and shoved the phone back in my purse. Laying my head back on the seat, I let out a long sigh as I closed my eyes.

Barely an hour earlier I was coming undone with the man I love, and now I was back in the madhouse that was now my life.

"I knew I was right," Patrick said, shaking his head.

"About what?"

"Everything. You need a break, more than my gift, though I do wonder why you didn't have a smile ear to ear when we picked you up."

Ignoring the subject of Nox, I asked, "How was my mom?"

His shoulder rose and fell. "I don't have anything to compare it to. The nurse said she's better. They couldn't give me much information, but they said she was better."

"I should have gone. Now I won't see her until tomorrow."

He reached for my hand. "Sweetie, you couldn't do anything for her. Despite the fact that you still look forlorn, you needed that break." His eyes widened. "You haven't lost him, you can't. Girl, that man loves you."

I shook my head. "I hope I don't. I love him too… I'm not marrying Bryce." Saying the words reminded me of the ring. I'd slip it on later.

"The road, tomorrow night?" Patrick asked.

"You know about that?"

"Yes, it was my idea."

"It's at least fifteen minutes. I don't know…"

Pat winked. "Girl, Cy and I are ready to take the heat. We'll be the life of the party. Your engagement may be a big deal, but a Fitzgerald officially coming out with all of Savannah watching." He waved me off. "Honey, I'm sorry, but you're going to be halfway down the society page. My man and I will have top billing."

"You want that?"

"Why the hell not? I don't care how our relationship started. Cy and I are real. Mom has accepted it, and Dad can speak civilly to Cy. It's a start. What better place to make all the rumors true than Montague Manor?"

He said *Montague Manor* as if it was a famous Broadway playhouse and they'd be center stage. I leaned closer and gave him a hug. "I love you."

"Yeah, I know," he said with a kiss to my forehead.

"You really do smell divine. I need the name of your cologne."

"And have that man of yours wear it? No way. He's got the tall, dark genetic thing happening. Let me have something."

As the car pulled along the curb, a glimmer of hope sprang to life, lighting a spark to my otherwise dark outlook. I used to love this shop. Leopold's had been in Savannah as long as I could remember and decades before.

Coming here had been my treat when I was young. Jane would bring me, letting me choose my favorite flavor. If it wasn't too hot outside, she even let me get a cone. The memories warmed my heart.

I took in the historic shop. Just like everything else in Savannah, it was exactly the same, from the red scrolled *Leopold's Ice Cream* sign to the old brick facade and large glass windows. As the driver opened the door, I caught a glimpse of the line of patrons, waiting their turn for the premium ice cream.

I stilled. "Seriously, Pat, I don't have time for this."

He nudged me with his shoulder. "I helped satisfy one need. Now let's take care of putting some more meat on your bones."

As we found our place in line, I whispered, "Nox said something about that."

"What?"

"He said I needed to get back to his cook's dinners."

Pat scanned me up and down. "Honey, you're beautiful, but they're killing you slowly. Not even slowly. You've been with them, what, a week?"

I nodded. "It seems like forever."

Step by step we moved forward. It took a few minutes before we were under the awning and out of the direct sun. As if finding solitude in the shade, Pat leaned close. "Talk to me."

"About what?"

My most innocent Southern-belle voice did nothing to stop Patrick's brow from furrowing. "How about we start with the meltdown in the car?"

"I'd rather talk about flavors."

"Oh, girl, you've always been vanilla."

I used to be. I tilted my head to the side. "Not anymore."

"There," he said, "look at that beautiful smile. Whatever dirty thoughts are going through your head, keep them on repeat. I like seeing you smile."

With the scent of sugar filling my senses, we inched forward, reminding my stomach that I enjoyed the simpler things in life, like ice cream and talking to a friend. "I'm sorry for the meltdown. It's not like me, but I'm not me. It doesn't make sense, but being with Nox…" I closed my lips and scanned the restaurant. Speaking softer, I went on, "…being with him for even a short time reminded me of who I am when I'm with him, and I miss her. I hate the person I am here.

"I'm on edge. I can't trust anyone."

"Hey?"

"Okay, only Jane…" I winked. "…and you. And what's the deal with Aunt Gwen? Does she know your plan… did she know?"

Pat shook his head. "Apparently my mother's not a fan of your future mother-in-law. It goes way back. Mom didn't spill the dirt, but I have my suspicions. When I told her I wanted to get you away from the wicked witch for a little while, she asked how she could help."

"Hmm. I wonder what happened?" I scrunched my nose. "I get the feeling Suzanna's after Alton. It seems like she's stepped in as his best friend and confidant. It pisses me off. She's supposed to be my momma's best friend, but since I've been back, she hasn't been to the hospital once."

"Has Uncle Alton?"

"Twice. Once when we met with the doctor. The other time he just showed up. I'm not sure if it was for her or just verifying that I was where I was supposed to be. He should have known. Normally I lead a damn parade." I looked around as we stepped to the counter. "I feel kind of vulnerable without the usual shadows."

"We lost them. Once they'd figured out where you'd gone—to Magnolia Woods—Mrs. Witt called and we left."

At the sound of Deloris's name, I turned toward Pat in disbelief.

"Can I take your order?" asked the girl at the counter, interrupting our conversation.

Scanning the cases, I whispered to Pat, "I should probably get yogurt."

"Because?"

I opened my eyes wide. "I have a wedding dress to fit into."

He shook his head. "Live dangerously."

"Believe me, I am." I turned to the young lady. "I can't decide between chocolate raspberry swirl and coffee chocolate chip. Which do you recommend?"

Before she could respond, Patrick said, "Give her a scoop of each and put some hot fudge on top. I'll take two scoops of Rum Bisque with caramel sauce on mine." He looked at me and grinned. "Oh, and add whipped cream and two bottles of water."

A few minutes later we were seated near the back of the shop amongst the picture-lined walls.

"Deloris helped with this afternoon?" I asked.

"Helped? She provided your alibi."

"My alibi?" I nearly hummed at the divine sweetness melting on my tongue.

"Wrong word," he corrected. "Because you don't need one. Somehow she hacked the cameras at Magnolia and spliced in images of you from before. We were never in a frame at the same time, but somehow it looks like you were there."

I sighed, leaning back. "I was worried about that. But don't you think this is a bit ridiculous?"

He tilted his head. "Have you really chosen a wedding dress? You can't do that without your man of honor."

"I told Suzanna I wanted you, but she nixed it."

"Wait a minute? Whose wedding is this anyway?"

"Since I don't want it to be mine, it feels like hers."

"I know Mr. Good-looking's plan to free the princess. Tell me yours."

"My plan is to get my mother better. If that means I have to play along until Christmas Eve, then so be it."

"I don't want you with that jerk—within his grasp for that long. I say you find another plan. Listen to your Prince Charming. Get out now."

"He told me once that he was no Prince Charming." I shrugged. "He's offered to steal Momma. To take her to someplace else for treatment."

"Well, I don't know the official definition of a Prince Charming, but I'd suspect he comes pretty close. That man is a keeper."

I pursed my lips as I dug my spoon into the frozen goodness and freed a piece of chocolate.

"Tell me what that was..." He waved his spoon toward me. "...that face."

"I didn't make a face."

"You most certainly did. What did he do?" He leaned closer and widened his eyes. "Is it kinky?"

"No." My indignation rose. "It was deceitful. And I shouldn't tell... but fuck it." I kept my words hushed, but they came out with more vigor. "Infidelity is the worst-kept secret."

"Don't tell me he wants out of your agreement. He knows you don't really want—"

"No, nothing like that. He... well, Deloris... Chelsea..."

Patrick shook his head. "The way that girl just sat there by you, after she's been all over your fiancé... tsk-tsk."

"It isn't how it looks. We've made up. I was mad, but now I know what happened. And after this afternoon, I know who's responsible."

"For her messing around behind your back for years? And you were so worried about her."

"No. It's an act. She's Bryce's cover for the whole Melissa thing. He'll probably be cleared of her disappearance because of Chelsea."

"And you're okay with that?"

I shrugged. "There are too many pieces to this puzzle to get upset about one or two. I don't know that he is responsible. I also can't say he isn't."

"But the fact he's using your friend as his cover? You're okay with that?"

I didn't answer as I plopped the chocolate chunk between my lips.

"Just like your momma," Pat said.

"What do you mean?"

He lowered his voice. "You know my mother would never say, but I think the reason she doesn't like Miss Suzanna is because of what you said… Uncle Alton. Mom hinted that it's been mighty convenient for him, and either your mom's been blind, clueless, or she doesn't give a shit. Either way, my mom thinks Miss Suzanna is a whore." He shrugged. "It'll be history repeating itself. Just like Uncle Alton, Spence will have a wife and her best friend—his own whore."

I laid the spoon down on the table and covered my stomach. "Jeez, Pat, I think I'm going to be sick. Besides, I'm not sure that could be true.

"I shouldn't say, but I learned that someone who works closely with Alton is also employed by Infidelity. I doubt he's that virile." I shook my head, freeing another piece of chocolate. "It's as if the employees are everywhere and I've never noticed."

"I think they are. I don't think it's as unusual as I'd first thought. But it doesn't matter. You're not going through with this. You're meeting Mr. Good-looking Saturday night and blowing this popsicle stand."

"It's an ice-cream shop and I'm afraid it won't be that easy. I'm not leaving without both Momma and Chelsea."

"I get your mom, but why do you even—"

"Because they set her up. She's not Bryce's cover because she wants to be. She's his cover because he bought her agreement."

It took a second, maybe two, but Patrick's spoon clanked to the table and his eyes grew two sizes. "Are you shitting me?"

I shook my head. "I told you, they're everywhere. And the bad part is that Deloris talked her into it. Chelsea's never had money. I'm sure the interview payment alone was more money than she's ever had at one time. Now she's been here for a few months." The whole thing made me sick.

"Why would Deloris send her here? Was it to spy on your family?"

"Nox said Chelsea wasn't supposed to go to Bryce, but to someone else and somehow the plan was messed up. And now she needs out."

Patrick sighed. "There's no out, not for a year."

"Yes there is… one."

Once again his brown eyes narrowed. "If you're fucking serious, I'm taking you back to the hotel. You're done with that scumbag."

"I'm serious, but I can't help Chelsea from the hotel. I can at Montague."

"I'm here for you. You say the word and I'll give him some of his own."

I smiled, taking in Patrick's physique. "I think you could."

"Oh, little cousin, I could, and more importantly, I would."

CHAPTER 32

—●○●—

ALEXANDRIA

LEAVING PATRICK IN the limousine was like walking in the final steps of a condemned man. It was *that* scene, the one in all the movies: the long corridor, flanked by shadows and impending doom. As I entered Montague Manor, the entire setting was there, all the way to the eerie lighting and hushed background voices. As they came into range, the voices sparked both recognition and curiosity.

Though the foyer was empty, the voices alerted me that I'd exceeded Bryce's deadline.

A booming laugh followed by deep male retorts confirmed that my stepfather was home.

Curiosity was a strange thing. My brain told me to go up to my room, shower, and prepare for dinner. However, my feet followed the sounds and voices as if taking me to answers I may not otherwise find.

The door to Alton's office was closed; nevertheless, I stilled near its threshold. The room beyond was quiet. The voices were coming from farther within the manor. I followed the corridor as it opened to a bright sitting room near the back of the house. It was the same room where Alton and Momma had taken my trust fund. The pristine windows glowed with the orange of the remaining early evening sunlight. The storm last night had cleared the air, literally. The sky was sapphire blue, cleared of moisture, except for the pink and purple of the impending sunset swirling near the horizon.

"That's the best news I've heard in months."

Alton's voice coming from the den refocused my mission. The doors were ajar. Was it an invitation or a trap?

"Mr. Fitzgerald, I wouldn't have missed this. Thank you for including me."

I turned the corner, needing to see the face of the man speaking. Like old recordings or songs, I tried to fit the voice with a name. I'd heard it before. I just couldn't place it. I stepped through the open doorway.

"Alexandria," Alton said, his gray eyes narrowing my direction. "I trust your excursion was worth it?"

A lump formed in my throat as I considered his dual meaning. At the same time, the gentleman turned, a tumbler of amber liquid in his grasp.

"Miss Collins?"

The temperature of the room rose. "Senator Carroll?"

"Doyle, you know my daughter?"

I extended my hand as the senator came near. He wasn't the only guest in the room. While we shook, I took in the strange gathering including Bryce, who was walking toward me.

"It's a pleasure to see you again," Senator Carroll said.

"Darling," Bryce said, placing his hand in the small of my back, "you didn't tell me you knew the senator."

I turned his way. "I guess it never came up."

Bryce extended his other hand, the one holding his crystal tumbler and made formal introductions. "Gentlemen, my fiancée, Alexandria Collins."

"Collins. Yes," Senator Carroll said. "That's what threw me off. Of course."

As my heart pounded with the likelihood that whatever was happening was not legal and could possibly affect Lennox and Demetri Enterprises, I tried to remain calm, exuding the perfect exterior.

"You remember Senator Grant Higgins," Bryce prompted, "from your welcome-home party and Severus Davis."

Graduation party.

Nodding, I forced a smile as each man came forward and shook my hand.

"Congratulations, Miss Collins," Mr. Davis said.

"On?"

"Why, your wedding of course."

The room broke into a rumble of laughter as the pressure from Bryce's hand increased on my back.

Playing off my mistake, I smiled. "Yes, how silly of me. I suppose I'm just overwhelmed with all the planning." I turned to Bryce. "Did your mother tell you we decided on the dress style for the bridesmaids?"

Though his eyes narrowed, his voice rang joyfully. "No, she didn't. That's wonderful. I'd love to hear all about your day."

"Nonsense, you're busy and I was about to clean up for dinner."

He leaned closer inhaling, his nose near my neck. Leaning back, he eyed me up and down. "That seems like a good idea."

What the hell was he doing? The lump from earlier was back. Pushing it down, I turned back to the room. "Well, gentlemen, it is a pleasure. I hope to see you again."

Senator Carroll spoke first. "Tomorrow night. We're happy to share in your celebration."

Though Bryce moved toward the door, I stopped, asking, "We? Is Mrs. Carroll with you?"

His cheeks rose as he exchanged looks with Mr. Davis. "Um, she isn't, but when Shirley learns this is your party…" He gestured about. "…and home, I'm sure I can convince her to jump on a plane and join me. She isn't usually much for traveling, but I'd expect that for you, she'd make an exception."

"It will be nice to see her again if she can make it. Please tell her I said hello."

"I will."

"Gentlemen," Bryce said, nodding and leading me toward the door and out into the hallway.

Severus Davis's voice bellowed as we walked away. "Well, I hope that doesn't mean I need to call Marisa." His comment was met with another round of hearty laughs.

As we approached the front stairs and I tried to wrap my mind around that grouping, Bryce stopped.

"What were you all discussing?" I asked.

"Where the hell have you been?"

His sudden change in mood made me take a step back. "At Leopold's with Patrick. We called."

"You left my mother over three hours ago. Your security detail had a hell of a time. Do you know how upset Alton was when they informed him that you were alone?"

"I wasn't alone. I was with Patrick."

"And that's supposed to make me feel better?" Narrowing his gaze, he scanned me again from head to toe.

"What is your problem?"

"It's... I don't know... something's different."

I shook my head. "You're delusional. You spend too much time with Alton."

"Where's your ring?"

Shit!

I fumbled for my purse, opening it and fishing the diamond from the depths. Pushing it on my finger, I smiled. "There. I'm not used to wearing it. It's so heavy."

Bryce narrowed his gaze and nodded. "Get used to it."

"I'm trying."

When I stepped onto the first step, so did Bryce. "Where are you going?"

"To your room."

"Why?"

"I haven't seen my fiancée alone in days."

Gathering my wits, I said, "And you have a room with two senators, my stepfather, and a lobbyist. Don't you think that I can wait? Besides, I need to clean up for dinner. Apparently, I'm *different*."

"Does Patrick wear cologne?"

I shook my head. "Yes, and it's divine. I don't know the brand, but I can ask." I had, but that didn't seem important.

"No, it's just..." Bryce shook his head. "I told you to be here before Alton."

"You didn't tell me what time that would be." I splayed my hand over his chest and faked a grin. "This is earlier than normal. Now, go. I'm confident that you shouldn't miss whatever they're discussing."

He leaned closer, his lips near mine, his Cognac breath teasing my nose. "Weed, that's what they're discussing. It's rather comical. I doubt any of them have ever tried it." He brushed my cheek. "Do you remember that one time at Duke?"

Weed? Pot? Marijuana?

I shrugged. "I remember. It made me sick."

I fought the urge to flinch as he brushed his lips over mine. Cold and tight. The connection was nothing like the electricity with Nox. Unconsciously, I sighed at the thought of the man I loved.

Bryce pulled me closer, misreading my body's clues. "Go on. Clean up. You've had a long day." He kissed me again. "And for God's sake, put on some perfume. You smell like... your cousin."

"I do?"

He kissed me again, this time probing my lips.

I closed my eyes as his wet tongue parted my lips. When he pulled away, he added, "But you taste like good whiskey and ice cream."

"I think it's you who tastes like whiskey."

Hurriedly I moved up the stairs, each step praying I wasn't being followed. By the time I reached the top, my heart was thumping in my chest.

"What the hell?" I muttered, unsure how to decipher the clues Bryce was giving. Did he have any idea where I'd really been? I should have cleaned myself at the hotel, but I'd been too upset to think about that.

A million thoughts fought for top billing as I made my way to my room.

Locking the door behind me, I relished the solitude. When had it happened? When had this room become a sanctuary? When had the rest of the house become so bad that my room became the least evil?

I sat on the edge of my bed and lay back. It wasn't the underside of the canopy that filled my vision, but memories of the afternoon before the spell was broken, when the world was right and safe. I wanted that with all my heart. I also wanted to tell Nox or even Deloris that Senator Carroll was in my house with Senator Higgins and Severus Davis.

Suddenly I sat up. Davis was old, not as old as Alton, but much older than Bryce. That was the person Chelsea was supposed to have been paired with. Did she know that? Did she know he was here? Had she agreed, knowing his age and that he was married?

Why?

Suddenly, getting ready for dinner lost its importance.

I rushed down the corridor and knocked on Chelsea's door. Slowly it opened.

"Where did you and Patrick go?" she asked.

"To visit my mom and then we went for ice cream."

She eyed me up and down.

What the hell? Was I wearing a sign?

"Hmm," she said, opening the door wider. "Do you want to come in?"

"I do. What's the matter? Did Suzanna get her panties in a wad?"

Chelsea shrugged. "No more than usual. I came up here as soon as I could, hoping to miss the drama."

I reached for her hand and tugged her toward two chairs near the window. As we sat, I noticed her view. It was neither of the front of the house nor the back. From this bedroom's window was a view of fields. As I looked more down than out—closer to the house—the tennis courts and small building were visible.

Reaching for my necklace, I took a deep breath. If I could slip out there, I could tell Nox what was happening.

I turned my focus back on Chelsea. "Tell me why you're here. How did you of all people become Bryce's alibi?"

"I can't. I don't know."

"That doesn't make sense. I mean, if what you've said is true, then you never met him until the night at the hospital. Tell me how you got from maybe having a job in D.C. to being with him."

Saying D.C. hit a cord. That would have been where she'd be if she'd been assigned to Severus Davis. Did he know that he could have had Chelsea? How did it all work?

Dressed in a pair of yoga pants and a tank top, not the attire for dinner, she pulled her knees to her chest and perched her bare feet on the edge of the plush chair. "Alex, I wish I could tell you. I'm dying to talk to someone about it, but I can't. All I can say is that we've told the Evanston police the same story. Bryce was with me when Melissa disappeared."

I shook my head. "But was he?"

"He was there in California before he told you he was. He has travel records proving he was there off and on during the full four years."

My stomach twisted. "You lied to the police?"

"I didn't have a choice. They were relentless. They even did tests on his cars and things. They came to Carmichael Hall... it was... scary."

"But... your testimony?"

She shrugged. "I don't think it's really testimony. It wasn't court. I pray it doesn't get that far. It was a deposition."

"God, you still falsified information. That's perjury."

"I didn't have a choice..." Chelsea's defense faded away.

I took a deep breath. "Because of the agreement."

Her eyes widened. "What did you say?"

"I know about Infidelity. I didn't know that was what you did, but I know about the company."

Chelsea jumped from the chair and stood, facing the window.

I waited, but instead of words, her shoulders quaked and head fell forward.

Standing, I slowly made my way to her. She wasn't far away, only a step, maybe two, but for a moment the distance seemed insurmountable. When I laid my hand on her shoulder, she spun toward me.

"I don't know how you know," she said between sniffles, "but since you do, now you know I *am* a whore."

I recalled Karen Flores's words, the ones I'd repeated to Nox. "It's companionship, not sex."

"How?"

"It's a long story, but let me just say... I understand the allure, the promise of the compensation for what seems like not much sacrifice. But it is. You and your body are more valuable than that agreement. I'm more valuable than that agreement."

She shook her head. "Look around. You can't possibly know what it's like. I've hated every day and yet in two months with the deal I made, Infidelity, and the HR job at Montague, I've earned enough to pay my sister's tuition for two years at a state school." She sighed. "It feels good to say Infidelity aloud."

"Babe, you're not a whore any more than I am."

"No, you're wrong. Bryce is all too willing to remind me daily of my title."

"Fuck him!"

"I'd rather not," she said with a grimace. "Besides, why would you even say that you're a whore? You didn't sign your life away."

"No, I didn't, just my companionship."

Her steps stuttered backward as her hands went to her lips. "Nox?"

"Yes, but it's complicated."

"Oh my God." The wheels of recognition turned in her head. "The trust fund. That's why. How? Did Deloris tell you about it too?"

"Not exactly. Deloris found my profile and she stopped it. Nox—well, his company—is an investor."

"He's not your client?"

"Not technically. Tell me what Deloris asked you to do."

Chelsea made her way back to the chair. "It wasn't supposed to be like this. It was supposed to be some guy. I saw his picture, kind of distinguished. He's married. I figured I'd only see him when he wasn't with his wife. The rest of the time I could have a life and at the same time earn this income. I'm not a prude, but that wasn't what happened."

"I know. I'm sorry. Do you remember that guy's name?"

"Yeah, it was like the teacher in *Harry Potter*, Severus."

"Did you ever meet him? Does Bryce know that was who you were supposed to be paired with?"

Her head moved back and forth. "No... and no. Bryce told me how he found me. He thought it was pretty funny." Her face contorted in disgust. "He was very proud of himself."

I sank back to the chair. "You don't have to tell me—"

She sat taller. "He put in specifics: hair length, body type, age. He described you."

"I'm so sorry."

"That's why you were right when you said I looked and dressed like you. He made me, even making me dye my hair."

"God, Chels, I don't know what to say."

"It's not your fault. I did it."

"But I told you to trust Deloris. I had no idea… Oh, but before I forget, the guy you were supposed to be with? He's downstairs."

"He's what?"

I reached for her hand. "Not for you. It's some political thing, two senators and Severus Davis. He's a lobbyist."

"But Deloris wanted me to spy on him. That was the plan. There must be some connection between him and Nox?"

"I don't really know. Maybe since we're both here, we can keep our ears open. But know this: I'm getting you out of here. You don't deserve—"

My words trailed away, stilled by pounding from the hallway. Bryce's angry voice echoed down the corridor and penetrated the door.

My gaze met Chelsea's.

"He's yelling for you," she said.

"Maybe if we stay quiet." I walked to the door, hoping to see if he had gone.

Just as I reached for the doorknob, Chelsea's door swung open wide with little regard for the other side. Quickly, I jumped back, barely avoiding a collision.

Bryce's expression —the one I likened to Alton—was back, complete with the red neck and ears.

"What?" I asked, wishing we'd locked her door. "What are you doing up here?" I looked to Chelsea and back. "Bryce, you should leave. We need to get ready for dinner."

He shoved the screen of his phone toward me. The picture was black and white and of poor quality.

"What? That's me." It was me, by my mother's bed, her hand in mine.

"Today?" he asked.

Shit! The floor suddenly fell out from under me—more accurately, from under my alibi. The dress was different.

CHAPTER 33

—●○●—

NOX

DELORIS INSERTED THE pen drive into her computer and pulled the documents up on her screen.

"I'll send it to your iPad," she said as her fingers flew over the keys.

"And mine?" my father asked.

Deloris looked over her shoulder. "Do you really need it twice?"

Oren shrugged. "Just curious if you have my private email address."

She laughed as my iPad dinged with the incoming email.

"I'll take that as a yes," he said, leaning back and bringing his tablet to life. "This is a long last will and testament," he continued. "I mean, I've seen some crazy shit, but old man Montague took control to a whole new level, all the way down to dictating his granddaughter's future. You can look at the entire document, but I suggest we all concentrate on Article XII for right now."

I looked over at Isaac. He was present, but silent. Instead of scanning the document, he was watching Charli's necklace app.

"Any change?" I asked.

"No, sir. She's back at the manor." He shrugged. "Sometimes I wonder if this heart-rate indicator works."

"Of course it does," Deloris said. "Why?"

"Like now, if it's working, her pulse is ridiculously high. One hundred and thirty. That's double what it is when she's sleeping."

My skin prickled. "If she just would have stayed."

Oren turned my way. "A week ago?"

"No, today. I had her for a short time."

"And you let her go?"

"She won't leave her mother or Chelsea."

"Fuck!" Oren stood. "You don't think they've figured out that you two were together, do you?"

"No. We took care of everything."

Oren turned on me. "We're so fucking close. Don't blow it because you're…"

"Because I'm what? I'm worried sick. I needed to see her, to touch her. I'm beyond frightened with every new thing we learn about Spencer. I knew he was a slime in business, but now… I'm not going to blow this. I'll storm that damn party if she doesn't get to that road."

"Gentlemen," Deloris interjected, "we have a document."

I took a deep breath and turned away from my father's icy stare.

Oren had to have the last word. "This isn't just about Alexandria. She's the strongest one of the lot. She can make it one more day."

His words made my skin bristle. I sat back down and picked up my tablet, praying he was right.

But if he was, then why the hell was her pulse elevated?

Focusing on the screen, I scrolled the pages, slowing for the subtitles until I reached: **Article XII Provisions for Montague Holdings.**

The room fell silent as we all read:

If at the time of my passing these provisions have not been satisfied, it is the responsibility of my heirs, Adelaide Montague Fitzgerald and Alexandria Charles Montague Collins, to willingly and legally satisfy the following criteria upon the appropriate dates. Failure to do so will result in the loss of all inheritance including but not limited to assets, property, company shares, personal properties, and the residence and remainder of my Estate.

As is now the case, it is essential that Adelaide Montague remain married to Alton

Fitzgerald for the remainder of their earthly lives. As Adelaide's husband, Alton Fitzgerald will have all rights set forth as the primary stockholder in Montague Corporation. If either party files for divorce or attempts to end the marriage, all Montague holdings revert to Alexandria Collins.

I stopped there. "Why on earth hasn't Alex's mother done that?"

"Divorce?" Oren asked.

"Yes, she would be free and the holdings would be outside of Fitzgerald's control."

Oren pressed his lips together. "I blame myself for not getting my hands on this document ten years ago."

Deloris turned toward my father. Her expression wanted more. I hadn't told her the history between my dad and Charli's mom, only that he wanted to help. Though she looked curious, I knew she wouldn't ask. Finally, she turned back to her screen and we all continued to read.

Upon the death of either A. Fitzgerald or A.M. Fitzgerald prior to the coming of age of A. Collins, all Montague holdings will be held in trust for her until the age of twenty-five or until she has completed a college degree, whichever comes first.

Once the age or degree completion has occurred, in order for A. Collins to inherit the Montague holdings and assets and to fulfill the requirements set forth in this legal document she must adhere to the following:

Being of the legal age of twenty-five (or having completed her college degree), Alexandria Collins must agree to a legal union with a husband who too will represent her and their biological children's shares in Montague Corporation as well as in the running of private Montague assets.

"I volunteer," I mumbled. It wasn't a proposal, but that didn't make it any less valid. Charli and I had never talked about marriage, but I'd do it, not because of this damn will or anything related to her family's money. I'd take her naked and penniless. The first part of those conditions brought images to my mind that were better left subdued.

I turned back to the tablet.

It is my desire, and thus forth the determination of this Will, that A. Collins will marry Edward Bryce Carmichael Spencer, the son of Suzanna Carmichael Spencer, as outlined below.

"How the fuck is this legal?"

"I'm not sure it is," Deloris said.

E. Spencer must first complete undergraduate and graduate school and prove himself worthy of Montague Corporation. Upon completion of his postgraduate degree, no more than eighteen months may transpire before their union.

"Prove himself worthy?" Oren asked aloud. "Does that include accusations of abuse and suspicion of foul play in a woman's disappearance?"

Though no one answered and we continued to read, for the first time, I was more curious about Melissa Summers's disappearance. Fuck Infidelity. If the entire company were to become public with the investigation, it was worth it if it saved Charli.

Upon their marriage, controlling interest in all things Montague will revert to A. Collins and E. Spencer, with provisions for the continued support and oversight by A. Fitzgerald and A.M. Fitzgerald until the time it is determined that either or both is no longer competent.

"Do you think…?" I began.

"That the bastard is making the case for Adelaide's mental competency before it is legally brought into question? I sure as hell do," Oren said. "I even have some information on that subject. I'll tell you later. Keep reading."

If this union does not occur, all Montague holdings and assets will be liquidated. The assets will henceforth be bequeathed to Fitzgerald Investments, leaving both heirs and their descendants without Montague assets.

If the marriage of A. Collins and E. Spencer fails to survive, resulting in divorce or premature death, all Montague holdings and assets will be liquidated and henceforth bequeathed to Fitzgerald Investments, with one exception: in the instance of a male heir over the age of twenty-five, the designated heir will retain all holdings and controlling interest.

If it is found that any one person mentioned in this article willfully and purposely hinders my wishes, that beneficiary will be stricken from receiving his or her share of the inheritance.

"This can't be legal. It would never hold up under appeal," I said.

"Beneficiary stipulations," Oren said, as if the phrase were something he referred to daily.

"What?"

"It's the imposing of stipulations for inheritance on beneficiaries. It's done more often than you think."

"Often it's something like completing school or where funds are only available to pay for education or housing," Deloris added.

"This is bullshit. Charli doesn't need this. She doesn't want it. Why is she going through with this?"

"Is she?" Deloris asked. "Or is she biding her time for her mother?"

We should have talked more this afternoon. I should have asked more questions.

"This doesn't change a thing," I announced after finishing. "We're going to go on with our plans. Fuck Montague."

"Not so fast."

We all turned to Oren.

"I told you that there's a codicil. Scroll to near the end."

Oren reached for his phone and sent a text.

"An important date?" I asked.

"In a way."

Before I could begin reading, there was a knock on the door.

"Expecting someone?" Deloris asked.

"As a matter of fact, I am," Oren said as he stood and walked toward the door. "Turn off the Magnolia Woods feed."

With a button, the TV screen went black and Oren reached for the handle.

A young man stood nervously at the door.

"Mr. Crawford."

The boy nodded. "Mr. Demetri."

"Come in," Oren opened the door wide, his invitation too gracious.

I stood. "Mr. Crawford? What is the—"

"During my perseverance..." Oren began as the young man shifted uncomfortably from one foot to the next and looked about the room. "...I learned of a job Mr. Crawford had recently lost."

The boy nodded. "You can call me Stephen."

"Yes, well Stephen was employed by Hamilton and Porter, the law firm who held this will. Stephen had the pleasure of working with Adelaide regarding this same will."

My father suddenly had my attention. "Mrs. Fitzgerald knew about it?"

"Yes," Stephen said. "I-I worked with her on several occasions." He looked toward Oren.

"Go on, son. These are my colleagues. We're all trying to help Mrs. Fitzgerald and if you can help us help her, we can help you."

He swallowed. "You have the will?"

"Yes."

"Um, okay. Well, there's a codicil."

"We just got to that," I volunteered.

"There are a few things you might not realize if you hadn't worked with Adela—I mean, Mrs. Fitzgerald."

"Like what?" Oren prompted.

"Sir, this is confidential information."

"Are you still employed by Hamilton and Porter?"

"No, but I signed a non-disclosure—"

"Did anything feel wrong about what Ralph Porter asked you to do?"

"I feel like I abandoned Mrs. Fitzgerald. She was really excited about the codicil."

Oren turned to Deloris. "Turn the feed back on."

I nodded.

The TV filled with a picture of Adelaide's room.

"Stephen, when was the last time you saw Adelaide?" Oren asked.

He stood taller. "It was right before I was let go. We had a meeting scheduled near the beginning of October, but I wasn't allowed to meet with her. The last time was nearly a month earlier. She would schedule and then reschedule."

Oren pointed to the screen. "Look closely. That's Adelaide."

He sucked in a breath as he walked toward the screen. "What happened to her?"

"That's what we are trying to find out. Could it be that she learned information she wasn't supposed to know?"

Stephen's eyes widened in horror. "Shit. I… this is dangerous. Surely…"

Oren's hand came down on Stephen's shoulder. "Son, no one will know your role or that you helped us. I can assure you of your safety and that of your young family. How old is that baby?"

My stomach twisted at the ease of my father's words. Deloris's eyes darted my way. It had been years since I'd witnessed this side of him in action, and yet at this moment, I didn't loathe his choice or strategy.

"Fifteen months."

"Stephen, you help us, and you and that pretty young wife and your little son will do much better. You can transfer to any law school in the country. I've seen your grades. You're a hardworking young man. It's a shame to waste your education at Savannah Law."

"It's a good school…"

"So is Stanford, Harvard, Yale…"

He turned back to the screen. "I liked her. Will she get better?"

"Yes," Oren replied unequivocally.

"Can I see the codicil?"

Oren nodded at Deloris and it appeared on the TV, replacing Magnolia Woods.

"Okay," Stephen said, scanning the words. "See this?" He pointed at the date and the initials CM. "This date is obviously the date the codicil was approved. What isn't stated is that according to Adelaide…" He looked at Oren as if he needed his permission to use her first name.

"Go on."

"According to her, that is the same date her father died."

"So this isn't legal?" Deloris asked.

Stephen shook his head. "No, it is. Mr. Montague passed away in his sleep that night from a sudden heart attack. He was legally competent when he approved the document."

When no one spoke, he went on. "I thought that was rather strange. I asked Natalie about it. She's one of the legal assistants. She told me not to worry about it."

"So you didn't?"

"I didn't say anything. But I can't shake the feeling that it's strangely coincidental."

"Can you explain the codicil?" I asked.

"You've seen the will, so you know about Article XII?"

We nodded.

"It's weird shit. I mean imposing beneficiary stipulations is a common practice, but I've never seen… even in school… anything as strange as the mandates in this one." He scrunched his features. "Can you imagine, some dead guy dictating who you have to marry?"

"The codicil?" I asked again, the agitation not lost in my tone.

"Yes, well. In a nutshell, it qualifies the provisions in Article XII, basically saying that any manipulation by any of the interested parties alters the provisions."

I shook my head at the reality. This addition to old man Montague's will said that if anyone does *anything* to dissuade, to interfere with the natural progression of, or to stop the planned arrangement, then that person null and voids his or her assets or any claim to said assets. It also nullifies the bequeathing of the liquidated assets to Fitzgerald Investments. Obviously he had some trust issues.

"So if the marriage doesn't go as planned, Montague Corporation will remain a viable entity, not being liquidated as originally set forth in Article XII?" I asked.

Stephen shrugged, scanning the document. "It does specify that the current board of trustees will be dissolved, and the entire corporate structure will become a publicly traded company. And if the marriage of her daughter to the guy named doesn't occur, or either person marries someone else, this will then enters probate where all interested parties must make a case for their rights. Assuming that the earlier mentioned interference isn't an issue, theoretically, the estate will be equally divided amongst the living heirs."

"So for clarification, this codicil null and voided the consequences of Article XII?" Deloris asked.

"Yes," Stephen confirmed.

"I wonder what made Mr. Montague change his mind," she added.

"Miss Adelaide wondered the same thing." Stephen turned back to Oren. "I hope this can help her. She was so excited about the codicil. She couldn't understand why she hadn't known about it. She kept saying, if only... if only."

Oren reached for the edge of the table, stabilizing himself as he turned back to the room. "Thank you, Stephen." He reached into his inner jacket pocket and took out a legal-sized envelope. From the look of it, I assumed it held cash. "This should help you to relocate. Contact my assistant. The choice of schools is yours."

Stephen held the envelope for a minute before passing it back. "Thank you. I appreciate it. I'd love to attend any one of those schools you mentioned. However, I can't." He shook his head. "Mr. Fitzgerald offered me money too. I didn't take it either. It's bad enough that I broke the non-disclosure agreement, but it wasn't for the money. I was serious. Miss Adelaide was a kind woman. She doesn't deserve to be wherever that is. I tried to help her." He shrugged. "I'm afraid the information I helped her find and understand may have led to what happened to her. For that reason, I'm happy to help you.

"I won't tell anyone, and I trust you won't either. Just help her. And if you can... that date thing has kept me awake at night. It just feels wrong."

I stood and stepped forward, fucking impressed with this man's balls. At the same time, I knew Oren's game—the indebtedness that fueled mutual obligation. I couldn't predict Oren's next move. Instead, I extended my hand. "Stephen, you're a good man. You'll make a fine attorney. I know someone else who believes in doing the right thing and helping those who can't help themselves. The law profession would be a better place if there were more like the two of you."

"Thank you, Mr. Demetri."

My grip tightened as Isaac's attention shifted from his phone to Stephen. "We weren't introduced."

His gaze shot between Oren and me. "I'm sorry if I presumed. It's the resemblance. Are you not related?"

"Mr. Crawford, take care of yourself."

"And that baby," Oren added.

Deloris stood. "May I show you to the door?"

"Can I...? Will I know if you help her?"

"I suspect there will be rumors."

CHAPTER 34

———•○•———

ALEXANDRIA

THE SCENE HAPPENED around me, with me, and yet I was always a step behind.

The picture on Bryce's phone was of me. Was it a trick?

"Bryce, what are you saying?"

He seized my upper arm, the same place he'd grabbed it the other day, pulling me closer. "I'm asking you a fucking question."

I fought his grip. "Let go of me. You're hurting me."

We moved about the room, all three of us in a dance choreographed by both rage and fear.

"As soon as I saw you in the den, I knew something was off. I couldn't put my finger on it, but then it hit me. The dress you were wearing…" Releasing my arm he shoved me away and scanned me from head to toe. "That you're *still* wearing… isn't the same as in the feed from Magnolia Woods." He paced a small circle. "I fucking warned you. When you first got here, I tried to tell you." He stepped closer. "I wanted this to be different, but I won't be made a fool of!"

Though every part of me wanted to back away from his approach, I didn't. I couldn't. I wouldn't give him that power over me. Not for a day, a week, until our wedding, or forever.

I lifted my chin. "Just spit it out. What are you accusing me of, because I have many more accusations to throw at you?"

The next second happened in a flash. Since I'd entered Alton's car, I'd been struck twice: once by him and once by Suzanna. Theirs were nothing like the power in Bryce's slap. It wasn't a slap, but a backhand, knuckles connecting with bone, flesh hitting flesh.

I staggered and screamed.

Not from the pain—I hadn't felt it.

From the shock.

My one word—"NO!"—rang through Chelsea's suite, the one syllable going on for what seemed like forever as my knees gave way and I fell to the floor beside my friend.

She was curled on her side, cradling her cheek with her chest heaving from the unexpected blow.

"What the hell did you just do?" I screamed up at him.

Who is this man?

Surely not my childhood friend. Not the man who'd begrudgingly left my virtue intact as a teenager. Not the man who was pretending to be my fiancé.

"Get up," he bellowed. His demand fell like a wet blanket as I stared up toward him, Chelsea's head now in my lap.

He didn't stop. "I said get the fuck up."

Gently I eased her head off my lap and back to the carpet. Slowly I stood up, ready to face the monster who'd been hiding, the wolf in sheep's clothing. As I rose, I knew without a doubt that Bryce Spencer was capable of hurting Melissa Summers. It was the accusations of his other crimes that I still didn't understand.

"Not you," he spat. "You."

I gasped as the toe of his shoe reared back and kicked Chelsea's leg.

I moved between them and put my hands out, trying to block him. My effort was similar to that of the buoys that floated out from the shore, capable of holding their own space, yet unable to slow the power of the waves.

"Bryce, stop it."

He ran his hand through his hair as Chelsea scooted back, away from him yet still on the floor.

"Get up!"

When I saw her begin to rise, I moved again. "No, Chelsea. Don't do it. Bryce, get the fuck out of here."

Glaring my direction, he bulldozed past, reached for her arm, and yanked her to her feet. "This is your fault, Alexandria. She can thank you later for what's about to happen."

"Nothing is about to happen," I retorted. "There's a room full of men downstairs. Go. Leave us alone. We have to get ready for dinner." It was a lame excuse, but my mind was a blur, scrambling for any shred of sanity.

His voice found an even-keeled, almost eerie calm. With his gaze now fixed on Chelsea, he said, "Leave the room, Alexandria."

What?

"No."

"Now!" No longer crimson as he turned to me, his face was red, bright red, a glowing contrast to his blond hair and light gray eyes. There was something different about them too, something I couldn't place yet felt hauntingly familiar.

I opened Chelsea's door and turned once more back to Bryce. He'd released Chelsea's arm as he turned to be sure I'd left. Instead, I pulled the door open wider and stepped toward him. As my chest met his, I thrust my key toward Chelsea and said, "Go now. Lock my door."

It happened so fast. She didn't hesitate as she took off running, her bare feet gripping the soft carpet as she sprinted away.

Bryce took a deep breath and moved toward me, each step enlisting my retreat, pushing me back and back until the wall stopped my progress. Caging me against the wall with one arm on either side of my face, he leaned closer. "You'll regret that. Not as much as her, but you will."

"What the hell is your problem? Is it Patrick?" *Because he's ready to kick your ass.*

I didn't say that last part.

"Right now, my problem is you."

"Fine, then don't marry me."

He seized my chin, his fingers painfully squeezing my face. "Shut the fuck up. Learn to keep your mouth closed and, I'll add, your legs together—to anyone but me. If you can manage to follow those simple instructions, things will improve for you and my whore."

His callous words bit more than his grip.

"Don't talk about her like that."

"You're right. I shouldn't differentiate, not when there were two whores in here."

Was her room bugged? Had he heard that I'd signed with Infidelity?

Shit! How stupid could I have been?

"Bryce... what's going on?"

"You weren't at Magnolia Woods today. I called. You weren't there, only Patrick. That means one thing. It means you were with *him*." He let go of my chin and caressed my cheek. The change from brutality to gentleness added to my queasiness. "Darling, if you can fuck, then I can too." His smile broadened. "I might even let you watch."

"I didn't—"

"Don't fucking lie to me. I warned you. I told you that you'd go along with everything, because if you didn't, you wouldn't be able to live with the repercussions." His tone softened, his timbre a mocking sweetness. "I can't do to you what I want, not right now."

The calculating coldness in his eyes sent a cold chill tingling down my spine.

"Because," he went on, explaining his psychotic reasoning, "in less than an hour you're going to be downstairs in a fucking different dress, wearing your ring, and playing the perfect fiancée. We have a party tomorrow. It's a shame Chelsea won't make it."

I had trouble keeping up. "But Suzanna and Alton want her there. A united front."

"But *you* don't. She's a whore. Everyone knows that and when asked, that will be your answer."

I shook my head. "No. I won't do that to her. I won't—"

His hand covered my lips. "You will or I'll tell Alton about today. I'll let him know that instead of visiting Adelaide, you were screwing a criminal. And then your visiting privileges with your mother will be revoked." He moved his head slowly from side to side as a grin came to his lips. "As I said, you will cooperate. Won't you, darling? Best friend or worst enemy. I suggest you work on reminding me why you want it to be friend."

"Leave Chelsea alone. She hasn't done anything. If you want to take this out on someone—not that I'm admitting to anything—then take it out on me."

"If only I could, but bruises won't go well with dinner tonight or the party tomorrow night. And, darling…" He allowed the endearment to hang in the air. "…I don't do sloppy seconds.

"Go now, it's nearly time for dinner." He reached for a bit of my hair. "Fix your hair and makeup. Make yourself beautiful." He ran his knuckles over my cheek as his tenor flowed like silk. "Because you can be stunning, Alexandria. I've seen it. I've watched you. From now on, you'll wear that gorgeous smile for me, won't you?"

I stared, terrified of his next mood swing.

He brushed his finger over my lips. "When I ask you a question, I expect an answer."

I nodded. It wasn't so much a concession as it was manipulation. By giving him the answer he wanted, I controlled his response.

Bryce smiled. "Now, here's a question for you. Tell me you don't want to be late for dinner; you don't want to be late *again* today, do you?"

I hadn't had a chance to respond when unexpectedly his fist collided with the wall, merely inches from my face. The plaster was no match for his punch as fine dust fluttered around us.

I gasped, shuddering as his growing erection pressed against my stomach.

"I asked you a question." The red crept back up to his ears. "Fucking answer it…" Before it could register, he reached down the neckline of my dress and under my bra, painfully pinching and twisting my nipple.

I screamed as I tried unsuccessfully to move away.

Bryce grinned. "…or, darling, I'll find places your dress will hide, places to leave my mark. Now answer."

"No," I replied quickly, gathering what was left of my self-control and pushing his hand away. "I don't want to be late."

He leaned closer, his nose touching my neck as he inhaled. "And shower. Exchanging you for her was supposed to rid me of a whore, not make another one my future wife."

Bryce took a step back, giving me the space to stand straighter.

Was he allowing me to leave? Would he follow me?

I stayed planted and softened my tone. "Please, Bryce. She's my friend. Please, don't do anything."

He let out a breath. "I know you may not understand, but I've paid a lot of money to do whatever I want." One side of his lips quirked upward. "As I said, she's a whore but for you... for now... I'll go back downstairs and make nice with your father." He tilted his head toward the fist print—the indentation in the wall. "Don't make any assumptions. Locks won't keep me out."

CHAPTER 35

---•○•---

ALEXANDRIA

BRYCE'S LIPS QUIRKED. "I don't give a fuck how many keys you have."

I held my breath and rebuttal as Bryce turned, leaving me alone in Chelsea's room. His last words, his menacing cold stare, fueled the rush of adrenaline flooding my system. Still standing, I reached for my own hands, gripped the large diamond, and tried to make sense of the shaking. I squeezed my hands in an effort to quiet the trembling, but as it registered, I realized it was no longer contained to my hands but racking my entire body, making my knees increasingly weak.

Like a jittery statue I stood waiting, fearful that he would return and yet more terrified that he'd look elsewhere to wreak his fury. As time stood still, air returned to my lungs and slowed my tremors. My breaths were the only sound as I searched for noise of him down the hall with Chelsea.

Though I wanted to help my friend, my body refused to move, paralyzed by what I'd seen and heard. Quietness prevailed as Bryce's footsteps disappeared in the distance, replacing the horror with relief. No longer rigid, my bones became pliable, giving way to the forces of gravity. With a suppressed sob, I melted against the pockmarked wall and puddled on the carpet.

Oh my God.

He's a monster.

With only my eyes, I rapidly searched the room for a clock. I needed to get ready. I needed to check on Chelsea, yet I didn't have the strength. Seconds became minutes as time passed and my heart beat out a cadence, a rhythm composed by dread. I couldn't marry that man. I couldn't spend another day with him nor would I allow Chelsea to. He was a psychopath, cold and without empathy or remorse. I'd never witnessed such uncaring eyes.

In a matter of minutes his anger had superseded rage, moving to a frigid terrain, colder than anything I'd ever seen. It was nothing like Nox's worst temper. It was even worse than Alton. Bryce was distant and disconnected.

When I closed my eyes, his calculating stare filled my unseeing vision.

Was that the last thing Melissa Summers had seen? What had she experienced? I may have doubted it before, but not any longer: Edward Bryce Spencer was capable of murder. I knew it in my soul.

"Alex?"

I blinked my eyes as Chelsea came into focus.

"Are you all right?" she asked, reaching for my hand.

Her right cheek was red and the contusion was raised.

"Me?" I gently touched the irritated skin. "What about you?"

Tugging my hand, she pulled me to stand. "I'm okay, because of you. I'm sorry I ran. I should have stood up to him, like you did. I-I told you, he scares me."

I nodded. "I see it. I do." I stilled our steps as we moved toward my room. "Chelsea, don't stand up for me. Don't. He said he will…" I could hardly make myself say the words. "…that he can hurt you, because he can do anything he wants to you. He can't hurt me. I have to be at dinner and the party."

Chelsea's arms wrapped about her midsection. "I-I can't stop him. You can't stop him."

I pulled her through my suite and into my bathroom, leaving two locked doors between us and the hallway. "I can. I'm getting you out of here. I have a plan."

WITH A FEW minutes to spare, I took a deep breath, made my way down the grand stairs and toward the dining room. I'd done as Bryce said, complete with a shower, washing away any scent of Nox or Patrick and replacing it with bodywash, shampoo, and perfume. My dress was new, even to me. It had been hanging in a garment bag, another costume for my new role.

I settled at the unoccupied dining table, happy for a moment of peace to collect my thoughts.

"Would you like a glass of wine?" the young lady manning the dining room asked.

I'd like a whole bottle, but I'd settle for a glass. "Yes, thank you. Cabernet."

"Yes, ma'am."

As she disappeared into the kitchen, Suzanna and Bryce entered. The calm was gone, yet I didn't turn to watch them enter. I was too terrified of what I'd see.

"Alexandria, how was your mother?"

Apprehensively, my head moved their direction, my gaze fluttering between Suzanna and her son. Was this another trap? Almost imperceptibly, Bryce shook his head, telling me to play the role. Perfect fiancée. That was what he'd demanded.

"She is getting better. The nurses keep saying she is."

"I need to go see her," Suzanna said. "Tomorrow morning I'll join you."

Before I could accept her proposal, Bryce spoke; each of his phrases poked another hole in my boat of hope. Soon it would sink, my titanic of dreams imprisoned in the ocean's depths.

"Mother, you're going to need to go alone. Alexandria will be occupied tomorrow. Perhaps," he went on, "she'll be available on Sunday." *It depends on her performance at the party.*

I heard the last part loud and clear, even though he didn't voice it aloud.

"Occupied?" Suzanna turned my way. "Doing what?"

The young lady placed the glass of Montague Private Collection before me as Suzanna sat. I shrugged. "It's news to me, too. You'll need to ask your son."

He lifted his glass of whiskey and grinned. "Our plans are yet to be determined." He circled his wrist, clanking the iced cubes. "There are so many variables."

The air cooled, not only with his words but also his too-calm tone. The chill settled over the room, leaving a trail of goose bumps on my skin.

"Nice dress," Bryce said, coming behind me and kissing my cheek.

"An unplanned excursion," Suzanna said excitedly. "That sounds like a great idea. Just don't get too carried away. Remember you have to be back in time to get ready for the party. The guests will begin to arrive at six."

The room fell silent as Alton entered.

Nodding, he grinned. "Now this is what I like to see. Everyone in place..." His eyes narrowed as he eyed the empty place setting. "Where is Chelsea?"

"Alexandria?" Bryce prompted.

Knots formed in my stomach as my mouth dried. My volume was barely audible. "I can't do it."

Everyone's eyes were on me: Alton and Suzanna's questioning and Bryce's warning.

"I think you can." His response was also soft.

I turned toward him, fighting the tears. "No. I can't."

"What is it?" Suzanna asked with a genuine concern in her voice.

Bryce's eyes narrowed.

I shook my head and turning to Suzanna, spoke louder. "I've tried, really I have, but if I have to face my academy classmates and the society of Savannah tomorrow night, I can't do it with that whore in tow." The word hurt my heart. I was thankful she couldn't hear me.

"Alexandria!" Suzanna shrieked.

I turned toward Alton as he sat. "Imagine how my mother would have felt sharing the stage with you and some whore you were screwing right under her nose."

"This isn't about your mother or me..." As his lame excuse rang out, there was something in Suzanna's expression that confirmed Pat's accusations.

"Or had she?" I asked.

"We're losing focus of the point," Bryce interjected. "Alexandria drew a line in the sand. Chelsea will stay, but not publicly. It's Alexandria's decision."

"I don't like it," Suzanna said. "Chelsea needs to work at Montague and face people in Savannah. If you snub her, you're sentencing her to public ridicule."

"And if I embrace her," I replied, "I'm sentencing myself to the same. It won't be as overt, but you know it will be there."

Alton lifted his hand as the staff entered with plates of salads. "That's enough." He turned to the young girl. "Take a dinner to Miss Moore's room. Apparently she won't be joining us."

"Sir?" The girl asked, looking my direction.

"I've already requested that. I let the staff know that she'd be eating in her room for the foreseeable future."

"That isn't necessary," Suzanna said in Chelsea's defense. "If you don't want her here, she'll move back to Carmichael Hall."

"No."

"Why not?" Suzanna asked. "At least there she won't be forced to face your animosity."

I turned to Bryce.

With a sweet expression of satisfaction gracing his thin lips, he lifted his glass. "Mother, I think that's an excellent idea."

The knots in my stomach multiplied.

"Fine," Alton said dismissively. "After the party. This is all too much drama. I've had enough. No more discussion about Miss Moore."

After the party. Thank God.

My boat of hope wasn't beyond repair.

Course after course came and went. The conversation—what little there was—focused on the unimportant and uncontroversial. I tried to bring up the subject of the earlier meeting in Alton's den, but each attempt was met with one-word answers.

"Really, Alexandria, you may be in law school, but many things are above you. Let the men worry about those things. That's why you're marrying. You concentrate on ladies' things."

It was the sexism sprinkled with negativity that I'd lived with most of my life. It wouldn't matter if I graduated with honors. I was female and obviously not bright enough to recognize illegal dealings when I saw them. Each passing minute burned another piece of my soul. I wanted nothing more than to end the family farce and make my way back to the refuge of my room.

Locks may not keep Bryce out, but I had a plan. I'd asked Jane to join me for a movie.

As dinner concluded and Alton stood, I dabbed my lips and placed my napkin beside my plate. Scooting my chair away from the table, Bryce's question stopped me.

"How about a walk, Alexandria?"

My thundering pulse warned me, yet I couldn't allow his attention to go back to Chelsea. "That sounds marvelous." My smile was too big. "Maybe another night. I'm exhausted. We could sit for a while in the sitting room?" In plain sight of Alton, Suzanna, and the staff.

His thin lips quirked. "Darling, I'm sure you can find the energy. After all, you had energy this afternoon. Surely you have time for me, your fiancé? Or would you like to tell us all about your afternoon?"

My breasts pressed upward against the satin lining of my dress. The tight bodice restricted my ability to take in a deep breath as a prickly sensation cut down my spine. "Of course I have energy for you. I-I'd love to walk. Maybe to the lake?" I asked, hoping for my childhood friend's return.

"I was thinking the woods."

What the hell?

"Nonsense," Suzanna interjected. "It's dark. You two have a big day tomorrow."

"Mother, we aren't children."

"You aren't, but before you go gallivanting off, I think the four of us have things we need to discuss before tomorrow."

"Such as?" I baited, hoping for a reprieve.

"While speaking to Gwen earlier this afternoon, I realized that there will be suspicions and questions. You both need to have your stories straight."

I nodded.

"The three of you handle this," Alton said dismissively. "I have pressing matters."

No one refuted Alton's claim as he stood. Seconds later he was gone leaving the three of us alone.

"Now," Suzanna went on, "with this abrupt change regarding Chelsea, we need to decide—"

"There's nothing to decide," Bryce said. "Alexandria is sticking by her conviction." He stood, giving me hope that he might be joining Alton.

"Well, yes," Suzanna said as she turned to me, "but, dear, you can't say that to others. You can't use that 'w' word."

Instead of leaving, Bryce moved to the chair beside me and splayed his hand over my lower thigh. His eyes opened expectedly. "Alexandria?"

The knots within my stomach churned with the little bit of food I'd managed to consume. Simultaneously, my skin coated with perspiration at the growing pressure of Bryce's hand. My teeth clenched as the pain increased.

"Suzanna," I fought to keep my expression from displaying what was happening. "I don't know if I can comply. It's the truth. There are too many lies to remember. I simply can't add another one."

The tips of Bryce's fingers continued to dig, pressing the material of my dress into my skin, near my kneecap.

"The truth?" he asked. "You mean the story you'll tell anyone who asks? Maybe you could remind us?"

The room dimmed, yet I obediently turned toward my fiancé, pleading with my eyes for him to stop the pressure. I reached below the table, yet I couldn't ease the force. My voice cracked. "Bryce?"

"We're waiting."

I couldn't move away, not without bringing attention to his actions. I swallowed the pain. "What story? You mean the truth that she's a whore?"

"Who will you tell?" His question was for no other reason than to make me speak, to make me recite his venom in front of his mother.

Suzanna was gone. Not in reality but through my anguished vision. The way his fingers dug near my kneecap sent excruciating jolts of pain through my entire leg. I clawed at his hand, yet each action only increased the pressure while at the same time, his expression remained curious and enthralled. Surely he wouldn't dislocate my knee… I wanted to believe.

I recalled the story I'd been fed, but never recited.

Letting go of his hand, I moved mine to his arm, visible to watching eyes, and concentrated on him. My volume rose above the blood coursing through my ears. "I'll tell everyone that I've always loved you. I'd tried to fight it. While in California I thought you'd given up on me. I didn't know that Chelsea was intercepting our messages, lying to me..."

I blinked with relief as the pressure eased a bit.

"Go on."

"...it wasn't until I came back for my mother and saw Chelsea with you that I knew."

"What?" he prompted.

"That we were meant to be together. That I'd been deceived by a gold-digging whore who'd pretended to be my friend."

My eyes closed and I sighed as he softened his touch. No longer forceful, his hand moved upward, higher on my thigh. For only a moment, the relief overpowered the reality. My hand dropped to his, stopping his progress.

Bryce's gaze narrowed in warning before turning toward his mother. "Is there anything else you want to discuss or may we take that walk?"

The entire room came back into focus.

Moisture glistened in Suzanna's eyes as she clasped her hands near her heart. "Oh, oh. You don't know how happy I am... I didn't think... I was worried..." She stood and rushed to our side of the table, her movement freeing me from Bryce's wandering hand.

Throwing herself toward me, Suzanna wrapped me in a hug. "This will work. It will. I'm so happy to hear that you agree. Wait until I tell your father."

Bryce's chair moved as he stood. "She does agree." He extended his hand. "Alexandria, my love, our walk awaits."

CHAPTER 36

ALEXANDRIA

HOW COULD BRYCE spew hateful, threatening things one minute and sound suave and debonair the next? Each word he uttered had me on the edge of my figurative seat, fearful of the other shoe dropping.

Placing my hand in his, I stood, searching for an out. I turned back to his mother. "Suzanna?"

Bryce's fingers wrapped around my hand, squeezing tighter and tighter.

"Yes?" she answered.

"Have a nice evening."

"Thank you, dear. I'm more than pleased with your change in attitude."

I feigned a smile. "You can thank your son for showing me the light."

Her cheeks rose higher, her gleaming smile radiating true appreciation toward Bryce.

Had she really raised a psychopath without knowing?

"You two have fun."

Pulling me closer, Bryce held my hand while circling his other arm around my waist. "Oh, we will, Mother. Right, darling?"

In a few short days I'd come to abhor that term of endearment. The way he said it was like a warning and threat, rolled in a thin coat of gallantry. A poisonous concoction sugarcoated to appear benign.

Soon we were to the back doors, the French doors leading out to the limestone patio. Once through and out under the starlit sky, Bryce paused and looked up at the manor. "I don't know if you remember," he began, "but I asked you a few months ago why you wouldn't want to live here and I told you that I would." He pulled me to his side. "And now I will. Just imagine, one day it will be our kids running around these lawns like we used to do."

I shivered as the cool chill of the autumn night air settled over us.

"Are you cold?"

"I suppose I should have grabbed a sweater."

With his arm still around me, Bryce ran his other hand up and down my arm. When he touched the area he'd seized earlier in the day, I involuntarily flinched.

"Don't do that."

"What?" I asked. "It's not my fault that my arm is sore."

We were to the edge of the steps, standing above the lawn with the lake in the distance. He turned me toward him, purposely clenching each arm. "It is. I want to hear you say that."

Bile came to a boil in my stomach, simmering higher and higher by the second as my internal temperature rose.

"What?"

"Say it, Alexandria. You did such a good job with Mother. I'm sure you'll have no problem telling anyone who asks about Chelsea as to what kind of a whore she really is. Now I want to hear you admit that it's your fault your arm is sore."

"Bryce? What's gotten into you?"

He took a step toward the edge, turning us both toward the flight of stone stairs. "I could ask you the same question, but I don't want to know the answer." He looked out beyond the lawn. "Have you ever thought about how high we are? How far down it is to the lawn?"

I tried to take a step back, but his grip of my arms increased. "Now, darling, your arm?"

Like the grip of Nessie—the imaginary monster in the lake below—his words and tone squeezed my chest, seizing my thundering heart and smashing it against my ribs. My chin moved upward at his forced encouragement.

"Look at me while you say it. I want to see that you're telling the truth."

I swallowed, searching for moisture. My tongue darted to my parched lips as I formed my response. "My arm... I shouldn't have stepped in between you and Chelsea."

"No, don't use her name. Say what she is."

I blinked away the tears. "Bryce?"

He looked to my bodice, reminding me of the agony he'd inflicted on my nipple. With a sickening grin, his eyes found mine. "Try again."

The words hurt my heart, squeezing it as if they were a knife, cutting not only me, but also Chelsea. "A whore."

Applying more pressure to my chin, he cooed, "Darling, this will go much better if you learn when to speak and what to say. She's not just any whore: she's mine. Start over and say it right."

Sick bastard.

"I shouldn't have stepped in between you and your whore."

"Go on."

I wasn't sure where I was supposed to go.

"Claim responsibility and I'll accept your apology."

My neck stiffened. *My apology?*

My head snapped back as Bryce pulled my hair. "Attitude is not acceptable. I believe your father told you that."

"I-I didn't."

He let go of both my chin and hair and then gently wiped a renegade tear from my cheek. "Don't cry, darling, you'll get the hang of this. After all, you're the one who was accepted to Stanford and Columbia."

"Bryce, I don't want us to be like this. I-I don't... you're scaring me."

He lifted my hand and brought my knuckles to his lips. "After what you did today, you deserve to be wary, don't you think?"

I still hadn't admitted anything.

"Bryce, I know what you think, but it's not true. If I'd been with Len—" I quickly remembered not to say his name. "If I'd been with him... think about it. Do you think I'd return here?

"I was with Pat. We went to see my mom. I didn't sign in. They know me now. I don't know why they told you I wasn't there, other than the shift may have changed."

"The dress?"

"I can't explain it. Maybe there's something weird with the cameras. Do you remember that dress that went viral a few years ago? Some people saw one color while others saw another." I took a step away from the stairs. "I wouldn't risk Alton or you," I added, "getting upset. And now…" My chest ached. "…dear God, with Chelsea, I wouldn't—"

His fingers covered my lips. "Not a name."

I closed my eyes, allowing my lashes to linger near my cheeks as I tried to settle the mayhem inside of me. "Your whore." I took a breath. "It doesn't matter why you think that, she isn't. She's my friend."

Taking my hand, he walked us again to the stairs, this time we descended step by step. "That was one of the problems with California. Savannah has better quality friends. After tomorrow night, you and I'll socialize with Millie and Ian, Jess and Justin, and Leslie and Hamilton. They never thought much of my whore."

Each time he said that, referred to her like that, my skin bristled and stomach twisted.

"Of course," he continued, "you'll need to confirm all their suspicions. The story you told my mother will do nicely. I'm sure that after tomorrow night, you'll have it down pat."

We reached the bottom walkway. With the manor's lights behind us, the lawn sparkled. The moisture was a combination of the aftereffects of the sprinklers and a thin layer of dew that had begun to form.

Small slivers of moonlight illuminated the lake and fields beyond the lawns.

I looked down at my feet, my high heels. "I'm really not wearing the right shoes."

"Then take them off."

As I considered the option, a breeze picked up over the fields and lake. Small waves shone in the silver cast as remaining leaves rustled. I wrapped my arms around my midsection.

"I'm cold."

With a huff, Bryce removed his suit coat and placed it over my shoulders.

My eyes burned at the scent of his unfamiliar cologne. I longed for Nox's woodsy scent or even Patrick's divine secret formula.

"There, now take off your shoes. We're walking."

Shivering beneath his suit jacket, I asked, "Why? What's your end goal?"

"My end goal? My end goal is to teach you a lesson, one about honesty and respect."

"Please, I get it. I do. I don't need to walk through wet grass to prove it. What do you want?"

"First, walking in the wet grass isn't my plan." He looked out toward the lake and then off to the horizon. "I'm sure we can get far enough away from the manor that no one will see us as you keep up this role." He eyed me up and down. "Second, I'm done waiting. If it means taking you in wet grass or Georgia mud, I don't fucking care.

"No matter what you say…" He blatantly reached for my core, thankfully still covered by my dress and panties. "…you're now mine. That means when those legs spread, it'll be my dick making you scream."

I took a staggered step back. "Not like this. No."

"As I said, I don't do sloppy seconds." He tilted his head. "But since we're being honest with one another and you're sticking to your story about this afternoon, then sloppy seconds is no longer an issue. Right, darling?" He encircled my waist and pulled me to him, bringing our hips together until his growing erection beneath his trousers probed my stomach.

I tried not to stiffen, not to show any outward sign of the repugnance seething through me. I was caught in a no-win situation, and with each passing second, my panic grew.

"Bryce?"

In the light of the moon, his complexion took on an eerie paleness. "Darling, I'm getting off with you tonight." The tip of his finger grazed my lips. "In your mouth." His touch moved lower. "On your tits." His hand moved toward my core. "Or inside your cunt, I don't care. It's happening."

Breath came too fast as panic rushed through me. "Why?"

He rubbed himself against me. "Do you need to ask? You asked me to 'take it out on you.' Your wish is my command, darling." He reached again for my hand. "Over there, by the tennis courts… I'm going to take it out."

My feet slid on the wet grass, still in my heels. "I don't want this."

He stopped, his voice again morphing to cold. "Wrong. You want it. Say you do."

I swallowed. "Please, Bryce."

His grin broke through the coolness. "Close. Begging is acceptable. Now, tell me you want me to take you. No, tell me you want me to *fuck* you. Come on, darling. No, I know! Tell me that *you* want to fuck *me* and you'll do it better than my whore."

I couldn't process. The words were nowhere to be found. Neither was air. Where had it gone? I tried to inhale as his fingers twisted my hair. My entire body went rigid.

"Alex! Alex!"

Bryce and I both turned. Like a release valve, the tension fled my muscles as I stumbled backward and took a ragged breath. Up on the patio, waving in our direction were Patrick and Cy.

"Fuck!" Bryce said through clenched teeth. His curse was louder than a mumble but not loud enough for anyone but me to hear. We were too far away.

"Pat! Cy!" I yelled toward them.

Placing my hand on Bryce's chest, I held him a few inches away. "Please, Bryce, I'm sorry you were upset. I played the perfect fiancée for dinner. It's your turn. Play nice with Pat."

He sneered. "I seem to remember that same speech years ago."

"You two always were..." I shrugged. "...not the most compatible."

"Well, obviously we have different tastes."

"Cyrus is a very nice man. He cares for Patrick and is good to him." Unlike how you've been tonight. "Isn't that what's important?"

As I turned toward the steps, Bryce reached for my hand and brought me back to him. "This isn't over. The only positive thing about this interruption is that I'll get to hear your story again. We can consider this a practice performance for tomorrow night. Remember: don't use her name, and she's not just any whore—she's mine. I want to hear every word."

"I-I... Bryce, Pat knows her, knows of her."

With us turned toward the manor, the patio lights illuminated his lips as they curled upward. "All the better." Bryce leaned down to kiss my cheek. "Don't mind me. I'll be the one enjoying the show." He tugged my hand one more time. "Do a good job. If you don't, you won't be the only one to face the consequences."

I didn't answer. Instead, I hurried toward the stairs and climbed the steps until I was engulfed in Pat's embrace.

"Problems?" he whispered.

I couldn't respond with Bryce only seconds behind me. Instead, I nodded and reached for Cy. His arms wrapped around my shoulders.

"It's been a while," he whispered. Kissing my cheek he added louder, "Nice little place you have here."

"Thanks." I wanted to say that I preferred Nox's apartment or theirs. I had so many things I wanted to say. Instead, I turned to Bryce. "May I introduce my fiancé, Edward Bryce Carmichael Spencer?"

Pat smirked "Are you sure there isn't another name in there? I remember a few you were called when at the academy."

Cy extended his hand. "I'm Cyrus Perry, but Cy is fine."

Bryce shook his hand, ignoring Pat. "Edward or Bryce. Nice to meet you."

I guess I'd never noticed how much Pat and Bryce truly disliked one another. At that moment, I didn't give a damn. I was too happy that once again my cousin had saved the day. "Can I show you around?" I asked. "Or how about a drink? Alton has an extensive liquor selection in the house."

"Oh girl," Pat said, "you had us at *can*!"

I walked beside Pat as Cy spoke with Bryce.

Soon we were all seated in the sitting room, Bryce glued to my side, attentive and touching. It took a few minutes and a finger or two of Alton's best Cognac, but soon Bryce was paying less attention to me, and more to talking business, companies, and banking, I didn't care what they talked about as long as it kept Bryce occupied.

"How about you show me around?" Pat asked.

Like a bloodhound, Bryce looked my way, splaying his fingers over my knee. Turning away from Cy, he said, "Really?" It was first direct thing Bryce had said to Pat. "I'm sure you know your way around."

Pat shrugged. "It's been a while." He winked at me. "Things change, right? And I don't know about the big plans. I want to hear about the party and reception. Mom said they're both here."

Cy leaned back. "That sounds enthralling."

Bryce smirked. "Girls will be girls."

Asshole.

Instead of taking offense, Pat rose and reached for my hand. "Tell me, do you plan on utilizing the patio? I've always loved the view…"

Cy swallowed more Cognac. "So, Edward, what do you think it will take for that to happen?"

Bryce turned back to Cy. "Distribution is the key…"

I sighed as they continued talking and Pat and I stepped back toward the patio. Once we were outside, he said, "When I first saw you… you didn't answer… did something happen?"

I turned toward the lake. "It is a pretty view."

"Little cousin?"

I held back the tears and shook my head. "So much… I can't. If I do, the tears will never stop."

His brown eyes narrowed. "Are you okay?" His questions were still coming low enough for only me.

"I suppose, but time will tell."

"Alexandria."

Pat and I turned as Bryce opened the French door.

"Come in, darling. I don't want you to get cold."

I caught Patrick's expression, but didn't respond to my cousin. I turned back to Bryce.

He kissed my cheek. "Good girl."

Once we were both back inside, Bryce went back to where he'd been sitting. Leaning back, he said, "Cyrus and I could use more Cognac. Why don't you get that for us, darling?"

Patrick's jaw clenched. "Let me help you."

Swallowing… biting the inside of my lip… I was doing anything to keep from giving into the tears bubbling just under the surface.

"The road… tomorrow?" Pat whispered.

272

I blinked the renegade tear away.

"Your mom will be okay," he spoke near my ear. "They have it worked out."

He stood with his back to the others and mouthed, "Do it."

"Yes." It was all I could say before stepping around him and carrying the decanter of Cognac to Cyrus and Bryce.

CHAPTER 37

NOX

"IF YOU DON'T kill him, I will," Pat said.

I paced back and forth in my hotel suite, holding my phone in a death grip. "You saw her again?"

"Yes. Cy and I went to the manor. We saw and talked to her, if you can call it that."

"What do you mean, 'if you can call it that'?"

"The ass was omnipresent. I even refused to leave until Alex retired to her room. I made lame excuses every time asshole hinted that we should go. Once she excused herself—she'd made plans with Jane for a movie night—then I wouldn't leave until Spence's car was pulled up."

I shook my head and walked again to the window and back. I'd wear a damn hole in this carpeting if I didn't get out of here soon. Storm the fucking castle—that's what I wanted to do. That's what my gut, or was it my heart, wanted me to do.

Hell, six months ago the damn thing had been a black hole in my chest, hard and uncaring. Charli had done this to me, made me feel, made me love, and now she was breaking my heart. It was breaking, thinking of her with him. "Fuck!" I said. "Twenty-four hours. She just needs to make it one more day."

Patrick sighed. "At least we got her through the night. I don't know what happened between this afternoon and now, but something did. She couldn't say, but I felt it."

The sky over Savannah had darkened. In the window's reflection I saw my image... I thought it was me. The bulging vein on my forehead, tendons throbbing in my neck, and clenched jaw were more pronounced than normal. My poor teeth wouldn't last much longer if I gritted them any tighter. "What do you mean? Do you think they found out about us, about this afternoon?"

Was it *this* afternoon or yesterday? I searched for a clock. Time didn't fucking move.

"If Spence knew," Patrick said, "he didn't let on, not to me nor Cy. He was all endearments and caresses. Sticky sweet. It was nauseating."

"I'll kill him."

"She... it wasn't like she enjoyed his attention. I mean she wore the Montague smile, but I know her. She looked... for lack of a better word... scared. Cy and I talked about it. I wish I could give you another assessment, but that's what I have."

"Scared? What do you think it is? Do you think that asshole would threaten her?"

"I wouldn't put anything past him."

The idea made my fingers fist. I'd show that fucker what it felt like to be scared. After all, Charli was the strongest woman I knew. I couldn't allow the thoughts to linger. If I did, I was hitting something: a wall? A door? I didn't care.

Patrick went on, "Even at the academy, he had a narcissistic air, but now... with his coronation into the royal Montagues at hand, there's something else... egotistical arrogance. I get the sense that he's feeling invincible."

There would be no quick death for that fucker.

My Charli deserved to be worshiped. The only thing that should ever scare her is one of the books she likes to read or if she'll make it across town in time for class. Never in her own home, never in her life, should her fear be real.

Patrick and I both knew that Spencer was using Charli for power and social status. What made it worse was that he was doing it with her stepfather's blessing. She'd been right. He was the devil, and that devil was selling her for his own future.

Now that we had the will, it all made sense. It was the codicil—without Spencer and Charli's marriage, Alton Fitzgerald could lose everything. It was the information Adelaide had recently learned with Stephen Crawford's help. After nearly twenty years with that ass, she'd finally found a way out.

Unfortunately, Fitzgerald learned that she knew. According to Oren's contact at Hamilton and Porter, Ralph Porter contacted Alton Fitzgerald... told him of his wife's discovery. The attorney was another name on my list. It was growing by the day... by the damn hour.

What happened next was systematic sabotage. Fitzgerald set Adelaide up for failure... the doctor overseeing her medical information found a metals test performed by Adelaide's primary care doctor nearly two months ago. He'd tested for mercury, arsenic, cadmium, and chromium.

Though the results were negative, what stood out to our physician was that Mrs. Fitzgerald's doctor was suspicious. She's ordered a hair follicle test. It shows all drug usage, including alcohol for the last ninety days. Isaac secured the sample a day ago, after visiting his 'father.'

The results should be available soon. Her hope is to see exactly what drugs were and have been in Adelaide's system and the amount.

As far as publicly, we all believe that the point of this illness was to deem Adelaide Fitzgerald incompetent. Under the influence of whatever was in her system, her behavior became erratic, her accusations easily dismissed. Eventually the chemicals in her system became too much for her frail body to handle.

It was a desperate play, but Alton Fitzgerald was desperate. He needed both his marriage and Charli's to Spencer. He needed the initial stipulations of old man Montague's will to go into effect so that no one would look for the codicil.

If for any reason it was brought to light, the life Alton Fitzgerald had enjoyed would come to a crashing end.

Patrick's end of the call went quiet. He'd been talking about tomorrow... or today. Where the fuck was a clock? I'd missed something.

"Is Cy good with the plan?" I asked.

"For Alex, he is. He said he's come out before, he can do it again."

"Did you see anyone else while you were at the manor?"

"Staff, but Spence dismissed them, happy to have Alex waiting on him."

"Are you fucking trying to get me to commit murder, because I'm ready?"

"Man, I want you as pissed off as I am."

"What about Chelsea?" I asked.

"I saw her at the restaurant this afternoon. She looked fine—not happy, but fine. I didn't see her tonight. Maybe she wasn't there."

Maybe it wasn't midnight yet. Why the hell won't the clock move?

"Isaac's been watching," I said. "According to him, she was taken back to Montague Manor and hasn't left. He's been watching the entrance."

Pat scoffed. "So I didn't need to let you know that I was there?"

"You didn't need to, but if you hadn't called, I would've called you."

"I assured Alex that you had it worked out to get her mother. Tell me that I didn't lie to her."

I shook my head. "You didn't. It's planned for during the party. We don't want to set off any alarms before. Once the guests begin to arrive, things will get chaotic. That's to our advantage."

"Are you personally getting her?"

"No. My father has that honor."

"Your father?" Pat asked. "I guess that's what families do."

It was my turn to scoff. "Well, that's not far off, but it's complicated. Apparently, Oren and Adelaide have met. He wants to help."

"Alex has a full corner of support. Looking at her tonight, I think she may have forgotten that. Man, she's hurting."

"What the fuck!" My growl resonated through the suite.

"No, not literally," Pat reassured. "She was thrilled to see us, yet anytime we started to talk, that asshole stopped it."

"She let him?" That didn't sound like my Charli. "She'd tell me to fuck off. Actually, she'd call me a dick." The thought made me smile.

Pat laughed. It wasn't real, but it broke the tension.

"If you hear anything," I said, "…call. I don't give a damn what time it is."

"I will. By the way, they gave her a phone. I held it when she was with you."

"Is that secret code for you've got her number?"

"It is. I'm sure it's monitored."

"I'd be disappointed in those assholes if it wasn't. I won't call it, but I want it."

"I don't know what it will do for us, but sure."

As I disconnected the line, I looked at the number I'd written.

Ten digits that would let me hear her voice.

Ten digits that could cause her more problems. I refused to be the source of any more of her anguish.

Instead of calling, I sent the number to Deloris and opened my app. Lying on the bed, I watched as she materialized. Not her, but her blue dot.

My cheeks rose. My Charli was the most beautiful blue dot in the world. I read her numbers. Her normal pulse gave me hope that she was safe with Jane, sound asleep, and ready for the big day we had coming.

I replayed Patrick's assessments in my head.

Scared.

Afraid.

With each recollection, sleep slipped further and further away. What had Edward Spencer done? What had he threatened? And why with a house full of staff, was the Montague heir waiting on him?

Fucking bastard wanted the power. He wanted others to see it. I knew his type. I despised his type. People who equated fear with power were bullies in the true sense of the word.

Just because my Charli could submit didn't mean she was weak. On the contrary, it took a strong woman to be submissive, to relent and trust. That was the woman she was.

Charli was fucking hot as hell when she gave herself—on her knees, her chin bowed, and eyes veiled. When she acquiesced, it was a gift, an offer to surrender her body and mind—her two most powerful assets. That's what submission was meant to be, a gift. Something given, not something that was required or taken.

Knowing that she'd willingly trusted me with all of herself, even in Del

Mar, showed me what an amazing and resilient woman she was.

I'd never forced her. I never would.

That was the differentiation between unique tastes and abuse. A true dominant—the opposite of a submissive—understood and respected the fact that the submissive was the one with the true power.

From our first meeting, the first time her golden eyes met mine, I never doubted that she was in control. I was captured by her spell.

Whether it was the pleasure of reddening her skin with my hand, a belt, or with the knots of a crop, it was never about power. Our power exchange was about pleasure—hers and mine. Whether I bound her with satin or a word, the anticipation was an aphrodisiac to us both. It wasn't only about her body, but also her mind. With someone as intelligent as Charli, the mind was as powerful as any bindings, and foreplay was as important as execution. With only words, her thighs would glisten, hips would writhe, and nipples would harden.

Charli was the most responsive and sexual woman I'd ever known.

That wasn't her only quality. Her sexuality didn't define her being. My Charli was also the smartest and most determined.

Fucking stubborn.

While I had plans to redden her ass for that, it was a trait I nonetheless admired.

I couldn't—wouldn't—think about what he'd done to scare her. Instead, I'd think about what could be done to frighten him. Bullies thrived on weakness.

"I have news for you, Spencer, I'm not weak. I'm also fucking smarter than you. You're going down and when you do, you'll be the one to suffer."

THE RINGING OF the phone pulled me from my sleep. I rubbed my face, trying to focus.

Since I was still dressed, I must have fallen asleep watching Charli's app. I reached for my phone. Isaac's name was on the screen.

"What?"

"Boss," Isaac said, "she's out of the manor."

I searched for the clock. What time was it? How late had I slept?"

"Where's she going?"

"It looks like Magnolia Woods. She's not alone."

"Spencer?" Just saying his name lit the wick of my explosive blood pressure.

"Not the one you think. She's with Mrs. Spencer."

His mother? "What makes you think they're going to Magnolia Woods? The last few times she's gone with his mother, they've gone on wedding planning excursions."

"That number you sent us last night? Mrs. Witt tapped into it. She's been listening to all of Miss Collins's calls. Mr. Spencer called her earlier this morning. Mrs. Witt overheard Miss Collins's destination."

I nodded. "I'm heading to Deloris's room. We'll keep an eye on the feed. Call if anything changes."

"Yes, sir."

Fifteen minutes later, showered and in clean clothes, I was in Deloris's suite, drinking coffee and watching the rotating feed from Magnolia Woods. The world beyond her closed drapes was alive with Saturday morning bustle. Tourists and locals walked the historic streets, going on with their lives as if there weren't others in the balance.

I waited. When Deloris didn't offer, I asked, "How did she sound?"

Looking up from her computer, Deloris smiled.

"I know," I admitted. "I sound like a pussy."

"No, Lennox, you sound concerned. You sound like a man who's worried sick over the woman he loves. While I'm sorry the two of you are going through this, I'm glad you've both realized how special your relationship is."

"Sometimes I think about Jo." There weren't many people I'd have this conversation with. Only two. Deloris was one of them. "I think about how I didn't know… how helpless I was. I don't want to be that way with Charli. I won't be."

"It's no secret that I loved Jocelyn almost like a daughter. She was a beautiful, naïve soul. Alex is different. If you'd had Jocelyn in your bed yesterday and told her that you didn't want her to go back to her family, she would've stayed."

I closed my eyes, remembering not Jo, but Charli in Patrick's suite. I could feel the softness of her warm skin, smell her intoxicating scent, and hear the echoes of her whimpers and moans.

"Lennox?"

I tore my gaze away from my nearly empty cup of coffee and pushed away the images. "I don't think that is a compliment for Charli."

"On the contrary. Alex keeps you on your toes. Despite what you may think, you don't control her."

The tendons of my neck stretched.

"Listen to me," Deloris went on. "She lets you. She's okay with it." She shrugged. "I could even go so far as to say that she enjoys it. There are some things I don't want to know. Nevertheless, it's not the same. What makes the two of you work is that you're both stubborn."

"Me?" I gave my most innocent stare. Honestly, it was a sad effort. There was nothing innocent about me.

"Yes. I can see that what's happening is hurting you, but it's hurting her too. If she hadn't done everything she could to save her mother, Alex would never have forgiven herself."

"And if I don't do everything to save her, I'll never forgive myself."

Deloris nodded. "Tonight. The plan's set."

Finishing my coffee, I set the cup down. "Now tell me about the call you overheard."

"I recorded it."

"What the fuck? Why haven't you said anything?"

"Because I'm not confident that I should share it."

"It's not your fucking choice. You work for me, in case you've forgotten."

"Lennox. Like I said, Alex is strong and stubborn. Wait until you have her in your arms. Wait until you know she's safe. I think… it's better if you wait."

"Play it."

Deloris shook her head. Pursing her lips, she typed on her keyboard. Seconds later, the recording began.

"Yes?"

My chest ached. Was it really only a day since I'd held her in my arms?

"Yes?" Spencer's smug voice resonated. *"Try again, darling. I'm sure that screen told you who was calling."*

What the fuck was his deal?

"Bryce, I just woke. I didn't read the screen."

"Then you're well rested."

"Not really. I didn't sleep well."

"That isn't my concern. Your concern is putting that stunning smile on your face. Do you think you can manage that?"

"I'll work on it."

"Hurry. Mother will be there soon."

"Why?" Charli asked.

"I think appreciation should be your response. Gratitude. Where are your manners?"

What the fuck? I stood, unable to listen and sit. My eyes met Deloris's.

Her lips pressed tighter together. "Lennox, you've heard enough—"

I raised my hand, silencing her. Charli was already speaking.

"...thankful for?"

"I'm agreeing to your request to visit your mother. That's what we do. We're going to be married. We want each other happy, right?"

"So I'm going to Magnolia Woods?"

"Mother will accompany you. I'd hate to have anything happen with today's visit. She'll be with you the entire time."

"Thank you."

"That's it, darling. After your visit she will bring you back here and you can elaborate on your gratitude."

"To Carmichael Hall? Why not here?"

What the hell? She's petitioning for Montague Manor. What the hell is up with Carmichael Hall?

"Manners," Spencer reminded her.

"Thank you for the invitation, but I need to prepare for the party."

"We have unfinished business. Carmichael Hall is a place where your fucking cousin won't materialize to disrupt our plans again."

My chest tightened. "What the fuck does—"

This time Deloris lifted her hand.

"Bryce, please."

"It's simple, darling, you or I'll send for my whore."

The muscles in my neck clenched.

"Maybe both? Perhaps you'd like to see what happens when—"

"Alton said she'd move back after the party."

"I didn't say I was having her brought here to stay, only to prove my point. She can return. Surely she'll still be able to walk."

"Stop. I'll be there."

"What did she just say?" I screamed at the computer.

"...my good girl. Be sure to tell my mother how much you appreciate her company."

"Yes. I need to get ready."

"You do that. I'll see you soon. I'm sure you'll enjoy our afternoon plans."

"Goodbye, Bryce."

Silence filled the line.

Deloris's eyes met mine.

My jaw ached as I said, "He needs to suffer."

"I've been thinking…"

CHAPTER 38

―●O●―

ADELAIDE

"MRS. FITZGERALD."

My eyelids were so heavy, so incredibly thick. Yet I knew the voice. I concentrated on opening them. Slowly at first, I allowed just a slit of light. It was there, the world beyond my closed eyes. I blinked once and then twice.

Light blue walls. White trim. Monitors and beeps.

I blinked again.

"Praise the Lord! Mrs. Fitzgerald. You going to open those eyes today?"

My lids fluttered as she came into view. "J-Jane? Is that you?"

"Yes, yes! Ma'am, I'm here. I'm with you."

I let out a long breath and closed my eyes. So tired.

Jane was here? Why? This wasn't my home. I wasn't in my suite.

That reality had been made painfully clear each time I'd awakened over the last few hours, or was it days? Maybe it was weeks? When had time lost its meaning?

I sucked in a deep breath as my tongue darted to my rough, crusty lips, snagging the flaking skin. "I-I'm thirsty."

A straw appeared at my lips.

"Here you go, Mrs. Fitzgerald. You drink."

I did. Slurp after slurp. I sipped the cool, clear liquid filling my mouth, covering my tongue and coating my throat. Each drop was heaven, like rain to parched Georgia clay.

When she pulled it away, I slowly opened my eyes. She was real. Jane was real. Her lovely brown skin glowed. I sought out her knowing eyes.

For the first time, in what seemed like a lifetime, my cheeks rose and lips parted. "You're the most beautiful sight I've ever seen." I lifted my heavy hand, searching for hers.

Warmth enveloped mine as she took it and squeezed. "Ma'am, you're a mighty good sight yourself."

I shook my head. "I-I doubt that."

The room beyond Jane came back into view. Sterile. That had been one of the words going through my head in recent memory. "How? What happened?" I lowered my voice. "Jane, did I take those pills?"

"Not the ones I took. I still has them."

"Then…" I tried to remember. "I don't understand."

"Ma'am, you get better. That's all that matters. You're talking. Wait until Miss Alex sees you."

My smile faded. Miss Alex, my daughter. I'd dreamt about her, but it wasn't real. I couldn't remember how long it had been since I'd seen her. Then again, my memories were fuzzy, distant, out of reach. "Maybe one day. Alexandria is busy with her life."

"No, Mrs. Fitzgerald. She's been here—every day. She's been takin' care of you. She's the one who's been bossing around your nurses."

"I-I thought it was a dream."

"No dream. It's real." Jane squeezed my hand.

My heart leapt as the beeps of the machines created an even rhythm. I tried to think. If Alexandria had really been with me, could Oren have been too? "Whom else, Jane? Whom else has come to see me?"

Jane shrugged. "I don't know exactly. Mr. Fitzgerald and Mr. Spencer, they come with Miss Alex.

"Ma'am, your head… does it hurt?"

I assessed my head. "No, it doesn't." Squinting my eyes, I asked, "Why would Alexandria be here with Mr. Spencer?"

"They… well, they engaged. There's a big party tonight at the manor to announce it, all official-like."

"What? Why? What happened to Lennox?"

"Her beau from New York?" Jane shook her head. "She came back. She's doing what she need to do."

I tried to lift my arm. "Jane, help me sit up." My right arm was attached to a web of tubes. There were only two needles, but each one divided and split. I tugged again. "I want out of here. I need to see my daughter, to talk to her."

She reached for the button and sat me up. "I was with her last night. She might not be able to be here today. She has that party, but, ma'am, she'll do her best to come Sunday."

"Sunday? What day is… try? What do you mean?"

"Mr. Spencer… he—"

No. I couldn't let her do that. I pulled harder. The needles tugged against my skin and pulled at the tape. "Jane, get these out. I need to talk to her. She can't…" I tugged harder. "This doesn't need…"

Alarms sounded.

Beep! Beep!

Sirens wailed and lights flashed their echoes and flickers filling the room.

"W-what's happening?" Jane asked as the door flew open. It bounced off the wall as person after person rushed into the small space, shouting orders.

"Ma'am, get out."

"Miss Collins said—"

"Ma'am…"

A man in scrubs pushed Jane backward as others rushed toward my monitors.

"Please, let her stay!"

Jane's big brown eyes opened wider as they backed her away.

"Wait! Jane, tell Alexandria…"

A woman pulled at my IV. I turned in time to watch her insert a syringe.

"Please, no. I want those out. Jane…"

Voices faded… the room disappeared.

Had it been real? Had I really talked to Jane?

Or was it make-believe? My mind playing tricks. Maybe it was a performance, a play, and the curtain had fallen. The scene was over… and now the theater was empty.

"J-Jane…" I tried to scream. "No!" The word didn't come. My lips no longer moved.

So heavy. Everything was so heavy.

"Wake up, Adelaide, I'm here. You're safe."

As his gorgeous blue eyes filled my vision, small crinkles formed in their corners. I pushed back toward the pillow and admired the incredible man in my bed. More accurately, the man in the bed we were sharing.

I lifted my palm to his cheek and savored the abrasive beard growth. Before my thoughts could wander, I said, "I'm sorry, Oren. Did I wake you?"

Warm lips peppered my forehead as his masculine scent filled my senses. Cologne mixed with intensity. It was an addicting potion, one I needed to quit, but like every other addiction, I'd been too weak. That was part of my nightmare, the part that I didn't want to do.

I inhaled, letting the magic scent enveloping us settle my taut nerves.

"I'd wake with you every day," he said.

"I didn't mean to… I was dreaming."

Oren sat up and pulled me toward him. Resting my head on his chest filled my ears with the rhythmic beat of his heart. Without thinking, my fingers found their way to his fine, dark chest hair. I twirled the softness with my manicured nails as I relished his strong arm around my shoulder.

His deep voice rumbled through his chest. "It sounded a little less like a dream and more like a nightmare."

I shrugged in his embrace. "I don't want to talk about it."

Oren shifted, laying me back on the pillow and hovering above. "Adelaide, how many years have we been seeing one another?"

I extended my bottom lip, playing up my Southern charm. "Don't you know?"

His nose came close to mine as warm breath skirted my cheeks. "I know the number of minutes. My point is that there's nothing you can say that I can't hear. You've heard my woes, my regrets. How, after that, could I ever hold anything against you?"

I lifted my lips to his. "You see, Mr. Demetri, I'm not a good woman. I'm an unfaithful wife. That's a mortal sin. I'm doomed to hell. There's nothing I can do about it."

His features contorted. *"Adelaide, that pains me. I'm the cause of your damnation, but I do believe there's one recourse for salvation."*

"You do? And what would that be... confession?"

"You just confessed."

"Then what can I do to do to find redemption?"

I knew the answer. I just didn't want to say it.

He reached for my hand, bringing it out from under the blanket. "You replace this ring with mine."

A lump formed in my throat. "I-I—"

"Don't say you won't...or say you can't... say not yet."

"Oren, my future is set. It has been."

"My love, you've already experienced damnation. It's time for you to experience the life you deserve. You've been in hell. Let me give you a slice of heaven."

I began to speak, but his firm lips captured mine, taking away my rebuttal.

"Not yet..." he encouraged. "You can say it."

I shook my head. "I can't hurt you any more than I have. I won't give you false hope."

"What about you?"

"What about me?"

"Don't you deserve hope?" he asked.

"No. I don't. I don't deserve any of this. But Alexandria does."

"She's still in high school."

"Yes, she has so much ahead of her."

"And so should you."

My eyes closed. It was my nightmare, the one I'd been dreading. "Oren," I took a deep breath. Securing the sheet over my breasts, I moved to the edge of the bed. "I-I came to see you this last time for a reason."

He moved behind me, his scruffy chin on my shoulder. "Adelaide, not the last. We have our entire lives. You can see me for whatever reason you want. The sky is blue. The grass is green. I'm available for you whenever."

I shook my head. "It's not fair." I stood and paced, the sheet creating a flowing train that twisted around my legs as I walked back and forth. "I've been thinking about Angelina."

"About Angelina? Why?"

"The two of you... you deserve to find that again. I'm holding you back."

Oren stood, his voice booming. "What the hell?"

It was my nightmare. The man I loved... I knew he was capable of darkness—he had to be. He couldn't have confessed to the things he'd said he'd done without a dark side. Yet, I'd never seen it.

Not until now.

As his features morphed I took a step back, anticipating the anger from my nightmare. The more I'd thought about this day, this goodbye, the more frequent the nightmares came. It was time. I had to face him. I had to face the change from Oren to Alton.

Maybe part of me wanted that. I needed to see it to truly walk away.

"Adelaide, I found that kind of love... in you. You are il mio amore. I don't want any other woman."

His love.

Tears filled my eyes. "No. This has gone on too long. For years—years that you could have been with someone out in the open, someone who could be with you day in and day out, and someone who could help you care for Lennox and Silvia. I've been selfish."

As Oren reached for my shoulders, I flinched.

"Stop it," he said, not letting me go.

"Please..."

"Adelaide, you know I'd never hurt you. I told you the truth. I wanted you to know what I'd done. Be honest with me. Is that the reason you want to end this, because of him? Because you can't be with a man like me?"

A man like him... A loving, kind, and forgiving man. A man whose mere presence makes my heart beat faster and whose words melt my insides until there's nothing left that could possibly stand without his strong arms. Was that what he meant?

No.

He'd asked me if I could live with a man who'd done dark, terrible things. A man who'd done what he needed to do, not only for his goals, but for his family and dreams. A man who'd done what my father had demanded.

I could live my life with him. I wanted Oren with everything in me.

Russell's fate was sealed with or without Oren Demetri the day he threatened to leave me and take Alexandria.

I would live with what Oren had done. I could love him for the rest of my life, but that answer wouldn't sever this relationship. It wouldn't set this wonderful man free.

I lifted my chin. "I can't. It was fun while it lasted, but no. I can't."

Oren's hands dropped, their gentle grip leaving my shoulders and falling to his sides. "I thought…"

"You thought wrong. I've had a good time, but it's time I work on my marriage."

"He's a pig. You'll accept him over me?"

A thousand times no.

"Yes." As his blue eyes lost their luster, it was confirmed. I didn't deserve Oren Demetri. Straightening my shoulders, I walked to the bathroom. "Goodbye, Oren. Please leave."

"Momma?"

I didn't try to respond. It wasn't any more real than Oren or Jane.

CHAPTER 39

◦●◦○●◦

ALEXANDRIA

As we approached, I saw Jane pacing nervously outside Momma's door.

"What happened?" I asked, rushing ahead of Suzanna.

Jane's dark eyes overflowed with tears, leaving her cheeks damp. "Oh, Miss Alex, she was talking. She was good... so good." She reached for my hands. "And then she got upset. She wanted to talk to you. I didn't know you was coming. She pulled at her IVs. Alarms and lights. They all came running in... They gave her more medicine."

"She was talking?"

Jane nodded. "Yes. I told her you were here. She thought she'd dreamed you." A hint of a smile blossomed behind her sadness. "I told her that you was real. You are."

"What's this all about?" Suzanna asked, coming up to us.

Jane stood taller and wiped her cheeks.

"Momma was awake and talking," I explained.

"And you're upset? Why? Why aren't we in there? What did she say?"

Jane turned toward her. "She asked questions."

"What questions?"

"She asked who visited her."

"Oh, Jane..." I said. "She's going to be better."

291

Jane nodded hopefully.

"What did she remember?" Suzanna asked. "Was she hallucinating?"

I turned. "Why would you assume she was hallucinating?"

"Dear, I'm not assuming. I know how delusional she'd been."

Jane spoke to me. "Miss Collins, whatever they gave her knocked her out real fast. I'm worried it's hurting her."

I looked past her into the room. There were three people standing around her bed. "I'll find out."

Suzanna reached for my arm. "They are doctors and nurses. I'd assume they know more about her care than a maid."

"Excuse me?"

"What?"

"Suzanna, thank you for coming here with me. I'd like some privacy as I speak to Momma's doctors."

"I didn't come *with* you. You wouldn't be here without me." She adjusted the purse hanging from her wrist and turned back to Jane. "Why are you here? Do you not have enough work at the manor to keep you busy?"

"She has plenty of work. I asked her to come here. Momma asked for her."

"She asked for *you?*" Suzanna asked, her nose wrinkling on the last word.

"Yes, ma'am, she did. Miss Collins, you let me know what I can do for your momma."

I reached for her hand. "Jane, come with me to talk to the doctors. You were there. You can tell them what happened." I turned to Suzanna. "Be a dear..." My tone dripped with sugar, sweeter than Southern sweet tea. "...give us a minute. There's a beautiful courtyard. If you go and have a seat, I'll have a nice cup of coffee sent out there. Once we know what's happening, I'll come get you."

"Bryce would not be pleased."

My eyes opened wide and hands flew to my chest. "I'd hope not! I'm sure someone as empathetic as your son would be devastated that my momma was on the edge of recovery and took a downward spiral." I leaned closer. "That is what you meant? Wasn't it?"

"Well..."

I waved to a man in an all-white uniform. "Sir, could you please get my future mother-in-law a cup of coffee with cream and two sugars? She'll be in the courtyard."

"Yes, ma'am." He turned to Suzanna. "May I show you the way?"

Her chin lifted. "Alexandria, I'll be back in ten minutes."

"I can't wait."

I reached for Jane's hand and tugged her into Momma's room. The bottom of the door scraped against the floor as it opened.

"I told you—" A man spoke without turning.

I stood taller. "Excuse me. Are you speaking to me?"

The man spun. "Oh, Miss Collins…"

"What happened?"

"Your mother had another incident. We had to medicate her."

"Have you tried to find out exactly what happened?"

"She was talking," Jane volunteered.

"We don't need to ask. Your mother is closely monitored. The alarms told us all we needed to know."

I took a step forward and gasped at the ties once again around her wrists. "Undo those restraints. What is your problem?"

"She was trying to remove her IVs. You don't seem to understand that these are for her own good."

"She is unconscious. Remove them now. I'll sit with her and assure her compliance."

"Ma'am, with the amount of medication she was given, she won't be regaining consciousness for quite a while."

My skin tingled as the incompetency unraveled my last nerve. "Then remove the restraints now."

I looked at Jane as the male nurse begrudgingly released the Velcro restraints. Immediately, we both rushed to her sides and massaged her wrists. "Is there anything else you need to do to *help* her?" I asked indignantly.

"No, I'm just being sure…"

"We have it covered."

"Ma'am?"

"Go. Tell Dr. Miller I want to speak to him and let my future mother-in-law in the courtyard know that plans have changed. I need to stay here until Dr. Miller arrives."

"Ma'am, the doctor isn't scheduled to be here until later this afternoon."

I pulled a chair beside Momma's bed. "Not a problem. I'll wait."

Once we were alone, Jane leaned close. "Child, I can stay."

"We can both stay."

"What about the party?"

"The guests don't arrive until six. I'll be back by then."

"I thought you said Mr. Spencer wasn't going to let you come here today?"

"I'm here. He wants me over at Carmichael Hall."

Jane grinned. "But you're staying here?"

"Yes, Jane. I am."

Her smile broadened.

The news didn't go over as well with Suzanna.

As she entered the room, it was obvious that it was her first visit. Her hand flew to her lips as she took in my momma, the bed, and the monitors. "Oh…"

Her feigned show of sensitivity didn't move me, nor did her list of reasons that I needed to return to Carmichael Hall. Though I knew my decision would come back to haunt me, I stood my ground.

"Something significant happened. I can't play nice at the party without knowing the doctor's thoughts."

Even while on phone calls with Bryce and Alton, I didn't falter.

"Jane, I do have one favor."

"Anything."

"Can you do anything to get Chelsea away from Montague Manor until closer to the party?"

Her gaze narrowed, but she didn't question. Jane had been at Montague too long. A moment later I heard her make a call. I wasn't sure to whom she spoke, but once she was done, she turned to me.

"Miss Moore will be busy today. She's going to help organize the deliveries. We've got a mighty big party happening and we need everyone's help."

"Will she still be at the manor?"

"No, Miss Alex. Miss Moore will be all over Savannah confirming the suppliers. It would've been me, but I'm busy."

I took a deep breath. "Thank you."

Once I'd upset everyone, I settled next to Momma on one side of her bed and Jane on the other. Even with the steady beeps of the monitors, cold room, and blind-covered window, it was the most relaxed I'd been since I arrived. I was with the only two people who cared for me—and whom I cared for—at Montague Manor.

"Was she really coherent?" I asked, keeping my voice low.

"She was," Jane whispered. "The other day, while I was out working with suppliers for the party, I stopped by Dr. Beck's office."

"You did?"

She nodded. "I don't know if it good or bad. The test... it didn't show any poisonous metals. He thought with the old house, maybe lead, but no. Everything show that the medicine in her... it was what he prescribed her."

My heart sank. "So she *did* overdose?"

"I don't think it's that simple. I told Dr. Beck, just like I told you: she didn't have the pills. I did. I still have them. Dr. Beck didn't give her more. The medicine they found in her with those tests was the same as what he'd prescribed. I just don't think it was hers."

"What about her preventive medication? They say she stopped taking it."

Jane shook her head. "She took it every day. I know what they say, but many mornings I watched her take it, even after she start having problems. I made sure she took it. I don't understand why..."

I took a deep breath, letting Jane's words penetrate my thoughts. Alton was a fucking genius. It was the perfect overdose: slip Momma more of the medicine she already took—a lot more.

After he and I had met with Dr. Miller, the minute I had my school-approved tablet, I'd looked up the side effects of opioids: headaches, dizziness, vomiting. Essentially, too much Vicodin and Momma would think she was having a migraine. Increase the dosage and get the added benefits of anxiety, shakiness, and erratic behavior. Combine that with alcohol, another depressant... memory and sleeping issues. Take away her preventive headache medicine. It was the perfect storm.

"This morning, was she really that out of control? Did they need to subdue her?"

"I've seen your momma more upset, a lot more. If they let me, I would have talked to her. She just wanted you."

Her words gripped my chest, squeezing my heart. "I-I…"

Jane reached for my hand. "She needs us."

"I'm trying."

"Is it wrong," Jane asked, "that I'm worried about her, more worried about her here?"

I swallowed. "No. I am too."

I wasn't sure how Nox's people planned to help my mother and get her out of here, but with each passing minute, I was thankful they were. I was also worried that they wouldn't succeed. Looking at my momma, I feared that if they failed, she was out of options.

CHAPTER 40

―●○●―

ALEXANDRIA

JANE AND I slipped into the back of the manor, forgoing the front door. Just before making my way up to my room, I remembered Chelsea.

I worked my way to her room, avoiding the first floor. After all, it was a madhouse. There were people everywhere, arranging flowers, setting up buffets, and stocking various bars. I'd forgotten to ask Jane how many people were invited. Maybe it wasn't forgetfulness as much as apathy. I didn't give a shit.

Gently I knocked on Chelsea's door and waited.

"Hello?"

"Chels, it's me."

The door opened. I hadn't seen her since last night. She was wearing slacks and a blouse with her hair in a ponytail. Though her cheek was covered with makeup, the purple showed through.

"God. I'm sorry that I arranged for you to go out like that."

She shrugged as she opened the door further, walked to a table, and picked up a pair of sunglasses. "The advantage of Georgia, even in November, is it's usually sunny." She slipped on the glasses, covering the bruise. "Besides, I was happy to get out of here."

"Have you seen him?" I asked, not having time to dance around the elephant in the room.

She shook her head. "No, but he called. He was pissed that I wasn't waiting here. He said you stood him up, so it was my job..."

She didn't finish. She didn't need to.

I took her hand and pulled her to the bathroom. Once the door was shut and she took off the sunglasses, shame and sadness shone in her hazel eyes, but there were no tears. It made me proud of my friend. Hopefully, she was done shedding them over bad choices and assholes.

"I'm afraid we screwed up," I confessed.

"Why?"

"Your room. I've assumed mine was bugged, but yesterday when we spoke..." The thoughts increased my pulse. "...I'm afraid they may now know about my connection to Infidelity."

Chelsea sighed. "Yeah, I'd hate for me to be the only whore."

I took a step back.

"No," she quickly replied. "I'm sorry. I'm mad. I'm scared. I'm lashing out at you... because I can. I didn't mean it."

Though I'd felt the impact, I understood. "I'm getting you out tonight. I told you my plan. It'll work. The downstairs is buzzing. By later, it will be total chaos and confusion."

"Did you know that there were thirty-two floral arrangements delivered?" Chelsea asked. "Thirty-two big ones! Helping to coordinate all of that was part of my job today. There's a kitchen with cooks and yet the caterers brought more cooks and over twenty servers." She shook her head. "I can't imagine your wedding."

"Well, don't. I'm getting out before that happens. He scares me, too."

"Alex, what will happen to your mom?"

I let out a long breath. "Hopefully Nox can help." I couldn't say more. What if the bathroom was bugged? What if Bryce got ahold of Chelsea and forced her to confess?

As he'd said about our day's plans... there were too many variables.

"You haven't been summoned to the party, have you?"

Chelsea shook her head. "The opposite."

I stood taller, tilting my head. "What does that mean?"

"When *he* called, he told me to stay here in this room. He said if things didn't go well at the party, he wanted to know he had an option..." She expelled a deep breath as her hands fell to her sides. "If you don't *behave*—that was the word he used—I'll be punished. He wants to know his 'whore' is available."

I reached for her shoulders. "No one, no one," I repeated, "deserves to be treated like he's treating you. I don't give a shit what the agreement says. Deloris will get you out of it." I touched her cheek. "Abuse is an out—I believe one that may even come with compensation. They should fucking screen their clients better."

"I don't even care anymore about the money. I did. I've saved most of it. But what good is putting my sister through school if I'm not alive to see her graduate?"

She paced a small circle. "But... are you sure? I don't want to leave you, and I don't want to stay."

"It won't be for long. I can't do this either. I've accomplished some of what I set out to do. I know things. I've seen things. If I wouldn't have come here... well, I did. Now I need to do what someone has asked me to do more times than I can count. I need to trust in him."

"You're not talking about Bryce?"

"Hell no!" I looked down at my watch. "I need to go get ready. I'll be back. When I do, it won't be for long. I know what Bryce said, but hang out in my room until it's time. I'll *behave*." The word tasted sour. "He won't have any reason to come up here. Keep the door locked. It'll make me feel better."

Chelsea nodded. "I love you."

"Like a sister," I said, kissing her unmarred cheek.

FRESHLY SHOWERED, MY hair dried but not yet styled, with a robe wrapped around me, I decided to assess the dress I'd be wearing. All I'd been told was that it would cover my breasts. I hadn't really been told that, but that's what Bryce implied as he pinched my nipple to elicit my attention. It was the area the dress would cover... where he could bruise.

I pushed those thoughts to the back of my mind. I couldn't revive the fright of last night, the inevitability of his threat… I couldn't do that and stand beside him playing the perfect fiancée role.

Instead, I worked to conjure thoughts of my childhood friend, the one afraid of Nessie—the monster our mothers had concocted to keep us from the lake. Ironic that they'd made up a beast to keep us safe when my living with one was their goal.

Even the childhood memories were tarnished. Had anything been real?

Of course not, this was the world of smoke and mirrors.

As I lifted the new garment bag from the rack in my closet, the sound of knocking warned me of another intrusion.

Fuck!

Please don't be Bryce.

"Hello?" I asked through the locked door.

"Alexandria?"

After releasing the wedged key, I pulled it open. Peering modestly around the edge, I eyed Suzanna up and down. Her dress was pristine, a sapphire blue with a scooped neckline and her hair was styled in some throwback beehive from the sixties. Okay, it was more of a bouffant, but it still looked ridiculous. Her eye makeup was overdone and lips were too red. If the intent had been to make her look younger, she'd missed the mark.

"Suzanna," I cooed. "Don't you look lovely? What can I do for you?"

Her lips pursed. "Open the door. I was going to tell you this morning, but… well, plans changed."

"What? I'm so sorry I wasn't able to spend the afternoon with you and Bryce. But yes, my mother is resting comfortably. Thank you for asking."

Clearing her throat, she stepped to the side, allowing her entourage to come into view.

"Open the door. Your team of stylists hasn't much time."

"Stylists? I don't need…" My protests fell on deaf ears as Suzanna and three other women bulldozed their way into my suite. Within minutes my bathroom was transformed into a salon. Straighteners and curling irons of all widths lined the marble counter while palettes of foundation, blush, and eye shadow littered any available spaces.

A chair was brought in, and I was encouraged to sit and obey.

Though I repeated my objection, soon I was doing as I'd been bid while Suzanna was filling me in on the upcoming festivities.

Looking at her watch, she laid out the schedule. "Though it's supposed to begin at six, guests may arrive sooner. The staff is ready to greet them. The bars and hors d'oeuvres will be ready. Your father and I will welcome everyone as they first arrive." She leaned toward the mirror and ran her finger through the creases of her open mouth, as if it could help the garish color. "Of course," she went on, "he doesn't plan to do that for long. He's expecting a list of distinguished VIP guests, many of whom he'll be entertaining privately in his den."

Did my stepfather sing and dance and I'd been blissfully unaware for over twenty years? I would've asked but the brush tugging my hair from one direction, sponges applying layers of foundation to my face from another, while at the same time my nails were receiving a glistening coat of gel, kept my rebukes to a minimum.

"I've told Bryce to join you up here—"

"Why?" I managed to interrupt.

I'd avoided him all day, minus a few calls. I didn't want to see him until we were surrounded by tens or hundreds of guests. The more the merrier.

"So… the two of you can make a grand entrance." She said it like it was as obvious as the too-low scoop of her neckline.

"And what time should we enter?"

"Not until after 6:30."

My stomach sank. "Is Bryce here?"

"Not yet. It's nearly 5:20. I expect him soon. Can you believe it? The cars have already begun to line up at the gate." She was almost giddy. "This is truly *the* social event. Your wedding… oh, it will be spectacular! I've told Bryce to come in another entrance."

I could barely form the words. "Y-you did? Which one?"

"The one near the curing barns is the closest."

I let out a breath. Thank God it wasn't the old road.

"The guards would never allow guests to enter there," she went on. "It's only for field workers, but on this occasion, I believe it will help Bryce avoid the traffic jam."

Suzanna reached for my shoulder as my hands were occupied. My nails were busy drying under little purple lights. "Isn't this the most exciting?" Her voice screeched with delight. "I bet Mildred Ashmore is green, just positively green!"

Mildred was Millie's mother. No doubt they'd been working day and night on Millie and Ian's wedding. After all, that was the reason Millie couldn't go on to graduate school.

As soon as the small contraption dinged, Suzanna pulled my hand from the light and stared at my engagement ring "And wait until they all see this! It'll be the talk of the town—no, of the nation. Who cares about the Kardashians? Quick-rich trash if you ask me. The Carmichaels and Fitzgeralds *and* the Montagues... this is what real American royalty is made of."

I began to remind her that the Fitzgeralds weren't part of the equation when the woman with a palette, one that looked like an artist's board, told me to close my eyes and open them wide.

"How do I...?" I began to ask.

She demonstrated. Her eyes closed, brow lengthened, and lips set to an oblong 'O.'

While I did as she said, Suzanna continued her monologue.

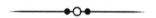

THE CLOCK SAID a little past six as two of the women secured an ivory lace dress over my head and fastened the row of buttons. It landed just above my knees; nevertheless, for some this could be a wedding dress. I suspected it cost as much as most. I'd seen the tag. The name alone added ten thousand dollars to the price tag, probably more.

Priorities at Montague Manor seemed to be awry. Alton called my law school education a frivolous waste of money. He threatened to stop all funding of my mother's private care, and yet he authorized a Gucci cocktail dress and a catered party for only God knew how many.

"Wait until you see these shoes!" Suzanna exclaimed as she opened a box.

Inside was a sparkling pair of strappy crystal sandals. The narrow heel had to be at least four inches. "They're Jimmy Choo."

"Yes, I recognize the name inside the shoe."

"Oh, Alexandria, don't you see? Once you marry Bryce, nothing is outside your budget."

What the hell? The woman was living in a fantasy world.

"You do realize that it's all mine, right?"

"What, dear?" she asked as she lifted a shoe, watching the colored reflections of light bounce off the embedded crystals.

"The money," I explained, "the name… it's mine. I don't need to marry Bryce for that."

My words sullied her joyous expression. "But you do. If you don't, you lose it all. You read the will. Consider your coming of age in this house simply a preview of the life you can have."

"Miss," one of the women said, "let me help you with the shoes. We don't want to risk the nail polish."

I sat, slipping my feet into each shoe while biting back my response. It wouldn't be productive, and it could alert her, if not to my plan, at least to my intentions. None of which included marrying her psychotic son.

Instead, I feigned a smile, perfectly maneuvering my painted lips. "You're right, and more than that, it secures your spot. Queen Regent?"

Suzanna's microexpression faltered, but not for long. She was the queen of illusion. With a dutiful grin, she replied, "Dear, I'm just here to help Bryce and fill in wherever your mother is unable to do so. Once she's back, it'll be as it always has been."

I wanted to ask how exactly that was, but I didn't get the chance.

Another clock had struck the witching hour. Not literally, but the demons were gathering nevertheless.

"And really," Suzanna went on, "I must get down to your father and help him greet the guests. You know how he is when people are late?"

"I'd say you already are."

She waved her hand dismissively. "Once he sees how stunning you look, he'll understand." Though I had my back turned, I heard her open the door.

"Mother?"

My neck stiffened. I didn't need to see to know who was standing at the threshold of my room. I hadn't let Bryce enter this room since we were teenagers, and now he was here.

"Bryce," Suzanna cooed. "Don't you look handsome? Come on in…"

It didn't matter. I wasn't the one to offer the invitation.

Slowly, I stood and turned. Our eyes met.

CHAPTER 41

─●○●─

ALEXANDRIA

"ALEXANDRIA, STUNNING!"

I secured my smile, the one Bryce had told me to wear. My gaze scanned him from head to toe, assessing him as he was me. His gray suit was tailored to fit, trimmer at the waist, wider at the shoulders. The legs were slightly narrower than the ones Nox wore, yet still considered stylish. He had on an ivory vest, tie, and handkerchief that matched the color of my dress and a white starched shirt.

I stepped closer, reaching for his shoulder. "You're very handsome yourself."

Lifting my hand, Bryce leaned toward me and inhaled. "Aww, is that perfume you're wearing? It's an improvement over cologne."

I swallowed my rebuttal and spoke words he'd want to hear. "The only cologne I want to wear is yours."

Bryce stepped back, holding me at arm's length. "This is an improvement."

I stepped forward, pressing myself against him, and kissed his cheek. "This is our party, our formal engagement. I know I've fought this outcome, but being with Momma..." I tugged his hand, pulling him toward the yellow bench at the end of my bed. As we sat,

I continued, "...being with her today..."

My long mascara-covered lashes veiled my gaze. "Thank you for understanding and allowing me to be there."

He didn't speak, but ran his hands over my arms. I consciously didn't flinch as he tested the area that yesterday was sore. It still was, but I didn't mention it.

"...when I was with Momma," I continued, "I realized that this is happening. I could fight you and Alton, but what good would it do? Bryce, she was better for a little bit. She spoke to Jane, but then they medicated her. I can't leave her. I won't."

"And this?" He motioned between us.

"Is my future. Momma tried to tell me. You tried to tell me. I didn't listen. Next week I want to transfer to Savannah for the rest of my schooling."

Bryce narrowed his eyes. "Alton thinks it's a waste of money."

"After we're married it doesn't matter what he thinks. That's what the will said. It'll all be ours... As my husband, you'll make the decisions, not Alton."

With each phrase his chest inflated, bigger and bigger, like a balloon. If I kept going would he pop or maybe fly away?

"Children?" he asked, not leaving any stone unturned.

"I suppose it's something we need to discuss."

He ran his hand over my knee. Unlike the night before, it wasn't forceful. On the contrary, it was meant to be enticing as he moved his splayed fingers under my dress.

"Talking won't make heirs."

Heirs. I hated that word.

I laid my hand on his, the fabric of my dress separating our touch. "No... and neither will coming in my mouth or on my breasts..." I was using his threat from last night. "I believe my momma would love to have grandchildren running these lawns."

"Like we used to do?" He moved closer until his chest was against mine. Removing his hand from my thigh, he laid it over my breasts. "Your heart is beating fast."

It was. Like a warning, it was about ready to leap from my chest.

"Because I'm nervous."

"Of?"

"Them… downstairs."

"Why?"

"What if they don't believe us? What if they assume I'm pregnant?"

His lips covered mine, stopping my questions. I moaned as his tongue probed.

It was more of a 'yuck' but I prayed that wasn't the way it sounded. "Bryce?" I finally managed.

"You're going to do this? You're going to behave?"

I shook my head. "No, it's not about behaving. It's about facing the facts. We're going to be married. Last night… you…" I stood. "I didn't like it. I don't want to be afraid of my own husband. I can't live like that."

He stood. Even in my four-inch heels, Bryce was taller. Not as tall as Nox, but tall enough to be threatening. I'd been working on my speech all day in my head while sitting with Momma and Jane, even during the useless meeting with Dr. Miller. I'd hoped I could deliver it in small snippets as mingling allowed. Never had I intended to be alone with him, but now that I was, I hoped I sounded convincing.

"Chelsea?" he asked, his neck straightening.

"Your whore?" I corrected.

A satisfied grin covered his face, his ruddy cheeks lifting under his gray eyes and gelled-back blond hair. "Go on."

"I-I don't want to share you, but if I have to, I'd prefer not to be reminded every day."

He nodded. "I believe we can find some common ground."

"Savannah Law?" I asked again.

Bryce lifted my hand, bringing the diamond near his lips as he kissed my knuckles. "Let's get through tonight. The most important thing is that you've come to terms with leaving Columbia."

I nodded.

"Say it."

I hated this man.

"I've come to terms with not going back to Columbia after finishing this semester."

"Nice add."

"Thank you. We won't be married until December 24. The semester will be complete and besides, Alton said—"

"Alton doesn't know what I know. He doesn't know about the magical changing dress. I suggest you concentrate on keeping in my good graces." He shrugged. "No doubt you've seen my whore today?"

Each time he casually referred to her in that manner was like a slap. The bruises just didn't show. Maybe that was his intention.

"Yes, we've spoken."

"Remember, only you can keep her from your punishment."

I reached again for his shoulder. "I want that too. I promise."

Again his lips covered mine. This time his hand roamed up and down my side, over the row of individual satin buttons. When his kiss ended, he reached for my hand and turned me, making me pirouette in my sparkling shoes on the balls of my feet.

"Tell me there's a zipper under those buttons."

My cheeks lifted and head tilted suggestively. "I can't. Just think how the anticipation will build."

"Go," he said. "I've smeared your lipstick. They'll be expecting us."

Once in the bathroom, I fixed the lipstick, taking away the smears and adding another coat. As I did, I secured my necklace in the gap of my bra and I lifted the diamond choker that had come with my ensemble. Like the ring I wore, it was ostentatious and would be noticed by everyone.

"Bryce?" I called through the cracked-open door.

The door moved as he stood in the threshold. "Yes?"

I lifted the choker toward him. "Could you help? The stylists left before they put this on."

He reached for the necklace and stood behind me. Our gazes met in the mirror as he secured the diamonds around my neck. Leaning down, he kissed the area behind my ear. I closed my eyes, blocking him out, hating myself, and again hoping it appeared differently.

"Alex, I want this too."

Alex.

Once the clasp was secure, I spun toward him until my arms were around his neck. "Can we forget yesterday?"

"That's up to you, darling."

"Me?"

"Tomorrow we'll discuss it."

In other words, it depended upon how well I played my role. I nodded. "Tomorrow."

He took my hand and led me toward the stairs. Just before we made it to the landing, I stopped.

"Oh, I forgot my handbag."

"Why do you need a handbag; you're in your own house?"

"I can't run up here every time I want to freshen my makeup." I pursed my lips. "You, Mr. Spencer, may have a history with women and whores but you have learning to do when it comes to getting used to a wife."

He smiled. "Hurry. We're supposed to be down there."

"I will," I called over my shoulder as I skidded around the corner and down the hallway. I moved quickly past my door to Chelsea's. One knock and the door opened. I reached into my bra and handed her what she needed for her escape.

"Are you sure?" she whispered.

"Shh," I whispered as I nodded and looked back toward the landing. As her door closed, I rushed back to my suite. Taking a deep breath, I ran toward the bathroom and found my purse. It was crystal encrusted, a Jimmy Choo, and matched the shoes. Before I could exit, I came to a stop, teetering on my heels.

"What?" I asked, assessing Bryce's expression. Had he followed me? Did he see me with Chelsea? I waited.

"I thought you said you were hurrying?"

Dismissively I shook my head and released a breath. "Again, you have some learning to do. This *is* hurrying." I lifted the tube of lipstick and dropped it into the purse. "My handbag's no good if there isn't lipstick inside."

Shaking his head, Bryce offered me his arm. Placing my hand in the crook, I looked up at his gray eyes.

"Are you ready?" he asked.

"Let's get this show started."

Dog-and-pony show. Things never change.

All eyes turned our direction as we descended the stairs. It was a sea of people. I smiled as I scanned for familiar faces. The foyer was becoming more crowded as people continued to flow in.

"It's the guards," Bryce whispered as we continued our descent. "Alton's stationed extra men. He's very specific about who can enter. They're doing a rigorous screening. It's taking longer than normal for everyone to arrive."

The foyer was almost full yet the door continued to open. As the stairs curved I saw the crowd extending toward the sitting room, parlors, and den. There were people everywhere. "There's more coming?"

"Over a hundred invitations were sent, so that's at least two hundred people."

I gripped his arm tighter. "For an *engagement* party?"

His gray eyes widened. "You should see Mother's guest list for the wedding."

"Alexandria! Edward!"

"Congratulations!"

We moved about the rooms. It was difficult and slow. Everyone wanted to talk to us, to hear our story, how our love had survived through the years.

"Alexandria," Shirley Carroll came up, extending her hand.

"Mrs. Carroll, let me introduce my fiancé, Edward Spencer."

Bryce gallantly took her hand. "Carroll? You can't be Senator Carroll's wife. Daughter perhaps?"

I nearly rolled my eyes. Was this seriously how he did business? No wonder Nox thought he was a slime. He had used-car-salesman written all over him.

"Oh, Mr. Spencer, aren't you the most?"

"He is," I confirmed. "And where is your husband?"

She shrugged. "I don't know. As soon as Doyle arrived, he was whisked off to some secret men's club."

Bryce's arm tensed under my touch.

I turned his way. "Do you think you should be included? This is *your* party." I was hoping I was reminding him that after our wedding, he would be in charge, not Alton.

"I…" He scanned the crowd, no doubt taking note of who was missing.

"Really," I cooed. "I'd love to show Mrs. Carroll around and mingle. I saw Millie and Jess in the crowd. I promise that I'll be fine. I'd hate for important discussions to happen without you."

His chest grew as the buttons on the ivory vest strained.

"Oh dear," Shirley Carroll said to me, "get used to this kind of thing. It's the way it is. The men always have life-and-death decisions in the balance."

Bryce turned, put his hand on mine, and leaned in for a kiss. "People are watching."

I feigned a laugh. "There are hundreds of eyes, now go."

A waiter approached offering Mrs. Carroll and I a flute of champagne. After we each took one, I nodded. "Can I show you around?"

"That would be fabulous. I've never been to Savannah before…"

"Alex," Pat said a few minutes later, coming up beside me. "Have you seen my significant other?"

"I haven't. I haven't even seen you." I turned to Shirley. "Mrs. Carroll, this is my dear cousin, Patrick Richardson. Pat, may I introduce you to Shirley Carroll, Senator Carroll's wife."

"From… California?"

"Why, yes. I didn't think that people in Georgia would know that."

Pat's lips quirked. "I am from here. However, now I live with my partner in New York. It's your husband's work regarding the legalization of cultivating marijuana that I'm familiar with."

I worked to not give Pat a double take.

"Yes, it's something he's hoping to push on a national level…"

Once Shirley Carroll stepped aside to speak to someone else, I asked, "What do you know about the legalized marijuana cultivation?"

Pat shrugged. "Nothing. Or I didn't until last night. While you and I were trying to talk, Spence was giving Cy an earful. According to Cy, Spence was spouting statistics about the potential of growing and manufacturing cannabis in Georgia and then shipping it to states where it's legal. Just as with tobacco, the environment here has great potential for marijuana growth. Unfortunately, that's currently illegal. Your friend Senator Higgins is working on a new bill.

"He was telling Cy that with the added support of representatives in states like California…"

CHAPTER 42

OREN

I CHECKED MY watch. Deloris was securing the video loop at precisely eight o'clock. The staff change at Magnolia Woods happened at seven. That meant that the nurse currently on duty was Adelaide's night nurse until five in the morning. Our surveillance had enlightened us as to much about the staff's habits. While some of the nurses—who Deloris discovered were rarely actually registered nurses—napped in a nearby chair waiting for alarms or commotion from their patients, others read or stared for hours on end at their cell phones, no doubt heightening their social media status with pictures of kittens and puppies or better yet, political propaganda.

Adelaide's nurse, a big burly man named Mack, was fond of his social media, yet he often chose sleeping as his favorite way to pass the time.

As I eased through the entry from the courtyard—the one that Isaac had left unlocked—I envisioned the scenes I'd watched multiple times. I recalled Mack securing Adelaide's hands. I heard his tenor as he mocked her social status, calling her an addict. I'd willingly taken the lives of men whose crimes were less offensive.

I scanned right and left. The hallway was clear. Though I kept my face down and away from the cameras, to the possible passerby I shouldn't be noticed. I looked the part, complete with the white lab coat—identical to the ones worn by the doctors on staff—and an electronic name badge.

My anticipation grew as step by step, I made my way toward her room. Though I'd watched her through the Magnolia Woods feed in Deloris's suite, it had been years since I'd seen her, face to face. That is, unless dreams count as reality.

It was 8:02. The surveillance from Adelaide's room was now on loop. To anyone viewing it, it would show whatever had happened in the last hour, over and over, until Deloris released the live feed.

Without hesitation, I opened the door. The swishing against the tile alerted Mack that I'd entered. It was unfortunate—for him—that the sound hadn't told him more about his future or lack thereof. Yet rarely was that as obvious.

Perhaps that was a blessing.

Immediately he stood. "Doctor?" He eyed me suspiciously. "Do I know you? Visiting hours are over."

"I think you misunderstand; I'm not visiting."

Adelaide stirred and began to mumble as her head turned from side to side.

Mack turned her way. "Damn depressant is wearing off."

"O-Oren?"

Though her voice was barely a whisper, my name was clear—to me.

My heart thumped against my chest. *Not now, not yet. Don't talk.*

"Don't mind her. She's delirious. She babbles about people and names that she's made up."

"Has she said that name before?"

He stepped closer, reading my badge. "Dr. Pope? Are you new?"

"No, I'm usually here during the day. Tonight I'm covering for Miller."

"Usually they tell us—"

"Usually I don't explain myself. Tell me what's happening."

Mack stood taller. "After what happened this morning, there are strict orders—as you probably know—that this patient isn't to regain full consciousness, not for a while."

I nodded. "I was informed about what happened this morning. Did you say the medications are starting to wear off again?"

"Yes, this morning they gave her eight milligrams of Versed. As you can imagine, she's been out. If you'll sign off, I'll give her four more milligrams and some fentanyl." He laughed. "She'll be sleeping like a baby for the rest of the night."

"Is that what you recommend, Mack?"

"Yeah, I mean, the standing order is only for two milligrams, but why open the door to trouble? Her husband was pissed off about her talking this morning. The morning shift is taking shit for it. I don't want that douche upset at me."

"Is that how you discuss all our clients and their families?"

Mack shifted from foot to foot. "Yes, no, well… I'm sorry, Doctor. I-I'm used to Dr. Miller."

I nodded. "Let me see her chart."

He tilted his head toward the corner of the room to a rolling cart and computer. It was conveniently located next to Mack's favorite chair.

Swiveling the cart toward me, I looked at the screen. "I'm recommending that we take her for a CT scan. I wouldn't want that *douche* upset that his wife's brain has turned to mush from too much sedation."

"Are you serious…?" His eyes opened wide. "Radiology is closed."

"I'll make a call. You get a gurney."

"This isn't protocol and I'm not an orderly."

"No. You're also not a doctor. If I don't have a gurney in less than three minutes, you'll no longer be a night nurse at Magnolia Woods."

If I hadn't known that Deloris was watching his every move through the Magnolia Woods security feed, I may have been concerned. I wasn't. My attention was focused on Adelaide. A few minutes later, Mack was back, pushing a gurney. "I'm not sure about this… I'm supposed to stay with her."

"There's an ambulance arriving shortly from Regional. You will accompany her. She'll get the scan and be back in bed before she or her douche of a husband realizes that you were on the verge of overmedicating her."

"I-I… it's not me… it's the orders."

"Mack, stop talking and help me move her."

He looked me up and down. "Doctor? Y-you're going to help?"

I put my hands behind her shoulders. As my fingers touched her soft skin, the dam I'd built around the memories of Adelaide Montague severed. The broken shards tore at my heart, bringing an onslaught of emotion back to the desiccated organ. "Lift."

As soon as Adelaide was disconnected from the monitors and secured with her IVs, I said, "Now, on her chart…"

Mack followed me to the computer.

It was good that he had a thing for benzodiazepines. The syringe slipped effortlessly through his neck. I've heard it said that delivering an injection is like piercing the skin of an orange. That wasn't true. The human skin gives much less resistance. A sharp needle penetrates like a knife through softened butter—so can a sharp knife, but that was a story for another day.

Mack's body went slack, falling into the chair.

He was right. Eight milligrams worked fast, even on a big man like him. The difference between his injection and the one he wanted to give Adelaide was that the one that he received didn't contain the fentanyl. There was no pain control for this asshole. Only sleep, to be followed by a headache from hell. I considered it my contribution to his training. Perhaps after experiencing the side effects firsthand, he'd become more empathetic to his future patients.

His girth slumped forward in the chair, leaving his chin resting on his chest.

I could have adjusted his windpipe. Theoretically, this position restricted his airway, a common cause of asphyxiation. I shrugged. Though that hadn't been my goal, if it happened, I wouldn't lose sleep.

Using pillows, I created the illusion of a patient. It was the monitors that had been attached to Adelaide that could have been our downfall if it weren't for Deloris's physician contact. She said that they would alert the main nursing station that their patient was no longer present. In moments I created a false loop. It was similar to the video surveillance but electrical, tricking the monitors into believing that they were still connected to a body and everything was registering normally.

My phone vibrated with an incoming text.

"AMBULANCE IS HERE."

"HALLWAY CAMERAS?" I replied.

"MOMENTARILY OFFLINE. FRONT GUARD OCCUPIED AND RECEPTIONIST INDISPOSED."

I shook my head. *Indisposed?* Was someone screwing the receptionist? I didn't care. Maybe it was the guard.

Covering Adelaide's sleeping face with the blanket, I eased the gurney into the hallway. The wheels turned effortlessly on the tile floor as we passed the other patients' rooms. Each door remained closed as we glided toward the reception area.

As soon as we arrived, the front door opened, filling the entry with a gust of night air. Dressed in the emergency-transport uniform, Clayton nodded. "You called for an ambulance?"

"I did."

He reached for the foot of the gurney. "Doctor, may I help?"

Within moments, Adelaide's gurney was loaded in the back of the transport, me at her side and Clayton driving. I didn't have monitors to tell me her status. Instead, it was my hand upon her warm, bruised wrist, the thump of her pulse beneath my fingertips, and the rise and fall of her chest that reassured me she was alive. Another indication was the way my heart drummed an erratic cadence as if it had just received a life-giving electrical jolt, because if hers were to stop, surely mine would too.

It wasn't until we passed the front gate that mine finally found its normal rhythm. I sent a group text.

"WE HAVE HER."

Smoothing back her long hair, I leaned close. "Adelaide, can you hear me?"

Again her head moved from side to side. "Not real. Not real."

"Oh, *amore mio*, it's real."

CHAPTER 43

—●○●—

NOX

MY SHOES POUNDED the Georgia clay. Back and forth I paced, watching my phone: the time, Charli's app, and Oren's texts. The sky was dark, barely a sliver of moon lighting the expanse from the woods to the manor.

"Are you sure she can find the way?" I asked Isaac.

"It's not difficult. You can see the lights of the manor."

I moved to the edge of the trees. We could see it. In the distance was Montague Manor, high on a hill, ablaze with golden lighting. Even from this far away, I could make out figures as people came and went on the back patio. Each one was smaller than ants, but they were there.

My phone buzzed and I read the text.

"It's from my dad. They have Adelaide. They're rushing her to the airport."

"Step one," Isaac confirmed. "Now as long as no one at Magnolia Woods is tipped off and informs Mr. Fitzgerald."

I shook my head. "Damn, my nerves are shot. I can do deals. I can spend millions, but tonight is almost more than I can take."

"It's almost there, boss."

I eased myself to the ground and settled on a soft, grassy spot near the trees. From my new position, I had a full view of the manor and the fields in

318

between. The barren tobacco stalks stood out against the night, as the air near the ground seemed to thicken.

Was it an optical illusion?

"Deloris hacked the guest list," Isaac said, sitting near me and breaking the tension. "One hundred and twenty-two invitations."

I didn't give a shit. Not one shit. I only cared about one person.

I reconsidered. I also cared about Patrick and Chelsea, because Charli did. It was more than that with Patrick. He'd shown me more than once that he loved his cousin. Throughout this whole thing, he'd been helpful, even instrumental.

"Any names you recognize?" I asked, less interested in the guest list than I was in making time move faster. If only I could hit fast-forward. If only I could have Charli secured in a plane as Oren was doing now with Adelaide.

My gaze moved about, from the soupy landscape up to the clear sky. Above us were stars, thousands of stars. Even in Rye there weren't as many.

"Doyle and Shirley Carroll, Severus Davis and guest."

Isaac suddenly had my attention. "Are you shitting me?"

His eyes opened wide. "No, sir, I'm not. Senator and Mrs. Grant Higgins." He continued with names that seemed unlikely to be at the same gathering. Was there more to this party?

Though I struggled with the possibilities—legislation, tax breaks, marijuana—I pushed them away. Those were thoughts for another day. Now I was concentrating on the task at hand.

Isaac jumped to his feet. "She's moving!"

His words seemed almost to be an illusion. I'd imagined them so many times for them to be real. I swiped my screen, pulling up Charli's app and praying that what he'd just said was true.

"Shit!" I held my breath. The blue dot—her blue dot—was moving away from the manor. Her heart rate was elevated, but then again, she was moving fast.

"God, princess," I spoke to the app. "Don't bring attention to yourself. Be careful."

I stood, searching the horizon, hoping and praying to catch a glimpse. There was nothing in the expanse between the light of the manor and us except darkness in varying shades of gray and black. As night had fallen, so had a sparse layer of fog. Though I longed for a clearer view, I hoped that the soupy air was the cover that Charli needed—the invisibility cloak she'd spoken of wanting in her childhood—an extra layer of protection to aid her in her escape.

"I wish I could tell her that we have her mom."

"Hopefully she got out of there before anyone learned that Mrs. Fitzgerald was missing."

"I hope." My hands fisted at my impotence. When had I relied upon hope and wishes? I should fucking be running, meeting her, and saving her. "Hurry, Charli," I spoke into the darkness.

After a few minutes of country-filled silence, Isaac asked, "Miss Moore?"

Animals scurried and insects sang their songs as my nerves continued to stretch. Frogs croaked a deep, brooding melody while the occasional screech of an owl nearly bolted my blood pressure even higher.

I shook my head. "I don't know. Patrick didn't know. Only that Charli had a plan."

Trust me. Her words came back as I once again paced, my shoes becoming covered by a fine layer of red dust. Trust—I'd asked that same thing of Charli many times. Now it was my turn. I fucking hated the wait. It was hell.

No, it was worse than hell.

Hell would be my own damnation. This wasn't me. I'd willingly sacrifice myself if it were possible. Instead, the one teetering on the edge of purgatory was my love, the amazing woman, the one who owned me heart and soul.

Without her, I was in hell.

"Fifteen minutes," I said aloud.

"Sir?"

"That's what Patrick had said. He said it was a fifteen-minute walk from the manor to this road."

Isaac shook his head. "She's not walking. She's running."

My throat clenched and eyes narrowed as I scanned the horizon. Fog played tricks, erasing images and creating others.

And then it happened.

The crickets and cicadas stopped their songs. The frogs became silenced and birds stilled on the branches above. Even the breeze forgot to blow.

In the distance, coming toward us... I saw her.

She was running as fast as she could.

I couldn't wait. I couldn't stand still.

"Sir, no."

I took off, my feet pounding harder and faster than they ever had on my treadmill. I pushed onward toward her figure. In the foggy darkness, I could make out her hair, a ponytail swinging back and forth as she ran. A goddess. I took in her figure: her curves became a dark, accentuated hourglass against the dim, impressionistic background.

"Charli!" I couldn't remain silent.

We were too far away from the manor. No one but Charli and Isaac could hear me. Isaac's footsteps were right behind me. I didn't give a damn about the guards posted around the property. My Charli was getting closer. She'd done it, entrusted me with her future, her mother's, and even Chelsea's.

Chelsea?

I turned back to Isaac. "She's alone."

"Sir? Where's Miss Moore?"

My gut twisted. "I don't know. I only see one..."

"Nox?" The female voice speaking my name stopped me in my tracks.

Gutted like a fish, I stood paralyzed as the figure came closer.

Her chest heaved with heavy breathing as she fell at my feet.

I lifted her shoulders until she was standing. It wasn't her face that I saw; instead, it was the necklace, the one Charli was supposed to be wearing. "What the hell? Where is she?"

Chelsea's chest rattled with sobs and ragged breaths as she leaned toward me. "S-she told me to wear it and to come. S-she said you'd help me."

The trembling started in my hands as my grip tightened. "Where is she?" My question came too loud.

With the closeness, her features were visible. No longer relieved, a new terror contorted her expression as she tried to back away. Her efforts were futile: my grip of her shoulders was iron. She wasn't getting away. Her body within my grasp shook as her breaths turned to cries. "I-I'm sorry."

Blood raged at record speed through my veins, thundering like a growing rumble pounding in my ears.

"Where the fuck is she?"

"Sir?" Isaac's voice was the calm to my storm. He extended his hand. "Miss Moore? We'll help you." She reached for him. "Sir… let go of her."

Common sense disappeared as I released Chelsea. Nothing mattered besides getting to Charli. One foot in front of the other, I took off running. Visibility limited the path to only a few feet in front of me as I blindly ran the same course Chelsea had come. That wasn't completely true. Above the ground, below the stars, the fucking manor was a blazing finish line, a shining beacon that with the fog appeared to be outlined in flashes of blue.

What the hell?

Was I the only one hidden by the fog, or were there others? As my feet continued to pound, I didn't care. No one mattered except Charli. I wasn't leaving without her.

CHAPTER 44

——●○●——

ALEXANDRIA

PATRICK'S EYES MET mine before he looked at his watch. It was his silent plea, and he was right. I needed to leave; however, since Bryce had left Alton's den, he hadn't left my side. With each glass of champagne or tumbler of whiskey, his enthusiasm for our marriage grew.

"I'm happy," Millie said, her expression displaying the opposite. "I'm just shocked. Why Christmas Eve?" She eyed my midsection. "Is there more we should know?"

"Only that we're in love!" Bryce said, kissing my cheek and leaving the stench of whiskey hanging in the air. "Right, darling?"

"We are." I smiled her way. Extending my hand and forcing my finger to support the giant rock, I asked, "Have you seen my engagement ring? I remember you showing me yours."

"I-it's beautiful."

As Bryce reached for another drink, I leaned Millie's way and scrunched my nose. "Do you really think so? I think it's too big, gaudy even?"

Her eyes widened. "No. It's perfect."

I couldn't help the smirk as she shoved her hand in the pocket of Ian's jacket.

"Now," I went on enthusiastically, "I don't know all the details. Miss

Suzanna is in charge, but there will be showers. You know, personal and family. Oh, you'll be there, won't you?" I reached for Millie's and Jess's hands. "I want you at every one!"

They both smiled, their desire to be part of the Carmichael-Montague wedding superseding their jealousy, if only for a moment. Millie and Jess nodded. "Of course," they said in unison. "We wouldn't miss them."

"And a bachelor party!" Bryce's voice rang out louder than necessary as he patted Ian's and Justin's shoulders. "I know…" He turned to me. "We can invite my whore."

My entire body froze as Jess's and Millie's eyes sprung wide.

I put my hand on Bryce's arm. "Dear, you're a little loud."

"And why shouldn't I be? It's *my* party." He leaned closer. "You said it yourself… this is all mine. It will be."

Like the beacon I'd been raised to heed, the reddening complexion from across the room caught my attention. It wasn't my fiancé—he was beside me. It was my stepfather. The crowd seemed to part as he moved toward us.

What the hell was wrong?

My mind spun with the things I'd done and things I knew.

Did he know about Chelsea? Had someone gotten to Momma? Had Magnolia Woods notified Alton that she was missing or did they catch Nox's man in the act?

My breath hitched as Alton came to a stop. His hand fell to Bryce's shoulder. "Bryce, come with me."

I inhaled at my momentary clemency.

"I'm a little busy," Bryce replied, wrapping his arm around my waist and pulling me closer.

Alton cleared his voice. "We need you in my office now." When Bryce merely took another sip of his drink, Alton added. "We need your decision."

Alton turned, no doubt expecting to be followed.

Bryce's eyes widened before they narrowed my way. "Did you hear that? *My* decision?"

"Yes, I heard."

He waved toward the group. "Go on, darling. While I'm away, tell them what you told my mother and your cousin." He whispered loud enough to be heard. "You know, about my whore."

I nodded. "I will. You go with Alton."

As Bryce walked away, Millie leaned close.

"Alexandria?" she asked with a note of pity in her tone.

Fuck this. I didn't need Millie Ashmore's pity. The story I was told to recite could just as easily have been about her. I looked up at where Pat had been standing. He was gone.

"If you'll excuse me, I need to find Pat."

Millie squeezed my hand. "Is he… is it true? Is Patrick…?"

"Excuse me," I repeated.

I soon found Pat standing near the open doors to the patio. Large silver heaters dotted the stone terrace, creating a comfortable area for guests to mingle. He reached for my hand and nodded.

This was it. Alton and Bryce were busy. It was my chance to escape. The seed of hope I'd refused to water sprung to life, its shell bursting open with anticipation, maybe even expectation. Soon, none of this pretense would matter.

Returning his small nod and with a hopeful grin, I turned toward the limestone steps. A thick layer of fog had settled near the fields, even obstructing the lake. Anything beyond the immediate lawn was masked in a cloud. No one would notice if I disappeared, at least not at first. This was the invisibility cloak I'd hoped for as a child. All I needed to do was make it to the fog. As I handed Pat my champagne flute, his eyes opened wide.

"Uncle Alt—"

A heavy hand landed upon my shoulder. "Where do you think you're going?"

I turned, perspiration dotting my skin as my shoulder shuddered with Alton's touch. Fighting the urge to flinch away, I nodded toward the lawn at the few people standing below and answered, "To talk to the guests out there."

"No, Alexandria. When I summoned Bryce, I meant you also. You're half of a whole now. Get used to it. Your presence is needed in the office too."

I wanted to scream for help. I wanted to hold on to Pat.

I couldn't.

Alton's stare took away my protest. Instead, I solemnly nodded to Pat and obediently turned toward Alton's office.

Everything was again happening in slow motion as my mind tried to make sense of the changing paradigm. The terrace outside and rooms inside hadn't changed. The voices of the guests combined with rings of laughter created the same low murmur. But now their song was a mysterious melody seemingly written to keep time with the rhythm of my frantic heartbeat.

As we made our way through the crowd, I reached for my necklace—my connection. Instead of the platinum-dusted cage, my fingertips met the diamond choker.

Oh, Nox. I'm coming, just a few more minutes. I took a deep breath. *Please let Chelsea be with you.*

It was my silent plea as I smiled politely toward the people we passed. Each one smiled and nodded. Was I paranoid? Had their expressions changed? Were they now somehow different, filled with anticipation, as if they knew the fate awaiting me?

"What's happening?" I whispered to Alton. "Is there something wrong?"

His hand, no longer on my shoulder, grasped my upper arm. As he hastened our progress, he leaned close, his stained teeth and thin lips set in a fake yet sneering smile. It wasn't aimed at me, but at the people we passed. "Keep walking."

With each word a gust of warm, sickeningly sweet, whiskey-ladened breath assaulted my senses, skirting over my cheek, and making my stomach churn. "Don't do anything stupid." His grip tightened as he spoke cordially to the people we passed. Once we were away from the crowd, he went on, "Nothing is wrong, *daughter*. Our schedule has just changed."

My mind was a whirlwind with possibilities.

What had happened? Had he learned our plans?

Was my mother free? Did Alton know? Or was the attempt thwarted?

Did Chelsea make it to Nox? Or was it a trap? Did Alton's men follow her? Had they done something to Nox?

My lungs forgot to inhale as I fought the bubbling panic. Who would I find in Alton's office? What had happened? I had visions of a bound Chelsea, maybe even Nox... my mother... dead...

It was no longer my conscious effort that made my feet continue to step. The cause was either continual motion or the forward momentum in Alton's grip. With each foot forward, my body and mind disconnected. Terror and dread fermented into a bubbling witch's brew. The poisonous concoction filled my bloodstream until oxygen no longer flowed. There was no water near. The lake was hundreds of yards away veiled in fog, and yet I was drowning from within.

All at once the chaotic din of guests faded. Nothingness rang like the fading clanks of a church bell as we crossed the threshold into Alton's office. Bryce had assumed the lead, the drum major to our parade, reaching our destination first. Alton and I were the middle with Suzanna following closely behind. To everyone we'd passed, we were the perfect family unit.

Smoke and mirrors.

I scanned the empty room. There was no one there. No bound Chelsea. No Nox or my mother. The unfulfillment of my fears filled my lungs, giving me the illusion of strength.

"What schedule change?" I asked, pulling my arm free. "What are you talking about?"

Alton's hand moved as his gray eyes blazed. At the same moment, Bryce stepped forward, reaching for my hand and hurling me behind him. I wobbled on my thin heels, balancing on the balls of my feet as I found myself pressed against Bryce's back, his body suddenly my shield protecting me from Alton's intended slap.

"Stop," Bryce proclaimed. His speech no longer slurred. "We have guests. Alexandria's question has merit. Why don't you inform us of what you want and I'll give you my decision?"

"Your decision?" Alton asked incredulously. "You'll give me *your* decision? Isn't that special? This isn't about your decisions. *I* built this…" He gestured about. "…all of this.

"*Your* decisions have gotten us to where we are today, where we are at this very moment. If you were anyone else…"

His volume grew and spittle rained with each phrase he spat.

"As it is, I'm not allowing you to make any more decisions." Crimson moved upward filling his saggy neck like a cloth-absorbing dye and creeping onward toward his cheeks and ears.

"Alton, calm down. Bryce didn't mean…" Though Suzanna's words faded into the background, her tone seemed to placate his sudden rage.

Had the world lost its tilt or was it suddenly in a tailspin?

I couldn't decide as the scene in which I was captive lost touch with reality.

Even from behind Bryce, I could see the growing glow of his neck, now also red.

The monster I'd created with my talk of his impending power was facing the monster I'd always known. Somehow I was a part of this. It was my life, yet the power was shifting—an alternate universe, one where Bryce and Suzanna were no longer my tormentors but my saviors.

I peered around Bryce's shoulder.

Without another word, Alton pulled out his phone and typed a text message. Once he was done, he lifted his beady eyes and smiled.

I shifted my feet, more uncomfortable with his faux happiness than I'd been with his anger. I was accustomed to his wrath. Bryce gripped my hand tighter. Alton's new demeanor sent a chill through the air that even he could sense.

"Did something happen?" I asked from behind Bryce.

"Something is about to happen," Alton replied.

We all turned to the knock on the door.

"Suzy, get the door and then secure it."

Secure it?

"We don't want to be interrupted," Alton added.

Without hesitation she obeyed, opening the door and quickly shutting it. I recognized the gentleman entering as one of the guests. I'd briefly spoken to him and his wife. There were so many people… I couldn't remember his name. That was all right; Alton was again introducing us as he handed the man a paper.

"Thank you for your service, Keith. Bryce and Alexandria, you know Judge Townsend?"

"This is a bit unusual," the judge said, "but I believe we can make it work." He turned toward Bryce and me. "Your guests will be ecstatic."

I looked up at Bryce. Was there comfort in the fact that we shared the same expression of confusion?

"Alexandria and Bryce," Alton announced, "Judge Townsend is here to marry you. Now."

"N-now?" My knees gave way as my stomach fell to my feet. Yet I didn't fall. My new savior was once again omnipresent. Bryce's arm caught me and pulled me upright again.

My vision filled with the man I was about to marry: his gray eyes, blond hair, and ruddy cheeks. This wasn't right. This wasn't what I wanted. I'd had a plan. My finish line was almost in sight.

"No!" I shrieked. "My momma." I turned to Alton. "You said my mother could be here. You promised."

"I'm afraid that's no longer possible."

What the hell does that mean?

Alton turned to Judge Townsend. "Keith, we need to expedite this process. You can predate the license?"

"B-but the wedding?" Suzanna protested, once again coming to my rescue. "This is just the legal part... right? We can still have the ceremony?"

Alton stopped Suzanna's objections with merely a look, one I'd seen many times.

He motioned for the judge to continue as the noise level from the guests increased. Their low din had grown to a rumbling roar.

What is happening?

"Keith?" Alton urged.

"Er, yes." He looked from me to Bryce. "Today we gather to celebrate—"

"No," Alton interrupted, his neck tensing. "Get to the legal part."

Judge Townsend nodded and looked down at the paper in his hand. "Okay, well, Edward Bryce Carmichael Spencer, do you take Alexandria Charles Montague Collins to be your lawfully wedded wife?"

Bryce's support of my waist increased, pulling me closer against his side. "Yes, I do."

My sinking heart seized as the doorknob to the office rattled.

"It's locked," Alton said as if to reassure us. "I told you we wouldn't be disturbed. Keep going."

Rapid-fire knocks came pounding on the wood. The banging grew louder. "Keep going!" Alton screamed.

Voices called from beyond the door. "Mr. Fitzgerald! Mr. Spencer!"

Alton reached for Judge Townsend's arm. "Keith, do this now if you ever want to see that bench again."

Judge Townsend's eyes widened as he turned back to us.

"Alexandria Charles Montague Collins, do you take…"

THE END of ENTRAPMENT

Find out what happens next in FIDELITY,
the final novel of the INFIDELITY series.

FIDELITY

—●○●—

CHARLI & NOX

Coming January 17, 2017, FIDELITY, the much-anticipated conclusion of Charli and Nox, the Montagues, Demetris, Fitzgeralds, and Spencers. Decisions have been made, alliances brokered.

When the vows are completed and the dust settles, who will be left standing?

Book #5 of the five-book Infidelity series, FIDELITY, by Aleatha Romig.

WHAT TO DO NOW...

LEND IT: Did you enjoy *ENTRAPMENT*? Do you have a friend who'd enjoy *ENTRAPMENT*? *ENTRAPMENT* may be lent one time. Sharing is caring!

RECOMMEND IT: Do you have multiple friends who'd enjoy *ENTRAPMENT*? Tell them about it! Call, text, post, tweet... your recommendation is the nicest gift you can give to an author!

REVIEW IT: Tell the world. Please go to the retailer where you purchased this book, as well as Goodreads, and write a review. Please share your thoughts about *ENTRAPMENT* on:

STAY CONNECTED WITH ALEATHA

Do you love Aleatha's writing? Do you want to know the latest about Infidelity? Consequences? Tales From the Dark Side? and Aleatha's new series coming in 2016 from Thomas and Mercer?

Do you like EXCLUSIVE content (never released scenes, never released excerpts, and more)? Would you like the monthly chance to win prizes (signed books and gift cards)? Then sign up today for Aleatha's monthly newsletter and stay informed on all things Aleatha Romig.

Sign up for Aleatha's NEWSLETTER: http://bit.ly/1PYLjZW
(recipients receive exclusive material and offers)

You can also find Aleatha@

Check out her website: http://aleatharomig.wix.com/aleatha
Facebook: https://www.facebook.com/AleathaRomig
Twitter: https://twitter.com/AleathaRomig
Goodreads: www.goodreads.com/author/show/5131072.Aleatha_Romig
Instagram: http://instagram.com/aleatharomig
Email Aleatha: aleatharomig@gmail.com

You may also listen Aleatha Romig books on Audible.

BOOKS BY NEW YORK TIMES BESTSELLING AUTHOR ALEATHA ROMIG

INFIDELITY SERIES:

BETRAYAL

Book #1

(October 2015)

CUNNING

Book #2

(January 2016)

DECEPTION

Book #3

(May 2016)

ENTRAPMENT

Book #4

(September2016)

FIDELITY

Book #5

(January 2017)

THE CONSEQUENCES SERIES:

CONSEQUENCES
(Book #1)
Released August 2011

TRUTH
(Book #2)
Released October 2012

CONVICTED
(Book #3)
Released October 2013

REVEALED
(Book #4)
Previously titled: Behind His Eyes Convicted: The Missing Years
Re-released June 2014

BEYOND THE CONSEQUENCES
(Book #5)
Released January 2015

COMPANION READS:

BEHIND HIS EYES—CONSEQUENCES
(Book #1.5)
Released January 2014

BEHIND HIS EYES—TRUTH
(Book #2.5)
Released March 2014

TALES FROM THE DARK SIDE SERIES:

INSIDIOUS

(All books in this series are stand-alone erotic thrillers)

Released October 2014

DUPLICITY

(Completely unrelated to book #1)

Release TBA

THE LIGHT SERIES:

Published through Thomas and Mercer

INTO THE LIGHT

(June 14, 2016)

AWAY FROM THE DARK

(October 2016)

ALEATHA ROMIG

Aleatha Romig is a New York Times and USA Today bestselling author who lives in Indiana. She grew up in Mishawaka, graduated from Indiana University, and is currently living south of Indianapolis. Aleatha has raised three children with her high school sweetheart and husband of nearly thirty years. Before she became a full-time author, she worked days as a dental hygienist and spent her nights writing. Now, when she's not imagining mind-blowing twists and turns, she likes to spend her time with her family and friends. Her other pastimes include reading and creating heroes/anti-heroes who haunt your dreams!

Aleatha released her first novel, CONSEQUENCES, in August of 2011. CONSEQUENCES became a bestselling series with five novels and two companions released from 2011 through 2015. The compelling and epic story of Anthony and Claire Rawlings has graced more than half a million e-readers. Aleatha released the first of her series TALES FROM THE DARK SIDE, INSIDIOUS, in the fall of 2014. These stand-alone thrillers continue Aleatha's twisted style with an increase in heat. In the fall of 2015, Aleatha moved headfirst into the world of romantic suspense with the release of BETRAYAL, the first of her five-novel INFIDELITY series. Aleatha has entered the traditional world of publishing with Thomas and Mercer with her LIGHT series. The first of that series, INTO THE LIGHT, will be published in the summer of 2016.

Aleatha is a "Published Author's Network" member of the Romance Writers of America and represented by Danielle Egan-Miller of Browne & Miller Literary Associates.

Made in the USA
Middletown, DE
31 January 2021

32850375R00208